THE MOUNTAIN OF KEPT MEMORY

ALSO BY RACHEL NEUMEIER

Winter of Ice and Iron

THE
MOUNTAIN
OF
KEPT
MEMORY

RACHEL
NEUMEIER

SAGA PRESS

LONDON SYDNEY **NEW YORK** TORONTO NEW DELHI

SAGA PRESS

AN IMPRINT OF SIMON & SCHUSTER, INC.

1230 AVENUE OF THE AMERICAS, NEW YORK, NEW YORK 10020

For information address Saga Press Subsidiary Rights Department, 1230 Avenue of the Americas, New York, NY 10020 • SAGA PRESS and colophon are trademarks of Simon & Schuster, Inc. For information about special discounts for bulk purchases, please contact Simon & Schuster Special Sales at 1-866-506-1949 or business@simonandschuster.com. • The Simon & Schuster Speakers Bureau can bring authors to your live event. For more information or to book an event, contact the Simon & Schuster Speakers Bureau at 1-866-248-3049 or visit our website at www.simonspeakers.com. • Also available in a Saga Press hardcover edition • The text for this book was set in Sabon. • Manufactured in the United States of America • First Saga Press paperback edition November 2017 • 10 9 8 7 6 5 4 3 2 1 • The Library of Congress has cataloged the hardcover edition as follows: Names: Neumeier, Rachel, author | Title: The mountain of kept memory / Rachel Neumeier. Description: First Edition. | New York : Saga Press, [2016] Identifiers: LCCN 2015050228 (print) | ISBN 978-1-4814-4894-9 (hc) | ISBN 978-1-4814-4896-3 (ebook) Subjects: | BISAC: FICTION / Fantasy / General. | FICTION / Fantasy / Epic. | FICTION / Action & Adventure. | GSAFD: Fantasy fiction. Classification: LCC PS3614.E553 M68 2016 (print) | DDC 813/.6—dc23 | LC record available at http://lccn.loc.gov/2015050228 • ISBN 978-1-4814-4895-6 (pbk)

FOR CAITLIN BLASDELL AND NAVAH WOLFE,
for their excellent taste in novels,
and for making this one the best it could be

CHAPTER 1

They were talking about her.

Oressa, curled beneath her father's throne, her arms wrapped around her knees and her knees tucked up tight to her chest, was precariously hidden behind generous falls of the saffron-dyed silk draped over the seat and back of the throne. This sort of thing had been easier when she was twelve. Or even sixteen. Now that she was a woman grown, she had to work much harder to stay out of sight.

At least she was still small. She was lucky Gulien was the one who'd gotten all their father's height. She breathed soundlessly through her mouth, tensed and relaxed all her muscles in turn to ease the painful cramps in her legs and back, and listened intently.

Oressa had known her father would spend the morning talking about important things. Her father never sent all his servants and attendants away unless he wanted to talk privately to his favored ministers. Sometimes the things they talked about turned out to be boring, as when her father and Magister Baramis had spent a whole afternoon arguing about whether to compel the dyer's guild to sell dyes and fixatives at a low flat rate to a favored merchant house that had just brought in a load of Markandan silk. Oressa had been stuck for far, far too long, listening to every possible ramification of the prices of dyes.

She had guessed that this morning's topic would be more interesting, though, because everyone knew the Tamaristan king had recently suffered a brain storm or seizure or something of the kind and was probably on his deathbed. The Tamaristan succession was often exciting, but especially this time because the Tamaristan king had collapsed without declaring which of his sons was going to be his heir and having the rest killed, which, cruel and horrible as it was, was usually how the Tamaristans handled their succession. So Oressa had expected that her father and his advisers would discuss the five living Tamaristan princes and which among them was most likely to defeat the rest and which one those Tamaristan ships out there in the harbor might belong to. Those ships looked suspiciously like narrow, fast warships rather than deep-bellied cargo transports. Or so people were saying. Oressa hadn't seen them herself.

She'd been right about the general subject of discussion. But she hadn't guessed her own name would appear in the ensuing argument. It happened after Lord Meric said, "Mark my words, sire. What we have out there is one of the younger princes who's decided that if he can't win his father's throne, he might as well get out of his brothers' way and try for *foreign* conquest. Naturally he looks our way. That gods-cursed white-crystal plague left us vulnerable—unless, ah, that is, of course, if the Kieba protects us, sire—"

"I think we should not depend on the Kieba's protection," said Oressa's father. His flat voice did not invite Meric to continue. Oressa could imagine her father's chilly eyes, the thin set of his mouth. Plagues weren't exactly rare, but her father had been furious about this one, almost as though the white-crystal rain had been a personal insult aimed directly at him. It *had* been pretty bad, and the Kieba had let the plague run its course instead of sending a cure, which was very unusual. Meric was right; that plague had left Carastind vulnerable. And Meric was right again: Of course Carastind really should be able to depend on the Kieba for protection. But everyone knew there was a problem between Oressa's father and the Kieba.

At least, Oressa knew it, and she could tell that Meric guessed. *She* knew, as Meric might not, that twice this spring the Kieba had sent one of her falcons to her father, summoning him to her mountain, and both times her father had declined to go. So far as Oressa was aware, he hadn't told anybody about that, but she knew. She watched her father very carefully.

After a brief, uncomfortable pause, Lord Meric said, his tone cautious, "Yes, sire, but then we must have a way to protect ourselves against this Tamaristan prince. There may even be one or two others on their way behind this one; the old man certainly left enough sons, and they say the eldest is ruthless. Ruthless even among the Garamanaji, I mean."

The eldest Tamaristan prince, Oressa knew, was Maranajdis Garamanaj, and he was indeed supposed to be ferocious. In Carastind, people said he'd murdered his youngest brother when their father had begun showing the boy too much favor, and there were doubts about the sudden illness of the king, too. If those tales were true, no wonder the younger princes might consider fleeing Tamarist rather than facing Maranajdis.

Oressa imagined a whole series of Tamaristan princes sailing in one after another to attack Caras. If she remembered correctly, there were two princesses between Maranajdis and the next eldest prince, Ajei, who was about thirty. Then there was another princess, and after her, Gajdosik, who was close to Gulien's age; and then, a year or two younger, Bherijda, and last—since the youngest prince had been murdered—Emarast, who was no older than Oressa was herself. And then the youngest princess, Alia, who was just fifteen or sixteen. Not that Alia or any of the other princesses actually mattered, since their lives were almost as circumscribed as those of their mothers.

Their very lack of power probably meant that the Tamaristan princesses were fairly safe from their brothers, but the way the Tamaristan succession was handled, the princes must have been at odds since childhood and surely could not be friends. But she imagined they might be *allies*, especially if they were all afraid enough of Maranajdis. It would not be good if they all joined forces to attack Carastind. Cannons guarded the harbor, true. But just how many ships could those cannons destroy if many came at once? Or what would Caras do if ships came in farther up or down the coast and Tamaristan soldiers marched overland toward the city? She found she had no idea. She wished suddenly that Gulien had explained military history to her, not just the ancient history of the dead gods.

Magister Baramis answered Meric. "If we have a clutter of Tamaristan princes looking for conquest, well, then, we had better look for options that depend on cleverness rather than forceful defense. Take this prince we presume is out in the Narrow Sea. Whichever one it is, right now he must still be considering his strategy. We'd better do something about him while he's still thinking and before any more of that lot decide to stir the pot. A dispossessed prince need not look at Caras itself, you know. A man so poor-spirited as to give up his birthright to Maranajdis without a fight might well be content to gain a little hayfield-sized kingdom of his own. Why not grant him one? We can give him those rocky hills up by the northern border. In a generation, his people will serve as a true bulwark between Carastind and Estenda. That would be useful."

Lord Meric snorted. "Useful! It would certainly give him a beachhead! One he'd use against *us,* not Estenda, and not in a generation, but now!"

"Not if we offer him the proper inducement." Oressa could hear the satisfaction in Baramis's tone and could imagine just what he looked like: smug, satisfied with his own cleverness, sure he'd hit on a perfect plan. He went on. "Oressa's twenty. That's well past marriageable age, and what better use could be made of her? Offer the princess to this Tamaristan prince!"

At that point Oressa twitched before she could stop herself. She froze, biting her lip hard, sure somebody must have heard her involuntary movement.

"We'll make the Tamaristan prince our ally against his brothers *and* distract Estenda all at once," Baramis declared. "It's perfect! And it means we needn't depend on the Kieba for anything."

The heavy throne that comprised Oressa's hiding place was solid, but it creaked as her father shifted position. The hilt of his sword rubbed against the side of the chair, and the concealing silk draperies trembled. Her father *had* heard her. He would catch her listening—

There was a loud slapping sound as someone else brought his hand down against the arm of a chair. Gulien spoke sharply. "Magister Baramis, that is a *Tamaristan* prince!"

Oressa had not even known till then that Gulien was in the room. He rarely spoke during such meetings, for though Gulien was a man grown, nearly twenty-five, their father expected him to listen and learn and be silent. But now, though Baramis and Meric both tried to speak at once, Gulien raised his voice. "You would offer *my sister* to a prince of *Tamarist?* To live the rest of her life in a *cage?* To watch her sons, my father's grandsons, raised by foreign nurses and finally murdered by her husband?" No one shouted in their father's presence, but Gulien was coming close.

"My son, enough," the king said flatly.

Oressa tucked her head against her knees and fought not to laugh, though it wasn't funny. It wasn't funny at *all*. Princesses seldom chose whom they would marry; she knew that; everyone knew that. But she couldn't imagine any woman voluntarily marrying a Tamaristan prince. Everything Gulien had said was true—everyone knew about the gilded cage in the Tamaristan king's city—Baija—the cage to which only the king had a key and within which his queen spent her whole life. It was a big cage, granted; tales claimed it was three hundred paces long and two hundred paces wide and held many graceful pavilions for the queen and her women servants and gardens filled with rare birds and flowers. But it was a *cage*, and the queen never left it.

Her brother seldom lost his temper. But at this suggestion he had, very rightly so in Oressa's opinion, and fortuitously distracted everyone, even their father, from the careless motion that might have betrayed her.

"We could certainly write more civilized terms into the wedding contract, Your Highness," said Baramis in a much more conciliatory tone. "The match would be advantageous enough that surely the prince would agree Oressa need not be pent as close as a Tamaristan queen. We could require exile for the extra princes, not death. But it's an offer that potentially wins us a great deal and costs us, in practical terms, very little. You know there's no obvious match for Oressa in Carastind, or she'd have been married years ago." His tone changed as he turned to the king. "I'm sure you agree, sire, that there's little benefit to bestowing your daughter on any rich merchant from Estenda or gilded lordling from Markand. And there's no unwed Illian prince except that boy in the northernmost province, but he's too young anyway. No, sire. Think on it: Such an alliance might offer quite enough advantages to justify offering Oressa to a Tamaristan prince under these circumstances. As Lord Meric reminded us, we remain vulnerable, especially if the Kieba—well, that is, of course Carastind will recover from its weakness, sire, but just at the moment—"

"Indeed," said Oressa's father, his voice dry.

Oressa bit her finger to keep from making a sound, but she knew Baramis was right about Carastind being vulnerable. Everyone must know, even in Tamarist, that the people of Carastind and especially those of Caras itself, had been weakened by the white-crystal rain.

There were always plagues: diseases brought by rains of cinders or blood or sharp slivers of iron or, worse, by creeping red or purple or black mists that even doors and shutters couldn't stop. Just a few days ago rumors of a lavender mist had run through the city. The resulting panic had sent palace servants and staff fleeing to relatives in the countryside. But those rumors had turned out to be all wrong; some fool must just have seen sunset light reflecting off sea mist and panicked.

The plague this past spring hadn't been anybody's imagination. It had been carried by a sudden swift rain of tiny white crystals out of a clear hot sky, a rain that had lasted only hours, so it shouldn't have been so bad. Only, like salt, the white crystals of the plague rain dissolved in water and afterward you couldn't tell the water was bad. Quite a lot of people caught the plague from the bad water before they realized what was happening.

Anybody who drank contaminated water got fever and then chills.

Then people seemed to get better. But after that, the fever come back again, only much worse. That higher fever brought on a terrible thirst, and there was so little clean water to give people, especially after many of city's cisterns turned out to be contaminated. Worse, the high fever brought hallucinations: People saw scattered images of long-dead cities from the deep past, from the time of the gods, and sometimes they forgot who they were and called out in languages no one today knew. Which would have even been interesting, and Oressa had almost wished to get the plague herself, but it was just as well she hadn't, because it turned out that a little while after the hallucinations, a lot of the fever victims went into convulsions, and then they died. And for some reason young men had been a lot more likely to die than women or old people or children.

Then the illness had passed. But by that time a lot of people had died already. Most of them were men, which besides weakening the militia was terribly hard for all the widowed wives. Oressa had pointed out to Gulien that someone might suggest to their father that taxes might be forgiven for the widows, at least for a year or two, but though he said he'd passed that idea around where it might do some good, nothing had happened. She knew there would be a lot of hardship in Caras because of that.

That was when a lot of people had started muttering that Oressa's father must have offended the Kieba. Oressa knew it was true, but she was pretty sure the rumors wouldn't have spread if her father had been nicer about the taxes. She now guessed that those rumors had spread even to Tamarist and that the Tamaristan princes believed them. And *that* meant they believed that the Kieba wouldn't protect Carastind against any enemies who suddenly decided to attack. And, most frightening of all, they might even be right. In that case, no matter what Baramis thought, a Tamaristan prince needn't be poor-spirited to think of trying to conquer Carastind rather than defeat the infamous Maranajdis. That would actually just be sensible.

So Baramis's suggestion actually made perfect sense. But Oressa didn't have to like it. She glared at the silk draperies, since she couldn't crawl out from under the chair and glare at Magister Baramis or her father.

Oressa's father said nothing. She imagined he had nodded or waved for Baramis to go on or looked at Meric—ah, the latter, because Meric said, "Well, sire, I have to admit, making one Tamaristan prince into an ally against the rest of them . . . I hadn't thought of that, but it's better than trying to fight them all. If we can get this first prince to ally with us, then very likely we can get any others that follow to turn aside from Carastind, to perhaps harass Estenda instead. Even if not, a strong settlement in the north would give Estenda pause." From his tone, he actually agreed, if reluctantly, with Baramis. He never agreed with Baramis about anything. Oressa thought this was a very unfortunate time for him to start.

Gulien started to say something, his tone sharp, but then he stopped. For a long moment no one spoke at all. Oressa thought probably her father had put up a hand for silence.

"Lord Meric, we will think over all you have said," the king said. "Magister Baramis, we will consider your suggestion." His tone remained flat, but it carried a finality that prevented anybody from trying to continue the argument. "Gulien—"

There was the sharp little click of the door opening. Oressa twitched, though this time at least she didn't bump the chair or make a sound. That had to be something important, because no one ever broke in on her father's council deliberations.

"Sire," said a deep, smooth voice, instantly recognizable. This was Erren, junior captain of the king's guard. Oressa didn't like Erren. He was handsome, yes, but he was a bully, especially with servant girls. Erren was thickset and muscular, and he had a mustache, which he wore long and waxed into points as though he were a Markand lordling. Oressa thought he'd probably been impressed by a mustache like that when he'd been young and had never gotten over it. She thought it was silly and affected, though she had to admit that lots of girls seemed to admire it. Not the servant girls, who knew better, but well-born girls, the kind who didn't have any sense.

Erren must have walked forward and bent to speak quietly into her father's ear, because though his voice was very low, Oressa nevertheless heard him say "Tamarist" and "soldiers" and something that sounded like "the sea-eagle" and, most alarming of all, "Paree."

Paree was a small town several days' ride south from Caras. There wasn't exactly a harbor there, but if the tides were right, even quite large ships could come and go from Paree. A cold feeling pricked across the back of Oressa's neck.

"So it's Prince Gajdosik, is it?" said Lord Meric. "The sea-eagle's his personal banner, isn't it? Well, we've never heard he's stupid, that one. Overland as well as right into the harbor, is that his plan? That's not the move of a half-committed man. He'll take Paree as a bridgehead if we don't stop him—and it's probably too late to stop him. With supplies from Paree to support his people, he'll come north at his leisure. He'll want to use that land force of his to support an attack against our harbor here—"

"Explain this to me, do," the king said testily, and got to his feet. The throne creaked, and the silk hangings swirled. Oressa tucked her chin tight to her chest and held very still. Cramps had started in both her calves, but she didn't make a sound.

Her father said to Baramis, "We shall send to Prince Gajdosik. Find out whether he's personally with that force in Paree or sitting out there in our harbor. Write a proposal along the lines you suggested. Something flowery, to flatter the man's vanity."

Over the magister's murmur of satisfied acquiescence, Gulien said, "But—"

"Sentiment does not keep enemies at bay," said the king, his tone flat and final, and walked out. Oressa could hear his unhurried steps and the heavier tread of Erren. There was plenty of movement suddenly, and she heard the door open, but she couldn't tell whether everyone had gone or whether somebody might linger in the room even yet. She was almost sure she hadn't heard the door close again. The cramps in her legs were worse, and there was an increasing ache in her back and shoulders and neck, and worse than the discomfort was the anger. She was *outraged*, and she couldn't make a sound. The worst thing of all was that she already knew it would never occur to her father to *ask* her to sacrifice herself for him and for Carastind. He would have Baramis write out a flowery letter for that Tamaristan prince and probably not even bother to mention it to *her* at all.

Then the door did close, a decisive little click, but she heard someone shift his weight, still in the room. Oressa tried not to make a sound. There was a pause.

At last her brother said, his tone resigned, "All right, Oressa. Come out."

Oressa rolled over to her stomach and crawled stiffly out from under the silk draping the king's chair. She'd been too cramped for too long to stand up, but she stretched her legs out gingerly, pounding her calves and thighs to unknot the muscles, concentrating on that so she wouldn't have to look at her brother. She asked, "How did you know I was there?"

"Heard you. You idiot."

"You distracted everyone on purpose?" Oressa hadn't realized that, though now it was obvious. "Thank you, Gulien. You're the *best* brother!"

"You, on the other hand, are the most annoying sister! If he'd caught you—"

"He never has. Nobody ever catches me but you." Oressa didn't admit out loud that this time somebody might have if not for Gulien. She stretched her neck out to one side and then the other. Her neck hurt. Her shoulders hurt. She was stiff all over. She glared at Gulien. "Would you have told me? Or let Father take me by surprise? 'Oh, Oressa, guess what! You get to marry a Tamaristan prince!' Gods dead and forgotten!"

"Don't swear, Oressa," Gulien said automatically. "Of course I would have told you." He came over to kneel behind her. "Here, let me—" He dug strong fingers into her shoulders.

"Ouch! Oh, that's better. Thanks. Gulien—"

"It's a stupid idea anyway. Marry *you* to Gajdosik? That'd be an act of war right there. He'd invade us again just to make us take you back."

Oressa smiled reluctantly. But she said, "Well, it *is* a stupid idea." It wasn't actually; she could even see the sense of it, and she knew Gulien had to as well. But she said stubbornly, "Anyway, I won't do it. Marry a *Tamaristan* prince? Ha! I'll . . . I'll . . ." There really *weren't* any obvious choices for whom she might marry. It wasn't as though she hadn't thought about this before, off and on for the past five years or so. But now a new and brilliant idea occurred to her. She sat up straight. "I know! I'll marry Kelian, quick before Father can stop me."

Kelian was a young lieutenant in the palace guard. He'd come to Caras only this spring, shortly after the plague, but he'd joined the militia almost at once and the guard very soon after that, and he'd been promoted quickly because the plague had left the guard so short of men. Kelian was obviously well-born. He had his own sword and horse, not to mention a beautiful strong jaw and melting dark eyes and the most wonderful northern accent, all long vowels and soft consonants. All the palace girls had fallen in love with him, but so far he hadn't shown special favor to any of them, though he never mentioned a sweetheart back home. He sent money back to his mother every week, but Oressa had never heard that he wrote to anyone else.

Not that she was in love with him herself. Naturally not. She had too much sense to fall in love with anyone, but she was sure she'd seen his gaze lingering on her from time to time.

But Gulien snorted. "You *idiot*. You will not."

"Why not? He's gorgeous and brave and nice to me and oh yes, not a *Tamaristan prince* with a stupid name like *Gajdosik*! I'll marry him and then it'll be impossible for Father to marry me off to anybody else." She glared at her brother. "What? It'd work."

"Father would hang Kelian," her brother said succinctly, "and then he'd lock you up in the highest tower room until he could marry you off to someone appropriate, which he would do so fast the gossip wouldn't have time to get outside Caras. If not to Prince Gajdosik, then to somebody else." Gulien gripped her shoulders and shook her gently. "Idiot. Probably Father will just dangle promises in front of Gajdosik, pull him into an alliance while he sorts out whatever trouble there is between him and the Kieba. Then he can find some decent Carastindin lord for you. Paulin, maybe."

Oressa rolled her eyes. "Paulin! I don't think so!" Lord Paulin's family, the Tegeres, had its principal estates in Little Caras, but the family had for generations had ties to Markand and Illian; Lord Paulin's father had bought a court title with the wealth he'd made in silk, dyes, alum, and finished cloth. On his death, both the title and the wealth had passed to his son, who was rich, influential, ambitious, and loyal to Oressa's father. Also indolent, corpulent, and nearly fifty.

Over the last year or so, Paulin, during his increasingly frequent visits to Caras, had begun courting Gulien. He invited him to his own town house to examine rare books or to attend special performances by Illiana dancers—not too often, but often enough. When he was at court, ostensibly to attend on the king, he made time to flatter Gulien's interest in old books and his knowledge of history. When some political question was under debate, if he had a chance, Lord Paulin made a point of drawing out Gulien's opinion and complimenting him on his understanding of politics.

In short, he did all the things a clever man would do if his family did not enjoy any particular favor with the king and he wanted to be sure his family's fortunes were poised to rise when Gulien took the throne. Lord Paulin had only one daughter, a long-married woman nearing thirty, or Oressa had no doubt he'd be dangling her in front of Gulien, too.

But for all his cultivation of Gulien, Lord Paulin still treated Oressa with a kind of benign disinterest. Though she imagined the disinterest might change in a hurry if her father suggested he might marry her and add a handful of princes to the clutter of sons he'd had by his first wife.

It wasn't that she blamed him, not for courting her brother's good opinion nor for ignoring hers—any practical man might do the same, and at least Paulin went about it intelligently. Besides, she was fairly certain he sincerely did like her brother. She believed she would be able to tell pure sycophancy from an honest like-mindedness, and she was sure Gulien could not have been fooled by any pretense of interest in history and rare books.

But marry Paulin herself? Hardly.

"He's clever enough, Oressa, and I know that matters to you—"

"Oh, he's *clever!* Clever enough to flatter *you* whenever he gets the chance!" Gulien, his eyebrows rising, started to say something, but Oressa raised her voice and went right on. "He talks to *me* like I'm just a pretty little lapdog, when he notices me at all. And he's *old!* I think Kelian is a much better idea." But of course she knew Gulien was right about her father's response. She eyed her brother. "You know what? If I can't marry Kelian, I'll run away to Markand. I'll be a temple maiden and carry the fire in the procession and dance around the golden fountain every solstice—don't laugh at me!"

"I'm not laughing at you."

"You are. Your eyes are laughing," Oressa said darkly. She glared at him harder. "I won't marry Gajdosik. I'm not joking. Live in a cage? Not likely!" She knew she might have to. She understood she might have no choice, but she refused to admit that even to Gulien—she hardly admitted it to herself.

It was on the tip of her tongue to say, *If Father insists on someone marrying into the Garamanaji, why not have you offer for Alia Garamanaj?* But she didn't say that, either. It would be a stupid suggestion, unless Prince Gajdosik was particularly fond of his sister, which she'd never heard, and had brought her with him, which she doubted. And worse, it would be cruel, because three years ago her brother had been engaged to a girl from Illian, but the girl had sickened and died; and then last year he had been engaged to Lord Bennet's daughter, but she had died in the spring plague. Gulien hadn't even known the Illiana girl, but he had liked Bennet's daughter well enough, and the whole thing had left him rather shy of getting engaged to anyone, as though he feared any formal offer from his father to a girl's father might carry illness and bad luck with it.

So Oressa only said, "You'd better tell me *exactly* what our father decides. Or maybe—" She cut that off. Maybe it would be better if she found a way to listen herself to her father's next meeting with Meric and Baramis. . . .

"If you try to sneak into Father's private rooms, they'll catch you for sure, and then he really will lock you up in the highest tower."

"Would I try such a thing?" Oressa laid a hand over her heart to show how shocked she was at this suggestion. She didn't tell her brother that she'd managed this exact feat once before, when she was eleven, just to see if she could do it. She'd pretended to be a servant boy, and actually she'd come pretty near being caught and hadn't even learned anything worth knowing. She'd sworn to herself she'd never try it again. But now she was afraid Gulien wouldn't tell her what their father said or did or decided. Not if he thought it was better she didn't know. Not if their father ordered him not to. She couldn't dress up as a boy anymore, but she'd thought of two other ways she might get in if she tried. She said, "You don't need to protect me, you know—"

"You don't try nearly hard enough to protect yourself! You've got to stop sneaking around, Oressa. If you're caught once—just once—you have no idea how seriously Father might take this."

Oressa found herself beginning to get angry again, this time with her brother. How could he say that? Of course she knew how angry Father would be. How could she not know? She knew better than anybody, better than Gulien did himself. *He* hadn't ever believed her about their mother, but *she* knew—

Her brother put a hand under her chin, lifting her face to make her look at him. He said seriously, "The next time I catch you, I'll call you out right then, in front of everybody."

"You—" *Wouldn't*, Oressa meant to say. But her brother looked very serious, and she wasn't absolutely sure.

"I would. I will." Gulien let her go, rose, and stood for a moment with his fists on his hips, staring down at her. "I'll check that the hall is clear, Oressa. But this is the last time I'll help you. You're twenty years old! Far too old to act like a servant's brat. You need to start behaving with a princess's dignity."

Oressa didn't protest that her brother was far too concerned about dignity, especially hers. It was true, but he wouldn't agree. So she only got to her feet, ignoring the hand Gulien held down to her. Then she brushed the dust off her skirt, straightened her shoulders, ran her hands through her hair, lifted her chin, and put on a proper royal attitude like a cloak. "You may check the hallway, if you like," she said as regally as she could. Once he had, she strolled away toward her own apartment as though she could imagine nowhere at all she'd rather go.

The king's chambers were on the lowest floor of the palace because the king was no longer young. His knees ached in the winter and ached worse when it rained, and he didn't like to climb stairs, and so two years ago he'd moved the royal apartment from the highest level of the palace to the lowest. That might have made it easier for Oressa to sneak into his rooms, only in actual fact, it didn't. The royal guardsmen hated the wide hallways that led right by the king's apartment from the more public areas of the palace, and they hated having three different doors to guard instead of just one at the top of a flight of stairs, and they most especially hated the wide windows that opened into the garden. But the king did not want to climb stairs, so the guard captains tripled the number of men on duty for each watch and made them all stand guard with an ostentatious zeal that was supposed to serve as a rebuke to the king for imposing this inconvenience on them, though Oressa doubted her father noticed. Or, at least, cared.

But the guards' fervor made things difficult. Sneaking in unobserved would be practically impossible. Oressa had decided that long ago. The trick would be to make the guardsmen think they observed one thing when really they were looking at something else all the time.

Dressing up as a boy was no longer very practical. Oressa had tried it, rather hopelessly, after she'd started getting a woman's shape, when she was thirteen, but it had clearly been no use: She had taken too much after her mother, and her curves were very soon too obvious. At first this had seemed purely inconvenient. Then it had occurred to her that if she married, she would leave her father's palace, and that had seemed worth the inconvenience. But then her father had delayed and delayed deciding whom she should marry, and now here was Baramis, with his brilliant idea that she should marry a *Tamaristan prince*.

"It's almost dusk," her maid, Nasia, said briskly, behind her. "What would you like to wear for dinner? Your green silk? I added cuffs to hide the mended place, so that's all right, and the color brings the gold highlights out in your hair."

The green silk did nothing of the kind, Oressa knew. There weren't any gold highlights in her hair, which was the most ordinary brown imaginable. But her maid, an efficient older woman with five grown daughters of her own, insisted on saying thing like that. Nasia had married off all five of her daughters and these days exercised her strong romantic streak by matchmaking for the servant girls and advising them all about their clothing and manners and marriages. This should have kept her busy, but somehow she always seemed to have time to fuss about Oressa's clothing and hair and jewelry too—more so every year that Oressa remained unmarried.

Oressa said, "The green will be fine."

"And those gold twist earrings and that necklace of hammered gold disks—"

"Yes, whatever you think." Oressa wandered away toward the bathing room. Getting past her father's guardsmen wasn't actually the real challenge. She could always just present herself at the door and ask to see her father and they'd probably let her in. But getting everyone to forget about her so she could linger and overhear everything . . . that would be a trick.

"You're very silent tonight," Nasia said, laying out the green silk dress and matching underthings and light slippers and the gold earrings and necklace. She took a towel from the warm stack and held it for Oressa. "You're not sickening with anything? Your moon-time hasn't arrived?"

"I'm only thinking."

"Well, it's certainly made you go very silent." Nasia laid the back of her hand against Oressa's forehead, just to make sure. "But you're not over-warm," she admitted. "What are you thinking about?"

"Kelian," Oressa said, to distract her.

"Oh, *he's* worth a thought or two," Nasia agreed, taking this bait with enthusiasm. "He's certainly not for you, of course, my dear, but no harm in thinking, is there? Would you like to go out to the officer's training yard tomorrow morning? I think they'll be practicing their footwork."

Practicing on foot with short sword and dagger, she meant. All the palace girls liked that best, especially on warm summer mornings when the men took off their shirts. Oressa thought about Kelian with his shirt off and blushed. Then she thought of Gulien saying, *Father would hang him*. She knew her brother was right. But it didn't stop her from blushing. She said in an austere tone, "I think we'll have more important things to think about tomorrow than watching the guard officers train." And, though she didn't say so, she suspected the guard officers would have more important things to worry about than impressing girls. But she wasn't supposed to know about that yet, of course. That was the hardest part about overhearing things: remembering what she wasn't supposed to know.

"Your father needs to stop all this fussing about and find you a husband," Nasia said, amused and plainly entirely ignorant about the sudden urgency of the Tamaristan threat. She couldn't know what echo Oressa heard behind her words when she added, "He should have done it long since. I know it's difficult to match princesses, but no father should let his daughter reach twenty without inviting a firm offer or two from suitable young men."

"I'm sure you're right," Oressa said mildly, and picked up another towel to dry her hair.

There was a polite rap on the door, the kind of firm tap that guardsmen used. Nasia rustled off to answer the door, leaving Oressa to dress herself, except for the buttons on the dress, which were innumerable and very small and mostly impossible to reach. She rubbed her hair with the towel, waiting for Nasia. She could hear the woman's voice, an indistinct murmur, and the guardsman's deeper voice.

Nasia came back into the dressing room, took the towel firmly away from Oressa, handed her a comb, and began to do up the buttons more quickly than usual. "Your father's sent a formal letter," she said in clear delight. "He might have been listening to me, it seems! The man's to deliver it directly to your hand, so it's *very* formal. I'm sure you're dying to find out what it is, child!"

Oressa clenched her teeth. Nasia was obviously sure that this must be the letter every father sent his daughter to give her formal notice that she was being courted by some eligible young man. And of course Nasia was probably right . . . in a way.

"Your hair's still damp. There's no help for that, but you can't go out to supper with it loose over your shoulders like some merchant's daughter. I'll braid it and put it up and it should look well enough. Don't fidget, please. Where did you put those gold bangles of yours? Those would look nice with the earrings and that necklace, and of course everyone will be looking at you tonight, child, won't they! The first days of courtship are such a wonderful time for a girl. All right. There. Don't look so solemn!"

Oressa took a deep breath and followed her maid out to her reception room to let the man give her the letter. Because the man would undoubtedly report her attitude and manners to her father, she took small ladylike steps and kept her eyes demurely down.

The man turned out to be a guard officer she knew slightly: Beriad, Lord Meric's cousin, an intelligent and good-humored man who had gone into the king's guard because he wasn't his father's heir. Oressa liked him, so she had never let slip any hint that she knew of his unsuitable closeness with a certain long-widowed lady of the court. But even if she liked Beriad, he was still her father's man. She tried not to show him anything but a blank court expression as she took the letter he held out to her and slit the fragile paper.

"Well?" Nasia asked, too polite to crane her neck and stare over

Oressa's shoulder, but understandably dying to know what name the letter contained.

Oressa glanced down at the few words—too neatly penned to have been written by her father's own hand—and found herself clenching her teeth, struggling against an outburst. She had already known what this letter would say. It was ridiculous to feel like this. She should have been prepared. Only guessing and knowing weren't the same, and now she found out how little prepared she had been. She smothered anger and fear and said as blandly as she could, "What a very interesting notion of my father's, to be sure."

She would live and die a virgin before she married a Tamaristan prince, but she didn't say that. She would climb out her window and run away to be a temple maiden in Markand, and nobody would ever guess except Gulien. But she certainly didn't say that. She swallowed her anger, determined that Beriad would not be able to tell her father that she'd had hysterics, like a girl, like a *child*. He was watching her worriedly—obviously her tone hadn't been quite as light and unconcerned as she'd tried to make it.

Nasia, her eyes narrowing, also guessed something was wrong. She plucked the letter from her hand, smoothed it out, and looked down at the thin spidery letters. Then she looked up to stare in confounded dismay at Oressa. "But," she said in a blank tone. "But this says—this is—a *Tamaristan* prince?"

"A Tamaristan prince? Surely not." Beriad, plainly just as surprised, shifted to look over Nasia's shoulder. Then he stared at Oressa.

"It's a sensible decision, I'm sure, under the circumstances," Oressa said coolly. "Naturally my father wants only what's best for Carastind." Despite her best effort, her voice wavered on the last words, and she turned and fled—in a decorous stroll, but it was definitely flight—back into her private rooms before she could lose her composure entirely. She did not slam her door behind her. Princesses did not have tantrums and slam doors. But she tried her best to make the quiet click of her door carry the same emphasis as a crash.

Gulien himself brought Oressa her supper, not so very much later. Ordinarily Oressa loved sharing supper privately with her brother. She actually did like the formal dining hall, with its carved and gilded tables and heavy crystal goblets and beautiful painted plates, but when she and Gulien shared their father's high table, Gulien had to sit all the way across the table from her and so they couldn't hear each other unless they shouted. And no one shouted at the king's table, ever. So she usually liked it much better when Gulien joined her for a late, informal supper.

But tonight, after all that had happened, Oressa could hardly bring herself even to look at her brother. She knew nothing of this was his fault. She knew it was all her father's fault, but she couldn't help some of her anger spilling over on Gulien.

"I tried to stop him, you know," her brother said tentatively.

Oressa still didn't look at him. "No one can stop him doing anything he wants."

"I think it must be true that he offended the Kieba somehow."

"Really? I can't imagine how."

Gulien sat back. "You're too hard on him. I know you don't want to hear it, but you are. Carastind *needed* a decisive king after our great-grandfather—"

Oressa sighed loudly to make her brother stop and said pointedly, "*Some* people think it's important to make the *right* decisions. Apparently Father thought it was just fine to offend the Kieba instead!"

"Anyway," said Gulien pacifically, "I did try to tell him that you couldn't marry a Tamaristan prince no matter how much gilding Gajdosik puts on the bars of your cage, and he said—"

"I know what he said!" Oressa jerked her head up and glared at him. "He asked what you thought a princess was for—the decoration of the court? Because he already has plenty of decorative objects and would prefer useful ones."

"Well . . ." Gulien opened a hand. "That's close."

"What, was it even worse?" Whatever their father's precise words, Oressa could imagine his exact scathing tone. She tore a piece of bread into little pieces and then littler pieces, until it was a pile of crumbs in front of her.

Two of her father's guardsmen had also turned up at her door. They were just like an honor guard, except they, like princesses, weren't there to be decorative. Oressa knew they were there to stop her from running away to, say, become a temple maiden in Markand. That was rather insulting. Oressa had every intention of sneaking out of her room later, even if all she did was stroll back down the hallway to her door so she could look puzzled when the guardsmen were shocked to see her. She could do this perfectly easily by going out the window and climbing around to the aviary. She did that all the time. No one expected a princess to climb around on the outside walls of the palace, though really there was plenty of fretwork and carving so it was very easy. And the aviary would be deserted at this time of night, so it would be perfectly safe.

But teasing the guardsmen wouldn't change anything. Prince Gajdosik's ships would still be in the harbor, his men would still be on their way north from Paree, and her father would still be planning to sell her to him in exchange for an alliance against his brothers and Estenda. With all that, teasing the guard almost didn't seem like it would be worth the effort. Running away to Markand, *that* might be worth some effort. If she had the nerve. She'd never been on her own in the city; she'd hardly ever even left the palace. And Markand was a long way away. And could Gulien cope with their father without her? It was all ridiculous and impossible. She scowled down at her pile of bread crumbs.

"Stay put," Gulien told her. Oressa might have been angry that he would dare command her about anything, only then her brother scrubbed his hands over his face and added wearily, "Will you? Please? This isn't the time for your tricks. Everything's upset—it's too hard to predict where people will be. You'll be caught. We'll find a way to get you out of this, Oressa, only you can't do anything foolish. It'll just make things impossible. But I promise you, I won't let anyone sacrifice you like a game piece on a board. All right?"

Oressa started to ask how he planned to stop their father from doing anything at all. But she saw then that he was desperately worried and that part of what worried him was herself. She said, in her meekest tone, "All right." Although she couldn't help but add, "For now."

Gulien looked at her silently for some time. Then he said, as she had, "All right." He rubbed his hands over his face again and went away.

Breakfast, like the previous evening's supper, was a silent, strained affair. Oressa had no one to share it with but Nasia, and her maid knew maddeningly little about what was going on. Oressa thought about sneaking out of her room and listening to the rumors, but it was easier to get rumors from her father's guardsmen as the shifts changed. Except that half the rumors contradicted the other half. The Tamaristan soldiers were advancing up the road from Paree toward Caras. No, they were still in Paree. No, they'd left Paree, but they'd gone inland rather than up the coast. Oressa personally doubted that one: She couldn't think of any obvious reason why a Tamaristan force would head into the desert when conquering Carastind so obviously depended on taking Caras.

Other rumors said that another Tamaristan force had landed north of Caras, up by Addas, near the border Carastind shared with Estenda. No, but more ships had been spotted out to sea and might be heading north. No, there were ships, but they clearly meant to come straight into the harbor at Caras.

Oressa supposed Gajdosik had a plan for dealing with the cannons at the harbor mouth. She couldn't imagine what it was. Maybe he just had so many ships he was willing to sacrifice some to get his men to the docks.

By the time Gulien came back to see her, near dusk, she was exhausted with worry and the effort of staying in her rooms like an obedient child. But Gulien looked worse than she felt. He was carrying half a dozen old scrolls and one fat book. He sat down on Oressa's couch, piled all the scrolls and the book on the cushions next to him, let Nasia bring him a cup of cider, looked at it with blank weariness as though he didn't quite know what it was, and set the cup down untasted on the flat arm of the couch. Then he looked at Oressa and said without preamble, "Gajdosik's rejected Father's offer."

"What?" said Oressa blankly. She was stunned. She'd been furious about their father's plan to give her to the Tamaristan prince. But she had never for a moment thought Gajdosik might turn that offer *down*. "He can't have," she said, and looked at Gulien, trying to figure out what he might really have meant.

But her brother only shook his head. "Our courier came back with a message. A very clear message. Prince Gajdosik doesn't want an alliance."

"But—"

"He's arrogant, but he must truly believe he has enough men to take Caras and then make himself king of all Carastind. Maybe he does. We're getting reports—well, all kinds of reports. But there may be two or more princes behind this attack. There are definitely a lot more Tamaristan soldiers than we expected. And there might be another force in the north after all. We thought not, but now we think maybe there is. But however many branches there are to this attack, we're fairly certain it's Prince Gajdosik making all the decisions. We're sure he's going to try to take Caras. We have no idea how much else he might try to take. He's an aggressive bastard, that's the truth. And arrogant. He declares—" Gulien stopped.

"What?" When her brother stared at her without answering, Oressa threw a cushion at him. "*What?*"

"Well, he says, while a Carastindin princess might be useful, he doesn't need his marriage bound about with concessions and promises," Gulien said finally. "And a strong man takes the whole loaf instead of being satisfied with a mouthful of bread."

Oressa jumped to her feet, glaring at him.

"*I* didn't say it!" her brother protested, raising his hands. "*He* said it!"

Oressa swallowed her first furious response with some effort and declared instead, "We're not going to let him do this!"

"No. No, we'll fight." But her brother's tone made it clear that he expected to lose. He said, "Even without the Kieba's help, we could throw them back in any ordinary year. And in any ordinary year, the Kieba would probably protect us. But this year . . . I guess those rumors about the plague and about Father offending the Kieba did make it across the Narrow Sea, and I guess they sounded more plausible than I'd have thought. . . ."

Oressa felt sick.

"So I'm going to go see the Kieba myself."

Every time Oressa thought she couldn't be more shocked, Gulien said something more shocking. But as she thought about it, she started to like the idea.

"I know it's not completely safe, even for a Madalin," Gulien said earnestly. "We don't intrude without invitation—that's always been true. But—" Gulien patted the scrolls he'd brought. "Our records show we've had a good relationship with the Kieba all the way from the reign of Oren Madalin. I looked it up. When the fire rain came and every Madalin except Oren died, that's when the Kieba extended her protection not just to Carastind, but to our family specifically. That long ago, Oressa! I simply don't believe our father could have offended her so badly she'd forget she's favored us for hundreds of years! Even if he has, surely I can persuade her to be generous and forgiving. Then, if the *Kieba* defends us, Gajdosik will have no choice but to tuck his tail and run back to Tamarist, and if he can't win mercy from his brother there, that's just too bad for him."

"Yes," said Oressa, nodding. "I'll come with you."

"Oh no, you won't—"

"Yes! What else should I do? Wait here to see whether it's Gajdosik or the Kieba who gets here first? Because I bet it'll be Gajdosik, and you'll get back to find him in this hall and me a married woman—"

Gulien held up his hands to stop her. "Our soldiers would be ashamed to know you think so little of them." He paused to let her realize this was true. When her eyes dropped, he went on. "As I say, we'll fight. Caras won't fall in a day, and we've men coming from Little Caras and farther east. They'll get here before Gajdosik, and the plague rain this spring didn't fall inland, so that'll help. We'll hold. You'll hold here. I'll take a pair of fast horses. It'll take me maybe two days to get to the Kieba's mountain if I ride fast and don't stop for the night. You'd slow me down, Oressa. But that's not why you can't come. It's dangerous right now for travelers, but that's not why either."

Oressa put together several things she should have understood more quickly. She said, "You need me here so I can tell Father where you went."

"When you think it's time," Gulien said quickly. "Not too early, not too late. I trust your judgment, Oressa. There's no one else I can trust with this."

This was definitely true. "All right," Oressa said, not very happily. She was half relieved, maybe more than half, to see her idea of fleeing to Markand become impossible. "All right," she said again. "I'll stay here. I'll do this. But if you don't come back, Gulien, I *will* come after you. You tell the Kieba that." She tried to smile. "You warn her how much trouble I'd cause her. Tell her that."

Gulien hugged her, briefly and hard. "Keep safe," he said. "Be careful. And if you aren't going to be careful—"

"Be lucky," Oressa finished with him, and hugged him back. Then she let him go and stepped back.

CHAPTER 2

The Kieba's mountain wasn't tall and sharp-edged like the great jagged mountains of Markand. Gulien had seen illustrations in books, so he knew what Markand's mountains looked like: ranks of jagged white-edged peaks against the sky, like knives or shark's teeth. Those mountains looked cold and forbidding, as though nothing could ever live there, although the books spoke of stocky white sheep that leaped up and down sheer cliffs on their way to high pastures and of giant eagles that could carry away half-grown lambs.

The Kieba's mountain wasn't at all like that. It rose out of the red desert in a series of knolls and humps. Its highest point was probably . . . Gulien tilted his head back, estimating . . . not much more than twenty times higher than the king's palace in Caras, and the whole mountain was probably no farther around than a man could ride in a single day.

On the other hand, the Kieba's mountain was the only mountain in all of Carastind. It shrugged upward from the flat drylands, brooding in solitary power over the sandy soil with its dusty sage and tamarisk and over the fields of drylands wheat and purple-leaved amaranth some farmers, bolder than most, had planted in its shadow. The farmhouses and scattered outbuildings were visible in the distance, beyond the wheat fields. The river, brown with sediment, wound its sluggish way through the nearest field and vanished around the low shoulder of the Kieba's mountain. The road followed the river, but Gulien drew his horse to a halt where the river turned, beneath the spreading shade of one of the cottonwoods, and stared instead up at the mountain. No path led toward it. No one would dare trespass.

The whole mountain was surrounded by a wall, making clear the Kieba's desire for privacy. It was a low wall, barely shoulder high on a man. The stones were rough, providing easy handholds, and the top of the wall was flat and smooth. It was not meant to keep out trespassers, that wall, but only to mark out the boundary of the land the Kieba claimed for her own. If anyone was foolish enough to intrude, well, the Kieba was certainly well able to deal with trespassers. Everyone knew that— certainly Gulien knew that: He knew *all* the stories about the Kieba.

Iskandar of Markand had believed that the Kieba turned trespassers into foxes or falcons, or that she fed them to her foxes and falcons in order to teach her creatures to take human shape. But the people of Markand did not live in the Kieba's own country, and Iskandar, like most foreigners, had been ready to believe anything of the Kieba, even long after she had ceased to be a god.

On the other hand, Maranas Madalin, Gulien's own distant ancestor, had written that the Kieba imprisoned trespassers in lightless cells below her mountain and kept them there until they forgot their own names and voices and bodies and turned into mere whispers of darkness. Then she let them go, but they were only wraiths, haunting the dark moments between sunset and moonrise.

Normally Maranas Madalin had written in a plain, level-headed style; he had not seemed much given to flights of fancy. But even so, he'd written about the Kieba's prisoners turning into *whispers of darkness*. That had seemed unlikely to Gulien, when he'd read Maranas's account.

Now he looked across that Kieba's wall himself and found all those old stories turning over in his mind until he was no longer certain what he believed. Now that he was here, Gulien found he was not quite so eager to meet the Kieba as he had imagined.

But even now Caras might be hopelessly trying to defend against Tamaristan aggressors. And he had promised Oressa.

The river was shallow enough to be easy to ford. Gulien left his horse by the river, in the shade of the cottonwood. He hobbled it, but lightly, with a string the animal could break if it was startled or became impatient. He heaved its saddle up onto the flat surface of the wall, where no one could miss it, and draped the bridle beside it. He hoped he would be able to reclaim both gear and horse very soon, but if anything prevented him, then at least the farmers who had been brave enough to plant crops here by the Kieba's wall should find his gear when they came to check on their ripening wheat. That would be better than leaving a good saddle to be ruined by the sun and the weather.

Then Gulien hopped up onto the wall, slung his legs over, and sat beside his saddle for a long moment. The mountain ran up and up before him, the slope easy at first and then steepening, gritty soil broken by rolling red stone. There was no path. Of course. But the climb did not look too forbidding.

Except for what one might meet, of course, on the way.

It was no use for him to sit here on this wall, too afraid to go forward and too stubborn to go back. Gulien took a deep breath, pushed himself off the wall, and dropped to the ground on the other side.

Then he stood still for a long moment, waiting. But the Kieba did not appear in a whisper of dusk or a blaze of lightning, demanding to know what he thought he was doing. So he took a step, and then another, and at last, since he didn't know whether one way was better than another, he simply walked up the slope by the easiest way he could see. He didn't walk too quickly: He looked all around as he went, trying to see the wonders hidden beneath the gritty red soil. He saw nothing but wisps of tawny grasses and dwarfed scrub oak and feathery tamarisk. Nothing moved but wind and half a dozen quick-winged sparrows, brown and russet feathers almost lost against the sandy soil and dried grasses.

Gulien wondered how long it would take a man to climb from the wall to the top of the mountain and whether a trespasser might reach the top without meeting any of the Kieba's creatures, and what he might find there if he did. A shrine like the ones the common folk put up in memory of the dead gods, with a few grains of wheat scattered on the stone at its foot?

Or a door, such as were said to stand here and there in the world: a door that would let a man step from the top of this mountain into some far country, Estenda or Markand or even Tamarist—that would be uncomfortable, for a Madalin—or some country farther yet, so far its very name had been forgotten. Gulien felt his pulse quicken at the thought. Though perhaps that was just the effort of climbing the mountain, which proved steeper than he had guessed from a distance. Besides, his father's heir could hardly dare step through a magical doorway into some far country, no matter how strange and wonderful—

Not twenty feet before him, a desert hare sat up on its hind legs and regarded Gulien out of dark eyes.

Gulien stopped and stared at it. He knew at once that it wasn't a real hare, but one of the Kieba's creatures. It was larger and lankier than any ordinary hare—larger than a cat, almost as large as the feist dogs that farmers used to hunt hares. And the way it acted was definitely not the way an ordinary hare behaved. It sat bolt upright, its long ears attentively forward, its round eyes unblinking. Shafts of dazzling light came and went as high clouds slid through the afternoon sky, and the light glowed red in the eyes of the hare, making it look very much a creature of the gods.

"Kieba?" Gulien said out loud, cautiously. He did not feel ridiculous speaking to a hare. It did not even occur to him until moments later that he might have felt ridiculous, and by then the hare had dropped down and begun lolloping slowly up the mountain, angling off to the side rather than heading directly up the slope. It did not look around, but Gulien was sure he did not mistake its invitation. He followed it, scrambling a bit for balance where the sand slipped underfoot.

The hare led him around a jutting ridge of red stone where a twisted pine grew. There was a kind of path after all, though it was very rough; Gulien only gradually realized how flat stones had been laid along the downward edge and how the pines and scrub oaks marked the way. He followed the hare out onto an almost-level shoulder of the mountain where a sheer drop lay off to the right and the jagged, broken, nearly flat face of a cliff came down on the left, and there it stopped. It rose up on its hind legs again and stared at Gulien, its ears stiffly upright, and Gulien stared back at it for a moment, panting slightly with the climb, and then turned to gaze down at the endless drylands below. He could see the farm, too, the fields of crops and a man walking behind a team of mules, harvesting the earliest wheat, and farther away the farmhouses and barns and outbuildings. The farm looked peaceful and quiet and prosperous. Safe.

No one in Carastind was safe if Tamaristan princes came across the Narrow Sea with fire and arquebus and sword. Unless the Kieba stopped them.

Gulien turned back to the hare. He waited for it to speak in some human language, as the Kieba's creatures were said to be able to speak. It only stared back at him, silent and motionless.

At last he looked at the cliff and saw that it was actually a door. Then he wasn't certain how he had mistaken it for an ordinary cliff at all. It was gritty red stone like any cliff, but veins of smoky crystal ran through it, as broad as his hand, clearly framing the doorway. The smooth dark crystal was . . . familiar . . . unexpectedly so, and Gulien reached without thinking to touch the fragment of similar crystal he wore as a pendant, carved into the falcon that was the sign of his family. He wrapped his fingers around the pendant falcon, reaching out with his other hand to lay his palm flat against the broadest streak of crystal running though the red stone.

The crystal was warm under his hand, which might have been merely the warmth of the sun after a long day, but it seemed somehow like a living thing—it seemed almost to purr like a cat at his touch, though soundlessly. Then the stone framed within the crystalline doorway wavered and vanished in a wash of heavy heat, and Gulien shut his eyes and stepped forward, into the heat and out again into cool air. Taking a deep breath, he opened his eyes.

He was standing, he found, in a huge and echoing hallway, floored and walled with dark, soapy crystal, nothing that looked like it had ever been carved out of the inside of a red sandstone mountain. In this hall stood a statue of every god and goddess that had ever lived, carved of cold white marble, or equally cold black, or now and then of polished jade or some dark red stone Gulien did not recognize. Every statue guarded a closed and dusty door, each door carved of stone to match its guardian. The doors were set into the statues' plinths or framed by the fold of carven robes or defined by the grip of stone hands.

The statues were all tall and beautiful, though many of the gods and goddesses had the heads of animals or birds. Gulien stared around at them, picking out familiar faces and forms among the many he did not know. There was dog-headed Eiròn, who had been the patron of truth and loyalty. Even today the people of Caras preferred dogs that possessed that elegant, narrow head and those pricked ears. He was glad to see the god; that familiar tilted head somehow looked friendly and welcoming even carved in cold marble. It was almost like recognizing a friend. And now he saw that beyond Eiròn stood the graceful hawk-headed goddess Tituvoel, her great wings arching up and up nearly to the ceiling. He knew her, too. She had been a goddess of wisdom and clear sight. But nearer at hand was the black marble statue of a god that seemed nearly human, save for the delicately rendered scales, each dusted with gold, that surrounded his slit-pupiled eyes. Gulien had no idea who he was. He had never seen even an illustration. His fingers itched for paper and ink. It would have to be an illuminated drawing, to capture those scales—

"Welcome, Gulien Madalin, to the Hall of Remembrance," said a cold, clear voice out of the air. "Welcome to the Tomb of the Gods." The voice was not loud, but it came from everywhere, as though the mountain itself were speaking

Gulien flinched in startlement and stared all around, looking for the speaker. The hare watched him from a few feet away. But the voice had not come from the creature. It had come from the air—from all around. But he couldn't see the Kieba, and it hadn't been a woman's voice anyway. Nor a man's voice. Maybe the voice of a god . . . but all the gods were dead. Clearing his throat, he said cautiously, "You know my name, then. Will you tell me yours?"

"I have no name," stated the voice. "I am the kephalos. You are Gulien Madalin. Your primary identity is recognized. Your key is accepted. Your secondary identity has not been established. Please state your affiliation, your principal aspect, your subsidiary aspect, and your position."

Gulien had no idea what any of this meant. He guessed that his falcon pendant might have been taken as a kind of key, here in this place that seemed to have been carved entirely out of similar crystal. He stroked the pendant with a fingertip a little warily. He wanted to ask the mysterious kephalos whether this was what it meant when it referred to his key, but if he revealed his ignorance, perhaps it would decide he had no right to be here after all and send him away. So he said nothing.

Years ago he had had the falcon carved out of a chance-found bit of crystal. He'd found the bit of crystal during one of Oressa's adventures in the less-explored parts of the palace. He'd liked it and kept it and slept with it under his pillow. He'd believed it brought him dreams, or he'd told himself he believed that, having, as a child, a fancy for such mysteries. He'd dreamed of strange places, and of strange voices speaking to him in languages he didn't know. Of course, everyone dreamed nonsense; he knew that. But he'd liked the crystal, the feel of it against his skin, and so he'd had the falcon carved from it.

And now he stood within a mountain that seemed to have been carved out of the same kind of crystal. That lent a different color to all his dreams, which now he wished he'd written down so that he might remember them better. But he couldn't recall . . . he didn't *think* he could recall . . . anything about a—or the—kephalos.

The voice that had spoken to him didn't sound like a living person, but he could not quite imagine what else it might be: a servant of the Kieba's, a companion, or like her, an immortal who once had been a god, or something else entirely? What did it mean that it had no name? What kind of title was "kephalos"? He hesitated, not certain what he should say, or ask. He said at last, cautiously, "May I speak to the Kieba?"

"Your affiliation is to the Kieba," said the kephalos, not like a question, but as though Gulien had answered a question. "Accepted. Your principal aspect is: undefined. Your subsidiary aspect is: undefined. Your position is: ancillary. Follow the golem."

Plainly this meant the hare, which laid back its long ears, swiveled around, and lolloped gently away among the statues, seeming almost as out of place in this hall as Gulien felt.

Gulien, his heart beating hard in his chest, took one step forward. Nothing happened. So he walked forward, not too fast, following the hare as the voice had commanded. Toward the Kieba, he hoped. He did not know what the kephalos was, but the Kieba . . . He didn't know her, but she cured plagues and outlawed slavery and created crops that flourished in the drylands, and she had been the patron of the Madalin family and of Carastind for a long time. Surely all that outweighed her reputation for dealing harshly with trespassers. And her mountain had opened for him. He hoped she might be easier to talk to than the disembodied voice of the kephalos. He hoped she would be willing to talk about Carastind and Tamarist and not just about mysterious aspects and affiliations.

He knew he should think only about finding the Kieba and putting his case—Carastind's case—to her, but he could not resist laying his hand on dog-headed Eiròn's door when he passed it. More than a little to his surprise, the door shimmered and vanished at his touch, leaving only the frame still standing. Gulien stepped back quickly, then stopped, staring, caught by the astonishing glimpse of a birch wood where a path floored with golden leaves led from the god's door, down and down, turning back and forth across the foothills of unfamiliar mountains. Far below he could see the slender white towers of a strange, beautiful city. Beyond the city, sharp ranks of lavender-shadowed mountains stretched up and out forever.

Looking up at the mountains made Gulien feel faintly dizzy. Looking down at the many-tiered towers of the city made him feel nervous and excited. He took a step forward without even thinking, longing to walk down that mountain path and explore the white city. But of course he couldn't. For any number of reasons. He shook his head, letting out his breath in a long sigh.

"Kansai," said the kephalos, its tone as flat and inexpressive as ever. But it did not seem offended that Gulien had opened the door, and the hare paused and turned and sat up tall, watching him with patient dark eyes. The kephalos said, "The city lies across the ocean, in Gontai."

"Which ocean?" It couldn't mean the Narrow Sea, because only Tamarist lay across the Narrow Sea, and beyond Tamarist only the remnants of barbarian tribes in lands too poor for Tamarist to bother conquering. And Gulien knew there was no city like that or mountains like those in Tamarist.

"The Altannac Ocean."

Gulien shook his head. He had never heard of it. He said softly, "Could I go there? Not now, but someday? Meet the people who live there . . ."

"Kansai is empty. The city has lain empty for one hundred and seven years."

"Empty? But—"

"The Kieba failed her principal aspect. There was a plague. She did not find its cure." The kephalos didn't sound upset or angry or judgmental. Its tone didn't change at all, even on such a statement.

Gulien said, stunned, "They all died? All those people died?" It had never occurred to him that sometimes the Kieba might actually fail to cure a plague. That sometimes a *whole city* might die. He said again, "How could that *happen*?" He started walking again without waiting for an answer, following the hare past a goddess he knew—Ailerel, patron of scholars, with a stylus in her hand and a grave expression on her round, almost feline face—and past two gods he did not know, one with the head of a boar and bristles down his back and the other almost human except for a peculiar delicacy of bone and delicately pointed ears. To his right stood one of Gulien's favorite gods, fierce Eneolioir, who had a feathered crest instead of hair, talons on his hands instead of nails, and high-arching wings that stretched up so high they almost brushed the ceiling of the gods' hall. Eneolioir was supposed to have been the patron of justice. Gulien felt reassured to see him standing here, although of course the god was dead and men must make their own justice, which sometimes seemed in short supply. He said, "Kephalos? How could that happen? I thought the Kieba never failed to stop a plague." He *had* believed she never failed. It was unsettling to learn otherwise.

"The plague was unfamiliar to the Kieba," explained the kephalos. "It shared few sequences or modes or characteristics with any of the plagues filed in the vault."

At this Gulien paused again. "A vault of plagues," he said. His voice came out flat and expressionless, even to his own ear.

"Before you," said the kephalos. "Where the golem is waiting. That is Ysiddre, and beyond her, Ysiddro."

The two goddesses, standing here at the far end of the hall, a little separated from the other statues, were identically tall and slim and goat-headed. Each held her hands out, palms upward, and each carried a slim sickle moon in one hand and a full moon in the other. They looked exactly alike, until Gulien realized all at once that the statue of Ysiddre radiated a wash of pale silvery light, while Ysiddro's statue was half hidden in the shadows. The hare sat directly between the twin goddesses, seeming no more familiar and hardly more mortal than they.

"Ysiddre was allied to mortal people," stated the kephalos. "She strove to protect the world. When she knew she must die, she made this place, and made me to inhabit it and guard it and keep its memories. Her doorway leads to the heart of the mountain, where memory is layered above memory and the Kieba now dwells. You must pass Ysiddre's doorway to speak to the Kieba. You may pass."

Gulien nodded. "But the vault of plagues?"

"Ysiddro was Ysiddre's sister and ally. Her doorway leads to the vault of plagues, for only in understanding each plague may it be destroyed. The Kieba is Ysiddro's affiliate and takes her aspects of healing and death."

Gulien saw that it did make sense, disturbing as the whole idea was. A vault of plagues! But he did not argue. He asked instead, "The goddess made you? What are you?"

"I am the kephalos."

Gulien wondered what exactly that meant. He wished he might linger and ask. He wished to ask a hundred questions, a thousand, but he knew he had to find the Kieba and ask her only one question: whether she would help Carastind against her attackers.

Ysiddre's door would take him to the Kieba, apparently. The door stood to the right of the goddess. It was of white marble struck through with veins of smoky quartz and amethyst. Its knob was crystal and the new moon stood above its lintel. The hare moved toward it, and it swung slowly open, revealing a stairway that rose toward misty light in a tight spiral, each step carved of the same amethyst-threaded marble. Gulien stared at this stairway. Then he left the hare, which leaped up one stair at a time while he delayed a moment to walk around the twin statues and both their doors and came back around to peer once more up the spiral stairway. It was quite wonderful: a stair that existed only if one looked through the goddess's doorway and not if one peered around it into the shadows. Light that glimmered above the stairway but shed no light into this hall.

The hare was out of sight. But he did not immediately step through the doorway to follow it. Instead, he turned, as though drawn, toward the other door.

The door to the vault of plagues stood to Ysiddro's left, one side of its frame formed from the folds of her stone robe. It was black marble threaded with veins of white and smoke-gray crystal; its doorknob was black iron. He wondered if it would open to a stairway of black marble that led down and down into the shadowed depths of the mountain. It seemed to him that would be appropriate. He started to touch it, then hesitated, fearing it might open and plagues pour out upon the world.

"Touch it, if you wish," the kephalos suggested.

"It's safe?"

"The plagues are not so easily freed."

So Gulien, curious, touched the iron doorknob. Unexpected cold lanced up his fingers all the way to his elbow. He bit back a yelp, jerking away, but the cold did not fade. His whole arm burned and ached. "Kephalos!" he said. "Why didn't you warn me?"

"So Ysiddro's door is not yet keyed to your hand," said the kephalos, its tone as flat and neutral as ever.

Gulien set his teeth. He didn't understand, and he was angry, but he tried to set that aside. He was sure anger was dangerous, sure that defying the kephalos must be dangerous. He had entered the mountain knowing it was a place of peril for mortal men. He couldn't argue that he hadn't known. He rubbed the back of his hand, very gently. The burn was beginning to subside to a sharp prickle, but his hand still felt tender, as though he had held it too near a fire. He asked, "What does touching Ysiddro's door do to a man?"

"Less to you than to many," said the kephalos, not sounding at all concerned. "Take Ysiddre's stair and inquire of the Kieba."

Gulien shook his head, but he went up the white stairway. Toward the Kieba. He tried to steady his nerves and think what to say to her, though he was distracted by the increasingly painful tingling that ran up and down his arm. He tried to ignore that. He felt he was walking up into a story, into legend, into the time of the gods.

The stairway ended at last in a small chamber that had been carved entirely out of the gray crystal. Nothing was in the chamber except a single chair, too small and plain to call a throne, carved out of the same soap-smooth crystal, and beyond the chair, a low dais of the same crystal. The chair and the dais and the entire room seemed to have been carved all in a piece out of the heart of the mountain: There were no visible seams anywhere. There were three doors evenly spaced around the chamber— no, two doors. No . . . Gulien looked again and all the walls were smooth and featureless, broken by no doors at all. He turned quickly to look behind him, but the door through which he had come was gone as well. But when he turned again, slowly this time, the Kieba was there.

She was smaller than he had expected, and younger than he had expected, and far less human than he had expected. He knew, everyone knew, that the Kieba had once been a goddess and was still immortal. But he had not understood how little like a mortal woman she would be. She did not have wings or a cat's head or anything of that sort, but her cheekbones were sharp in her too-thin face, her mouth was narrow and her lips thin, her eyes enormous and a strange color, not really a color at all, translucent as water. When he looked in them, he saw nothing he recognized. Nothing human, or mortal, or approachable.

The Kieba was seated in the chair, her back straight, her arms resting along its arms, her long, bony fingers curling across the carved finials. She sat perfectly still, as though she had grown out of that chair, crystal herself, and only just taken on the color and warmth of life. She gazed at Gulien with a disinterested expression, as though she only half saw him and did not care for him at all. If she was breathing, he could not tell it. She did not speak. A marble statue could not have looked less welcoming. The hare sat upright at her side, its long ears turned forward, its dark eyes fixed on Gulien's face.

Now that he faced her, Gulien had no idea what to say to her. He finally bowed, neatly, rescued by his father's training: A prince learned to always be graceful and never show when he was at a loss. "Kieba," he said. He made sure his tone was quiet and respectful, as though he spoke to his father. Then he waited for her response.

"Prince Gulien," answered the Kieba. She tilted her head to look at him, but there was something wrong about the way she moved: quick and abrupt, a little like a bird rather than a mortal woman.

Gulien flinched and blinked. He realized he had half expected that she would ignore him—that he had half believed she was a statue after all. But her voice was more human than her appearance. Her tone was neutral, almost indifferent, but its timbre was that of an ordinary living person. He said, "Kieba, I have come to ask—"

"You laid your hand to Ysiddro's door and took injury of it," she interrupted him. "The kephalos informs me. Not a great injury, but potentially distracting." She looked Gulien up and down, as though she could look directly through his skin to his jumping nerves. Perhaps she could. It was impossible to tell whether she meant the injury distracted Gulien or herself.

"I—"

"The kephalos should have prevented you. Sometimes its inclinations are obscure," said the Kieba. She held out her hand, and a short, thick rod about the length of Gulien's forearm fell out of the air and into her hand. Gulien stared at it, and at her. It was a caduceus. He recognized it, though he had never seen one. They were not the most rare of the artifacts of the gods, but they were among the most prized. The loss of the Madalin caduceus had been the worst of the many damages inflicted on his family by his own great-grandfather's improvident rule: That had been a loss to everyone in Caras.

This one was longer and more heavily ornamented than the one that had belonged to the Madalin family. It was about as thick as Gulien's thumb, made of twisted black iron with a thread of black crystal running around it from one end to the other. From the way the Kieba held it, Gulien guessed it must be heavier than it looked. The Kieba traced a fingertip down the line of the crystal, from one end of the rod to the other and back again. Then she met Gulien's eyes and held out her hand in clear command.

After a moment Gulien obediently set his hand in hers. The nerves twitched and jumped under his skin, and her touch burned as though her skin contained fire rather than mortal flesh, but he tried not to let himself flinch. The Kieba grasped his wrist firmly and drew the tip of the caduceus quickly down his arm, from elbow to palm. Then she did it again. First the tingling came back, but not unpleasantly; then the cold numbness faded. Warmth flushed through his arm, then through his whole body. Gulien let his breath out in a long sigh.

"So," said the Kieba. She let him go abruptly and set the caduceus aside, laying it down on empty air as though on a side table; rather than falling to the floor, it vanished.

Gulien stared after it. Then he met the Kieba's opaque gaze and began. "Thank you—"

"Do not thank me," the Kieba said flatly. "The injury was slight. I do not know why the kephalos was concerned. You would most likely have recovered in some small measure of time without aid." She lifted one hand slightly to signify dismissal and went on. "You have come to ask me to intervene for Madalin against the Garamanaji princes. I am aware of events in Tamarist and in Carastind. I am not surprised that your father sent you to me. But I am surprised that Osir Madalin would expect me to be swayed by any request of his."

"There *is* more than one Tamaristan prince?" said Gulien, trying to decide whether this was good or bad and finding it on the whole unwelcome news. The various princes might quarrel with one another and that might be useful, but he feared they would ally against Carastind and that would surely be very bad. He collected himself and looked the Kieba in the face. "I ask your pardon, Kieba, that I must correct your misapprehension, but my father did not send me. I came on my own. I must beg you to excuse my boldness in trespassing upon your privacy. You know everything already, so you must also know I had no choice but to come. If you will not help us, we will surely be defeated."

"Why should that matter to me?" asked the Kieba.

Gulien bit his tongue hard to keep from exclaiming out loud. He said at last, "My father has indeed offended you somehow, then. I feared that might be so. Tell me now what amends I can make, Kieba, that will restore my family and my people to your favor."

"If you recovered Parianasaku's Capture for me, I would favor Carastind. You cannot. Your father will not give it to you, you cannot take it, and if you did, you would not give it to me. No Madalin will give up Parianasaku's Capture. It was most unwisely bonded to the blood of the kings of your line."

Gulien tried not to stare at her. He dropped his gaze to the floor, rapidly running through the whole list of fragmentary artifacts his family had ever collected, whether known to contain splinters of the dead gods' power or otherwise, but he could not think of anything with that name. He began at last. "Kieba, I assure you—"

"It was a gift to the Madalin line," the Keiba told him, sharply impatient. "Well intentioned, to be sure, and it seemed harmless at the time, even wise. A gift to aid folk to flourish here in the drylands; one could see no harm in that, and much good. It is always better to establish towns and nations as widely as possible, lest one lose too much when one city or nation perishes. And the drylands are not quite so susceptible to plagues as gentler country."

Gulien thought at once of the empty city of Kansai, the white towers pristine and dead. He felt chilled at the implication that such disasters might have happened before, perhaps more than once—that they might not even be rare.

The Kieba was going on, her voice no more expressive than before. "Even allowing Parianasaku's Capture to bind to the blood of one Carastindin king and then another seemed well enough at the time; artifacts such as the Capture must be fed and tended to maintain potency. For many years your ancestors put it to good use drawing in the spring rains, gentling the midsummer dust storms away from your croplands, capturing the winter mists. All this was well enough. But now Osir Madalin has discovered a secondary function of Parianasaku's Capture and put the artifact to a use for which it was not intended. Thus he has created a situation which is even now causing me considerable difficulty. Your father's attempts to capture and control plagues might be laudable, if pursued with the proper tools and an accurate understanding for the inevitable complications. Neither of which he possesses. Fortunately, a suitable recourse now presents itself, as clearly one or another of the Garamanaji princes will shortly relieve Osir of his crown. That will end the terms under which Parianasaku's Capture was lent. Then I will recover it without difficulty."

Gulien protested, "But—"

"It was bonded to your family for so long as your family should rule," the Kieba said flatly. "Those were the terms of the gift. It exists half in

Osir Madalin's flesh, half in his mind, and hardly at all in the world. Thus I cannot simply take it. He must give it to me. And he will not. Perhaps he cannot."

"Kieba, *I* would give—"

"You say so now. But you cannot take the Capture save if you take the kingship of Carastind. And if you should do so, if the artifact should forsake your father and enter your blood and bond to your flesh, what then, Gulien Madalin? Do you think you would be able to give it up then?"

This was more and more disturbing. Gulien hardly knew how to answer.

The Kieba went on. "Now Osir Madalin puts it to serious misuse. A plague your father cast out of Caras now burns in Elaru. Worse, it has attained a far more virulent form because of his mishandling. Worst of all, it possesses a long latency, or it would never have spread so widely before I discovered it. I warned him. I did warn him most strictly. Now he does this. Perhaps I will be able to destroy the plague, or perhaps I must burn a firebreak about Elaru and allow those within the city to die, lest it spread. Then there would be two dead cities in Gontai. So you see I have little fondness now for Osir Madalin."

"I understand. I am sorry, Kieba, for the errors my father has made. I swear I had no idea of this. But, Kieba, I *would* give up this artifact," Gulien promised her. "I—"

"You would not. And even if you would, it is not yours. You are not king."

The Kieba sounded completely inflexible. Gulien had heard that tone many times from his father. When his father used that tone, everyone knew he would not change his mind. But the Kieba was not Osir Madalin. Maybe she could be swayed. Gulien paused and then began again, carefully respectful. "Your anger with my father may be just, Kieba, but are you so angry you will leave all the people of Carastind to suffer under a foreign king? Is *that* just?"

The Kieba lifted her eyebrows almost imperceptibly. "Kingdoms rise and fall, young prince, and it matters very little. Your family has done well by Carastind in the past, but families, too, rise and fall. It is a mistake to grow too fond."

Gulien had no idea how to answer that. He took a step forward, holding out his hands in urgent entreaty. "Kieba, the people of Carastind do not know that you have decreed they should become a subject people! They will fight. They may be fighting even now. Even weakened by the spring plague, our men will fight to protect their families, to keep their wives and their children from being made the slaves of a foreign king. And well they should! All know how folk live in Tamarist: poor and unlettered, forbidden to take up arms though brigands prey upon them. Will you leave my people, who are your own people too, to suffer—"

"You will not sway me, young prince."

Gulien knew he had to sway her. He said forcefully, "Kieba, as my father has offended you, dispossess him! As the Madalin line has lost your confidence, dispossess us. Then you may take back your artifact at your pleasure." He found he dared not think too closely about what he was suggesting. He went on quickly. "Only set some symbol of your power between Tamarist and my people before you tear down the Madalin falcon—let all the Garamanaji princes see that your hand is between their ambition and the people of Carastind. Then they will take their quarrels elsewhere, and you may choose another king for us from among our own people. Anyone who pleases you. There must be a man of Carastind who would please you!"

The Kieba shrugged, a minimal gesture. "Allowing a Tamaristan prince to throw down the Madalin falcon is far simpler. I must attend to Elaru."

"But—"

"The plague there, Prince Gulien, is one for which your father is *directly* responsible, and even now I delay working with it to speak with you."

Prince Gulien opened his hands, pleading, casting aside pride. "Kieba! I swear I *will* bring you this artifact. I will take it from my father and bring it to you. I will set it into your hands myself. You need not trouble yourself at all! If you are angry with my father, with my house, then let your anger fall on my father and on my house. But"—he straightened as a new thought struck him and said, still more urgently—"Kieba, leave my sister to wed a new king. Then even my father's partisans must accept the change of lineage. Kieba, please! Intercede now, only a little, and there need not be years of strife and fury, and everything will be as you desire—"

The Kieba moved her hand, and Prince Gulien fell silent, swallowing. She did not look angry, exactly, but he did not dare defy her gesture.

"Prince Gulien, go back to Caras. Let events play themselves out. It is time for the Madalin line to be dispossessed of its crown, that the gift may achieve its finite term. If you would reduce your people's hardship, then persuade your father to yield quickly to the strongest Tamaristan prince. Gajdosik would do best, I think. Giving Carastind into Prince Gajdosik's hands would do more than anything else to achieve your aim. Let Prince Gajdosik take Carastind. He will do well enough—and Parianasaku's Capture will return to its proper place and role."

Gulien stared at her for a long moment. He asked at last, "Can I say nothing to sway you?" But he already knew there was nothing he could say.

"Go back to Caras," the Kieba told him, with an indifference worse than unkindness. "I must return my attention to Elaru. When I am able to spare time and attention for minor problems, I shall return and then I will see to it that Carastind does not suffer unduly under its Tamaristan king. But you would do best to return to Caras. There is nothing for you here."

Gulien might have tried to argue further, but she only lifted a hand, flickered twice like a candle in a breeze, and like a candle flame, went out suddenly. Her chair was empty, as though she had never been there at all. He turned quickly, looking for her, already knowing he would not see her. She was gone. To the city of Elaru, he assumed, abandoning Caras and all of Carastind. Because of his father. Gulien scrubbed his hands across his face, sick and furious. He did not know what he would tell Oressa. Or his father. If his father indeed held this Parianasaku's

Capture, and Gulien had no doubt that he did, then the Kieba was right. Whatever it was, whether it was bonded to him somehow or not, he would never give it up. Osir Madalin never gave up anything of power.

Gulien said out loud, "Oh, gods!" But the gods were dead and could not hear him, and he supposed they might very well only have said, *Kingdoms rise and fall, and it matters very little. . . . It is a mistake to grow too fond.* He said, half a groan, "Carastind is going to fall. Caras might already have fallen! How could I even know? Kieba!" But though he hoped, despite himself, that the Kieba might answer, she did not return.

"Gulien Madalin," said the flat voice of the kephalos. "Your key has been accepted. Your ancillary position has been recognized. Do you wish to envision Caras? Your predisposition should be confirmed. It may prove adequate to allow further ties to memory. If you wish to confirm your predisposition, ascertain your status, and establish your secondary identity, you may try the Kieba's chair and venture the memories of the mountain."

Gulien looked up, trying to parse this peculiar suggestion. Then he looked across the room at the Kieba's empty chair. It was a heavy thing, carved with bold, smooth strokes and no flourishes whatsoever. Except, he saw now, the finials of its arms, where your hands would rest if you sat in the chair, were carved with thin grooves and glittered as though dusted with tiny jewels. Other than that, the chair was completely unornamented. That it was a thing of the gods was highly probable, though Gulien had never heard of so large an unbroken artifact. That it was part of the Kieba's power seemed likely. That it might be dangerous to dare take her place in that chair also seemed likely.

But, apparently, he had the kephalos's permission. And a key. Gulien lifted a hand and curled his fingers around the smooth, warm crystal falcon set into his pendant. Its familiar warmth reassured him.

The kephalos said he might see what was happening in Caras if he sat in that chair. He thought that was what it had meant. The Kieba might not know what the kephalos had proposed. Probably she didn't.

If she did, she would probably be angry. But the Kieba was not here. Though he waited another moment, and another after that, she did not come.

At last Gulien made his way across the room and laid a cautious hand on the back of the chair. The crystal's faint, familiar warmth was reassuring. Like his own crystal, the chair felt to him like something alive, like something he knew.

Turning, he sat down in the chair, not permitting himself to think more about it. Though made of a kind of stone, the chair was surprisingly comfortable. It had looked small from across the room, sized to the Kieba, but now it seemed made to fit Gulien's height and length of limb. When he stretched his arms along the arms of the chair, his hands fell exactly on the finials.

But as soon as his hands touched the finials, needles grew out of the arms of the chair and pierced his hands and wrists. Some of the needles were black, some white, and some clear as water, and all of them were fine and sharp enough that Gulien barely felt their bite. But he would have jerked away, only he couldn't. From the first instant, a sharp cold radiated outward from where each needle pierced his skin. Somehow the cold pinned him in place. He blinked. Even that tiny motion felt slow and strange, and he wasn't sure afterward whether he'd opened his eyes again or not. His vision dissolved, not to blackness, but to a broken storm of images and memories that sleeted through his mind, sharp and glittering as shards of crystal.

He glimpsed patchwork fields amid the drylands far below, and Caras like a jewel beside the sea, and ships running over the waves and docked in the harbor. Above the ships flew banners showing an eagle with serpents in its talons. He recognized the device: It was the sigil of the Garamanaji, the royal family of Tamarist. And those ships were docked already in the harbor; the harbor defenses must have failed already—the defenses must have failed almost at once.

Gulien slid down the wind, his wings tilting . . . all his wings; his vision multiplied, dizzyingly, so that suddenly he saw the countryside from a hundred different angles and heights. He *was* flying, but it wasn't him. Only in a way it was. He could *feel* the wind rushing through the feathers of his wings. He knew it wasn't real, couldn't be real, but it *felt* real.

There were Tamaristan soldiers outside the city gates, too, and not only outside: He saw a great plume of black smoke and red dust hanging in the air, slowly shredding away inland because of the sea breeze. The gates were strong and heavy and had not been breached. He saw that. But the wall beside the gates had shattered, broken stone like gravel scattered out into the city streets. And he could see the Tamaristan soldiers moving, in an advance that seemed slow, but he knew they were actually rushing into Caras and he could see that the narrow line of defenders would not be able to stop them.

He groaned and did not know if he made a sound at all, and then he suddenly he saw the whole city from far above: He saw a rain of fire and everywhere homes burning and a tide of blood rolling into the harbor. Horror struck him, yet he saw then that the city was both afire and peaceful; that men both fought and did not fight; that the harbor was both stained with blood and clean. He didn't understand what he saw, except it came to him after a shaken instant that the fire and blood were nothing that was happening right now: That was memory, only not *his* memory. The anguish that shook him with sudden violence wasn't his, either; he knew that, but it *felt* like his. He wanted to weep for the grief of it, but he didn't understand what he grieved *for*. But someone knew. He almost remembered.

A falcon banner flew over the gates of Caras, but the banner was burning. Fragments of ash and charred cloth whirled away on a hot wind. A voice he almost recognized said, in grief and rage, "The falcon cannot outfly the fire," and Gulien knew that someone had once stood under a banner like that, high up on a balcony of golden stone, as he stood now. . . . It wasn't him. Yet he could almost feel the balustrade under his palms. Someone had turned, his heart breaking, to see . . . to see . . . He didn't know. Someone or something that was lost, or would be lost, or had been lost, far in the past. The vision shattered before he could grasp it, shards of memories scattering out of his grasp.

Through the discordant fragments of vision, he caught a sudden glimpse of an unfamiliar city, all white stone and red brick, sprawling in the midst of amazingly green pastures and thick woodlands—a countryside that had nothing at all in common with the drylands and desert around the Kieba's mountain. He flew through the cold air high above, watching the folk of this city barricade their homes against the creeping violet-black mist that spread outward from the heart of the city. The sound of drums came to him distantly, and the tolling of great bells, and above both a high-pitched wailing of women's voices. He knew the city. . . . *He* didn't, but a voice out of memory said, "Elaru. Elaru is burning."

Horrified, he flinched away from the creeping mist and the lamenting women, and vision shattered and re-formed around him once more, but he could not find Caras again. So he looked for himself, for the Kieba's mountain, for the place he remembered he was, but he couldn't find the mountain or himself, either. He tried to remember his name, but the names that sleeted through his memory weren't his—he didn't know his name; he couldn't pick one out from among the rest—

"Gulien Madalin," said the kephalos. "Gulien Madalin."

Gulien jumped up, staggered, lost his balance, recoiled, took a fast step to catch himself, and nearly fell anyway. His hands were shaking. He didn't even care. There were tiny pinpricks of blood on his palms and wrists, and a residual cold that seemed to have spread right through his whole body. He wanted to sit down, but not in that black crystal chair. He collapsed on the floor instead, like a child. He couldn't begin to frame what he'd seen. Or thought he'd seen. Or felt. Or remembered. He didn't know whose memories those had been. They were *still in him*. He could see Elaru dying in his mind's eye. He could see Caras burning, even though it hadn't happened yet—hadn't happened again. It was in the past, but it felt like yesterday, like today, like it was happening right now. The memory of black smoke choked him. But it was memory, and not *his* memory.

"Manian Semai," the kephalos stated, its flat voice making him twitch as it seemed to read his thoughts. "That was his memory. You seem inclined toward Manian Semai for your secondary identity. That will do. Your overall predisposition seems clear and strong."

"I don't—you didn't—it wasn't—" Gulien pressed his hands over his mouth. He was shaking. Memories that weren't his crowded his mind's eye. "What is this predisposition?"

"Close dealing with living crystal often yields a strong predisposition. This is generally stronger in the scions of lines that have long possessed a potent artifact."

Gulien shook his head, not understanding any of this. But he remembered ships flying the eagle banner, and the soldiers on the road, and the falcon banner above the closed gates of his own city. That part was real. That part was *now*. He remembered standing on a balcony of golden stone, feeling afraid—no. Not afraid. Guilty. He didn't have any idea why he should feel *guilty*. He couldn't *remember*. But that memory wasn't his, hadn't been his. Shattered bits of disconnected visions and memories and that terrible feeling of guilt . . . fire in the sky and the sea turned to blood . . . Nothing he seemed to remember made *sense*. He couldn't stop shaking.

"Ancillary memory is generally perceived as disturbing," said the kephalos. "Your predisposition is well established, however. Do not be concerned."

"Concerned!" said Gulien, and laughed, but it was half a sob, and he cut it off, pressing his hands over his mouth again. He tried to think only of what was most important. Tamaristan aggression. Prince Gajdosik. He would first take Caras and then conquer the rest of Carastind, and there was nothing Gulien could do about it. The Kieba meant to let it happen.

Gulien could still hardly believe it.

Although he understood it. His skin tightened with horror when he thought of the city of Elaru, of that violet-black mist creeping among the brick buildings, and the high, thin voices of the women wailing. If his father had sent that terrible plague to Elaru . . . No wonder the Kieba was so angry. That was a *terrible* thing to do. Gulien wondered whether his father had known that he was sending the plague away to another city rather than destroying it. If he had . . . if he had, then the Kieba was right to be angry. Gulien discovered that he was furious with his father himself. And furious with the Kieba. He shook with anger at them both. He said, not letting himself think too much, "Kephalos!"

"Yes, Gulien Madalin?" answered the calm, inhuman voice.

"The Kieba is not here. Is that so? She is gone to Elaru?"

"That information is restricted," said the kephalos without emphasis. Then it added, "However, the Kieba is now unavailable."

Gulien took a deep breath. "But she can't spare time or attention for *minor problems* here in Carastind. Not right now. Isn't *that* so?" He knew it was.

"That is so," agreed the kephalos.

Gulien nodded. He said cautiously, "I need an artifact, so that I can protect Carastind against our enemies. Since I . . . I have an affiliation to the Kieba, and an established secondary identity, and an ancillary position—" Or was it supposed to be an established identity and a secondary position? He hardly remembered and hoped he had gotten it right. He said, trying to sound firm and confident, "I have the right to take—to borrow—an artifact. Is there something—what do you have that I could take with me back to Caras and use to drive out the Tamaristan invaders and protect my city and my country?"

There was a moment of silence. Then the answer came, flat and level and uninflected: "A war golem would effectively answer your need as you have defined it."

A war golem. Gulien hesitated, glancing down at the hare. That was a golem. It did not look like an ordinary animal. But it hardly seemed adequate to drive away an invading army. He said cautiously, "A golem? Like that hare?"

"It is not a hare. It is a golem. An accessory of mine."

Gulien nodded, though he wasn't certain what the kephalos meant by "an accessory of mine." The creature *looked* like a hare. "An accessory?"

"An appendage. The golems are my eyes and hands. Also the eyes and hands of the Kieba."

Gulien studied the hare. Its fur ruffled when it moved; it tilted its ears and turned its head like a real animal. "They say—" He stopped, wondering whether it was wise to ask. But he wanted to know, and went on at last. "I've read accounts that claim the Kieba turns trespassers into foxes or cats or crows or owls. Or hares. That's not—that isn't—that isn't how golems are made?" He'd read worse than that, but he wasn't certain he wished to ask if the Kieba really fed trespassers to her creatures, or if she really flayed people alive and used their skins to give her servants human shape.

"No. A golem is not a creature."

The hare tipped its ears back, dropped to all fours, and shook itself.

Gulien jerked back. Then he leaned forward, staring. The hare had come apart into two halves, which was appalling, but it was not at all like an animal on the inside. It was solid all the way through, soft like putty, a gray-blue color flecked with silver and black. "What *is* it?"

"A golem," repeated the kephalos.

Gulien shook his head, not in denial or disbelief, but in a kind of wonder.

The front half of the hare stood up again, and so did the back half, and the two halves came back together and sealed, leaving only a faint ripple in the fur to show where it had divided itself in two. Then it shook itself again and folded inward and opened out, and it was a falcon.

It looked exactly like a real falcon: a large one, nearly the size of an eagle, but with a falcon's buff chest and narrow copper-colored wings. The falcon drew itself up to its full height, opened its wings, and leaped into the air. It flew exactly like a real falcon: fierce and sudden and neat in the air, turning on a wingtip and flying in a swift circle before dropping to perch on the back of the Kieba's chair.

Or, thought Gulien, it didn't move *exactly* like a real falcon. The difference was subtle. But he *thought* the falcon moved just a little more sharply, a little more jerkily than a real bird.

"My eyes in the world," said the kephalos.

Gulien stared at the falcon. "You have many such golems, then? You see through the eyes of all the golems at once? And so you see everything." He could hardly imagine. A thought struck him and he asked, "Do the golems—do you—see through the Kieba's eyes as well?"

"Sometimes," said the kephalos. "And sometimes the Kieba sees through my eyes."

Gulien nodded and took a breath. "And if falcons are your eyes, what is a war golem, may I ask, kephalos?"

An image flashed into the crystal behind the Kieba's chair, an image of an unfamiliar city, and stalking through the streets, a great spidery shape made of steel and glass, which had assuredly never been anything so harmless or small as a hare or a falcon.

Gulien took a step back involuntarily before he caught himself. He put a hand out for balance, though there was nothing to take hold of except the Kieba's chair, and he would not touch that. But he wished he had *something* to cling to. He felt as though the mountain had shifted under his feet, as though if he moved he might fall from a great height. But that wasn't real. The stone under his feet might be made of layers upon layers of crystallized memory, but it was solid. No matter what he did, he could not really fall.

There were tales of those golems, from the beginning of the age, from the time when the Kieba had first established her authority and taught the kingdoms of men that she would enforce her decrees. Sketches had survived, though they did not agree one with another. Gulien asked, half dreading the answer because he could already imagine coming too late—too late for his city, too late for his sister—"But how fast could that kind of golem get to Caras?"

"If the golem passed through Berakalan's door," stated the kephalos, "it would require four and a half minutes to achieve that destination."

Four and a half minutes! There was a *door* to Caras, right from the

Kieba's mountain. Of course there was. Gulien shut his eyes and tried to think. *You need do so little*, he had pleaded with the Kieba. *Only let Gajdosik see that your hand is between him and the people of Carastind.* A war golem would be clear proof to everyone that her hand *was* set between the people of Carastind and all their enemies. "But if she finds out . . . ," he whispered. "*When* she finds out, what will she do? And would I be able to *use* a golem, anyway? I'm not the Kieba!"

He had said it only to himself. But the kephalos answered. "When the Kieba's attention returns from Elaru, she will be able to countermand any measures you requested and recall any golem you have deployed. But if you agree to consolidate your ancillary position and establish your secondary identity within the mountain, I will construe your position as permitting you to direct the resources of the mountain within reasonable limits, until such countermanding instructions should be issued. The use of a single war golem would be well within those limits."

Gulien turned this over in his mind. He had not understood before that the kephalos might have its own design, that it might not be strictly the Kieba's servitor. But he thought so now. He thought it intended to use his appearance at the mountain—with his own key, and apparently his own position, whatever that meant—to pursue some goal of its own. He didn't know whether he should find that frightening, but he could see that it could be useful. The Kieba would find out he'd taken one of these war golems. She would be furious. But . . . perhaps that would not matter. After all, it would be done. The Tamaristan soldiers would have been thrown out of Caras, and everyone would have been shown that the Kieba still favored Carastind. What happened to Gulien himself after that hardly seemed to matter.

He said to the kephalos, "Yes. Yes, I want a golem. I will agree to all you say." He looked again at the great spider reflected in the crystal. One would be enough. He had read Malke's account of these creatures, when the Kieba used them in Markand, to tear down the court of Sedmenam during the third Taran Dynasty. He was sure that one would be enough.

And the kephalos said tonelessly, "I will send the golem to Berakalan's door."

Berakalan turned out to look almost like a human man, only with eyes that were too big and slit-pupiled, and with short, blunt tusks set obliquely in his lower jaw. His door, on which one of his stone hands rested, was a huge arch of glittering pinkish gray stone. Gulien, resting his hand cautiously on the arch, found the center of the arch dissolving, so that he looked down toward Caras from a gritty, barren drylands slope. The city was small in the distance, but the black smoke streaking the air above it was plainly visible. Gulien turned grimly to look for the promised golem.

After what seemed a long time but was probably only a few minutes, it came, picking its way carefully through the Hall of Remembrance because it was too big to fit easily between the statues. Gulien stared up at it—and up. It was huge. It was *splendid*. He had not expected such splendor, and found himself breathless with awe. Truly it was a thing of the gods.

The golem was, as he had expected, a little like a giant spider. At least, it had many legs, like a spider, except the golem had twelve legs instead of eight, and some of the legs had gripping claws that were almost like hands. And it had slender little arms in the front with real hands, too, though its fingers were longer and more slender than human fingers, and seemed to be jointed oddly.

The golem was about eight feet tall and at least that big around, but its head rose up on a slender jointed neck, much higher than its body, strange and elegant. It had clusters of black crystal eyes all around its head so it could see in all directions at once and delicate antennae on which more crystals bobbed and swayed.

Despite its size, the golem moved with a neat, precise, abrupt motion that was almost dainty. It looked like it was made out of steel, only its body and legs were covered with slender needles of glass so fine that it might have looked like coarse fur, except for the way the spines glittered.

After it reached Berakalan's statue and stopped, Gulien touched the tip of a spine very carefully, then shook a drop of blood from his finger because they were even sharper than they looked.

The golem was perfect. He thought if this golem stalked toward even the bravest soldiers, they would break and flee in terror. Besides, the Tamaristans would know immediately that something like this had to belong to the Kieba. That alone should terrify them.

He asked, "Can I ride on top of that golem?"

"Yes," said the kephalos. "That is expected. The back of the golem will provide a safe position for you under most anticipated conditions of the modern battlefield. Simply instruct it as to your intentions and desires. It is partially autonomous, though largely containing my own awareness."

Without waiting to be instructed, the golem tipped a bit to the side, canting a long leg to provide a step, its spines all rippling to the right and left so, Gulien realized, he wouldn't be shredded on the way up. He climbed up, careful of the spines. The metal beside the golem's neck was smooth, and there was a good place to sit if you tucked your legs up. Gulien eased himself down to his knees, then grabbed a handy spike as the golem heaved and straightened.

He stared out at the Hall of Remembrance. Sitting up on top of the golem wasn't like sitting on a horse. It was so much taller, and it didn't feel exactly alive underneath him the way a horse would have. He felt, sitting here, perfectly stable and unreachable. He took a deep breath, put a hand on the golem's neck to steady himself, and said, "Let us proceed at once through Berakalan's door and to Caras!"

The golem lowered its round head on its long neck, and Gulien ducked *his* head, and the golem carried him through Berakalan's door and out into the hot drylands. Distance and brilliant light and a hot wind smelling of the sea and the distant city with charcoal streaks of smoke above it. Behind them, when Gulien looked, there was no trace of the god's door. "Kephalos!" he said, alarmed. "Are you here?"

"Yes, Gulien Madalin," said the flat, dry, familiar, reassuring voice of the kephalos, not sounding any longer as though it surrounded him, but seeming to speak from the head of the golem.

Gulien took a deep, relieved breath, trying to pretend he had never been frightened. "Let us move quickly toward the city," he commanded.

The golem immediately strode forward, its many legs going *tock, tock, tock* against the sandy ground in a fast rippling motion. It moved faster and much more smoothly than a horse. Riding the moving golem, Gulien decided, was like a cross between riding a huge bull and riding a boulder: It felt alive and massive and dangerous. It was *splendid*. He said impulsively, "That stone up ahead, the one with the smaller rock on top of it, attack that stone as though it were an enemy soldier!"

The golem's head swiveled, and one of its legs twitched. Three glass spines flashed through the air, glittering, and struck the boulder—and exploded, each with a sharp *crack* like a dry branch breaking, only louder. The stone shattered. Shards of rock flew in all directions—Gulien bit back an exclamation and ducked, covering his head with his arms, but he was laughing, too. The golem was *perfect*.

CHAPTER 3

Oressa stood on the highest peak of the palace roof and stared out over Caras, toward the harbor. She couldn't see the harbor even from this height, but she could see black smoke billowing into the sky. There was a great deal of smoke. Somewhere, something important was on fire. Ships, maybe, which would be good, as long as they were Tamaristan ships. Or the dyers' guildhouse, which was near the harbor—that would be bad. A guildhouse on fire would mean the Tamaristans had gotten right into Caras.

The defenders should have been able to use the cannons mounted at the harbor to keep enemy ships out, but though she had heard some explosions from that direction earlier, she couldn't hear any cannons firing now. She could hear the sharper sounds of arquebuses way to the south, so she knew there must be fighting near the southern gate, but none of the deeper voices of cannons. She tried to think of good reasons the Carastindin defenders might have decided not to use the cannons, but everything she came up with seemed unlikely. Maybe that smoke meant the docks themselves were burning. Oressa thought if she'd been defending the harbor and found herself for some reason unable to use the cannon, *she* would have burned the docks.

Of course, if she'd been in charge of the Tamaristan attack and the docks were fired, she'd have at least one ship prepared to run straight against the stone quay. It would be worth sacrificing a ship to establish a bridgehead at the harbor. She wished she could see. She could hear well enough: All the shouts and cries and screams seemed to rise to her high perch. But the distant clamor told her nothing. It rose and fell and seemed at first nearer and then farther away.

Oressa wasn't supposed to be on the roof, of course. She was supposed to be in her rooms, waiting obediently for the eventual summons that would tell her whether it was still her father who controlled the palace and the city, or whether it was Prince Gajdosik, or maybe somebody else. She felt much safer on the roof. She stood behind the carved statue of an old god, a god with feathered wings. Gulien would have known his name. Oressa only knew she was grateful for his wings, which stretched out behind him, curving inward at the tips to enclose the peak of the roof. Sheltered by the god's wings, she was safer than if she'd stood on a balcony with a sturdy railing. She leaned her elbows on the carved feathers and stared out toward the smoke.

It was only getting up beside the god that was a little tricky. And getting down, of course. But Oressa was barefoot, so she wouldn't slip. She had her slippers in a pouch at her hip, along with a skirt, the one of crushed green and gold silk that never showed extra wrinkles because it was supposed to look like that. She'd braided her hair and wound the braid around her head, but she had a comb and a long strand of pearls in her pouch, too. She had everything necessary to turn herself back into a dignified princess. She could climb back down the roof and into the palace through any number of windows, and then all she would need was a minute or so of privacy. But Oressa thought she might spend the whole night on the roof instead. It wouldn't matter, because her father was already as angry as he could possibly get. She had told him about Gulien. At dawn, when the Tamaristan soldiers had come into sight of the city, she had finally told him.

"Oressa," her father had said, his voice flat, when she'd found him in the green map room with his war advisers. He didn't glare at her. He wasn't interested enough in her to bother glaring. "I have no time for you now. Go back to your room."

Oressa had ignored this. "You've noticed Gulien's missing," she'd started.

"Your brother seems to have gone south to face the Tamaristan army."

Oressa had abruptly found that she was blindingly furious. Their father thought Gulien might have gone south and died or been captured, and not only had he not sent someone to tell her—she wouldn't have expected that—but he didn't even seem to care. She'd said, unable for once to keep the fury out of her voice, "He didn't go south! Do you think he's so stupid? He went east to the Kieba's mountain. He told me to tell you."

There had been a short pause, during which Oressa's father really looked at her for the first time since she'd come into the room. "You stupid girl," he'd said at last. "Why did you not tell me at once?" His tone, still flat, had hidden anger under the indifference.

Oressa knew all about the king's anger. She'd smothered hers immediately, lowering her eyes in case some of her rage might still show, and answered as docilely as though she never had a thought of her own in her head and always did exactly as she was told. "But he said I should wait until the Tamaristan army arrived at the gates of the city."

Magister Baramis began, "If Gulien—"

An army officer said at the same time, "If the Kieba—"

Suddenly everybody was talking at once. Somebody shouted, and somebody else shouted back, and her father actually raised his voice to shout over them both. Since nobody was looking at her, Oressa had fled, quickly, before anybody could think of her again.

That was when she'd climbed up onto the palace roof. The roof was the safest place she knew, especially the highest peak, where only the pigeons came. Maybe she *would* stay here, tucked up between the god's wings, all night. Tomorrow, too. Although she hadn't brought up any food or even a flask of water, so she supposed she'd have to sneak back into her room at some point. But she didn't want to leave the roof. It was the first time she'd felt safe since Gulien had left, and wasn't *that* ridiculous, because of course she wasn't safe at all. But then, she hadn't been safe when Gulien had been with her either. Her brother couldn't protect her. Nobody could protect anybody, not really. She knew that.

Even so, she *felt* safe here with the god, stone though he was. She didn't want to venture back into the palace until she had to.

She looked out across the city again, trying to judge whether there was more smoke now, or maybe a little less. The smoke billowed upward in huge black clouds and then spread out to darken the whole sky. It wasn't at all like the haze from cooking fires that rose above the city during a normal day.

Gulien had been gone for two full days and now most of another day, and she didn't see how he could bring help back for at least two or three more days. If he brought help at all, it was going to be too late, unless the Kieba sent stinging wasps to paralyze the Tamaristans or something of that kind. Maybe she would. If she did, she had better do it soon, because Oressa thought there was real doubt about who might hold the city and the palace when dusk fell: her father, or Gajdosik, or the Kieba, or possibly fire—the city was mostly whitewashed plaster and red stone and hard-baked tiles, but there was plenty of wood in the palace. She could imagine her father burning the palace himself, just for spite, if he thought a Tamaristan prince was going to take it. And here she was on the highest roof. She tried *not* to imagine that.

There seemed less noise out in the city now. For a moment Oressa thought that the fighting might have stopped, that the city's defenders might have thrown back the Tamaristan soldiers. But she gradually realized that this was only a lull. It was nearly dusk; maybe the Tamaristan commander meant to wait for morning to press his attack. She could see barricades in the nearer streets: overturned carts and wagons and stones from walls the defenders had thrown down. She could see that all kinds of people had come out to join the defenders: not only properly armed militia, but also ordinary people with broom handles and axes. The Tamaristan commander might well be reluctant to press ahead into a hostile city at night.

If *she* were in charge of the attackers, on the other hand, *she* wouldn't let up. She'd wait just long enough so that everybody would *think* she meant to wait for morning, and then she'd do something instead. She'd want to take the palace if she could. She'd want to cast down the Carastindin king and capture the Carastindin princess and claim a decisive victory before the hostile city and countryside could defeat her limited forces. How would she—

An enormous crashing sound roared through the dusk, and a brilliant, burning light smashed across the palace. It was as though all the cannons in the world had fired at once, as though all the gods had come back to life to hurl simultaneous lightning bolts at the city. Oressa reeled and would have fallen, only she grabbed the winged god's legs and clung. She thought at first that it was only sound and light, but then she staggered again and realized that the roof really had lifted under her feet and then plunged down again—not a huge movement, but wholly unexpected. Tiles cracked and shattered under her feet, and the god swayed—he actually *swayed*; Oressa was certain of it—and she set her teeth against a cry of shocked terror and let go of him, leaping back in case he should topple from the roof and sweep her down with him. She was furious—terrified, but furious, too. Gajdosik had ruined her safe place for her, and she was blazingly angry.

The roof steadied under her feet after that one sharp rise and fall. Oressa crouched low, one hand gripping the god's wingtip and the other flat against the tiles, trying to decide whether to scramble for a window or to stay where she was. One of her feet was bleeding: She had cut it on a broken tile, and not only did the cut hurt, but she knew the blood might make her slip when she tried to move. The shouting below intensified, and the clash of weapons echoed around her. She couldn't see what was happening, but she thought maybe the Tamaristans had somehow blown a hole right through the palace walls.

There would be no safety in the palace and probably less out in the city. But the tiles under her feet shuddered again, and she knew she had better get down at least to a wider, flatter part of the roof. She took a deep breath. Then she turned and let herself skid in a controlled fall down to the carved dogs at the edge of the high roof. She caught herself there—it wasn't hard, except that she'd also cut her other foot now. She wished she dared put on her slippers, but cut feet were better than losing her footing, especially for this next part, where she had to swing over the edge of the upper roof and climb down the sheer wall to the next level. From there she could go lots of different ways, or simply tuck herself up amid the carved monsters that stood along the edge of the lower roof and wait to see what happened—

The world crashed around her, and the roof heaved up and dropped abruptly out from under her. Oressa clung, gasping, to the stone forequarters of a snarling mastiff. She jammed her arm into its mouth, clinging hard as the palace shuddered and swayed. Broken tiles fell around her. One struck her a glancing blow, bruising her shoulder and back. She cried out in terror as the blow nearly knocked her off the wall. Her grip on the mastiff's jaw saved her, her arm jammed tightly enough that the carved fangs cut her, but even when she lost her foothold and swung for a moment dizzyingly free, she kept that hold until she swung back again. The statue of the winged god plunged past her, huge and silent, so close she could have reached out and touched it, and smashed right through the roof below.

Oressa found she was weeping with rage and fear. She rubbed her other arm fiercely across her face to clear her eyes. Her shoulder ached and her back hurt; she couldn't tell whether the tile had cut her or only bruised her. But she couldn't stay where she was. She scrambled down again, faster now because it was obvious that she had to get off the roofs before the whole palace was torn down around her.

She was still above the lower roofs; she had to get down that far at least, avoiding the hole where the god had fallen. The ground was two stories below that. She knew a window must be over to the right, somewhere below her. She had lost track of exactly where it was, but if she could find it, that window would let her into a tower room meant for important guests. She couldn't remember whether anybody was staying in that room now and didn't care.

The shouting below her, already loud, intensified again, and she swung herself sideways to a god with the arms and hands of a man and the flat head of a snake. She swung a leg over his shoulders and clung with her knees. Her braid had come undone. She shook her head impatiently to get her hair out of her eyes, then scrubbed her free hand across her eyes and tried to see what was happening.

Then she almost wished she hadn't, because there were men on the roof below her, and she saw at once that they weren't Carastindin soldiers: They were Tamaristan. She guessed they'd been crossing the roof to break in against the defenders from an unexpected direction, and even though this surely meant that nobody was going to blow up more of the palace, which was good, it also meant they'd spotted her, which wasn't good at all. Especially because of course they didn't know who she was, and they *all* had bows, except one with an arquebus. In a moment they *would* shoot her, and even though Oressa had finally spotted the window she wanted, and even though it was open, she knew she couldn't possibly reach it before a dozen arrows feathered her like a pigeon. At this range, even the arquebusier wasn't likely to miss, and that was worse. She saw, almost as though it were really happening, a brief, vivid image of an arquebus ball smashing her skull and her own headless, arrow-pierced body following the winged god's plunge.

She screamed down at them, without even thinking about it, "I'm Oressa Madalin! I'm Osir's daughter!" which, after she took half a second to think, still seemed like a good idea because they didn't shoot her after all. So she caught a carved bit above her, got a foot on the upraised hand of the snake-headed god, and flung herself for the window. She didn't remember her bruises or cuts until she tumbled through the window and scrambled to her feet, and even then there wasn't time to do anything about them. She actually had the pouch with her slippers and skirt, for a wonder: The pouch still hung on her belt, only there wasn't time to get her slippers out and put them on, but if she didn't, she was going to leave a blood trail—she bolted for the door, scrabbling at her pouch at the same time.

The door was locked.

It took Oressa far too long to remember which of the closets hid a secret door and then even longer to remember how to open it—one of the carved oak leaves outside the closet controlled the catch, only she couldn't remember which one. She should have remembered, she *did* remember, only she tried one leaf after another and they were all wrong. She found it at last, weeping with frustration, by closing her eyes and reaching blindly to where she knew it was, and it *was* there, but then the panel was locked from the other side. And then the Tamaristan soldiers arrived, just as she kicked the panel as hard as she could and broke the latch.

They brought her to Gajdosik, of course.

Prince Gajdosik was not in the palace. He had established his headquarters at the harbor, in a warehouse that smelled of fish and rendered oil, but now had a sea-eagle banner flying by its door. The prince himself was in an upstairs room that must have once been an office, giving orders to dozens of other men. Men would run in and say something and Gajdosik would give a command, or a string of commands, and the men would run out again. He almost never hesitated about any decision. Oressa was impressed, even though she tried not to be. All the Tamaristans spoke Tamaj, of course. Oressa concentrated on not letting anyone see that she understood them. It was always better if people didn't know everything you knew.

Five different magicked windows, set right into the ordinary wall of the warehouse, showed views of the palace and the main roads that led to the south and the north. A man in the black robes of a magister stood near them, touching one and then another. The views changed whenever he touched a window. The fires burning along one side of the palace and near the south road looked especially impressive. But Oressa could see, too, that men were working to put out the fires. There was no sign now of actual battle anywhere.

Two ordinary windows on the other side of the office looked out over the harbor. There, too, fires were burning, and there as well men were working to put them out. Oressa looked for the cannons, but saw only burned timbers and shattered stone where the platforms ought to have been. No wonder she hadn't heard those cannons firing: They never had. The explosions she'd heard early, before the fighting, must have been the ones that brought the cannons down. Oressa wondered whether Prince Gajdosik had bribed Carastindin soldiers to destroy those platforms or whether he'd sent his own men into the city to do it.

The regular docks and piers had all been destroyed too, but the Tamaristans had put in floating docks, just as Oressa had guessed they'd do. All the men hurrying back and forth along those docks and at the water's edge moved with urgency, but everything they did was orderly.

Prince Gajdosik didn't seem to notice Oressa at first. Then the officer who had captured her finally snatched a quiet moment to go and mutter to him, and he swung around and stared at her. The officer muttered to him some more, no doubt explaining how they'd caught her. "On the *roof*?" the prince said, plainly incredulous. Oressa raised her chin and glared at him, putting on her most imperious princess manner like a mask. She had never felt that she needed a mask so badly.

The Tamaristan prince wasn't that tall, though a lot taller than she was and maybe a little taller than Gulien. He had a close-cropped beard, which was not the custom in Carastind, but many of the Tamaristans wore beards. The beard was a brown so dark it was almost black, darker than his hair. Somehow it made his jaw look more sharply angled, though Oressa would have expected it to have a softening effect. His skin was dark, darker than any Carastindin farmer would have tanned no matter how hot the sun. His eyes were narrow, a sharp, startling blue, set obliquely under winging eyebrows.

The Tamaristan officer, an *addat*, which was almost the same as a company captain, had allowed Oressa to wash her face and put on her skirt and her slippers. He had even bandaged her feet himself, and stitched the gash on her back too, when he saw the blood on her blouse and realized she was cut. He had apologized—in good though accented Esse—for being forced to take liberties, but he had been as polite as possible, dismissing his men from the room while he cleaned the cut across Oressa's back and closed it with nine stitches, as neatly as any good physician. Then he had apologized again for having no clean blouse to give her. She had tried to get him to let her go back to her room for another one. He had refused, which she had expected, but it was too bad. She *had* taken down her hair and looped it up again with a strand of pearls, but she knew she probably didn't look like a princess. But she apparently didn't look like anybody who ought to have been climbing around on roofs, either, judging from the disbelief in Gajdosik's blue eyes.

"You wrecked my father's palace," she said. It came out in a tone of angry accusation, which she hadn't intended. She hadn't exactly planned to say that at all—she hadn't known what she was going to say—but the gaping holes and missing wall were very obvious through Gajdosik's magic windows, and all her anger at the ruined palace came back to her forcefully.

The Tamaristan prince's eyes narrowed, and his mouth tightened. Oressa couldn't tell whether he was angry or amused. Maybe both. He said in Esse, sounding neither angry nor amused but merely matter-of-fact, "Only part of it." Like his officer, he spoke Esse very well, with very little accent.

Oressa glared harder. He didn't seem ashamed at all of blowing up the palace. She thought of the winged god plunging past her, smashing through the lower roof to shatter below. That god had been almost as old as the city—older than anything else in the palace. She demanded, "How could you?"

Gajdosik opened a hand in a gesture of apology, answering the accusation instead of the question. "I was sorry to damage the beautiful palace of your family, but I did not want to lay a long siege or destroy this city—"

"You don't have the men to destroy Caras, and you *certainly* don't have either the time or the resources to lay a siege!"

The prince blinked. He looked at Oressa for the first time as though he actually saw *her* and not merely a painted game-tile. After a moment, he said, "Well, yes. Or no. That's true, too. I needed a faster way to end the battle." He shrugged. "Blowing up part of the palace was fast. I had men of mine place powder below the walls. But I am sorry you were on the roof. I had men looking for you, but you were supposed to be in your rooms. They did not guess you had gone out onto the roof." He glanced at the officer who brought her to him, then looked back at Oressa. A slight note of incredulity crept into his voice. "Laasat says you climb as skillfully and bravely as any young man. He says you almost got away. Did you think to find safety from my men on the roof?"

Oressa started to shrug, then winced.

"Laasat tells me you were injured," said Gajdosik, observing this. "I will have my physician attend you. I will personally oversee your care—"

"I'm fine," Oressa snapped, outraged at his sympathetic tone. "You needn't take any trouble. I'm sure you must be busy. After all, a strong man who won't take charity must have lots of loaves of bread to claim."

There was a moment of perfect silence. Then the magister hastily turned his back to stare intently out one of his windows, and Laasat coughed, sounding strangled. Gajdosik didn't take his eyes off Oressa. He said at last, in an extremely neutral tone, "I did not mean those words to come to your ears."

"Oh," said Oressa. "That's perfectly all right, then." She thought she had better stop there. Although she could think of quite a few other things to say. She bit her tongue to keep herself from saying them. She didn't know Gajdosik, after all, except that he hadn't had the nerve to fight his older brother for their father's throne, so he was trying for Carastind's instead. Oressa hated her father, but she hated the idea of a foreign prince conquering Carastind a lot more. Especially a foreign prince who was arrogant and ambitious, even if he was clever enough to arrange to blow up palaces at just the right tactical moment.

"You—"Gajdosik stopped. "I—" He stopped again. Then, in Tamaj, he said to Laasat, "Take the princess somewhere safe and clean. Preferably a room without access to high rooftops."

"Of course, Your Highness," said Laasat in the same language. His tone was perfectly sober, but there was glint in his eyes that made Oressa think he was still trying not to laugh. He beckoned to her, tilting her head to the door, so she gave him a hostile look, turned on her heel—which hurt her foot, but she didn't let herself wince—and headed for the door, walking slowly because that hurt too. She was already wondering whether she might get out of whatever room Laasat put her in. Not every building had useful carvings all over the walls like the palace. And Laasat might make sure she didn't have even a window. It was a pity Gajdosik had given her into the keeping of a man who had already seen her scrambling around on the walls and roofs of the palace.

She didn't realize until she'd stalked all the way to the door that she hadn't thought to ask Gajdosik about the attack on the palace—about her father. She almost turned back. Her step faltered. But then she asked herself why she should even think of asking. If her father was still alive, then Gajdosik would surely capture him soon, and what did she care, anyway? But she was glad Gulien, at least, was not in Caras, but safe with the Kieba—

There was a sharp, hard screaming sound behind her. It was loud and yet strangely muffled. It wasn't any kind of sound a man would make, or could make. It was a little like breaking wood, but not the same. She turned, staring.

The view from the ordinary windows hadn't changed, but the view from all the magicked windows was now exactly the same. All of them now looked down on Caras from above, as though the warehouse had suddenly lifted up into the sky and tilted over on its side. Of course it was only the view in the magic windows that had changed, but the illusion that the warehouse had flown up into the air and flipped over was so compelling that Oressa staggered. The officer caught her, though he missed a step as well and flung a hand out to brace himself against the doorframe. Everyone else had done the same—the magister had actually fallen, perhaps because he had been more tightly focused on the magic windows than the others. Prince Gajdosik was helping him up again. Only the prince was standing straight, seeming unaffected by the illusion of movement—and part of that was bluff: Even he had one hand set flat on a table.

From the view they now had, they could see almost the whole city. They could see the fires, most of which looked like they were fairly well under control or else at least nearly burned out. They could see the palace, with gaping holes on two sides and broken stones and timbers littering its courtyards. They could see orderly Tamaristan troops around the palace and more in the streets. The Tamaristan companies looked very few and far between in the city streets, but there was little other movement in the city, so apparently they had Caras under good control. Or they *had* had. Now—now Oressa wasn't sure what she was seeing. Though it was now long past dusk, the city wasn't dark. Something in the sky filled Caras with light: a paler, whiter, colder light than any sunlight. The same light came into the warehouse through the ordinary windows, which made the view through the magic ones even more disorienting.

But they could all see a huge spider thing stalking through the brightly lit streets. It was huge, but it moved quickly and lightly. It was not anything Oressa recognized. Except it *was* like a spider. A really, really big spider. It had a lot of legs. More legs than a spider, she thought, though she wasn't sure how many a spider actually had.

The spider thing moved in a neat, deliberate way that looked slow but she suspected was actually pretty fast. It was covered with glittering hairs that seemed to be made of glass or crystal. It seemed to be made of steel, like a sword. Like a sword, it looked like a weapon.

"A war *autajma*," said the magister, staring at his magic windows. He spoke in Tamaj, and Oressa wasn't certain of the word he used for the spider. "But only one. I might be able to stop it, even take control of it. . . ."

Yes, thought Oressa vengefully. *Try it, you, and see what happens when the Kieba really takes notice.* She honestly hoped he would.

"No," said Prince Gajdosik, also in Tamaj. "If the Keppa indeed remains living and attentive . . . no. We are not yet in a position to challenge her. I would not like to see her bring fifty of those *autajma* against us if you took that one."

"What, then?" said the magister. "Would you have us go back to face Maranajdis? I tell you—"

"You need not," said Prince Gajdosik sharply. "I am perfectly well aware. Of course we cannot go back. But we cannot press forward either. Not yet, not that way, not until we know what we face. No." He cut off the magister's attempted answer with a sharp gesture and glared at the images the magic windows showed them, his mouth set. His startling blue eyes narrowed suddenly.

Oressa, following the prince's intent gaze, realized that a man was perched high up on the spider's back. She knew at once this must be Gulien and did not try to suppress a triumphant smile. Let Prince Gajdosik see she knew that he might have won his battle but lost anyway. And she would be certain to tell the Kieba, when she met her, that the Tamaristan magisters spoke of stealing her spider artifact. Let Prince Gajdosik explain *that* to the Kieba.

The spider moved on its own path through the city, in a straight line from the outer part of the city toward the center. It was hard to see where it was heading. To the palace, Oressa assumed, and wondered what her brother would think when he saw the holes.

When the spider met a column of Tamaristan soldiers, the soldiers hesitated. The spider didn't hesitate at all, but stalked straight forward. The soldiers tried to shoot it, but they hardly had time, and even the arquebus balls that struck it seemed to do nothing but strike sparks from its steel body. The spider could throw things that looked like slivers of ice, or shoot them, maybe, because the glittering slivers flew a long way, and the front ranks of the men fell. . . . It was awful, but very impressive.

The men gave way, not in wild flight—Oressa admired their courage—but backing away in decent order, yielding the road to the spider. The spider ignored them once they were out of its way. It went right past them, and the men closed up again and followed it cautiously. The spider still ignored them, continuing along its path toward the palace. No, not toward the palace, Oressa realized. But she couldn't figure out what its goal actually *was*.

"It's coming here," Gajdosik said suddenly. "It's coming *here*." He swore viciously in Tamaj.

Oressa let her smile widen. She said, in her blandest, most regal tone, "Gulien went to ask the Kieba for help. I think"—and she smiled at Gajdosik deliberately—"I think she said 'Yes.'"

The magister rather than the prince answered, in Esse, his tone biting. "The Keppa is dead. *All* the immortals are dead."

Oressa stared at the man in honest astonishment. "Is that what they teach you in Tamarist?" She pointed at the magic windows. "Well, look! I think the Kieba isn't so very dead after all! What do you think?"

The magister began, "*I* think—" But then Prince Gajdosik held up a hand in sharp command and he stopped.

Then the prince issued a very fast series of orders, mostly in Tamaj, sending his men running in all directions. *Get the men out of the path of the spider. Give orders they are not to attack it. Recall the men to the ships. Are the ships adequately provisioned for a run out to sea? Well, see that they are provisioned with fresh water immediately, and tell the captains to abandon everything else if they must. Withdraw our men from the palace. No, just let the fires burn if they're not out yet. No, don't do anything with the king.* This was how Oressa learned that her father was alive, because Gajdosik said absently, as though it weren't important, *Don't do anything with the king. Just get the men clear of the palace.* That was what Gajdosik ordered.

Twice the magister tried to say something. The second time the prince led him away to a far corner of the room. They spoke for several minutes, or at least the magister spoke. Gajdosik mostly listened. Finally he made a sharp gesture and said a few brief words. Then the magister went out, looking surprisingly satisfied with whatever decision had been made. Oressa couldn't see how any decision that involved abandoning their victory could satisfy any of the Tamaristans, but the prince came back just then and she didn't have a chance to think about it.

"Your Highness," Laasat said to him in Tamaj, very stiffly and formally, not looking at her at all. "You know the princess will be a valuable hostage—"

Gajdosik cut him off with a sharp gesture, frowning. But he said in the same language, "Yes, of course, and we may all have reason to be very grateful for your quick eye." He stared at Oressa. The he asked her, now speaking Esse, "What will your brother give me for you?"

Oressa glared at the prince, humiliated and furious. His people didn't seem careless enough to let her get away, which was too bad, because if the Tamaristan prince was determined to treat her like a painted game-tile, she longed to take herself right off the board and let him try to deal with Gulien without her. She said fiercely, "Not much! Don't bother asking for a quarter of Carastind or anything like that. You'd better ask just for leave to withdraw your men. If you ask for a night and a day to get your people clear of the city, my brother might give you an hour."

The Tamaristan prince looked at her for a moment. Then he said, "Bring her," to Laasat, and went brusquely past and down the stairs.

The officer laid an apologetic hand on Oressa's arm. She didn't shake him off. Her feet hurt, and her shoulder and back ached more every moment. She thought she might be unable to manage the stairs without help. Besides, there was a tight pressure behind her eyes as though she might cry if she wasn't careful, which was ridiculous. There was no reason to cry *now*. Scowling at Laasat helped her keep the tears behind her eyes.

She thought, from how fast the Kieba's spider had been moving, that her brother might even be out there waiting for her before she made it down to ground level. She was *sure* it was him. She tried to move a little faster, gritting her teeth against the pain.

CHAPTER 4

The golem was, in fact, almost too powerful. When they approached the eastern gates of Caras, Gulien told the golem to clear a way through the Tamaristan soldiers there, and it immediately knocked down a lot of the wall on top of the soldiers and then cleared a path through the rubble and the crushed bodies. This *worked*, but it wasn't what Gulien had had in mind at all.

"I'm doing more damage to Caras than the Tamaristans have done!" Prince Gulien snapped. "It's important to look strong, like I've already won, but can't you make your golem act with a little more subtlety?"

Then he thought that perhaps he should not snap at the kephalos as though it were a human servant. But the kephalos only answered, as flat and calm as ever, "Yes."

Gulien didn't exactly relax, but he hoped the golem wouldn't knock down huge chunks of the wall again. Nor, he hoped, any buildings or houses, either. At least the people of Caras didn't seem to care about the wall. They opened their shutters and came out onto their rooftops and threw pieces of brick and tile after the retreating Tamaristan soldiers and cheered Gulien. Gulien made himself smile. He stood up on the golem's back and waved, and the people cheered louder and shouted his name and "Kieba!" And quite a lot of them came down into the streets to follow the golem. Gulien waved again encouragingly, because it might be dangerous for them to take such risks, but he thought it was important for his people to feel they had had a part in forcing the Tamaristans to withdraw.

"Kephalos, do you know where I can find Prince Gajdosik?" Gulien asked. "It *is* Gajdosik commanding these Tamaristan soldiers, isn't it? Is he at the palace?"

The Tamaristan prince was down by the harbor. The kephalos said Gajdosik had five crystal mirrors through which he could envision the whole city. Gulien found, rather uneasily, that he knew exactly what the kephalos meant. Some part of his new, uncertain memories seemed to encompass such strange oddments of knowledge. Those mirrors must have given Prince Gajdosik a great advantage through the fighting, but now the kephalos found him through those mirrors, so Gulien supposed it all balanced out.

"Can you control those mirrors?" he asked. "Can you show Gajdosik that we are here—that I am here—and that I am driving his people out of the city?" It was important, he suspected, for the Tamaristan prince to *know* he was beaten, or else he might keep fighting—and then who knew what might happen? Gulien knew that the Kieba might return from Elaru at any moment. It was important that Gajdosik understand that passing time was not his friend but not realize that time might not be Gulien's friend, either.

It was good, probably, that Gajdosik had been commanding his invasion from the harbor. He'd better not have lost his ships; they'd be the only good way he had to get his men out now. If anything had happened to those ships, if the Tamaristan prince was actually unable to retreat, that could be very bad. He wondered whether he could possibly use this golem to slaughter all the Tamaristan soldiers. It would be an ugly thing. He had already found that the golem's glass needles did worse to a man than he ever wanted to see. Sometimes one of the foreigners tried to shoot Gulien from a concealed location, but the golem always seemed to know the enemy soldier was there before the man could set a match to powder or aim a crossbow.

Every time the golem killed a Tamaristan soldier, the people of Caras, now crowding close behind, cheered fiercely and stamped their feet. Gulien knew how they felt. He knew because he also felt fierce and proud and vindicated to see Carastind's enemies helplessly retreat, but even so he didn't want to think what it would be like to drive those soldiers back against the sea and slaughter them all, like a dog killing rats. He didn't think he would be able to tell the kephalos to do it. He was perfectly certain that he didn't want to.

He said, "It would be best if the Tamaristan soldiers all over the city could see that the Kieba is on our side, and it's growing too dark to see much. Can you put lights in the sky?" There were tales of such things, but even so, Gulien was taken by surprise when lights flicked into place high overhead, lights that burned with a painfully brilliant radiance. The light was colder than sunlight but almost as bright. He thought the lights might have been enough to frighten away an enemy all by themselves; they were so clearly god-magic and showed so clearly that the Kieba favored Carastind and not Tamarist. But it was probably just as well to have the golem, too.

When he got to the harbor at last, he found a great many of the Tamaristan soldiers there before him. Some had already gotten onto ships and retreated out into the Narrow Sea, but boarding was painfully slow because the docks had been burned. All the men left were just waiting their turns to board or else working to provision the remaining ships. Only a few men stood out in the open, between the warehouses and the quay, waiting.

"Our cannons," Gulien said out loud, sharp and angry. "That son of a cow destroyed our cannons!" The cannons that guarded the harbor at Caras were famous. Now there were only four piles of broken stone and splintered timbers, the dull gleam of black iron visible amid the rubble. No wonder Gajdosik had managed to take Caras so quickly; if he had destroyed the harbor cannons first, the city would have immediately become vulnerable.

And Gajdosik still expected him to *talk*. There he was: That had to be him in front there, the dark man with the beard and the closed expression; he was not as old as Gulien had expected, though he'd known Gajdosik was only a few years older than Gulien himself. He had the high Garamanaji cheekbones and the dark Garamanaji coloring, and certainly the fierce Garamanaji arrogance. All of that was familiar to Gulien from portraits, because his father thought it was important to know one's enemies and collected portraits of every nation's kings and princes.

Arrogant Prince Gajdosik might be, but he was also clearly waiting for parley. Gulien supposed he had better see what the man had to say. He rested his open hands on his thighs and tried to look older than he was, and confident.

In fact, Prince Gajdosik looked quite confident. That was almost offensive under the circumstances, though Gulien guessed that the confidence might be a habitual mask. Beneath the confidence was something else: something darker and quieter. An intense, tightly contained anger and behind that a grim patience. He didn't look like a man who would give up easily. Yet he was here, rather than in Tamarist. Perhaps he was a man who preferred to battle strangers and capture a foreign throne rather than fight his own brothers for the throne that might be rightfully his. Maybe he and his brothers had decided to divide up the world and he had drawn the lot for foreign conquest; Gulien would have believed that, too, from the other man's intensity.

Prince Gajdosik came forward a few steps, toward the war golem. He looked up at Gulien, shading his eyes against the unnatural white light that poured down across them all. He ignored the crowd of ordinary people who had followed the golem to the harbor. He didn't seem frightened at all, but inclined his head, graciously conceding with that one wordless gesture that the advantage now rested with Gulien.

Gulien, unwillingly impressed, leaned forward, resting his elbow on his knee, put his chin on his fist, and stared down at the other man. He tried hard to look arrogant and confident and angry. He said loudly, so the people foremost in the crowd could hear him, "Your Highness, what are you doing in my city?"

"Leaving," said Gajdosik, not quite as loudly, but also pitched to carry. "If Your Highness will permit me." His Esse was very good, though he had a definite accent. He still didn't look afraid, for all his words contained an acknowledgment of his own disadvantage and implicit surrender.

"Should I?" Gulien asked him. He wished he had had time to think all this out more carefully beforehand. He wished he could ask the kephalos for advice—though he doubted its advice would make sense and suspected its priorities had nothing to do with his. He asked, careful to keep his tone level and inexpressive, "And what would you do then, Your Highness? Take your people back south to Paree? Seize land there, despoiling Carastindin people, until we were forced to come against you? Or, if we would not, until you returned once more to throw yourselves against our gates?" He wanted the Tamaristan prince to offer him a guarantee, his word against any such intention.

Instead, Prince Gajdosik said smoothly, "I can hardly argue. But allow me to offer you a compelling reason to deal with me, and perhaps we may come to an accord that benefits us both." He snapped his fingers, and one of his men came out of the little gathering, leading Oressa.

For an instant Gulien could not think at all. He was too shocked. His sister did not seem to have been harmed. She looked coolly unimpressed, which he knew meant she was probably seething. But the cool look, meant to get her through tedious court functions and even more tedious etiquette lessons, served her perfectly. She looked, at this moment, every inch the proper princess, despite a torn blouse and untidy hair and a streak of dirt across her face. She carried herself proudly, as though she had never suffered a moment of doubt in her entire life. She lifted her shoulders in a tiny shrug when she met Gulien's gaze, it seemed by way of apology, though what his sister had to apologize for escaped him. This situation was the foreign prince's fault, not hers, though he understood how deeply offended she must be to be used as a game piece against him. He gave her a long look back, hoping that she would not take this moment to insult or revile her captor, however strong the temptation.

"What will you give me for her?" asked Prince Gajdosik. He paused, then went on. "Caras is yours, of course. Clearly it is impossible for me to hold the city now. I ask only for a night and a day to withdraw my men from your city. When the last of my men are aboard ship, I will release your sister to you."

Games with hostages held no attraction at all. Gulien snapped, "I'll give you an hour, and I'll take her now."

"There, didn't I tell you?" Oressa said to Gajdosik. She jerked her arm free from the man holding her and scowled fearlessly at the foreign prince. "You can agree to an hour. He'll give you two if it comes to that. He'll keep his word, you know. You won't argue if you're wise."

Gajdosik lifted his eyebrows at her. Oressa only tapped her foot and said, "Well? Let's get *on*," in a sharp tone, as though she were speaking to a servant.

Gulien thought the Tamaristan prince looked as though he might laugh at Oressa, or maybe shout at her. He looked as though he was having trouble deciding which. Gulien found himself unexpectedly sympathetic; he knew just how the other man felt. But he didn't think it wise to give the foreign prince time to consider his reaction. He leaned forward, staring down at him, and said crisply, "I could kill you all before you harm her." He tried to sound grimly certain of that, though in fact he wasn't at all certain it was possible.

"Perhaps you can," answered Gajdosik, turning back to face him at once. "Let us not test the possibility. Promise me time to get my men away and I'll release her to you."

"An hour. Two, if it comes to that. You may go. You may all go. I don't care where, so long as you don't touch Carastindin soil again. You might find better luck in Estenda—or go back across the Narrow Sea. I don't care. But if you return, I shall assuredly destroy you all."

He stared down at Prince Gajdosik, trying to look resolute and determined and as though he were perfectly certain the foreign prince would obey him. "You have an hour to get off Carastindin soil. Or two, if it comes to that. But not three. Do you understand?"

Prince Gajdosik drew breath as though he would say something, but then he didn't. He only opened one hand, a gesture of concession, which he then turned into a wave that invited Oressa to go.

She gave him a wary glance. Then her mouth firmed. She tossed her hair back with deliberate scorn and stepped away from him, toward the war golem. She walked slowly and carefully. Gulien thought this was simply a show of royal dignity at first, until he saw how her face tightened with pain as she moved.

At first he could hardly believe it. Then she took another step, and he *had* to believe it. "You're hurt," he said, stunned, and then, with gathering intensity, though barely above a whisper, "Oressa, you can *barely walk*." Fury rocked him, all the more intense for being wholly unexpected. He had been angry and upset and ashamed when the Kieba denied his plea for help, but the rage that struck through him now was of an entirely different order. Gulien came up to one knee on the golem's back, one hand closing so hard into a fist that his knuckles whitened. He said to Gajdosik, biting off each word with bitter force, "Of course, a strong man takes what he wants. Isn't that what you said?"

Gajdosik's head went back a little at this accusation, as though he had been struck. Then he went ashen as he understood what Gulien meant and realized the depths of his fury. He obviously realized Gulien meant now to destroy him and all his men and knew there was probably nothing he could do to stop it. He stood perfectly still, though his breathing had quickened. In a moment he would say something, but it didn't matter what he said, Gulien would be *glad* to deny any plea for clemency—

"Gulien!" his sister said urgently. "I'm *not* hurt! Anyway, it's not his fault. Well, it *is*, of course, but not like that!"

Gulien turned his head slowly to stare down at her, not certain that he understood her—not certain that he believed her. He felt a bit as though he had turned to stone and only now might have begun to turn back.

"I cut my feet! And a tile fell off the roof and hit me. That's all! His people took care of me. He wasn't—he didn't—anyway," Oressa said, recovering her dignity, "he *did* blow up the palace, so that part is his fault. You can blame him for *that*, if you want." She glanced over her shoulder at the Tamaristan prince, who was staring at her. The color had come back into Gajdosik's face, but his expression was odd.

Gulien took a breath. Another. He closed his eyes. He had been so angry. He had been *so certain* that he was going to kill Gajdosik and all his people. Now he didn't know what he felt, or thought, or should do. Then he opened them again and said, not quite steadily, "He blew up the palace?"

"Well, not all of it. But I expect you're going to be pretty upset when you see it."

"You weren't on the *roof*, Oressa—"

"I didn't know he was going to blow *holes* in it." His sister hesitated. She said at last, "His people were perfectly polite to me. Prince Gajdosik certainly didn't, well—" She began to shrug, then winced.

Gulien stared at Oressa for a long moment. Then, at last, he turned back to the Tamaristan prince. "I misunderstood," he said stiffly. "I beg your pardon."

The Tamaristan prince bowed his head at once. "A natural mistake, under the circumstances. I must in turn beg your pardon, and Her Highness's pardon, for a stupid boast that I should never have phrased so offensively."

Gulien hardly knew how to answer this. He said at last, "You blew up the palace?"

"Do you want me to apologize for that as well?"

Gulien stiffened. "Two hours," he bit out. "You may have two hours to get your people out of Caras."

Gajdosik nodded. "You are generous. Thank you." He glanced at Oressa. "As Her Highness is generous."

"Oh, please," Oressa said, unimpressed. She stepped stiffly forward and looked up at the golem, obviously wondering how she was supposed to get up on its back.

Gulien didn't have to say anything. All the glass needles rippled away sideways to clear a place for her to put her hands and feet. He nodded, and Oressa kicked off her slippers to climb onto the golem. He could see that both her feet were indeed bandaged. But she put a confident foot on one of the golem's legs, grabbed another angular leg, and clambered up as casually as a boy climbing an apple tree, flinching and hissing under her breath only when she had to reach upward with her left hand. Her skirt caught on a cluster of needles and ripped, but of course she didn't seem to mind that.

Gulien caught her hand to steady her, and the princess waved to the crowd that had gathered at the edge of the harbor—they cheered her, too, though Gulien wondered if they could see well enough from that far away to know whom they cheered—then turned and dropped down to kneel beside him, casually claiming the place with the best view.

Then she gave him a quick sideways look and a flashing smile. "A splendid rescue! Thank you, Gulien. You're the best brother."

Gulien put an arm around her shoulders and said, ignoring the Tamaristan prince and his people, "I suppose we had better go see how much of the palace is left. I'm certain there won't be any trouble here." He didn't even glance at Prince Gajdosik when he said that. But as soon as the golem started moving, he added in a much quieter voice, "We'll get all our own people to follow us to the palace—we don't want trouble between our folk and the Tamaristans, not now, and anyway, we're more likely to find trouble there than here now."

"You mean Father," Oressa surmised. "You're right. He didn't like it one bit that you went to the Kieba, and not even this beauty is going to change his mind." She patted the golem on the neck admiringly.

"He still lives, then." Gulien felt simultaneously intensely relieved and somewhat dismayed, a sickening mix of emotions, worse because until that moment he had more or less successfully refused to think of their father and was now worried by the idea of facing him in person. He rubbed a hand across his mouth.

"Yes, I think so. Prince Gajdosik said something that made me think so, at least. In Tamaj. He didn't know I understood him, so it was probably true."

"It may not surprise you to learn that the Kieba doesn't like our father at all. Though she's not likely to be very happy with me, either. She was going to let any Tamaristan prince take Caras. She told me to persuade Father to yield Caras if I wanted to save Carastindin lives. Instead, I borrowed her golem, and now . . ." He hesitated.

"Borrowed?" said Oressa.

"The kephalos allowed it, but . . ." He didn't know how to finish this sentence either, especially since he knew the kephalos was within the golem, listening. He warned Oressa hastily, "The kephalos seems to be foremost among the Kieba's servants, or . . . anyway, it's here with us, in the golem. Kephalos!"

"Gulien Madalin," answered the golem, in the flat voice of the kephalos.

"Oh!" said Oressa, and was silent, her eyes widening. Then she said, her tone just a fraction too cheerful, "Well, I want to hear *all* about it later, Gulien! It's so unfair! *You* got to meet the Kieba and the, ah, kephalos and you got this amazing spider-golem and all *I* got was taken hostage. Though," she added firmly, "I would have escaped if you hadn't come."

Gulien was sure she would have. "Meeting the Kieba was . . . not something I would actually recommend." Seeing his sister's skepticism, Gulien tried to gather his thoughts. He didn't know what he could safely say with the kephalos listening. He didn't know if he dared explain that the Kieba hadn't been what he'd expected. That she had seemed so . . . indifferent. It had been as though all the caring had worn out of her over the years, and now all that was left was . . . habit, perhaps.

Gulien hadn't precisely realized this until he thought about it now, but he thought that it was true. It seemed to him, remembering the Kieba, that she hadn't even really *cared* about the plague in Elaru. He didn't know what to think. The Kieba he had expected, the Kieba from all the old tales, was not like that. What if the years really had at last worn out her compassion for the many peoples of the world?

"The Kieba frightened you," Oressa said, frowning.

She had. Thinking about her now frightened him more. Though not as much as facing their father. Gulien waved this away and told his sister, "What she seems to want most . . . Listen, have you heard of an artifact called Parianasaku's Capture?"

"Gulien. How would I know? You're the one who remembers all those peculiar names and everything."

"Well," Gulien conceded. "But you hear things."

Oressa shrugged and glanced thoughtfully up at the head of the spider-golem, thinking, perhaps, about the listening kephalos. "If Father has an artifact called anything of the kind, he never said so where I could hear him. But he wouldn't talk about it, you know. He's so secretive."

"Said the lump of coal to the iron kettle," Gulien said, recovering his balance. "Whatever it is, the Kieba wants it back, and Father won't give it to her. Maybe *can't* give it to her, to hear her explain it. But I need to get it, and apparently the only way . . . the only way is to . . ." Gulien could hardly make himself say it, and the words came out in nearly a whisper: "I need to depose Father."

There was a short, shocked pause.

Then Oressa said in a bright, brittle tone, "Well, it's terrible, of course, if the Kieba doesn't like Father, but if deposing him is the price of her help against Tamarist, who could argue?"

Gulien winced, looking away.

"I'm sorry," Oressa said, much more gently. "I'm sure you hate the idea, and I'm sorry about that. Truly. But you know I won't be sorry if the Kieba requires you to take the throne and set Father aside. It may take some careful persuasion to get people to accept it, but I'm sure you can do it. I mean, here you are with the Kieba's spider, saving Caras from the Tamaristan invaders! You *own* this moment, Gulien. Oh, you'll have the occasional awkward moment later, I'm sure, after Father's supporters realize they've lost their influence and start trying to make trouble for you. I'll help—you know that—but Baramis will be difficult, and so will Erren, and that's just to start with. But that's for later, and by then lots of other people will support you."

Gulien shook his head, far less confident. "I know few people love our father, but he's been a good king for Carastind—tough-minded, deci-sive. He's kept us strong. Without him we might well have been trapped into a second Little War with Estenda. Or worse. A lot of people trust Father to keep us safe."

Oressa scowled at him. "Strong!" she said derisively. "I suppose so! Ruthlessness may make a king *strong*, but if a king's to be trusted, he has to be just; and if he's to be loved, he has to be kind. You'll be a far better king than Father. You'll show people you can be ruthless when you depose him, and then you'll show them you're also just and kind, and of course they'll support you! Besides, you were always going to be king *someday*, which everybody knows. Why not now? Give people a month and they'll forget why they ever worried."

Gulien slanted a look at his sister, appreciating her confidence, though he feared it was misplaced. He said after a moment, "I grant, riding into Caras on the Kieba's golem will surely help."

"I should think so!" Oressa agreed with great enthusiasm. She patted the golem's steel neck with a proprietary air. But then she asked in a more cautious tone, "Just how angry with you is she likely to be about you *borrowing* her golem? Even if her—her kephalos, or whatever, let you, so it hardly seems fair for her to blame you, does it? Kephalos, is the Kieba going to blame Gulien for anything?"

The kephalos didn't answer. Gulien asked, "Kephalos?"

"Unknown," stated the kephalos.

"You see," said Gulien, and sighed.

"Well," said Oressa in a bracing tone. "Even if she does blame you, maybe she won't still be angry about it after you depose Father and get Parian-whoever's Thing back for her. Here's what we'll do: You tell everybody that the Kieba hates Father and wants you to be king instead. Tell everyone she saved us because you went to her and asked her. Then, when she comes to take back her artifact, it'll already be arranged. Everybody will cheer and celebrate and tell her how wonderful she is and how grateful they are that she supported us against Tamarist. Then she'll be ashamed to punish you."

"I suspect the Kieba will do exactly as she pleases, no matter what we do."

"Well, but can it hurt? Anyway," said Oressa firmly, "if she wants somebody to be angry with, she can be angry with *Father*. That's fair, especially if he stole an artifact of hers. Anybody can see that's true."

Gulien began, "Oressa—" Then, finally glimpsing the palace ahead of them, he said, horrified, "All gods dead and forgotten! *Look* at what that son of a misbegotten cow *did* to our palace!"

The white lights in the sky were a little dimmer now, but still more than bright enough that he could see exactly what Gajdosik had done to the palace.

"I told you," said Oressa. "I *did* tell you. He said he had people put black powder under the walls."

"He had agents in Caras?" Gulien was outraged.

Oressa only shrugged. "Obviously. I guess they blew up our cannons at the harbor too."

Gulien stared at the broken stones that littered the courtyard, then tipped his head back to gaze at the ragged timbers dangling high above. A roof tile fell suddenly, shattering on the stones below with a clearly audible sound.

"And you were on the roof!" said Gulien, turning suddenly to stare at his sister. "You little *fool*!"

Oressa said in a small voice, "After I told Father where you'd gone, I wanted to get out of his way. I thought the roof would be safe."

Gulien put an arm around her shoulders, hugging her against his side, forcing his mind away from thoughts of his sister falling, her body broken on the lower roofs or the flagstones of the courtyard, crushed by falling rubble. He might have come home to that. He didn't know whether to curse Prince Gajdosik for blowing up the palace, or whether to be grateful his men had gotten her safely away from the wreckage. He stood up on the golem's back, putting a hand against one of the spines to balance himself, looking more closely. He could see that the eastern wing of the palace was less damaged—well, it must be less damaged, or the whole structure would have come down.

He was right about that, at least. The east side of the palace was in much better shape than the south. The courtyard there was crowded. Everyone in the whole city seemed to have followed them here. Gulien had never realized there could be so many people in one place. Or how disorderly and noisy they could be. But the noise ebbed. All the people, as they glimpsed the war golem and turned to look, stared and nudged their neighbors and stared some more, and silence spread out from them until all the clamor had died away. People coughed and muttered to one another, but that wasn't the same. The war golem shone brilliantly in the pale light that filled the courtyard. Absolutely everyone was staring at it. Gulien was used to being the center of attention, but this was different and he knew he had flushed.

"Do you see Father?" Oressa asked, not seeming to notice the crowd. "Gulien, you *are* going to depose him, aren't you? Gulien?"

"I don't . . ."

"Gulien!"

"I know," Gulien said, helplessly wretched. "Don't go *on* about it!" Then he stopped, as their father appeared between the wide-open doors at the top of the stairs. Everything stopped. King Osir Madalin, tall and grim and disapproving, seemed somehow entirely in control of the situation, even though that was outrageously untrue.

"Gulien . . . ," Oressa began, her voice going small. She tried to tuck herself behind her brother, but there wasn't room. Instead, she knelt down on the golem's back, bowing her head, seeming suddenly diffident and meek. But she whispered, "You *have* to tell everyone that the Kieba supports you and wants you to be king. Gulien, you *have* to tell everyone that! If you stole her golem and now you defy her again—"

"I know. I know! He won't give it up to me or to her just for the asking, Oressa. I know that." Gulien took a deep breath. "I'll do it," he said. "I will. The Kieba's the important thing. We can't let her turn her golem against *us* and call Gajdosik back—"

"She won't! She can't!" Oressa said. "We'll make sure everyone cheers you, and her for supporting you, until she has to forbear for very shame.

You'll be fine. Look, everyone's here. There's Baramis and Erren. I don't see Ramak. Or Meric. Oh, I hope nothing's happened to Meric! But there's Lorren. That's good. You need influential men as witnesses. Oh, *look,* Gulien, there's *Lord Paulin.* He *is* showing his age, isn't he?"

This made Gulien laugh, though he still felt rather sick. He said, "Kephalos, can you tell the golem to carry us toward the king, slowly? Give people time to get out of the way."

The golem moved smoothly forward.

"That statue in the center of the courtyard is close enough," Gulien said after a moment. "Stop us when we get that far."

But the golem didn't stop at the statue. Even when Gulien repeated more urgently, "Stop the golem now, kephalos!" And then desperately, "Kephalos!"

There was no answer.

"Gulien!" Oressa said, sounding frightened.

Gulien swallowed. He knew exactly what had happened. He whispered, "Gods remembered and forgotten," but very quietly, almost like a prayer. Then he said, much more clearly and formally, "Kieba, please. I beg you will grant me just a little more time. I am so nearly finished here. Please, let me finish this." It was surprisingly difficult to speak to her when he could not *see* her, even though he had found her unreadable in person. He closed his eyes and said, "Of course you are angry—you are justly angry—but grant me the use of your power for just an hour longer. I'll depose my father. I swear I will." His voice shook but then steadied. "I'll take back the gods' artifact and return it to you. I swear I will. This will be so much faster and more certain than working your will through the Tamaristans, Kieba!" He stopped and waited.

There was no answer. The golem did not pause.

Gulien said in a low, intense tone, "Kieba, please! Do anything you wish with me and with my father—"

Oressa opened her mouth. Gulien caught her arm, shaking her to make her be quiet. She hissed in pain, but he ignored her. He said urgently, "But before you punish me, let me help my sister take the throne. Let me help her set Caras in order—I swear to you, she'll do well by Carastind! You have been our patron for hundreds of years! Surely we still matter to you at least a little!"

The war golem stopped. It had come nearly all the way to the foot of the stairs. All around them, people pressed back out of its way. Osir Madalin stood above, gazing down at them.

The king of Carastind was a tall man, and thin, with a lean face and hooded eyes. There was a small crease between his brows, which made him look disapproving and faintly disdainful. He wore a sword, but it was only for show, with pearls on the scabbard and a ruby set in the hilt. Gulien was faintly surprised none of the Tamaristan soldiers had stolen it. Maybe Prince Gajdosik had meant that as some kind of empty courtesy toward a defeated king.

King Osir looked mildly interested and mildly annoyed. That was false—a mask. Gulien knew that none of his father's real thoughts or emotions were out on the surface. One always had to wonder what was hidden behind the king's indifferent gaze. *Then* one started to be afraid of what might be hidden. The king created that effect that on purpose, of course. It worked on everyone. Even on Gulien.

Gulien could not meet his father's eyes. He gripped one of the golem's spikes to steady himself. His other hand was shaking, and he tucked it into his belt. He said quietly, "Golem, move one step closer to the stairs and then stop."

He was sure the golem would not respond. But it did. It took one precise step closer to the base of the stairs, and then it stopped. Gulien let out the breath he had been holding. He let go of the spike he had been holding, straightened his shoulders, and looked directly into his father's face. He was distantly surprised to find that they were almost exactly at a level: the king at the top of the stairs and Gulien on the golem's back.

The king began to speak, but Gulien cut him off. "The Kieba is willing to be Carastind's ally!" he declared in a clear, hard voice that sounded amazingly confident, considering how tense he felt. "But she is not *your* ally, Osir, king of Carastind. She declares you have misused her gift, and now for dislike of you, the Kieba would allow any Tamaristan prince to ravage here as he pleases before she would set a hand between Carastind and our enemies!"

In the whole courtyard, there was hardly a sound. Nobody spoke. Nobody coughed. The king gazed at Gulien in mild surprise, as though at a child who spoke out of turn. Gulien wondered what his father was really thinking. His father drew breath to speak, but Gulien cut him off. "I have given the Tamaristan prince Gajdosik an hour to clear our lands!" he declared. "In another hour, Gajdosik and all his people will be gone! But we will still have men who are injured! We will still have rubble in the streets and a shattered palace! If we have time to heal our men and repair our city, it is because the Kieba has chosen to be our ally! She will not abandon us—unless we choose to be ruled by a king who has defied her, a king she reviles!"

His father took one precise step forward, to the very edge of the landing at the top of the stairs. He said, "That is enough." His voice was flat and hard. "The Kieba does not choose the kings of Carastind."

This one statement would probably have swayed most of the gathered people back to the king's side, except that everyone in the city had just seen Caras conquered by Gajdosik's swift, unexpected campaign and then seen the Tamaristan soldiers thrown out of Caras just as unexpectedly by the Kieba's war golem. Gulien, standing high above the crowd, atop a golem made of magicked steel, with the Kieba's white lights shining down on him, was so clearly master of the moment that no one at all moved to support the king.

"She will depose at least one," Gulien said, not declaiming for the crowd this time, but speaking more quietly, directly to his father. "Indeed, she has. I'm sorry for it. I am most heartily sorry for it. But it's done. It is the price of her support against Carastind's enemies. You should have returned her artifact when she asked."

"I have no doubt *you* will hurry to do her bidding," said his father, his contempt like the flick of a whip.

Gulien did not let himself flinch. When he looked deliberately from one of his father's attendants to another, each man dropped his gaze. When he said, "Magister Baramis. Lord Paulin. Magister Lorren. I will see you all in half an hour, in the green map room—is that still there? Good. Lord Meric as well, if he—if possible. Captain Erren, you may escort my father to his tower apartment, if those rooms are still intact."

All of the men he addressed moved to do as he said.

The king said nothing at all, but gave Erren a disdainful look that stopped him in his tracks and turned on his own to go into the palace. Erren looked nervously at Gulien, bobbed his head in apology, gathered up two guardsmen, and followed the king.

"He's too shy of Father," Oressa said to Gulien, lifting her head and straightening her back now that their father had gone out of sight. "And too full of his own splendidness, and nothing like as clever as he thinks he is. Ramak's cleverer, but even if he were here, he's mean and a sneak and I hate him. Kelian would do better."

"Tomorrow," Gulien said distractedly. He stared after their father, who was no longer in sight. "We'll sort it out tomorrow, Oressa."

His sister gave a little nod. "Well," she said optimistically. "That wasn't so hard, was it?" Her voice was bright and brittle again. She said, "You're doing everything right! You see, the Kieba has forgiven you after all! But fast is better than slow."

"Yes," said Gulien, though he wasn't nearly so confident of the Kieba's forgiveness as his sister. When the war golem crouched and eased forward until it touched the stairs, he took a breath and followed the implicit command, stepping down to the stairs and holding out a hand to steady his sister as she followed him.

"Kieba," Gulien said, turning to face the golem because it was as close as he could come to facing the Kieba herself. He hoped he did not sound tentative or nervous. To his surprise, he actually did not feel nervous now. He felt tired almost beyond bearing. He gazed up at the glittering black crystals that served the golem as eyes and asked, "Will you tell me how long I may have to establish order in Carastind?"

The golem spoke. It spoke with the voice of the Kieba, not the kephalos. The Kieba's voice said clearly, "You may have one year, Prince Gulien. One year to see to Carastind's stability and to arrange for your sister to marry appropriately so that she may secure the throne. Then you will step down in favor of your sister's lord, ending the Madalin claim on the throne."

Oressa, obviously both startled and horrified, started to frame some kind of argument or protest. Gulien realized at once he should have warned her about this other notion of the Kieba's, but dared not dispute it now. He gripped his sister's arm hard, warning her to be silent, which for a wonder she was. Then he said merely, "Just as you say, Kieba. It shall all be just as you say. But I may have a year first."

"You may. So long as you return to me the artifact that your father holds so close. Do so without delay, young prince."

Gulien drew a breath and inclined his head to the golem. "I shall, Kieba. I thank you for your lenience. I am ashamed to ask for further generosity, yet a falcon of yours . . . a visible sign of your favor, a living symbol of my family, sent from your hand to mine. If I might yet request such a grace, in order to be certain the people of Caras remember it is by your will that I have set down my father . . ."

"Good. That's clever," Oressa muttered under her breath.

Gulien shook her slightly, afraid her forwardness might offend the Kieba. He said quietly, "Please, Kieba. My father's supporters will wish to forget your power. They will raise questions of right and authority, and as most men abhor disorder and strife, they may sway the people of Caras to their opinion. Though I know I do not deserve your favor, yet I must ask for a sign that will make your preference clear to all men, and hope for your tolerance of my boldness."

But she did not answer, and no falcon fell from the sky. The golem merely straightened, drew back, swiveled nearly in place with a rippling movement of all its legs, and strode away. Above them, one at a time, the Kieba's strange white lights were going out, leaving Gulien to sort things out for himself. He let his breath out, trying not to feel betrayed, knowing full well the Kieba might have dealt with him far more severely than merely declining a sign of her favor.

"Rude!" said Oressa right out loud.

Gulien shook her again, a little more forcefully. He glanced after the golem, but if the Kieba had heard, there was no sign of it. He let his breath out. "It's all right," he said. "I can do this. *We* can do this. Don't worry, Oressa. We'll find someone you favor, someone who'll respect your wits. Someone at once ruthless and just and kind, who has all the qualities a man needs to be a good king."

"Oh, will we?" Oressa muttered. But she didn't immediately refuse to even consider the possibility that Gulien might have to step down himself or that she might herself have to marry in order to secure the throne.

Not that Gulien believed his sister would continue to be meek, but he was grateful for her kindness in leaving those arguments for another day. He said firmly, "We got rid of that Tamaristan prince; we can surely deal with our own people."

But, though he was pleased with how assured and determined this statement sounded, Gulien only wished he believed it was true.

CHAPTER 5

Gulien tapped the table gently to compel everyone's attention, a trick of their father's, which, for some reason Oressa didn't understand, seemed to work better than hitting the table and yelling. Perhaps because its very restraint suggested that escalation was possible if everyone didn't cooperate.

"This artifact, Parianasaku's Capture, has to go back to the Kieba immediately," her brother declared.

After that, a little space stretched out. No one argued. Not even Magister Baramis, although Oressa could see perfectly well that he wanted to object simply on general principles: He, of all their father's advisers, had been the only one to press Gulien to give up his usurped authority and yield the crown back to his father. But even he said nothing to Gulien's statement. Out of all the disaster and confusion of the past day, this one thing seemed abundantly clear: The Kieba's artifact had to be returned to her immediately.

They had gathered in the green map room, which was one of the few functional rooms remaining in the western wing of the palace. Every now and then something creaked or a tile fell outside the windows, and everyone looked up and flinched. But it was a traditional setting for important meetings, and Gulien had wanted the support lent by formal surroundings. Oressa agreed it was important for him to make every possible show of authority and confidence. She still wasn't certain her brother could succeed in permanently usurping their father's power. The Kieba could do anything, but she wasn't here and their father *was*. Oressa had no faith in the guardsmen to keep Osir Madalin pinned up in his tower apartment.

She was sitting beside her brother at one end of the table, right out in full view, which felt peculiar and not entirely safe. In some ways she would rather have been crouching under the table or hidden behind the false panel at the far end of the room, but Gulien wouldn't hear of it, and she supposed it was a ridiculous idea. Even though she knew just how openly people spoke when they didn't know you were listening, and *her* idea had been to let everyone else arrive first and talk among themselves before Gulien even came in. She'd suggested that, but her brother wouldn't hear of it and insisted instead that she sit beside him. Sometimes Gulien was a little . . . conventional.

Magister Baramis was seated at the other end of the table, which was fair since he was their opponent; Magister Lorren and Lord Paulin took the spaces at the sides of the table. Lord Meric had been killed in the brief, violent Tamaristan attack. Oressa was sorry for that; she'd liked Meric. Gulien had insisted on Lord Paulin in Meric's place, which she didn't think was an improvement. Her brother had followed Oressa's urgent advice about the guard, though, dismissing Erren as junior captain on the grounds that he was too clearly their father's man and promoting Kelian to take his place.

"Just promise me you won't seduce Kelian," Gulien had begged Oressa. "I can't afford to hang him by his thumbs from the palace walls. Besides, I'm not sure the palace walls could take his weight." It was true that pieces still tended to break off the shattered walls at random moments. For now the stonemasons and architects had just shut off those parts of the palace while they worked to repair the damage, but the work was slow.

Oressa had laughed and refused to promise, but she had also been scrupulously careful to behave like a proper princess around Kelian, who stood now in his proper place by the door, his arms crossed, silent and frowning. But then, no one was very cheerful at the moment.

"I think we all understand that," Baramis said at last. "But—"

"I'll ask him for it, and I have some hope he'll give it to me. But if he won't give it up, I'll have to take it. The Kieba made it clear that this artifact somehow belongs to the Madalin kings. She was willing to see Carastind conquered to break my father's reign. If he won't give up her artifact, then his reign will have to be broken *somehow*, so that it can be taken from him."

"We *know* all that," snapped Baramis. "But—"

"Do we even know what this artifact is?" asked Lord Paulin, smoothly interrupting what promised to become a tedious repetition of an argument they'd been through half a dozen times already.

"Well, once I'm through the formal coronation and have taken the throne, I suppose it will come to me somehow. And then I'll find out." Gulien did not look happy contemplating this prospect.

"Your Highness, it's not that simple," Baramis argued. "If you act too swiftly or too—too ruthlessly, then you'll lose all your father's partisans." He didn't have to say himself foremost among them. "And if that happens, I honestly don't know whether you will be able to hold Caras, and if the situation in the city becomes too chaotic, Gajdosik's still out there, and for all we know all the rest of the Tamaristan princes lined up behind him—"

"The Kieba no doubt has more golems where the first came from," murmured Oressa.

Baramis shut his mouth with a snap.

"She did say Gulien should move 'without delay,'" Oressa pointed out. "Just how long do you think we should wait?"

This produced an uncomfortable silence.

Oressa glanced at her brother, frowning when he evaded her eye. She was afraid that the *real* reason Gulien hadn't yet simply gone on and claimed Carastind's throne and their father's crown was that he hated having been forced in between their father and the Kieba, hated to have people like Baramis think he had ever wanted to depose their father, and most of all *hated* to have their father think that. So he put things off. *She* thought that if he was going to have to take the crown and the throne and the artifact, he had much better go on and do it. But Gulien could be stubborn when pressed. She bit her lip to keep from arguing.

"I'll start by simply asking him for it," Gulien said quietly. "And we'll go on from there. I promised the Kieba I would take the crown. It may be possible to work out a, well, a compromise, of sorts. But not one that will see my father on the throne in the coming year. I don't think any of you would advise me to break my promise to the Kieba." He looked around the room. No one said anything.

Baramis glowered and looked away, then looked back. "What—" He stopped, hesitated, and started over. "What do you intend to *do* with . . . your father?"

Gulien looked blank, as though this question hadn't crossed his mind. Paulin frowned. Lorren looked quietly concerned. Oressa said, her tone a little more vengeful than she had intended, "Oh, I don't know, I suppose Gulien could send Father to one of those desert retreats where men go to mourn the deaths of the gods. That would be *perfectly suitable* for a king who's abdicated and left the active world."

Everyone except Gulien looked moderately shocked. Gulien said, "Oressa . . ."

"Well? It *would* be perfectly suitable."

Gulien didn't seem angry. He just said, "We shall discuss the matter once the artifact has been recovered and returned to the Kieba. You may propose your solutions to the problem at that time. I thank you all for your support." He stood up expectantly, and everyone rose, murmuring, and began to make their way out.

Oressa rose, too, but leaned on the back of her chair and waited. Once the others were gone, she said, "Do you . . . want me to come with you?" She didn't want to. There was almost nothing in the world she wanted less. But she was afraid that once her brother found himself actually facing their father, he would give way. He was always the one who tried to please their father and win his regard, to be the good son. Oressa had always put all her efforts toward simply not being noticed, but at least she didn't have to try to break a deep habit of obedience. But she knew she couldn't say *that*. There were a lot of things she couldn't say. She could only summon up all her courage and offer to go with him, in case that would help.

Gulien didn't answer immediately, occupying himself instead by carefully lining up all the chairs exactly parallel with the edges of the table. Eventually he said, not quite looking at her, "I know things have always been difficult between you and Father. And I know it's his fault, mostly, though it doesn't help when you . . . Never mind. I only mean, you might try to be a little more generous. Father's been a good king in a lot of ways. You're too young to really remember Great-Grandfather and what happened to Grandfather and Uncle Mikel, but Father's got reasons to be the way he is."

Even though she'd just resolved to hold her tongue, Oressa couldn't help herself. "Oh? You mean deceitful, manipulative, and cruel?"

"Oressa . . ." Gulien stopped, sighed, and made a helpless gesture with one hand. "Never mind."

"*You'll* be a thousand times the king *he* ever was—"

"Never mind!" Gulien slapped the table, not eschewing such gestures when it was only her. "At least there won't be such a hurry about the rest of it, if he'll only give me the Kieba's artifact. Once I return that to the Kieba—"

"You can't leave Caras! Not yet! Not when everything's unsettled!" Oressa said, more sharply than she'd meant because she was upset.

"I know that!" her brother snapped. "Anyway, she said I have a year. I'll get Parianasaku's Capture today, send it to her . . . gods remembered and forgotten! There must be someone I can trust with the gods-cursed thing." He ran a hand distractedly through his hair. "Anyway, I'll tell Father he can give it to me freely or else I'll have the coronation this very afternoon, take the throne and the title, and take the artifact that way. We both know what he'll choose, given those choices."

Oressa had to nod. "But, Gulien, even if you get this artifact, it's *dangerous* to wait to claim the throne and the crown. You have to make everyone recognize that you're king, and you have to get rid of Father somehow, and I don't know what's wrong with a desert retreat, especially since—"

Her brother held up a hand. "Oressa, we'll talk about it *later*." He paused, and sighed, the annoyance draining out of him. "First I'll have to get Parianasaku's artifact. Don't *worry*. I'll get him to give it to me."

Oressa couldn't help but worry. In the end her brother went up to get the Kieba's artifact all by himself, though Oressa was ashamed of how she relieved she felt that he wouldn't let her come with him.

"It's all right," Gulien told her, leaving her at the foot of the tower stairs. "I know I have to do this. It will be easier for him if I'm alone." He added in a lower voice, "Easier for me, too, I hope."

Oressa nodded unhappily. Her hands were actually trembling. It was stupid to feel like this, all shaky and small, when *she* wasn't the one who had to face their father. No, she would stay out of sight and leave the hard part to Gulien. No wonder she thought it was so easy to tell her brother what he should do. It was always easy to give other people advice. She was disgusted with herself, but she still didn't suggest again that she go with him.

"I can do this," Gulien repeated, as though trying to convince them both. "You just wait here for me. Give me twenty minutes," he added, smiling, "and then bring Kelian and a dozen guardsmen and come rescue me."

His smile was tense. Her brother was joking, but not really. Oressa nodded mutely, privately resolving that she would do exactly that, if she had to.

Oressa had done her best, in the whirl of events after her brother had seized authority and made their father back down, to help Gulien choose guardsmen who might actually be loyal to him and not to their father. This meant men who had seen Gulien riding into the palace courtyard on the golem and also men who really *understood* that Carastind couldn't possibly exist as an independent country without the Kieba's favor, something that not everyone remembered because it had been a long time since the Little War, when Estenda had tried to reclaim northern Carastind as its southernmost province, and longer still since Carastind had been carved out of Greater Estenda in the first place.

Oressa knew that Kelian was intelligent and had once heard him mention a grandfather who'd told stories about the Little War, so she hoped he understood how important the Kieba was for Carastind, even more important than she was for the rest of the world. But what she knew for sure was that a man who had joined the palace guard only at the turn of the year could not possibly be as loyal to her father as a twenty-year man who'd served Osir Madalin his whole life. Kelian had certainly gone rather quiet and extremely professional when Gulien had promoted him, though, a little to her disappointment, he was also extremely professional around her. But she had to admit that this was probably for the best. Anyway, the moment Gulien actually went up the stairs to the tower apartment, she sent for Kelian.

Kelian looked harried and busy, and if he was secretly in love with her, he didn't show it. Oressa might have liked him to be just a little less sensible, but she only nodded politely when he joined her with a frown and a formal little bow.

"Your Highness. All seems well," he told her, with an uneasy glance up the stairs.

"I'm sure it won't really be necessary to rescue my brother," Oressa assured him. *Almost* sure, but she didn't say that.

Kelian really was *extraordinarily* handsome. He had a strong jaw and a generous mouth, a straight nose and high cheekbones, and it all came together in perfect proportions. He looked like a carved statue. Like a god, Oressa thought. Only of course without boar's tusks or a dog's head or anything of that kind. His skin was a dark tawny color, his eyes large, his eyebrows narrow and elegant, his hair the exact color of ripe wheat and curling just enough to make a girl want to run her fingers through it and watch the curls spring back. His worst habit, according to the servants' gossip, was that he gambled now and then, but not too much. And whether he gambled or not, he sent frequent letters home to his mother in the north—as she knew from the girl who sorted the mail that came and went from the palace; the girl sighed over Kelian and was practically in raptures about his dutiful kindness and respect for his mother.

Naturally she only cared about any of that so that she could advise Gulien.

She cleared her throat. "You might send for Evan and Tadlen, though. They'd be good choices if we need more men to, um, escort my brother back down from the tower. Evan's not too smart, but he's completely honest. He's never taken a bribe in his life, and if he says he supports Gulien, then he really does. And Tadlen *is* smart—too smart to think it's all right if the Kieba detests Carastind's king."

Kelian stared at her. He said, "Your Highness, I had no idea you thought about such matters." His voice was beautiful too: low and warm.

Oressa shrugged. "Oh, well. I hear things, you know." Probably it wouldn't be a good idea to let Kelian understand just how much she knew about everyone's private business. She cleared her throat. Although now that he was captain, even junior captain . . . and she *did* trust him, and Gulien needed men he could trust, too. "You know—," she began

Then her father's man Kedmes came down the stairs, stepped out into the hall, saw her standing there with Kelian, and stopped in his tracks, glowering.

Oressa straightened her shoulders and glared back. She knew plenty about Kedmes, too, who was her father's bodyguard as well as his personal servant. Or, well, *mostly* what she knew was that Kedmes never took bribes to get anybody an audience with the king, that he occasionally visited a certain house in town but didn't bother the servant girls in the palace, that he was big and not stupid and didn't like her, and most of all that he would never, ever forgive Gulien for deposing their father. That last part was what worried her. She hadn't heard anything—there had been no sound of a fight. She hadn't even heard Gulien yell.

"What were you doing up there?" she demanded. "I know Gulien ordered all of Father's people to stay in his other apartment!"

But after the spring plague and the Tamaristan invasion and now Gulien's getting rid of the ones Oressa told him he couldn't trust, there weren't nearly enough guardsmen still on their feet and at their posts to keep somebody like Kedmes where he didn't want to stay.

He sneered, lip curling, unimpressed by her—not impressed by Kelian, either, obviously. "Don't fret," he said shortly. "I'm going there, and there I'll stay, I guess, less there's some reason why not. You tell your brother t' keep his promise to me, hear? He listens to you, all of us know 't, for all you're flighty and bird-witted—"

Kelian moved a deliberate step forward. "Watch how you speak to Her Highness, man," he said sternly. He didn't touch the hilt of his sword—a guardsman wouldn't so threaten a servant, even a servant like Kedmes. But he meant it.

Kedmes glowered at him, too, for a long moment. Then he lowered his eyes and jerked a reluctant nod at the guard captain and another at her. "Your Highness," he said to her. "I'm going there, as His Highness ordered, if I've got your leave."

For half a honey cake, Oressa would have told Kelian to escort her father's servant to the other apartment. For less than that, she'd have ordered the new guard captain to escort Kedmes to the dungeon and see him chained up where she could be sure he'd stay. But she wanted Kelian with her, right here at the foot of the tower . . . just in case they had to rescue Gulien after all. She definitely didn't want to imagine storming up those stairs and into her father's apartment and trying to extricate her brother from their father's clutches all by herself.

"All right," she said at last. "Go, then. It's a two-minute walk from here, I think. Kelian will check later to be sure it was a two-minute walk for you, too."

This time the look Kedmes gave her was no more fond, but it held a shade of respect. "Your Highness," he repeated grimly, and strode away, ill-tempered but with no sign of disobedience.

"Two minutes, is it?" said Kelian. "I really will check."

"You really should," Oressa agreed. "And you'll have to time it, but

I think it's about that." She knew better how long it took to get from one place in the palace to another via the secret passages. Plainly she should consider pacing off and memorizing some of the distances when one took the ordinary hallways, too.

She was deliberately trying to distract herself from her brother's confrontation with their father, she knew. She stared worriedly up the stairs. "In fifteen minutes . . . ," she began, though she was by no means sure she'd have the nerve to go up those stairs herself, even with Kelian and a dozen guardsmen.

"His Highness will get that artifact, just as he intends," Kelian assured her, clearly understanding that look. "Any man who would brace the Kieba in her mountain isn't likely to flinch from much."

Oressa smiled at him gratefully and didn't say that there was a world of difference between facing the Kieba and facing Osir Madalin.

CHAPTER 6

It had been simple for Gulien to promise the Kieba he would depose his father and recover Parianasaku's artifact for her, and simple to give Oressa the same assurance. Grandiose promises were always simple to make. In the pressure of the moment, perched high atop the Kieba's golem, with her intangible but forceful presence filling the air around him, around them all, it had been amazingly easy to compel his father to step aside. Osir Madalin was not a man to be forced into a public confrontation he couldn't win—as Gulien very well knew.

But there was all the difference in the world between a public confrontation and a private one. Gulien knew that, too. He had tried hard not to let any of them see his apprehension—not Lord Paulin Tegeres nor Magister Lorren nor Magister Baramis nor anyone else. It didn't help that all of the important men whose backing Gulien needed so badly were so much older than he. It didn't help that he knew any of them— well, at least Magister Baramis, and probably many of the others—would far prefer to have his father back in command and never mind the recent string of disasters. He didn't blame them. He wanted that himself, except it was impossible.

It was almost equally impossible to imagine actually *facing* his father, now that the ferocious flood tide of events that had carried him along had ebbed and left him stranded to make his way forward by his own strength and will.

Though he'd so bravely strode up the stairs while Oressa was watching, as soon as he turned around the first landing and was safely out of sight, he found his steps slowing until he came to a complete halt on the second landing. He leaned against the wall for long moments, furious with himself but unable to make himself go on up the final flights of stairs.

Perhaps he should have let Oressa come with him after all. If his sister had been with him, he wouldn't have been able to lose his nerve. Or even if he *had* lost it, he'd have had to keep moving. That was sometimes all you could do, hide the fact that you'd lost your nerve and just keep moving. Especially with their father, who didn't *have* nerves and despised cowardice almost more than stupidity.

But no. Oressa brought out the worst in their father. If Gulien had let her come, she would have gone all meek and biddable and stupid, and then their father would turn impatient and imperious—more imperious—and once Osir got into that sort of mood, Gulien would never be able to get him to give up the Kieba's artifact. Never.

He wished fervently that the Kieba had left him a falcon, as he'd requested. He had wanted it to show everyone, especially his father's partisans, that he was the one who held the Kieba's favor. More than that, he found now, he had hoped to draw confidence from it himself. But she had refused him, and he must depend on his own unsupported will to face his father and make him yield the Kieba's artifact.

Only Gulien could take Parianasaku's Capture from his father, and only if Osir yielded it to him; so the Kieba believed. It was in the king's blood. What had the Kieba said? That it dwelt half in his flesh and half in his mind and hardly at all in the world . . . something of the kind. Gulien didn't understand any of that, but he supposed it must be true and he knew he could not *take* that artifact. He had to persuade his father to give it up.

Halfway up the stairs and Gulien still could hardly imagine his father giving up *anything*. Even to his own heir.

Osir had been king for a long, long time. He would never accept being deposed—not by the Kieba and certainly not by his own son. He could never accept any kind of defeat, not in anything. Even though he had already seen all his advisers and counselors and . . . well, Osir didn't really have friends . . . his allies, then. He had seen them either killed by that Tamaristan prince or forced to accede to Gulien's demands. But accept that he had lost his throne and his crown and his absolute authority? No. He would never accept any of that.

Gulien let out a hard breath, pushed himself away from the wall, and took the next two flights of stairs two at a time.

The landing at the top of the stairs was broad, all but empty. Polished boards stretched from one side of the tower to the other, with a window piercing the thick stone walls on each side. Generally, with the king in residence in this apartment, there would be a guardsman or two on duty here. But there were so few guardsmen Gulien trusted—well, he trusted most of the guardsmen, of course; but that meant he trusted them to go about their ordinary duties, not stand watch over the man who had been king of Carastind until just hours past, the man who had probably taken their oaths personally, who had certainly been king all their lives. Out of desperation, Gulien had ordered bolts and a chain brought from the dungeon, fastened the outer door of the tower apartment with that, and kept the key himself. If no guardsman had the key, no one could disobey orders to open the door.

But his father's servant Kedmes was sitting there on the hard boards next to the locked and chained door, his powerful hands folded around one drawn-up knee, his back against the wall. The man had heard Gulien coming, clearly—and just as clearly had chosen to stay seated. It might have been a deliberate insult; it probably was. But Gulien suspected it was also probably an attempt to look harmless. This was not easy for Kedmes, who was a bodyguard as well as a servant, and entirely loyal to the king.

His father's servants Gulien trusted not at all, except to be loyal to his father come what may—Kedmes more so than any. That was why he had ordered them all confined to the king's newer apartment on the ground floor of the palace. All but two of the oldest servants, nearly his father's own age, whom he had sent to the tower to see to Osir's comfort during this period of transition. Now, finding Kedmes here on the landing, he took an involuntary step back toward the stairs and thought of calling down for Kelian, having his father's servant arrested and confined somewhere more daunting than simply the other apartment. If the man dared lift a hand against Kelian, far less Gulien, then without question Gulien would have every right and reason to chain him down in the dungeon below the palace and leave him there.

Kedmes knew just what Gulien was thinking, of course. He was not stupid, or the king would hardly have tolerated his service. The big man got to his feet, but carefully, opening his hands in token of submission. "Your Highness. I figured you would come up eventually. I only wanted to ask leave to go in. To stay by His Majesty. What if that Tamaristan prince comes back? Or if the Kieba sends one of them falcons of hers, or something else, something worse—"

Gulien held up a hand, and Kedmes fell silent, glowering but ducking his head deferentially. "The Kieba won't send a golem against my father," Gulien said, making sure his tone was level. "She has no need to. She sent me." He wished this were precisely true. But he only went on. "Nor will Prince Gajdosik return. He would hardly dare now. I ordered you to the lower apartment, did I not?"

After a barely perceptible pause, his father's servant admitted, "You did, Your Highness. But—"

"Go there now. Stay there." Gulien stepped aside, gesturing toward the stairway. "Get out of my way and give me no reason to think ill of you, or think of you at all, and I give you my word that when I decide where to send my father—" And where *could* he send him, where he wouldn't have to worry about him? One of the ascetic desert retreats, as Oressa had suggested? Some loyal noble's country house—didn't Lord Paulin's family have a house in the southeast, by the Markand border? The idea of simply leaving his father in this tower, an ominous presence just out of sight, was insupportable.

Drawing a breath, Gulien went on with hardly a pause. "When I decide, I will send you with him, if you wish. But not if you will not obey me now."

The big man scowled, but he also lowered his eyes and ducked his head again. "Your Highness," he muttered, and strode past Gulien and down the stairs, unhurriedly but without argument. And if Kedmes kept quiet and did as he was told, Gulien supposed he would have no choice but to keep his promise to send the man with his father. Even though he knew that by so doing, he put a weapon in his father's hand.

He wanted to go down those stairs himself, back to his own apartment, take a few hours to think everything through, set it all down in order—what he needed to accomplish and what essential obstacles he faced and what advantages were available to his hand and what everyone was likely to do. If this, then that, all in neat order. But it wouldn't help. Whatever complicated plans Gulien laid down, his father would undoubtedly confound. Osir was almost as unpredictable as Oressa.

No, Gulien simply had to keep matters simple, hold to what he knew was true, and never let his father distract him. Get Parianasaku's Capture, return it to the Kieba, take the next year to set Caras and all of Carastind in good order. Settle Oressa with a reliable man who was not Madalin and had not earned the Kieba's anger, ensure that his sister and whatever man he found for her would have the support they needed to rebuild Carastind's safety and prosperity. He could do this. He had to do it, and he would.

But the first step was to get Parianasaku's Capture from his father.

He had been, he acknowledged, deliberately putting off the moment when he must set key to that lock and open that door. He had almost welcomed the confrontation with Kedmes; he almost regretted the man had not given him more trouble—grateful, yes, but almost sorry for it as well. Because he did not want to go into that apartment and face his father.

Recognizing that, he had no choice but to put the key into the lock and turn it.

The apartment was a big one, of course, with several sitting rooms beyond the antechamber, a small kitchen and a large dining chamber to the left, and its own private library to the right, and at the back, no fewer than three bedchambers and a solarium with potted lemon trees that could be brought in or set out on the balcony depending on the season. Gulien was familiar with the apartment, of course, for though the king had moved down to the ground floor years before, he had long been accustomed to request and require his son's attendance for the occasional private supper. So, despite the small noises of activity from the kitchen, Gulien automatically turned to the right and made his way to the largest sitting room.

His father was, as he had expected, seated in one of the straight-backed chairs. He had been reading—the book was a heavy leather-bound volume with silver lettering deeply embossed across the spine: a history of the great kingdom of Estenda prior to the breakaway of Carastind and Markand. Gulien had read it, and he suspected his father had chosen to examine it now for its accounts of the earliest history of the Kieba's alliance with the Madalin family, for it was the Kieba's choosing to dwell in Carastind that had enabled that early rebellion.

Osir Madalin must have heard his son at the door, or recognized his step, for he had arranged the ribbon in the book to mark his place and closed the volume. Now he unhurriedly laid the book aside on a glass-topped table and raised an eyebrow at Gulien. "Well, my son? I gather the Kieba has sent you to make her requirements known to me?"

Gulien had known that nothing about this encounter would be easy. Pretending to be untouched by the sting of his father's contempt, he said, "Let me be plain: To recover her artifact, she intended to allow that Garamanaji prince to conquer us. She meant us to become a subject people. If she allied with anyone, it would have been the Tamaristan, not us! That was what you achieved with your defiance."

Osir's eyes narrowed. "My son, the Tamaristan prince would have found himself in difficulty soon enough. I gather you compelled his departure. That, at least, was well done, but you were not well advised to seek the Kieba's intervention in the matter. In time you will find, as I have, that an artifact constantly in the keeping of the Madalin kings is far more reliable than the Kieba's fickle nature. If you had come to me—"

Recklessly, Gulien interrupted him. "Or I might have applied to Prince Gajdosik for his thoughts on the matter, sir, since despite your claim to have the matter in hand, by the time I returned to Caras, the Tamaristan prince was clearly well positioned to cast down the Madalin falcon."

Osir sighed soundlessly. "My son, you know less of these matters than you believe. Of course the Kieba does not wish Parianasaku's artifact to remain in Madalin hands. Of course she would use any tool that set itself conveniently into her hands. It is in the nature of power, as you yourself are surely finding now, that that it must be used. However, as you would have discovered had you composed yourself in patience rather than dashing carelessly off to the Kieba's mountain, once mortal men learn to handle certain artifacts appropriately, our kingdoms may safely dispense with her arbitrary, outmoded rule."

"More likely we would have found Carastind required to use whatever artifacts we might possess against both Tamarist and Estenda at once—or will you tell me the Estendan merchant-princes would not seek advantage in our weakness once their agents brought them word we had cast off the Kieba's friendship? Do not tell me that *your* spies suggest the merchant-princes have failed of ambition, for I will trust the goodwill of Estenda no more readily than the peacefulness of Tamarist."

The king regarded Gulien with chilly amusement. "Both the merchant-princes and the ambitious Garamanaji princes would find we had cast it off because we no longer depend upon the friendship of the immortal Kieba for anything."

"Indeed, sir? Or they might have discovered, as *you* might have discovered, to your cost, that you were not superseding the Kieba's rule, but actually unleashing plagues upon the world. Then every man's hand would turn against you and against all of Carastind for permitting it—"

"Really, Gulien. Is that what the Kieba told you? You cannot be so easily gulled."

It was a mistake to have let his father draw him into argument. Gulien knew that. It was a worse mistake to allow his father to stop him with that cool scorn. He *knew* that. He set himself to lay out the Kieba's demand and make it clear this was also his own ultimatum.

Before he could quite manage to speak, his father went on. "The Kieba has never truly set her strength against the plagues that ravage the world. It is the nature of the powerful to use what tools come to their hands to enhance their own power, and thus the Kieba uses the plagues that beset the world. She wishes us to remain frightened and ignorant. She declares that she is a friend and ally to Madalin and Carastind, that she is a friend and ally to all mortal men. But in truth she wishes us to remain dependent on her kindness and generosity. That is why she gave Parianasaku's Capture to our ancestor and yet taught him only the least of its powers, never how to use it to destroy plagues. That is why she has turned against Carastind and against me: She wishes to punish our temerity in daring to protect ourselves rather than come crouching at her feet like dogs, begging for her protection."

Gulien said, "I'm sure you're mistaken, sir." It was true. He remembered Caras burning, and grief; he remembered the violet-black mist creeping through Elaru. Wherever those memories had come from, he knew they were true memories. He *was* sure his father was wrong. He *knew* the Kieba truly stood between the world and all the endless plagues and ills that would devastate it. But though he hated the feebleness of his own tone, he could not seem to manage to speak firmly.

His father gave him a chiding look, expecting him to back down. "My son, I assure you, had you never gone to the Kieba's mountain, even so the Garamanaji prince would have discovered, to his cost, that Carastind was not so helpless as he supposed."

"Indeed?" said Gulien. Gathering his nerve, he forced himself to go on more strongly, raising his voice when his father tried to cut him off. "You were awaiting the perfect moment to strike Prince Gajdosik and all his men dead, I suppose? When precisely would that moment have arrived? Will you declare it served your aim to allow the Tamaristans to destroy our cannons or to stand aside as our own folk poured out their blood in our streets? I'm sure you don't mean to suggest that it's the nature of the powerful to allow their enemies to slaughter their own people and blow up their own palaces. It seems to me, sir, that possibly you failed to protect our folk from the Tamaristan soldiers because in fact you could not protect them; yet it took only a single one of the Kieba's golems to do so."

This time he had truly touched his father's temper. Osir Madalin set his hands flat on the arms of his chair and leaned forward.

Even though Gulien *knew* he had had no choice but to depose his father, even though he knew that the people of Caras would accept what he'd done just so long as he didn't falter, even though he knew he had all the power now and his father had nothing—even knowing all that, it took every bit of nerve and resolution Gulien possessed to lift his own hand and say quickly, before his father could speak, "Carastind needs the Kieba's favor, and we have it, so long as we return the artifact she demands. She cannot take it. Nor can I, not while you remain king of Carastind. But give it to me freely, sir, and I swear to you, I will beg her to forget your defiance and permit you to take back your rightful place."

He *would* do that; he meant every word of that promise. He didn't admit out loud that he could hardly believe the Kieba would listen to any Madalin plea. Besides, maybe he was wrong. Maybe she would after all surprise both of them with forgiveness. He said, "You are still king in name and by right, until I call for a new coronation and the succession is formally proclaimed. Once she has this artifact in her own hand, perhaps she may be inclined to be generous. Then she may not require any such disruption to Carastind's succession. She cares very little for such matters, I believe. So then you may have an opportunity to make peace, which I fervently advise; or, if you *must* defy her, then you must see how much better it would be to do so from a position of strength, not while Carastind is so weak!"

Eyes narrowing, his father started to answer him, but Gulien went on quickly, as forcefully as he could. "Do *not* argue for the strategic advantage of allowing Carastind to fall under the rule of a Tamaristan prince, sir, for I will not agree with you. If you refuse, sir, if you refuse my very moderate and reasonable suggestion, then I will formally divest you of your title and rights and have the coronation this very afternoon, and then this artifact will come to me anyway. Then *I* will make peace with the Kieba, for I think it most unlikely I will see any advantage in dispensing with her rule, arbitrary and outmoded though you may consider it."

Osir leaned back in his chair, considering Gulien. He said after a moment, "You are set on this course, I see. You will not be dissuaded."

"No, sir. Nor will I wait for your answer, but require your decision immediately."

"You are mistaken in all your intentions, my son. But the fault is mine as well. I should have kept you closer to my counsels this past year or more."

"Perhaps, sir, but I think we would still disagree." But now that he'd thought of the bare possibility that the Kieba might relent, Gulien couldn't help but hope that he might win enough time to persuade his father to go to the Kieba himself, to speak to the kephalos, to sit in that crystalline chair and see for *himself* the Kieba's memories. . . . If he could only persuade his father to agree *now*, to yield in this one thing, to give up this one artifact, to accommodate the Kieba's demands just so far . . . then just possibly he might bring his father, eventually, to change his mind. The Kieba had insisted he wouldn't, even that he couldn't, but surely the Kieba didn't understand the depth of Osir's strength of will. Gulien knew his father could do anything he set his mind to. Even give up an artifact the Kieba swore no one had the strength to give up. Even apologize to the Kieba and ask her pardon. Osir Madalin *was* capable of admitting fault when he had been wrong. Gulien had seen him do it. He was merely unaccustomed to the necessity.

Gulien hardly dared hope he might yet persuade both his father and the Kieba back into the traditional alliance. He certainly did not dare speak of any such hope now. He said instead, "I must have your answer now, sir."

For an endless moment Osir did not give him one. Then his father tapped his fingers impatiently on the arm of his chair and, regarding Gulien with narrow attention, brought out from an inner pocket a medallion strung on a silver chain.

It was blue and green and gold, its face inlaid with spidery lines of smoky crystal. Gulien recognized it at once. It had long been a treasure of their house. His father had often worn it on court occasions when Gulien was little. Then he had given it to Gulien, who had worn it himself for some years. Only a year or so ago, Osir had taken the medallion back and put it away somewhere; Gulien had not seen it at all during this last year or so. That suddenly seemed significant. Plainly his father had taken it back once he'd learned how to awaken it; of course he would have kept it close once he'd learned its name and its use. Or something of its use. Enough to do harm.

Certainly it looked different now. Brighter. Smokier. The crystal had seemed like quartz before. Now it was obviously the same smoky black crystal as Gulien's own falcon pendant. He recognized that much instantly and hesitated to touch the medallion at all, wary of what that crystal might do or become under his touch.

"Take it, my son," Osir commanded, holding it out. "You will feel the power in it, I am certain, now that it has been woken. But I enjoin you: Do not trust the Kieba. She desires to extend her own power by crushing the kingdoms of men beneath her foot. You mean to ask her for favor, but she will give you nothing save that her gift rebounds to her own benefit."

Gulien made no answer, but took the medallion quickly, before his father could change his mind. The traceries of crystal glittered. He could feel the life in the artifact the moment he took the medallion into his own hand. It purred warmly against his skin, so that he moved quickly to hold it by the chain instead lest it should send fragments of foreign memory scattering through his mind. It was unmistakably allied to the kephalos of the Kieba's mountain; he could *feel* the similarity and connection.

He had not truly expected his father to yield Parianasaku's Capture to him. He had never once believed that it might be possible to walk into this apartment, argue with his father, and win any concession at all. Meeting the king's eyes, he said sincerely, "Thank you, sir."

Osir made a small, dismissive gesture. "You have severely disappointed me, my son. But the fault is partially mine, and I shall hope you may yet learn better."

Gulien didn't argue, but bowed his head again and retreated, in better order than he had ever hoped.

Kedmes was not on the landing, so that was reassuring. And even from the top of the tower, Gulien could hear his sister's voice below, indistinct but familiar. That was even better. Gulien locked the chain behind him with hands that seemed shamefully inclined to tremble even now that it was over and he was out of that apartment. Even now that he had won. He could still hardly believe he had won any victory against his father, but the medallion was heavy in his pocket and he could feel its life even through the cloth.

He took a breath, let it out, waited a moment to make sure he had managed to compose himself, and did *not* run down the stairs—though he still went down much faster than he had come up.

Oressa had been talking to the guardsman she liked, Kelian; too handsome by half was Gulien's opinion, but Oressa approved of him and his sister wasn't easy to fool. But the moment Gulien came down that last flight of stairs, she jumped up from her bench and darted forward, taking his hands and looking anxiously into his face. "Gulien! That was quick! And you didn't need to be rescued after all! Kedmes came down after you went up, but he said you'd sent him down and told him to stay out of your way—I thought he was telling the truth, although Kedmes! You know he'll be loyal to Father forever. Are you all right?"

Gulien wouldn't have claimed so much, but he made himself smile reassuringly. "Kedmes *was* telling the truth. He'll do well enough, I think. It's the men who aren't honest about their allegiance who might make trouble." He took the medallion out of his pocket to show her. "Recognize it? When you pick it up, you can feel, now, that it's an artifact."

Oressa touched it with a fingertip and looked impressed, whether at the artifact or at the fact that Gulien had gotten their father to give it to him. He could tell she was sorry he'd had to do something so difficult, afraid of what their father might do in retaliation, and anxious about the Kieba. She hugged Gulien hard. "You're so brave."

Gulien pressed her hand gently. "Father said . . ."

Oressa patted his hand anxiously. "I'm not sure I want to know."

Gulien didn't blame her. But he needed her opinion. He put an arm around her shoulders, leaned his cheek against the top of her head, and said in a low voice, "He says the Kieba is our enemy. That she allows plagues to strike the cities of mortal men because she wishes us to be frightened. To depend on her protection. To remain ignorant and afraid of even the least traces of the dead gods' power. He said that Parianasaku's Capture can be used to destroy plagues. . . ."

"He *would* say so! Well, I don't believe it," Oressa declared instantly. "I don't believe a single word of it, and neither should you. The *Kieba* letting plagues run across the world? It's ridiculous. It's nonsense from front to back, Gulien, and you know it!"

"Yes," Gulien said, relieved. "I know it can't be true." He *did* know, but somehow he was still glad to have Oressa say it so firmly. He wouldn't tell her what else their father had said. *You have severely disappointed me, my son.* He flinched from that memory.

Nor would he tell her what he had offered in exchange for their father's cooperation, either. Not, he decided, unless it seemed likely that the Kieba would indeed accept his request to allow his father to take back the kingship. A year to set Carastind in order; that could also be a year for the Kieba to forget her anger and for his father to learn better than to mistrust her. Then everything could go back to the way it was supposed to be. But Oressa wouldn't like that at all.

It would probably take the whole year to talk her around to the idea.

Oressa said energetically, "You've done exactly what had to be done. Right from the start. If you hadn't gone to the Kieba, everything would be awful. That Tamaristan prince would own not only Caras, but also me *and* Parian-whoever's artifact, isn't that right?"

"Only Madalin kings can own Parianasaku's Capture as our father did, apparently. I grant you, I wouldn't want either you or Caras in Prince Gajdosik's hands." Gulien smiled down at his sister, then turned the medallion thoughtfully over in his hand. Light glittered across its face: enamels of blue and green and gold cut through by whorls of smoky-dark crystal.

"Your Highness, be careful!" Kelian edged a step closer, craning his neck to get a look at the medallion. "If that's a god's artifact, and awake, then it's probably dangerous. You shouldn't touch it or keep it close to you—you should let me take care of it."

"I'm sending it out of the city tomorrow," Gulien told him absently. "It must go back to the Kieba." He rubbed his thumb across the medallion's face again, a lingering gesture, feeling the half-familiar purr of the crystal against his skin. But he did have to send it back to the Kieba, and as soon as possible. He looked sharply at Kelian. "I need someone to take it to her. Someone I can trust. Can I trust you, Kelian?"

Kelian, looking startled, drew himself up. "Your Highness—I mean, Your Majesty—"

Gulien dismissed this confusion with a flick of one hand. "Until my coronation, my father is still king. Let that go for now. It's an important task I ask of you, but it shouldn't be dangerous."

Kelian, collecting himself, said firmly, "Of course you can trust me with this errand, Your Highness. I will set the artifact directly into the hand of the Kieba herself."

Oressa was smiling. Gulien knew she was relieved and proud because she was the one who had brought Kelian to her brother's attention.

"Shall I take the Kieba's artifact now?" the guardsman asked. "I can leave at once—"

Gulien shook his head. "I think we need not require quite so much haste! I'm certain you will have a great many things to see to tonight. You may leave in the morning. Early, to be sure. You may collect the Kieba's artifact from me an hour past dawn." He clapped the new guard captain on the shoulder and added less formally, "I must say, I will be sorry to lose you, even for a few days. I have too few men here I can trust."

CHAPTER 7

Oressa couldn't sleep that night. She was worried about Prince Gajdosik and what he might do; she was worried about the Kieba and what *she* might do; she was worried about Magister Baramis and everyone else and what *they* might do. Most of all, she simply couldn't forget that her father was in his tower apartment and still—until Gulien's actual coronation, which for some reason Gulien seemed deliberately to be delaying—still officially king of Carastind. She couldn't forget that *she* knew of two secret panels in that apartment, and though neither would let her father actually get out of the tower, she had to wonder whether there might be more *he* knew about and she didn't.

When she finally slept, she dreamed she was running through the dark, empty rooms of the palace. Some of the rooms were missing ceilings, some of the walls had been torn open, and all of the secret doors were standing wide open. Oressa knew that her father had discovered all of her hiding places; *everyone* knew about them; there was nowhere to hide. She ran across the rooftops of the palace, but the winged god wasn't there. She saw his shattered face and broken wings lying far below, shards of white stone scattered across the red gravel. She was on the roof, but it broke beneath her feet—she was going to fall—she *was* falling—she jerked hard and woke herself up.

After that dream, she lay awake for a long time. The ordinary night sounds of the palace were not the same as they had been. Too much of the building had been damaged, and too many of the servants' routines had changed, and everything was just different. It was much too easy to believe that she heard people walking through the hallway and standing outside her door, even when she knew this was impossible. Or at least very, very unlikely. Even so, Oressa found she couldn't rest unless she slipped out of her bed and curled herself under her dressing table instead. The table was hung with yellow silk, and it was big enough that she could be almost comfortable under it, especially since she'd wrapped herself up in her dressing gown and taken her best pillow with her.

She knew her father must be plotting. He was always plotting. Maybe that sometimes made him a good king, or at least an effective king, as Gulien said. But if he thought all those awful things about the Kieba . . . What would he do if he truly believed all that? She could *feel* him brooding, a dark presence on the highest level of the palace, thinking and thinking about how to use everyone to get what he wanted while all the time making them think they were getting what they wanted. It was amazing how nobody ever seemed to notice that in the end Oressa's father always got things his way.

"Not this time," Oressa whispered. "This time will be different." But she was afraid to go back to sleep even though she was hidden under the table.

At dawn she appeared exactly where everybody expected her to be: at breakfast in her room. She drank tea and nibbled nut bread and creamed eggs. Everything was exactly as it should be on any ordinary morning. She chatted with Nasia and with the girls who brought her breakfast, finding out the kitchen gossip, just as on any morning. But the minute the girls took away the breakfast things, she tossed her light house slippers under her bed, took off the frilly silk Nasia had helped her put on, dressed again in a practical traveling outfit of plain linen, took the pearls out of her hair and rebraided it with a simple ribbon, and found her riding boots. The right boot was a little tight over the bandage she still wore on that foot, but she could walk without limping if she tried. So she walked, with a carefully firm step, to her door.

Then she paused. She *could* change her mind and her clothes and find something else to do. Something more sensible. Something less big and dramatic and a lot less likely to upset Gulien. She could slip unobtrusively around the palace and find out what everybody was saying, all the courtiers and the important people from the town who would be coming and going from the palace today, and, even more important, the servants. All of that would be easy and familiar and interesting, and she nearly decided to do that instead.

But she didn't. She couldn't. Her skin crawled at the thought of spending another hour, another day, or especially another night in this half-ruined palace with Tamaristan agents lurking who knew where and her father locked in the tower. Though she hesitated for a long moment, when at last she took a deep breath and went out her door, it was to go down the stairs and out to the east courtyard, where Kelian was speaking to a handful of guardsmen while one of the stable boys led out his fast bay mare. No other horses were in evidence.

He turned in surprise when she said his name.

"I see you were planning to ride fast and alone," Oressa said in her most cheerful, confident tone. "But, you know, there might yet be a handful of Tamaristan soldiers out there somewhere! There's not such a need for haste that we must take rash chances." Turning, she signaled to the most senior of the guardsmen, pleased to see it was Tarod, whom she trusted, and whose family lived away to the east, very near the Kieba's mountain. It could hardly be better. "Tarod," she said, making sure she still sounded cheerfully confident, "please gather up half a dozen guardsmen and see that everyone is properly outfitted for a few days on the road." As the man bowed, she turned and smiled at Kelian. "I hope you don't mind a slightly larger party. It's true I'm not an experienced rider, but I'll try not to slow us down."

Kelian said helplessly, "Your Highness—I mean, of course not, but—I assure Your Highness, I am altogether capable of—"

"Of course you are," Oressa told him warmly. "But Gulien and I have decided it's best if a Madalin personally returns the artifact to the Kieba. He, of course, cannot leave Caras at this time, so I have taken on this task. Of course I will need a respectable escort. I'm sure it won't take a minute to put one together. After all, there's no need for pomp. I'm sure the Kieba would hardly be impressed." She said to the stable boy, "A gentle horse for me and enough mounts for my escort."

The boy, eyes wide, bobbed his head and ducked back into the stable.

Kelian began, "Your Highness, truly—"

"It's perfectly all right," she assured him. "I'm longing to see the Kieba anyway." This was actually perfectly true, though Oressa had never thought she would have the chance. It felt a little strange to realize that she planned to just ride openly across the drylands and right up to the Kieba's doorway.

"But—" Kelian hesitated. "It is hardly right for Your Highness to risk herself on the road—"

Oressa raised a surprised eyebrow at him. "Really, Kelian, I'm sure you and a handful of guardsmen can keep me perfectly safe. I'm sure Gulien would be astonished to hear otherwise. Brigandage is not such a problem as that between here and the mountain, surely? You must see how important it is for my family to show the Kieba that we value her good regard. Do stop arguing and let's get on, shall we? Oh, but you had better go ahead and let me have the artifact now."

The new young captain said, in a somewhat stifled tone, "Yes, Your Highness." He patted at his shirt. "I have it safe. You should permit me to carry it. His Highness gave it to me in trust. I promise Your Highness I won't lose it—"

"Of course you won't lose it. That's not the point." Oressa was surprised he didn't understand. "I need to be able to tell the Kieba truthfully that I carried it to her myself. Surely you see that! I promise you, I won't lose it, either! Go ahead. Let me have it."

With a set mouth and palpable reluctance, Kelian brought out the pouch and handed it to Oressa.

"That's the way," Oressa said approvingly, glancing into the pouch to admire the glitter of the medallion. Then she tucked it away in her skirts and patted Kelian's arm. He really didn't look at all happy. Handsome, undeniably, and she did like him, but possibly he might be a bit stubborn. At least he seemed to have given up arguing.

Oressa actually felt a little bit guilty for stretching the truth, although she really *did* believe it ought to be a Madalin who returned the Kieba's artifact. She could apologize for her father and offer the respect of her family, explain that Gulien would be a great king and would never defy her. It was obvious that Gulien had in fact taken the Kieba's golem without permission, and Oressa knew her brother wouldn't speak on his own behalf. Their father had taught him never to argue or explain or justify himself, which meant it was up to her to see the Kieba and explain. So it *really did* make perfect sense to go see the Kieba herself.

So she shouldn't feel guilty at all. And the sharp need she felt to get away from her father wasn't any part of her decision. Not really.

She glanced around, but no one seemed to be questioning her presence or her right to commandeer an escort and accompany Kelian. She hoped Gulien didn't plan to come to the courtyard himself to see Kelian off. But they were nearly ready. The boys were bringing out more horses, and Tarod was striding back across the courtyard with four other guardsmen—Oressa knew all of them, at least slightly. She beckoned to Tarod to help her mount her horse, a gentle-looking sorrel gelding, and said, "Your family lives near the Kieba's mountain, isn't that right? Have you ever actually seen her? I've always known she was out there, in her mountain, but I never thought I'd actually *see* her. Perhaps you can tell me about her while we ride."

Tarod, it turned out, did in fact know *all* the stories about the Kieba, once he relaxed enough to talk to Oressa. He was an animated, cheerful young man and a good storyteller, and she liked how he seemed to forget she was his princess once he was in the middle of a story. "I think some of the tales are made up, though," he confessed, then grinned and added, "I made one up, myself, once." He told it to her, about how the Kieba turned people who offended her into cottonwood trees and then when the wind blew and the branches creaked, you could hear their voices, pleading to be turned back.

Oressa laughed. "Did you get anyone to believe that?"

"People like unbelievable stories," Tarod assured her. "The more unbelievable the better. Anyway, I'm not sure the Kieba couldn't turn people into trees if she wanted. Though I don't think you'd hear them pleading afterward."

"*I'd* believe it," declared the youngest guardsman, who had been riding close beside her in order to listen. His eyes were wide. "I wouldn't want to hear a story like that at night, with only a little fire between us and the dark. Are you sure we're riding the right way, Your Highness?"

"You're safe," Oressa promised him. "No one needs to actually cross her wall except me."

Kelian cleared his throat. "Your Highness, your brother entrusted this task to me. Surely you will permit me to intrude upon the Kieba's mountain while you remain below. I promise you, I will—"

"No, no, returning it myself is the whole point of my coming, after all." And if there was any trouble—though she didn't know why there should be!—then Kelian could take word back to Gulien. Oressa winced a little, contemplating that prospect, and asked Tarod to tell another story about the Kieba. Preferably one without lonely voices wailing on the night breeze or anything.

They were well out in the countryside by that time. Just riding though the city had been exciting—Oressa had hardly ever left the palace in her whole life. She'd studied maps of Caras and of Carastind and of the wider world, but always rather wistfully. For all her casual threats to run away and become a temple maiden in Markand, she hadn't actually expected ever to see most of the landscapes captured in ink. Now she found that maps weren't the same at *all*. The city was so much more crowded and busy and noisy and smelly than she'd expected. The streets were narrower and far dustier and the buildings taller and much more colorful—not just whitewashed plaster or the natural colors of the stone, but as they got farther from the palace, many of them painted poppy red or eggshell blue or a delicate pale green. How strange that she hadn't even known how the people of Caras painted their homes.

Even the sunlight seemed hotter in these crowded streets, which were filled with hundreds and hundreds of people, all of whom, even the children half Oressa's age, seemed to know just what they were about. To them these crowded neighborhoods must be as familiar as the palace was to her. It seemed very strange that she hadn't thought of that before.

And once they left Caras and passed through the farmland that stretched out inland into the true drylands, she had been surprised again at the very flatness and aridity of the land. Oh, there were wheat fields still, and fields of amaranth, and occasionally some other grain she didn't recognize, and here and there a carefully tended stand of fruit trees where there was a summer well that never failed. But there were also increasingly vast stretches of scrublands where nothing grew but tamarisk and scrub oak and pitch pine. The land was so very open, and there seemed so much more of it than she had imagined. Tarod's stories were doubly welcome then, for being told in a familiar voice and for reminding Oressa of the purpose of her journey.

She wondered whether her brother had realized yet that she was missing. But then, she was often missing, and she always turned up again. By the time he figured out where she must have gone, it would be far too late for him to send somebody after her, or come himself, which was what mattered. And he ought to know he could trust her to take care of this anyway. She was sure he did know that, really. Or would remember it, once he got over being angry that she'd slipped away.

It was strange being out of the palace, out of the city, out in the countryside—just *out*. To be riding between fields of wheat stubble and scattered goats looked after, casually, by young children. The sky seemed much wider out here. The world itself seemed wider. "How far is it to the Kieba's mountain? How long will it take us to get there?" Oressa asked. She ought to know, but it had always seemed unreachable. Everything outside the palace had always seemed unreachable to her. Princesses did not go about the city like the daughters of common merchants or tradesmen, far less out into the countryside. She hoped it was a long way. She felt safe, somehow, enveloped by all this space. Not a secret door anywhere, nowhere for her to hide—but nowhere for anyone else to hide, either. No place for secrets. Though it was ridiculous to feel that way, really, because she knew perfectly well that secrets always hid in people's hearts, not in the earth or sky.

"Five days, but that's with farmers' wagons," Tarod told her.

"Three, for us," Kelian said. He slanted a look at Oressa. "Two, if I were riding alone."

"I'm sure three will be perfectly all right," she assured him blithely.

They stayed the night in the one public house in a little town, hardly more than a village, called Terand. "The mill's down that way," Tarod told her, gesturing vaguely. "We always used to stay at this end of town when we brought grain to be ground. My cousins still do, I expect." He looked around and grinned. "Ah, there's a cousin of mine now, with his eldest! With your leave, Your Highness—"

Oressa waved Tarod away, peering curiously at the big bluff man who rose to greet him with a wide grin and a buffet on one shoulder. The man had been sitting with a boy and a girl alike enough to be twins, who also jumped up to welcome Tarod. Both appeared several years younger than she was, perhaps sixteen or seventeen, but *they* seemed perfectly familiar with how to go on in a public house. She was surprised to feel a twinge of something almost like envy at the easy knowledge of the farmer's children, who knew how much a meal in a public house ought to cost, and how to buy one, and whether it was proper to speak to chance-met strangers. She hadn't even known until this moment that she didn't know any of those things, and now she felt the lack.

Of course, the guardsmen knew all those things. A couple of them went off to order food while Kelian arranged for a supper and also for a private chamber for Oressa—which proved, when she glanced in curiously, to be starkly plain, with only a straw mattress on the bed and not even a rug on the floor. But it seemed clean enough, and she supposed one could not expect feather mattresses when one ran away on an adventure.

"You didn't announce who I am to the whole room, though? I wouldn't want to create a fuss," she said to Kelian as they sat down to platters of mutton stew and dark bread, butter and ripe pears. She thought he looked tense and worried and didn't understand why. Everything seemed to be going perfectly well as far as she could tell.

"No, no," he assured her, a touch impatiently. "Of course not. But rough men stay here, Your Highness, and anyone can see you're a lady of breeding and wealth."

Oressa glanced around, surprised. The public house was too small to have private parlors, but the common room was not terribly crowded. It seemed to be mostly families here, men and women both, many of them with children. "All these folk look perfectly pleasant to me. Six guardsmen and you are surely enough to guarantee our safety."

Kelian didn't seem to be listening. He said, "And you have no maids to care for you! This is hardly proper. You must hire one of these village girls, but what if the girl proves to be untrustworthy? All our supplies will be perfectly secure with the men, but the Kieba's artifact—it's a beautiful thing; anyone might covet it—"

"Kelian, I'm sure you're worrying over nothing!" But Oressa glanced around with a touch of unease. It was true that she did not know anything about any of the people here, and it was equally true that she ought to have a girl with her. She beckoned to Tarod, at the other end of the table. "Your cousin," she said. "He's an honest man, I'm sure. And I'm certain his daughter is a pleasant and honest girl. Would she be willing to stay with me tonight, as I did not bring any of my proper maids?"

The girl was awed and delighted with Oressa's request, for though no one told her straight out that she was being asked to serve the princess of Carastind, Oressa was obviously an important lady. The girl's father was first wary of the request for his daughter's service and then, on seeing Tarod's bluff confidence, cautiously pleased. Oressa felt smug. It was a problem she ought to have foreseen, but it was perfectly simple to solve. She couldn't quite resist giving Kelian a complacent nod. That should show him he could stop *worrying* about every little thing.

Oressa thoroughly enjoyed the public house. She'd never stayed in one before. She watched Tarod, who knew how to manage. One had to order bathwater separately, for example, which she would never have guessed. Servants carried steaming water into the bathing room in huge pots, two girls to each pot, and tipped it into the tub. There wasn't any running water. There weren't drains, either. The servants had to carry the water away again. Probably they watered the kitchen garden with it—nobody would waste water in this dry country. It was almost real desert even this close to the coast, which Oressa hadn't actually realized. She was appalled but not actually surprised when Tarod's cousin's daughter, whose name was Tania, told her how much the bathwater cost.

"How does anybody grow anything here?" Oressa wondered. "I thought it was all farmland once you got away from Caras."

"There's rain in the spring for the wheat," Tania explained. "The Kieba made the wheat for us, you know, long ago at the dawning of the age. It's special drylands wheat, and plumps up the grain despite the summer drought. And amaranth is tough enough to take anything. Goats don't need much water, either, and people have wells. And there's the river, of course. Nobody else uses it once it loops toward the Kieba's mountain, but my family has our farm along that part of the river and the Kieba's never minded."

Oressa was delighted to have found such a talkative girl. She gave Tania a silver ring set with a pearl and asked her if she was willing to be hired for a few days. "Since Tarod is your father's cousin, surely it's all right," she suggested.

The girl laughed. "It's better than all right! This ring is far too much, but you can all stay at my father's farm and get supplies for the ride back, too."

So every obstacle fell down before her. Oressa went to bed feeling very satisfied with herself despite the prickly straw mattress, and dreamed of riding through wide-open drylands and not of her father at all.

From Terand, the road, Oressa found, mostly paralleled the river. There were indeed farms along both banks of the river, and the next night they stayed at one of them. Oressa shared a room in the farmhouse with Tania, but the men had to sleep in the barn, which they seemed to expect and didn't object to. Only Kelian seemed displeased, and by then Oressa was used to ignoring his displeasure, since he plainly was never going to approve of her presence on this journey.

On the third day, the Kieba's mountain finally came into view, and Oressa noticed how the farms vanished and the road narrowed and turned into a rough track as soon as the mountain began to loom against the distant horizon. Very few people came this way, Tania told her. Mostly travelers heading for Kamee, beyond the mountain, went around through Little Caras, and came up from the south. The girl sounded mildly scornful at the idea of people going out of their way to avoid the Kieba's mountain, which Oressa found comforting.

A little while later Tarod straightened in his saddle and peered ahead. "We'll be there by midafternoon," he told Oressa. "I can't believe how much faster everything is with good horses and no wagons."

Oressa squinted her eyes almost shut against the hot glare and watched the Kieba's mountain grow gradually larger and taller before them. It wasn't a very large mountain, she realized, and was obscurely disappointed. Then the river turned so that she saw the cottonwoods against the bulk of the mountain and changed her mind. It was large enough after all, though it still didn't look to her like the abode of an immortal woman who had once been a goddess.

But for the first time, it looked close. She could see they would indeed arrive well before dusk.

In fact, they rode beneath the long shadows of the cottonwoods and guided their horses splashing across the river, here hardly more than a slow and lazy creek, two or three hours before sundown. Tania pointed, and Oressa saw, beyond the fields of drylands wheat and amaranth, the farmhouse that belonged to Tania's family, the barns and other buildings beyond, and looming to the immediate north, the great bulk of the mountain. She grinned at the other girl and nudged her horse into a trot, riding out in front of the little troop, leaving Kelian to frown disapprovingly at her back.

That was why she was the first of them to run into the Tamaristan soldiers who had come to the Kieba's mountain mere hours before them.

CHAPTER 8

Gulien was ashamed to realize how long it had taken him to notice that Oressa was missing.

There was just so much to *do*. The streets had to be cleared, the walls repaired, rubble from the golem's violent demonstrations of power cleaned up, the injured seen to—some had no families to care for them, and those were rightfully Gulien's responsibility. When he made time to visit these wounded and guarantee payment for their care, he found a few were Tamaristans, left behind because they were too badly hurt to move, and those were *definitely* his responsibility. The guildhouses had provided space and pallets for the injured men, but of course Tamaristan soldiers could hardly be left among the other injured. Gulien rather desperately had them all moved to the palace, where they could be both cared for and guarded, pressed for space as all of them were with the western wing mostly in ruins.

Two guildhouses had been burned, and the guilds were rightfully due aid in rebuilding. The debris at the harbor had to be cleared and work started to reset the cannons, those that were salvageable. A massive amount of gunpowder had been used and more had to be made by the cannonsmiths, and though neither charcoal nor sulfur were in short supply, Gulien had to approve the release of royal stores of saltpeter.

Worse, a great deal of the gunpowder had all too obviously been stolen and used by Prince Gajdosik's agents. One expected foreign spies in any large city; Gulien knew there must surely be Estendan agents in Caras as well, and probably a couple Markandan or Illiana spies too, though neither Markand nor Illian were nearly so likely to try to take advantage of Carastind's awkward situation as Estenda. Estenda had always resented Carastind's independence; Gulien was almost more worried about what Estenda's merchant-princes might decide to do than what else might come out of Tamarist.

But generally, whatever the relationships and tensions between one state and another, a foreign power's agents confined themselves to gathering information. What Prince Gajdosik's agents had done made it urgently necessary to find any who might yet linger in Caras. Unfortunately, Gulien had no idea how to find such agents. That was why he first looked for Oressa, the same morning he sent off Parianasaku's Capture; he hoped she might be able to do exactly that, now that they knew of the problem.

But when he went by her apartment, she wasn't there. Her maid, Nasia, only said that Oressa had seemed perfectly cheerful and lighthearted during her customary early breakfast; the woman had no idea where Oressa had gone after that. Gulien should have suspected the truth right then, because cheerful and lighthearted was exactly how his sister *would* seem when she was plotting the most appalling mischief. He should immediately have remembered all the times when, as a boy, he'd had to search out his little sister from the farthest dungeons or from some dusty secret passage in the attics.

He had all but gotten himself permanently stuck in a particularly cramped crawlspace in the attics, in fact—he remembered the incident vividly. His lantern had burned out, leaving him flat on his belly in the close dark, trapped because the secret panel had snapped closed behind him and, crawling forward, he'd found only what seemed a solid wall of cracked plaster and stone ahead of him. He'd had no idea where Oressa could have gone that time, either; he'd been sure she was right ahead of him until he'd found that wall.

As he recalled, before Oressa had wiggled back through the crawlspace and showed him the trick of opening the second hidden panel,

Gulien had cursed his little sister in the name of every god he could remember, which, since he'd had a good memory even as a boy, was quite a few. More than once in the years since, he had found it satisfying to curse his sister with cat eyes and bat ears, with a pig's tail and dog's feet. She had generally deserved it, and besides, it was perfectly safe to invoke the gods since they were all long dead. Except the Kieba. But even the Kieba wasn't a goddess any longer, so praying to her wouldn't do anything anyway. Though Gulien had been in the habit of leaving her out, just to be safe.

Now, of course, he knew that he might as well have invoked the Kieba with the rest of them. At least, she seemed to have been keeping an eye on his family regardless.

Well, the wall that time had turned out to be a trick panel, actually, and the secret room on the other side *had* been interesting, if not nearly so filled with hidden treasures as his sister had insisted it would be. The only thing of interest had been the shard of crystal he'd found, and that merely in the crawlspace itself, not in the secret room at all. He'd bruised his knee on it, but the shard had caught his interest because it hadn't been sandstone or marble or quartz or anything familiar, but a dark gray crystal, roundish and flattish, more like melted glass than like a broken bit of stone. When he'd stroked it with the tip of a finger, it had felt almost like soap or wax, but . . . smoother or warmer or softer, or something. Later, once they'd got out into the light, he'd found one could sort of see into it, though it was not transparent like glass. He hadn't found it beautiful, but it had been interesting. "I don't think it's magic, but I bet it's the only thing we're going to find in there," he had told Oressa. "Do you want it?"

His sister had shrugged, dismissing the unshaped bit of stone.

So Gulien had kept it. He had carried the crystal in his pocket, liking to think about the kind of medallion or staff or dagger hilt it might have once decorated. Eventually he'd had it shaped into a little falcon, something his father could not object to, and set into a pendant so he could wear it on a chain around his neck, though he assuredly hadn't guessed the Kieba's guardian kephalos would recognize the crystal he'd made his pendant from, or call it a key. So Oressa had been more right than she knew, about finding secret treasures in that hidden chamber, fragments of artifacts long unrecognized or forgotten. Had he remembered to tell her that, in all the rush of events since he'd returned to Caras? He would be sure to tell her once she turned up.

But she didn't turn up. Only, when Gulien couldn't immediately find his sister, he assumed she must have disappeared into the servants' parts of the palace. Everyone was so overworked, and tucking up her skirts and helping sweep out hearths, or pinning back the lace on her sleeves so she could help gut fish or peel turnips—that was just the sort of thing she'd do. This habit was one reason their father thought she was lack-witted, but Oressa always said she found out more by chatting with the chambermaids and potboys than she ever could from Nasia's staid gossip. Gulien had his own quiet arrangements to make among the palace staff, and then his attention was pulled away by other matters, and he didn't even realize he'd gone the whole day without once setting eyes on his sister until he fell into bed. *Tomorrow*, he thought fuzzily, sinking exhaustedly into sleep. Tomorrow he would certainly ask Oressa what she thought they might do against foreign spies.

But as soon as he woke, he was immediately pulled away into consultations with Magister Toen about how much of the west wing of the palace could be salvaged, and then one of the physicians, Magistra Itea, urgently asked about the palace's supplies of feverfew and boneset, and could he possibly assure her that the palace's stores of medicaments would soon be resupplied? Gulien promised he would see to the matter at his earliest opportunity and made yet another note about that.

Then he had to find reliable men to send north and south, to assure he had a better idea of what had happened in Paree, where the Tamaristans had landed, and what might be happening in the north. The palace guardsmen were stretched so thin, he was forced to apply to Lord Paulin and Lord Bennet for men, which required courtesy visits to each man's town house. So with one thing after another, it was after noon before Gulien once again realized he hadn't yet seen his sister.

She must, he decided, have slipped away onto the roof, or into the maze of secret passages that she knew so well, listening to private conversations from behind peepholes and tapestries. His sister had never been as interested as Gulien in poking through the dusty knickknacks and broken furniture in the highest attics, but even as quite a young a child she had loved nothing better than finding her way through the secret doors and passageways and attics. She had always longed to find real treasures—jeweled crowns or forgotten artifacts. Gulien had always known that no king would ever lose track of anything important once he recognized it and claimed it and held it in his hand. Certainly it was impossible to imagine their father forgetting about anything *he'd* ever hidden.

Sneaking about and eavesdropping was an appalling habit, as Gulien had told his sister more than a few times, but now when he needed Oressa's particular talents—not merely to find Tamaristan agents, but to discover whether his own people mostly supported him privately, as they assured him to his face—where was she? He told one of his own servants to tell Oressa's woman Nasia that he must see his sister at the earliest possible moment.

When his sister didn't join him for the noon meal, Gulien wondered again, absently, where she might be. But by that time he was busy trying to sort out the news that was beginning to arrive from up and down the coast—*had* there been another Tamaristan landing north of Caras, or were those sightings merely nervous men worried over ordinary sea traffic? If the reported ships were Tamaristan, did they belong to Prince Gajdosik, in defiance of Gulien's order, or to one of his brothers? Lord Paulin thought the former; Magister Lorren argued equally adamantly for the latter; Magister Toen did not believe a second Tamaristan attack was likely at all.

Gulien hoped Toen was right and that all the Garamanaji princes would simply stay in Tamarist and murder one another at home, but he had no confidence in such good fortune. And no confidence in the quiet from the north, either. Estenda would hardly fail to try to take advantage of Carastind's weakness and confusion. Of course his father had his own agents in all the foreign courts, but no one held a secret closer than Osir Madalin. Gulien had no idea who his father's spymaster might be, or how to make reports flow to him and not just run aground when they couldn't reach his father. He could not possibly go back up to the tower apartment and ask his father for help or advice.

Not possibly.

It all gave him a pounding headache. No wonder Oressa was staying well out of it. Though he hoped she wouldn't put a foot wrong on a rooftop that seemed more solid than it was. Surely she would have the sense to stay to the more sound parts of the palace and out of the shakier attics.

As evening approached, though, Gulien nodded as Magistra Lara, a scholar-mathematician associated with the architects' guild, finished explaining how it would be necessary to finish pulling down part of a wing of the palace before they could start rebuilding it. They were both standing in one of the courtyards outside the most damaged part of the palace. The lowering sun showed the broken walls mercilessly. Gulien half expected the rest of the nearest wall to crash down before them, it was so badly damaged.

"Talk to Magister Toen about this," Gulien told Magistra Lara. "I agree it's important to preserve access to the cisterns, regardless of what other work must be done. Tell Toen that I leave this in his hands, and yours, of course, Magistra." Then he turned distractedly to the next person who was waiting for his attention and found it was Beriad, the man he had, on Oressa's advice, made senior captain over the guard.

"Beriad was loyal to Father," she'd explained, "but loyalty in itself is just what you want, and he's far too sensible to look at the Kieba's golem and want to set Caras against the Kieba—especially not after the plague this spring, and Prince Gajdosik, and everything. Beriad has got the rank and the experience—he's senior lieutenant, and he'd have been a captain ten years ago if his family weren't in trade. His father's only a cobbler, you know, but I'm sure Beriad really is loyal and honest. His wife is Ellea, one of the cooks. All the girls trust her, and his sons are all in the city guard, married to respectable women, honest men, by everything I've heard."

Gulien hadn't even been surprised by this flood of information. He'd simply nodded and followed Oressa's advice, glad to have one decision that was easy to make.

Now here was his new senior captain, looking stiff and unhappy. And Gulien hadn't seen Oressa all day, nor yesterday. Gulien found all the pieces suddenly fitting together, when he hadn't even known there was a puzzle to solve.

"Oressa?" he asked.

Captain Beriad's small, curt nod showed that he was angry, or perhaps embarrassed, or else wary of Gulien's temper, or perhaps all of that at once. "I knew a handful of my men were out of place. I knew that last night. But the roster's still confused, and I didn't check the duty book near as quick as I should have. But Tarod's a responsible man, and he signed 'em all out proper. Six of my men as an escort for Her Highness, though Kelian told me he'd be off about your mission on his own." The man paused. Then he said, even more stiffly, "I ought to have realized much earlier."

"So should I," said Gulien. He pinched the bridge of his nose and sighed. Then, dropping his hand to his side, he added, "Captain Beriad, everything in the palace—in the whole city—is still very much out of order, and will be for days, I expect. We are all doing the best we can, but it's going to be a scramble. I hardly see how you can be held to account for my sister's whims. Nor are your men to blame. I'm sure Oressa could talk anyone into anything and make it all sound perfectly reasonable. She took six men?"

Beriad's shoulders were no longer quite so stiff. "Seven, Your Highness, counting Kelian, which was more than I'm glad to spare, but not so many as I'd have sent if I'd known Her Highness meant to ride out."

"Still, I hardly think they'll encounter anything seven men can't handle between Caras and the Kieba's mountain," Gulien said. He was both relieved and surprised Oressa had swept off with so many guardsmen, though on second thought that wasn't fair. His sister was bold, not stupid—and besides, even if she'd suggested it, she would *never* have been able to persuade Kelian to let her run off with him, just the two of them. Not if Kelian valued his place here, not to mention wanting to avoid being hung from the palace walls by his thumbs. Unless he were in love with her after all, and Gulien didn't believe he was, and anyway Gulien was perfectly certain that whatever she said, Oressa didn't really care in that way for the new captain, however handsome Kelian might be, or she'd never have spoken so flippantly about marrying him.

He didn't say any of that. He only said, "I should be grateful Oressa had the sense to hoodwink your men, I suppose, if she was going to hoodwink me." He *was* grateful, and angry at the same time, and not in the least surprised at the trick his sister had pulled, now that he finally understood what she'd done. Run away to visit the Kieba! Of course she had—not just on his behalf, either, but because she was surely furious at Gulien himself for leaving her behind, pinned between their father and that Tamaristan prince.

"The Kieba has no reason to be angry with *Oressa*," he said out loud, partly to Beriad and partly just to reassure himself. "Especially since she'll bring her Parianasaku's Capture, after all. It's quite fitting that a Madalin return the Kieba's artifact to her hand. Oressa has too much sense to try her tricks on the Kieba. . . ." Surely Oressa had too much sense for that. But no, she would no doubt put on her meek, biddable manner, as she always had for their father. There would be nothing in that which could possibly cause offense. "Yes," he decided. "I'd never have agreed to it, but this may be as well." He nodded to his new guard captain. "And I'm certain you'll have your people organized from top to toe by this time tomorrow."

Beriad gave him a firm nod, plainly much relieved by Gulien's reaction. "Yes, Your Highness, you may be sure of it."

"Of course," agreed Gulien. But he couldn't quite let it go at that and added, "But send a man. Two, though I know how shorthanded you must be, and I'm sorry for it, but please send two men after her, with mounts and remounts. Just to make certain she's well and bring back word. I doubt they'll be able to persuade Oressa to let anyone else go up onto the Kieba's mountain, so I won't require they try. Only bring me word when she's gone up and again the moment she returns. We'll all worry less when we know she's on her way back, eh?"

On the captain's acknowledgment, Gulien dismissed him and turned distractedly back toward the more-or-less sound eastern wing and his own apartment. He might hope for as much as twenty minutes of quiet to think, perhaps, before he must meet Lord Paulin and Magisters Lorren and Baramis and begin to consider what matters might be so urgent that they had to be dealt with this evening and what might reasonably be left till morning.

He didn't get ten steps before someone called out, stopping him.

Turning in surprise, Gulien found not merely Baramis, but also several other magisters as well as Lord Sanric—all his father's partisans, as he knew very well. Gulien's stomach clenched; though he was not precisely surprised, he had to jerk his head up to keep from flinching.

Worse, they were accompanied by half a dozen guardsmen, including Erren, whom on Oressa's advice Gulien had demoted. Now it was plain he should have dismissed the man from the guard entirely, for though his arquebus was still at rest over his shoulder—for the moment—he could see that Erren looked tense and angry and aggressive. Magister Baramis was flushed and pale by turns; it was obvious he had nerved himself for a confrontation. Gulien would have liked a little more warning to do the same, but the timing for this had never been something he could control, just has he had not been able to control the exact circumstances. But he was surprised Baramis hadn't chosen better than this public and well-traveled courtyard.

Beriad had come back and waited now a few steps away, his expression professionally blank, but his thumb hooked into his belt right behind the hilt of his sword. Magistra Lara, who had lingered to make some more extensive evaluation of the damaged wall, turned as well, frowning. Gulien met the magistra's eyes briefly. Then he looked thoughtfully at two hostlers and a stable boy who had been leading horses through the courtyard but had paused when Baramis had called out. At Gulien's glance, one of the hostlers took the boy's horse and sent him running with a jerk of his head. Three woman with the tucked-up sleeves and reddened hands of laundresses also paused. Two of them ducked their heads and hurried away when Gulien nodded to them, the third moving to join the hostlers, who bent their heads toward her, muttering.

If it came to a pitched battle here in the courtyard . . . But Gulien had no intention of letting any of this go that far.

"This farce must end!" declared Baramis. "Your Highness, I acknowledge your intentions are good, but your father the king—"

Gulien interrupted, cutting across the magister with his best imitation of his father's flat tone. "Magister Baramis. Magisters. Lord Sanric. Whatever your concerns, this is not the place and certainly not the appropriate manner. As you know, Magister Baramis, you are due in thirty minutes for a supper meeting during which your concerns may properly be brought forward. All of you may attend." He glanced thoughtfully at Erren. "Well, not the guardsmen; their services are required elsewhere. Captain Beriad, see to your men."

"Your Highness," Beriad acknowledged, and started forward as though he hadn't any concern at all. Erren shoved forward to meet him, half raising his arquebus, but Beriad said curtly, "Enough, man. Start that kind of thing and who knows where a bullet might go? Anything happens to His Highness, *you* can explain it to His Majesty. Or do you think he'd thank you?"

That made Erren pause, and one of the other guardsmen with him grabbed his arm. Erren shook himself free, but his momentum had been broken and Gulien doubted he would go on with any such effort now, particularly when Beriad shook his head disgustedly and said,

"Arquebuses in a crowded courtyard! I hope I won't see guardsmen lose their heads like boys right off the farm!"

The guardsmen, even Erren, shuffled their feet exactly like boys right off a farm. Before Baramis or one of the others could rally them, Gulien took advantage of the general hesitation. "You know," he said, striving for a tone that was merely thoughtful, "one might reasonably be concerned about the possibility of a second attack, from Estenda as likely as from Tamarist. Internal strife does not serve Carastind, as any sensible man must plainly acknowledge."

Baramis began again doggedly, "Your father, the king—"

"His Highness is right," Magistra Lara said abruptly, and one of the hostlers put in, "Don't be a fool, man. Quarrels don't serve the city, I say, nor riling the Kieba. Less you have one of them spiders in your pocket, eh?"

Baramis had clearly never expected to be answered by common folk, and by this time there was beginning to be quite a crowd in the courtyard. The stable boy had roused up not only the stable master and most of his people, but also all the townsmen who'd gathered for bread and beef after the day's work of clearing rubble; and those laundresses had clearly passed the word to what seemed the entire domestic staff. Against the still-growing gathering of common people, the magister's group suddenly looked paltry. Ineffectual.

"Remember them lights in the sky?" asked one of the laundresses, an older woman with strong arms and a plain face. "Takes a lord or a magister to think of spitting in the Kieba's eye after that. Ordinary folk have more sense. No offense," she added to Magistra Lara.

"Not at all. Quite right," the magistra said, and frowned sternly at the magisters with Baramis.

"Lights!" said another woman, even older and less impressed by the group of challengers than the first had been. "Remember the plague this past spring? I ask you!"

"And us without our cannon to see off Tamaristan ships," added a townsman whom Gulien faintly recognized—one of the bakers who supplied the palace and noble houses, he thought. "Who let that happen under his nose while His Highness was away getting the Kieba's attention, eh?"

Gulien lifted his hands. He meant merely to quiet the gathering, say something that would give Magister Baramis and Lord Sanric and the rest a chance to back down gracefully. Then he would have to speak to the people. He hardly knew what to say beyond expressing his gratitude for their trust, his hope to earn it—but he was rendered speechless as a falcon plummeted unexpectedly from the sky to perch on one upraised hand. Its talons pierced his thumb and wrist, the pain so unexpectedly sharp that Gulien just barely managed to convert a startled cry to an unvoiced gasp.

Though a casual glance would have taken it for a real falcon, one of the little ones that hardly took anything larger than a mouse, it was heavier than a real bird, and its eyes were smoky crystals that glittered red in the light of the setting. Everyone knew that when the Kieba wished to send one of her servants to a Madalin, she sent a falcon, symbol of the Madalin family. The bird-golem ducked its head and mantled its wings, and when it snapped its beak, the sound was clear and distinctive in the sudden profound hush.

Gulien straightened his shoulders, lifted his chin, and deliberately met Baramis's eyes. He said, his voice pitched to carry, "The Kieba herself told me to set Caras in order. You know that, Magister. You were there. Don't now persuade yourself into folly while the rest of us work to defend Carastind. No one will follow you."

Indeed, Lord Sanric and the others were edging carefully away from Magister Baramis, who—give him credit—made no excuse for what he had tried to do, but held his head up and met Gulien's eyes with credible directness.

Gulien found he had no heart to draw out the confrontation and only nodded dismissal to Baramis and his allies . . . not so many as had seemed at first, really. There were many more common people gathered in the courtyard. Indeed, he didn't think that he had needed the falcon at all. That made him wonder at it all the more, of course. It had meant to demonstrate its presence, but to Gulien's opponents, or to Gulien himself? He asked quietly, not quite knowing whether he hoped for an answer or not, "Kephalos?"

But the falcon flung itself into the air again without a word, beating its way into the sky until it was quite invisible in the fading light, leaving Gulien with only thin trickles of blood running down his wrist from his pierced thumb and wrist and the knowledge, both reassuring and disquieting, that the Kieba—or the kephalos, perhaps—had him under her eye, and wanted not only him but everyone to know it.

The sunset seemed to be creating bursts of light that swelled and faded around the edges of Gulien's vision, and he was ashamed to discover that his knees felt shaky. His injured hand stung and ached, the pain ridiculously intense for such small wounds. He knew all this intensity of reaction must surely be due to the shock of the confrontation—for it *had* been a shock, even though Gulien had also expected it. But he was humiliated to find himself so shaky. He moved a few steps so that he could lean, he hoped unobtrusively, on what was left of the nearest wall. If the rest of it tumbled down because of his weight, he would surely look a complete fool. But if he were stupid enough to faint right here in the courtyard with all these onlookers, that would be a thousand times worse.

Trying to shake off his shameful unsteadiness, he said to Beriad, pretending to a confidence he was far from feeling, "Well done. See to your men. Dismiss Erren if you think it wise; or keep him on the rolls if you think that better. The same with the rest of them, all that lot. Do as you see fit." Then he smiled as one of the laundresses brought him a cloth with which to wrap his injured hand. The weakness was passing off, which was a great relief, and in a moment he would stand up again and go to speak to the others, the hostlers and the other laundresses and townspeople, and Magistra Lara, of course, whose support was at least as important. He was perfectly well, the confrontation with Baramis was behind him, his authority in Caras was secure, and if there would be no less to do tomorrow than today, at least he knew he had little need now to beware of active rebellion.

All this was true. But even so, that night the sting of his pierced thumb and wrist followed him into sleep, and he dreamed that he was a mouse, hiding in terror from an enormous falcon with eyes that were sometimes the yellow of a living bird and sometimes gray crystal, but always fixed on him with cruel, inhuman intent.

CHAPTER 9

Oressa didn't know who was more surprised at that meeting, but she knew who was most horrified by it. The Tamaristan soldiers—there was a whole company of them—realized almost immediately that there were only seven Carastindin guardsmen. Worse, they immediately realized who Oressa was, because the man in charge of the Tamaristan company was the very same *addat* she had met before.

"Incredible," he said, staring at her. "Your Highness."

Oressa rolled her eyes, hoping she looked exasperated rather than frightened. "Laasat, isn't it? I thought you and your prince and all the rest of you would all be halfway across the Narrow Sea by this time."

"And I'm sure we all thought you'd be climbing about on the roof of your palace, overseeing repairs," the officer told her. He didn't quite smile, but his eyes crinkled at the corners. "What, by all the dead and absent gods, are you doing *here*?"

"She came to speak with the Kieba, of course," said Prince Gajdosik, when his men brought Oressa and the rest of them into the main house. "Whom else should her father send? One imagines he and Prince Gulien are otherwise occupied at the moment and yet require to consult with their ally."

"She's a girl," objected the officer.

Gajdosik dismissed this objection with a brief, impatient gesture. "A woman grown, and a Madalin. And she's clever."

Oressa's eyebrows rose at this. She said nothing, not even to correct Gajdosik's idea about who now ruled in Caras.

Tania's parents, and her brothers and their wives, her sisters and their husbands, and her cousins and all their children, were gathered in the main farmhouse of the sprawling family compound. No one seemed to have been harmed. None of the Tamaristan soldiers even had a weapon drawn. Their presence was all the threat they needed, Oressa supposed. Farmers were hardly going to do battle against hardened Tamaristan soldiers, even if their children hadn't been implicitly taken hostage for their quiet behavior. Tania looked anxiously around the room at her family and then, her eyes wide, at Oressa, clearly expecting the princess to do something. Oressa tried to think of something clever, but Prince Gajdosik's opinion aside, her wits seemed to have deserted her entirely.

Gajdosik said to Oressa, "In Caras, your brother was plainly controlling the Kieba's *autajma*." Only he didn't pronounce the Kieba's name right. As she had noticed before, he said "Keppa." He went on. "If your brother is capable of claiming the Keppa's power, well"—he nodded to the black-robed magister standing by his side—"Djerkest should certainly have no trouble. Which is just as well, as I have a dire need for the gods' power."

"To conquer Carastind, I know!" Oressa said scornfully. "Because you hadn't the nerve to stay in Tamarist and fight for your father's throne!"

She had thought the Tamaristan prince would become angry, perhaps scrambling his own wits a trifle and giving her some small advantages, but Gajdosik only shrugged. "It's quite true I daren't return to Tamarist without an artifact of great potency. My brother Maranajdis is too powerful there. Nor could I hope to hold Caras against my other brother Bherijda without such an advantage. So I will acquire one." He slanted a warm sideways look toward his magister. "Or Djerkest will, on my behalf."

"Really?" said Oressa in her haughtiest tone. "Who is Djerkest, to dare trouble the Kieba's privacy?"

But Gajdosik still did not seem offended, and the magister only said, amused and scornful, "Oh, the Keppa's *privacy*." His Esse, though competent, was much more heavily accented than either Laasat's or Prince Gajdosik's.

"Oh yes, that's right: *you* think the Kieba is dead," said Oressa. "You ought to know better, after seeing Gulien's golem! Gulien *met* her, you know! He told me all about it. Believe me, you don't want to challenge the Kieba. Surrender to me now and I promise I'll speak to my brother for you." Parianasaku's Capture felt heavy and obvious in her pocket. She tried not to think about it, in case she somehow gave away its presence to Gajdosik. Or to his magister.

"To your brother," Prince Gajdosik said thoughtfully. "Not to your father?"

He was clever, too, Oressa thought. One little slip and he started figuring things out. "My father, too, of course," she told him. "But Gulien is the one who knows the Kieba. It seems quite likely you're going to need him to intercede for you with both!"

Magister Djerkest snorted, glanced at his prince for leave to speak freely, and said to Oressa, "The Keppa never was a god. You say Kieba; in Markand they call her the Kebba. In the lands of Gontai, they say Gebba. Everywhere she is the same: the immortal woman who used to be the goddess of healing, who banishes disease and esteems physicians. Everywhere she hates slavery and piracy; everywhere she is powerful but slow to act. But my people"—it wasn't clear whether he meant the Tamaristans or his own school of magisters—"have come to suspect this is not quite the truth."

"Oh? So what is the truth, then?"

The magister glanced at Gajdosik once more, who turned a hand palm up in permission. So the magister said, "You see, it's all the same word. It's a corruption of 'Keeper.' The Keppa was a servant of the old gods, the keeper of the old magic after the gods destroyed themselves in their war. But she was never a god herself. She seems powerful to us, but she holds only a shadow of a true god's power." He paused. Oressa didn't say anything, and the magister, looking faintly disappointed, went on. "The Keppa is a mortal woman, or mostly mortal, and the power she commands can be commanded by anyone." He paused again, then added dryly, "As your own brother has demonstrated."

Gajdosik looked expectantly at Oressa. She said, with all the sincerity she could muster, "I think you have *no idea* how powerful the Kieba is. I think you're going to find out the hard way, and then you're going to wish you'd stayed in Tamarist after all—or accepted my offer to speak for you."

The prince said equably, "Perhaps that is so. But if the Keppa is still so powerful, then one wonders why she has not acted herself to protect your people. I think she cannot. Her power has waned. I think it has greatly waned. I think she is afraid to face Magister Djerkest."

Oressa could hardly believe he was serious. "*One* of her golems gave my brother the strength to cast you and all your people out of Caras! Just one. And so you came here, so your magister can challenge her in person?"

"Some risk attends every great endeavor," Gajdosik said gravely. "If I had taken Caras and then Carastind, I might not need the Keppa's power so badly, or at least I might not need such haste to seize it. Now I must hope that you are mistaken, Your Highness, and your friend the Keppa not quite so impervious as you believe her."

Oressa glared at him. "There's risk and then there's madness. You won't succeed, you know."

"Ah, well. You may tell me everything about your brother's visit to this Keppa. Perhaps I might change your mind."

"Nothing will change your mind," snapped Oressa. "It's not just that you're unbearably arrogant. No, the truth is, you don't dare change your mind. You *need* a powerful artifact before you go back to Tamarist, or else you need it so that you can conquer Carastind after all and stay here. So either way, you *have* to have Magister Djerkest's story be true."

There was a pause. Prince Gajdosik said at last, "Then I shall certainly be delighted to find it *is* true." He looked searchingly at her.

"How did your brother get into the mountain?" he asked. "You do know how, I'm quite sure. Tell me everything your brother told you." When Oressa hesitated, he leaned forward, adding, "I would not like to have to threaten you, Your Highness. Or any of your people." He glanced thoughtfully at Kelian and the other guardsmen, then around at Tania and her family, making it clear what threat he might employ if she was stubborn. Then he raised his eyebrows at Oressa and tilted his head inquiringly.

"No," Oressa said grimly. "I'll tell you. But it won't matter. The Kieba will just send a golem to destroy you all, and you'll deserve it, too." She only hoped the Kieba could tell the difference between a Madalin princess who had a right to be here and an arrogant Tamaristan prince who emphatically didn't.

Except Gulien had told her how the Kieba intended to dispossess the Madalin line and let Prince Gajdosik conquer Carastind. So she might decide his right was better than hers, which was ridiculous, but she *might*. But Oressa couldn't do anything about that. She lifted her chin and gave Gajdosik a cool look, refusing to let her doubts show on her face.

"Perhaps you may be right," said Gajdosik, but with no sign that her warning troubled him. "Tell me your brother's tale, Your Highness. How did he enter the mountain? What did he find there? Tell me everything."

So she told him about the door that opened in a wash of heat when Gulien touched it, emphasizing that her brother had had a key and it wouldn't open for Djerkest so easily. She didn't mention the kephalos. Neither Djerkest nor Gajdosik seemed to know anything about the kephalos, so why mention it? She implied her brother had spoken only to the Kieba and assured Gajdosik, in her most sincere tone, that the Kieba had been pleased to let Gulien borrow one of her most terrible golems because she favored the Madalin family and Carastind. She described the Hall of Remembrance with all the statues of the dead gods and goddesses, but she didn't mention the twin goddesses who guarded both the way to the heart of the mountain and the way to the vault of plagues. She couldn't think of a way to turn that knowledge to her advantage, but it was always, always best not to tell anybody everything you knew.

"Well," Gajdosik said, when she had finished. He traded a thoughtful glance with his magister. "We shall have to contrive." Rising to his feet, he gestured Oressa up. "If you would be so kind as to lead the way, Your Highness."

The Tamaristan soldiers had been up and down the Kieba's mountain already, Oressa gathered, and though they hadn't recognized the door when they'd passed it, Magister Djerkest recognized her description at once. Oressa hadn't expected that. She'd thought they could waste hours searching for it. She ought to have lied and told them that Gulien had found a doorway right at the top of the mountain; then she could have acted all astonished when they found no doorway there now and said, *Well, the Kieba plainly doesn't welcome you; you'd better stop this nonsense before she loses patience.* But she hadn't wanted to lie right at the beginning of her story. It was almost always better to begin with something true in case someone knew more than you hoped. People were much more likely to go on believing you when you began lying if you'd started with the truth.

"This door will open for you as it did for your brother," Djerkest told Oressa confidently, "Or if it won't, I'll open it."

Oressa hoped he was wrong, although it had occurred to her that since she had Parianasaku's Capture tucked away in a pocket, the Kieba might very well open the door for her. Or the kephalos might, because it seemed to make a lot of decisions, and for all Oressa knew, the Kieba was still distracted by Elaru or some other plague-stricken city. But she certainly didn't intend to *try* to open the door. She would just pretend.

Gajdosik left nearly all of his men at the farm. "We won't need them with us," he said. "Or if we do, we won't have enough men, no matter how many we bring." He told the officer he left in charge to respect the family and even to have the men help with the work of the farm, so Oressa didn't have to fear what the Tamaristans might do in their prince's absence, which was a relief.

But Gajdosik brought Laasat—he didn't say so, but Laasat's job was clearly to keep an eye on Oressa. And he brought three soldiers to run errands or carry messages or whatever they might need. And Magister Djerkest, of course. Then he gestured to Oressa to lead the way across the pasture toward the Kieba's wall.

The Kieba's wall was no more a barrier for them than it had been for Gulien. Gajdosik simply set a hand on it, vaulted over, and turned to assist Oressa. Oressa lifted her chin, gathered up her skirts, stepped up on a rough stone and then to the top of the wall, and leaped neatly down.

Gajdosik merely lifted an amused eyebrow at this snub. "I am glad to see your shoulder no longer troubles you, Your Highness."

Oressa fixed him with a scornful look, then turned to gaze up the slopes of the mountain. It all looked the same to her: small, twisted oaks and pines clinging to the scant soil and the gritty red stone. She had no idea which way the door lay.

Djerkest, unfortunately, seemed to have an excellent memory and set off confidently up the slope, bearing a bit to the east. As soon as she saw it, Oressa recognized the cliff that was really the door from Gulien's description. There were the veins of smoky crystal running jagged and glittering through the red stone; there was the single stunted pine with its roots twisting their way into the mountain. Gajdosik gave Oressa a meaningful look, so she shrugged, stepped forward, clapped her hands, and said, "Kieba! Open your door!"

Nothing happened, of course. Oressa turned to Gajdosik with a scornful little shrug: *You see? I told you.*

The prince wasn't looking at her, though. He was watching his magister.

Magister Djerkest ran his hands over the red stone. His eyebrows went up. "Hmm." He stroked his hands across the stone once more, as though he were blind and trying to define something by its shape. He closed his eyes. Then he reached forward with one hand. He reached into the stone. His hand disappeared, and then his arm up to the elbow. He said, "Ah yes." Then, as Oressa stared, he walked forward and disappeared.

Prince Gajdosik took a step forward and reached out to touch the cliff face. His hand, too, disappeared into the stone. He looked at Oressa. His expression held not smugness, but satisfaction and a little tension. He gestured to her to come forward. After a second she obeyed. She stepped forward into a stinging heat that clung to her skin, and then into a great echoing hall carved out of dark crystal and crowded with all its statues of dead gods, exactly as Gulien had described.

Magister Djerkest was standing perfectly still, peering into the far reaches of the hall. He glanced at Oressa when she joined him, but immediately turned again to examine the gods and goddesses. "Remarkable," he said absently. "Not merely the statues, though those are remarkable enough. We have always believed this sort of crystal"—he scuffed his boot across the floor—"rare and precious. No Tamaristan tale describes the Keppa's mountain thus. Were you aware that this place was made of, or carved from, living crystal?"

Oressa didn't know exactly what the Tamaristan magister meant by "living crystal" and wouldn't have answered him anyway, but the hall *was* remarkable, though she thought this was more for the statues than the floor and walls. She spotted the winged god whose statue had once stood on the roof of the palace in Caras, and wished she had ever asked Gulien to tell her his name. She looked for the god Gulien had said guarded the doorway that led right back to Caras, but she couldn't see him. By looking for moonlight and shadows, she spotted the two goat-headed goddesses with their important doorways and deliberately looked away again, keeping her expression bland.

Gajdosik stepped out into the echoing crystal hall, and then Laasat and the soldiers. The soldiers stood up straight, staring around, pretending to be alert rather than impressed. They couldn't quite manage it. The prince made no such pretense. He set his hands on his hips, revolved slowly in place to take in the expansive, crowded hall, and whistled quietly, a low sound of amazement.

Magister Djerkest turned to him, looking rather blank. "Hmm. How very . . ." His voice trailed off. Clearing his throat, he took out a chip of stone—no, Oressa saw it was a piece of the same kind of crystal that this whole hall was made from, gray and smooth. Gulien had a crystal falcon like that, though she had forgotten about it until this moment. She wished she'd known about the crystal being important somehow. Gulien should have *told* her, and then she'd have known to worry for whether Djerkest had a piece, too. She had a sinking feeling that she might have made a mistake, showing the magister the way into the mountain.

Djerkest tilted the bit of crystal to one side and then the other, studying it. It changed, and changed again, and Oressa moved a step closer, fascinated despite herself. The crystal glimmered with formless light at first and then rippled with a brown swirl that looked like mud stirred into clear water, and then a jagged red shape darted from one side of the crystal to the other like a frightened minnow, and then the light came back again. "Hmm," murmured the magister. He tilted the crystal a different way again, then tapped it firmly with a fingernail. It rang like a bell.

Magister Djerkest tapped the crystal a second time. It went quite blank, then flashed with light, and finally cleared to show at last the magister's own face, like a mirror. Djerkest cleared his throat and said, to Oressa's horror, "Kephalos!"

"Name?" asked the neutral, flat voice of the kephalos. "Affiliation? Aspect? Position?"

Oressa said sharply, "Kephalos! I'm Oressa Madalin! Listen to me, not—" But though Gajdosik caught her shoulder and put a hard hand over her mouth, the prince need not have been concerned. The kephalos did not answer her.

The magister said carefully, as though he were answering examination questions and was not certain of the answers, "Djerkest Manajarist. Ininoreh. Fire. Superior."

"Your primary identity is recognized," said the kephalos. "Your key is accepted. Your affiliation is accepted with reservations. Superior position unavailable."

"Ancillary, then," Magister Djerkest said quickly.

"Your principal aspect is: undefined. Your subsidiary aspect is: undefined. Ancillary position accepted," said the kephalos.

Magister Djerkest let out his breath, straightened his shoulders, and said, this time as though he knew exactly what he expected, "Kephalos."

"Yes, Djerkest," answered the kephalos, perfectly readily.

The magister darted a swift look at Prince Gajdosik and asked, "Where is the Keppa?"

"The Keppa is unavailable. Do you wish to request the Keppa's attention when she becomes available?"

The magister began, "No—"

Oressa jerked herself away from Gajdosik and shouted, "Yes! Kephalos!" Then Gajdosik got his hand over her mouth again, though she tried to bite him. But he needn't have bothered, because although they all waited a breathless moment, the kephalos did not answer Oressa. *She* had no key, and the Madalin name alone was obviously not enough to get the kephalos's attention. Gajdosik gave her a little warning shake but took his hand away from her mouth. Furious, she tried to shake off his grip, but his grip did not loosen. He was not even looking at her, but at his magister.

"How long will the Keppa be unavailable?" Magister Djerkest asked the kephalos.

"Unknown," said the kephalos.

"I need to see . . ." The magister looked around. "Everything," he concluded.

"We don't have a year," Gajdosik reminded the magister, who looked like he was ready to begin exploring at the bottom of the mountain and work his way to the top. "A few days at most. Can you make the kephalos recognize me? Obey me?" He might have sounded greedy or vain: a prince seeing a swift path to power. He might have sounded like that, but he didn't. He only sounded intense.

Djerkest opened and closed his hands. "I don't..." He looked around, this time seeming rather lost and uncertain.

"Can you make it give me *autajma,* of the kind the Keppa gave the Carastindin prince?" Gajdosik pressed. "A dozen or so? Can you make it tell them to obey me?"

"I . . ." Djerkest stared around. "Kephalos! I need war *autajma*—"

"Following the recent unauthorized use of war golems, the Keppa has restricted the use of golems to those of superior position," stated the kephalos.

Oressa let her breath out and straightened her shoulders. "You see! You thought you could come here and take the Kieba's golems and she might not notice, but it's not so easy, is it? When the Kieba comes back, she'll find out what you've tried, and what then? You can't hide what you've done from her." She tried to sound more certain about all that than she actually felt.

But Magister Djerkest only said, "Hiding what I do is not my aim. I need to find the Keppa. If she can be removed, the superior position will surely become available to me." The magister looked around as though he might find the Kieba hiding in the shadows behind one of the gods' pedestals. Then he looked back at Oressa. "Do *you* know where she goes when she is 'unavailable'?"

"No!" Oressa said, and looked warily at Gajdosik.

But the prince did not seem inclined this time toward threats. He only said to Magister Djerkest, "We have days, not years."

"Yes, true." The magister looked around again. "I think we will find that each dead god guards a door. Many lead outward, but some should take us farther inward, toward the center of the Kieba's power."

Oressa said nothing, but she could see that Djerkest knew a lot more than she had hoped. She was struggling with the realization that the magister really did think he could defeat the Kieba, kill her, and take her power for his own. He was wrong. He had to be wrong. But what if he was right?

"There should be . . . There is a place here," Djerkest muttered. "The heart of the mountain. Let me just see . . ." He glanced around at the crowding gods and goddesses as though one of them would tell him which way to go.

"You'll find the Kieba and she'll destroy you all! What you *need*," Oressa declared, seized by sudden inspiration, "is a thing of power that you can really *control*. Something potent but small enough that the Kieba won't miss it. Then you won't need the superior position after all, isn't that right?" She turned urgently to Prince Gajdosik. "You don't need to challenge the Kieba or conquer Carastind! All you need is an artifact powerful enough that you can go back across the Narrow Sea and take your father's throne! You actually have a *right* to the throne of Tamarist. Wouldn't it be better to fight for something you have a right to hold instead of making trouble everywhere else?"

Gajdosik gave her his full attention. "Do you know where a thing like that might be, Your Highness?"

"My prince—" Laasat raised a warning hand. "If this were true, why would Her Highness tell us?"

"Because she has begun to fear Djerkest," Gajdosik said impatiently. "Because she has begun to wonder if she knew less than she thought, and Djerkest more, and so she has begun to fear for the Keppa, whose presence in Carastind is the source of her country's security."

Oressa dropped her gaze. It was not at all difficult to look angry and frightened. She said, "There's a vault. My brother told me. A treasure vault, but not for gold. For powerful artifacts left over from the age of the gods, that the Kieba might find a use for one day. The Kieba didn't let Gulien see it, but she told him about it." She looked up, met Gajdosik's eyes. "It's at the bottom of the mountain. It's buried in shadows. Ysiddro's statue guards it." She paused. "I'll show you where it is if you swear to leave the Kieba alone. To make Magister Djerkest leave her alone. Take whatever you find back to Tamarist. Do whatever you want on the other side of the Narrow Sea. I don't care. But leave the Kieba alone and leave Carastind alone. Promise me, and I'll show you."

"You think you can trust my promise?" Gajdosik asked her.

"What choice is there now?" Oressa asked him. It took no effort to sound bitter.

"She probably means to seize one of the Keppa's artifacts for herself," said Djerkest.

"Very likely, but not a great concern." Gajdosik turned to her and said firmly, "Done! Show us this treasure vault and you will find you may trust my promise, Your Highness. I will do my utmost to leave the Keppa be and Carastind in peace."

Strangely, though Gajdosik was an enemy, his careful qualification made Oressa feel like she *could* trust what he said. And it made her feel worse about her own lies, even though she knew she had no reason to feel guilty.

Light glimmered from the statue of goat-headed Ysiddre. The lightless statue of her twin sister Ysiddro, veiled in shadows, was not so easy to see.

"Ysiddro," Djerkest murmured. He laid a hand on the statue's foot, tilting his head back to gaze up at her slender neck and goat's head. "Goddess of shadows and hidden things. Unseen treasures and kept secrets and forgotten powers." He didn't look at Oressa. He did not, as far as she could tell, suspect anything. He traced the door in Ysiddro's pedestal with the tip of one finger. Gulien hadn't been able to open that door, but Oressa watched anxiously as light followed the line the magister traced. And when he laid his palm flat against the door, it opened before him. She thought the kephalos might speak in warning, but it did not.

The goddess's black door opened to show an equally black stairway that led upward, wider than it should have been, curving smoothly around as it climbed.

"Well, that's unusual," Oressa commented, trying to sound confident. She set one hand on the edge of the doorway, putting her head in to gaze upward. "Gulien told me about this, but it does look very strange, doesn't it? How far up does it go?"

"We'll find out," Gajdosik said, and invited the magister to proceed with a gesture.

Oressa wished she could suggest that she might be left behind, but unfortunately she couldn't think of a way to do it that wouldn't immediately make Gajdosik realize that she had set a trap for him and his people. Djerkest went first, and then Oressa, and then Prince Gajdosik, and then his handful of soldiers and Laasat at the rear, so she didn't see any way to get clear of whatever trap they sprang, unfortunately. On the other hand, *she* was almost certain that a trap was going to snap closed, and they had no idea. She would just have to be quick when it happened. She would get away. She could get out of anything. She told herself so firmly, and tried to believe it.

It occurred to her only when they were all partway up the black stairway that it was also *possible* that Magister Djerkest would be able to open the vault of plagues.

Surely not. Surely no one whose position was merely ancillary would be able to open the vault that the kephalos had told Gulien was so closely guarded.

The stairway was made of polished black stone shot through with veins of some green mineral. It seemed to go on for a long time, turning and turning in a widening spiral until it seemed they should have climbed right out of the mountain. The stone was slippery, and the treads not quite even, and despite the sourceless white light, shadows lay thickly across the stairs. It would have been easy to fall. Before many minutes had passed, Oressa longed to get to the end of the stairway, no matter what they might find there.

Nevertheless, when they came to the end, at first she didn't realize it. The rise of each stair was simply a little less than the one before until the stairs melted almost imperceptibly into a narrow hallway of green-shot black stone. Then, almost before they started forward again, the hallway ended at a blank stone wall. Green and white crystals glittered randomly in the polished black stone, but there was no sign of any kind of door or lock or anything that might ordinarily secure a vault.

Djerkest reached out to run his fingertips across the black stone. "Hmm."

One of the soldiers started to mutter something, but Laasat touched his arm and he stopped. No one else made a sound. Oressa glanced at Gajdosik and away, then watched the magister with open interest.

Magister Djerkest touched the wall a second time, frowning. He glanced at Oressa, frowned more deeply, began to say something or ask a question, but then shook his head and said nothing. He got out his small piece of crystal instead, holding it angled so that it reflected the wall of the vault. "The door . . . ," he murmured, speaking to himself rather than to any of them. "The lock . . . Hmm." He tapped the mirror he held with a fingernail, which made no sound at all. Then he reached out and tapped the black wall.

The wall tolled like a great iron bell.

Oressa flinched. Everyone did, even Prince Gajdosik. Reverberations rose around them, echo building upon echo, so that they seemed to stand within a huge bell, its voice surrounding them and filling them until all their bones vibrated in sympathy.

Djerkest put his hand against the wall, but before he could do anything, the dispassionate voice of the kephalos said, "Attempted breach of vault." There was a slight pause, and then the kephalos added, its tone unchanged, "Kieba unavailable." A second pause and then, "Presumption of hostile breach. All positions below superior interdicted. All gods and mortals present presumed hostile. Limitations of response—" A very slight hesitation and then, "Limitations disallowed."

Magister Djerkest hissed under his breath, a sound of disbelief but not fear. Oressa was terrified enough for them both. She took a step back and sideways, away from the vault wall, which had gone suddenly translucent. *All* the walls were translucent. Shadows moved within the walls, slowly and far away, then suddenly fast and much closer.

Prince Gajdosik closed a hand on Djerkest's arm and hauled him away from the walls, back toward the stairs. He had a knife in his other hand—he had no sword. The soldiers closed ranks in front of their prince. *Their* swords were out, for what good that would do—none at all, Oressa was certain. She was already darting back toward the stairs.

The walls that had all seemed to be black stone rapidly became transparent as water. The surfaces of the walls *rippled*, and suddenly the hallway was filled with golems. They were many legged and crystal eyed like the huge war golems, but smaller, no larger than large dogs. They moved with swift aggression, and Oressa saw the stairway wasn't *there*; it was *gone*. The hallway ended now in a blank wall, exactly like the wall of the vault. She turned back toward the others, then stopped again, not knowing what she should do. There didn't seem anything she *could* do, not now, and suddenly this all seemed like a terrible idea—

Magister Djerkest stepped between Gajdosik and the golems, his crystal in his hand. One of the golems flung a silver needle at him. He blocked it with the crystal, but the golem's weapon only flashed once, brilliantly, as it hit the crystal, and then went straight through and struck the magister in the throat. The crimson blood was shocking in the black and silver hallway. The magister looked surprised. He put out a hand toward Gajdosik, lifting the other to touch his throat. He half turned, opening his mouth. But blood came out of his mouth. He made an awful choking sound and crumpled slowly to his knees. The crystal fell out of his hand and rolled away across the floor.

Two of the soldiers crowded around to get in front of their prince and were instantly torn apart, their swords useless as broomstraws against steel-and-glass golems with crystalline weapons and deadly aim.

Laasat efficiently hit Gajdosik's wrist to make him drop his knife, kicked the prince's legs out from under him, and flung himself down on top of him. The only remaining soldier threw away his sword and dropped to cover them both. Oressa dropped to her knees and cried, "Kephalos, kephalos, we surrender! I'm Oressa Madalin. I'm Gulien Madalin's sister. Kephalos, stop. We surrender!"

There was no answer, but Oressa knelt where she was, panting, and nothing killed her. There was a long horrible moment when all she heard was the light, quick tapping of steel and glass on stone: the sound made by small war golems moving near at hand. But nothing else happened, and after a moment she started to believe that maybe the kephalos had accepted their surrender after all.

CHAPTER 10

Gulien was much relieved to have Magister Baramis's challenge behind him.
He had expected that Baramis, or someone, would make an attempt to set Gulien himself back and restore his father to power. He had anticipated that attempt, predicted with reasonable accuracy who might take part in the challenge, guessed that it would be a public contest but carefully out of the way of Gulien's own partisans. Having correctly predicted all of that, he had taken steps to counter his opponents, and won. He was cautiously proud to have done it on his own, without depending on the Kieba's support—he was *almost* certain he had carried the issue before her falcon had blazed out of the sky and made her will clear. He was grateful for her support, yet at the same time he almost wished she had not sent her falcon at all, so that he could have been sure of his own mastery of the situation.

Today Magister Baramis and his allies had been very quiet. Two of the magisters had retired to their guildhall, in fact, staying clear of the palace, until Gulien had sent for them and ruthlessly set them to assisting with the continuing efforts to brace and repair the damaged wing of the palace. He was not entirely happy with his own satisfaction in their discomfort, but it *was* satisfying. He could hardly imagine that Baramis—or anyone, once word of the falcon ran through the city, as likely had already happened—would dare challenge him again, and that was also satisfying.

But he was also aware that meeting this one early, predictable test was hardly proof that he would master the next. The thought of a second Tamaristan invasion woke him early; anxiety about how Estenda might take advantage of Carastind's situation prevented him from falling back to sleep; awareness of the endless tasks necessary to restore and strengthen the city drove him to his feet and kept him upright through one long day and then half of another, and always in the back of his mind, he waited for the men he had sent east to return with news of Oressa, assurances that she was well and smug with her successful adventure. He waited for that every moment, even though he knew it would be at least another couple of days before his couriers could possibly return.

He would have welcomed the piercing talons of the falcon, if it had stooped down to light on his hand again. He was sure Oressa was well, but he would have been glad of the chance to ask after his sister. But though he glanced up at every pigeon that whirred overhead, hoping for a crystal-eyed falcon, he saw no birds that seemed to be anything other than natural birds.

On this day, just past noon, he stepped out of doors to cross to the storeroom that had been converted for the care and comfort of the few injured men who had not yet either died or recovered enough to leave the care of the physicians. A round dozen Tamaristan soldiers still lived, and one of the physicians, Magistra Ilia, had brought him news that one, a *karanat*—a rank roughly equivalent to a Carastindin lieutenant—was now deemed well enough to be questioned. Though the man would not admit to speaking any Esse at all, it was her opinion he understood at least a little.

Gulien wished again for his sister, who was far more fluent in Tamaj than he was. Still, he could manage, more or less, and knew he had better question the man himself. He was determined not to be tempted to any base cruelty, which in any case would severely offend the physicians. But he wanted very badly to know what Prince Gajdosik might have decided to do after being forced to withdraw from Caras. Even if the *karanat* would not speak of his own prince, he might be able to explain more about the current political situation in Tamarist. Gulien also wanted to know what the clutter of other Garamanaji princes might be up to, whether any of them might follow Prince Gajdosik across the Narrow Sea, whether any of them might already have done so.

But he had not quite reached the storeroom when Lord Paulin called out.

Gulien turned, concerned but not alarmed. But Paulin was so obviously upset that Gulien took a step toward him before remembering his proper dignity—he half thought he heard his father's acerbic voice: *If a prince would not be mistaken for a farmer's son, he had best behave like a prince.* So he checked himself, waiting instead for the older man to come up to him. It was a ridiculous game, but he knew the steps of it did matter and made himself remember to follow them.

He knew Paulin's first loyalty was to his own house and family; he knew the man was playing his own game. But Gulien was confident Lord Paulin did not desire an abrupt return of Osir Madalin to power: Gulien's father had many advisers but hardly listened to any of them. Gulien, on the other hand . . . Paulin had been at some pains to make certain that he, of all men in Caras, was Gulien's friend. But he truly *was* a friend. Gulien did not doubt that.

Of course Paulin did not yet know that Gulien had promised the Kieba he would abdicate in favor of his sister's eventual husband. So for the moment, at least, Paulin was an ally, very possibly Gulien's most important ally in Caras. He was wealthy, influential with the court and the guilds, intelligent, and perceptive. Oressa thought he was a flatterer. It wasn't that this was precisely untrue, but Gulien believed Paulin's studiedly offered friendship was sincere, even if he had also deliberately used his own interests in history and rare books to court Gulien's favor. Anyway, Gulien trusted that the older man's interest in a strong, secure, and prosperous Carastind was likewise sincere. And the man did have good sense.

So the urgency in his tone, and the speed with which he was making his way across the courtyard, was worrisome. Especially as Lord Paulin was not ordinarily a man who hurried. He moved rather like a ship under sail, in fact—not a sleek warship but a round-bellied galley. Not that Gulien would have dared express the idea in quite those terms, even to his sister.

Then Paulin came close enough to speak and began before he had even caught his breath, so urgently that Gulien immediately lost any impulse to smile: "Word from the north, Your Highness—a man of mine, with news. It's Gajdosik again. Reports are that it's the sea-eagle come to harbor up near Addas—"

"Gods dead and forgotten," Gulien said, but though he was immediately furious, he realized almost at once that he was not actually surprised. He said, and heard the grimness in his own tone, "I *told* the man I would destroy him if he touched Carastindin lands a second time. Does he think I didn't mean it?"

"He's desperate, Your Highness—or despite your demonstration, he thinks he's found a way to defy the Kieba as well as you. Whatever he means to do, likely he's had time to set it in motion. My man rode hard, but at best it's three days' ride from Addas—"

"Yes." This was obvious. Gulien turned decisively toward the repurposed storerooms, beckoning for Lord Paulin to accompany him. That he would have to do something was plain. That it would be far better to know first just what that cursed Tamaristan prince was actually about was also plain.

Half a dozen men and several women looked up in startlement as the door flung open, Magistra Ilia straightening from beside one of the pallets with a frown for the violence of this entrance.

The wounded Tamaristans, clean and tended, clad in the plain linen shifts the physicians provided for indigent patients, rested on pallets, the most ill at the rear of the storeroom where it was coolest and those more nearly recovered closer to the door. Two physician's attendants, both women, had been moving quietly about to tend the wounded, though because these men were Tamaristan, two guardsmen also stood by the door—now at attention in respect of their prince's presence, but still watchful.

The windowless, thick-walled storeroom, pleasantly cool even during the heat of the day, was lit by oil lamps that swayed overhead on chains. The floor was stone, but with rush mats laid across it on which the attendants might kneel while tending their patients. The ordinary smells of a sickroom were not absent, but the dominant scents were of lamp oil and astringent herbal unguents.

The *karanat*, nearest the door, had jerked up onto an elbow in alarm. He was a young man, surely no older than Gulien. Though he could not know precisely who Gulien was, he could hardly mistake him for a physician or servant, and he had surely expected an officer to come with questions. One of his legs was splinted, and his opposite arm as well, but he met Gulien's eyes with commendable composure, his mouth tight with what Gulien feared was stubbornness as well as pain.

Some few of the other Tamaristan soldiers also seemed certain to mend; several were sitting up and alert, looking now from Gulien to their officer and back in understandable anxiety. The others, some half dozen who had hardly stirred, must still be fevered or were worse injured.

At Gulien's sharp gesture, the attendants backed away toward the far wall; the guardsmen laid their hands to their weapons, and Magistra Ilia said in rebuke, "Your Highness, moderation, if you please!"

Gulien ignored her. He said to the nearest guardsman, speaking clearly but not too loudly, "Those six in the back don't look likely to recover, so why are we wasting effort on them? Dispose of the lot of them and then we'll see what we can do with these others."

The *karanat*, horrified, exclaimed, "No! Your Highness, please!" even before Magistra Ilia could explode.

Gulien held up a hand to check the guardsman, who had hesitated in disbelief anyway. Giving the magistra an apologetic nod, he turned to the *karanat* and observed, "You do speak Esse. Let's have no more pretense of that kind. I have questions, which I can put to you in civilized fashion here, under Magistra Ilia's eye, or elsewhere, under no concerned gaze. Not only your own well-being depends on your answer, but that of all these men. Don't tell me you don't understand."

The *karanat* was pale but steady. His good hand was clenched, white-knuckled, on the linen shift he wore—undoubtedly he was wishing for proper clothing and boots and to be facing the Carastindin prince on his feet. In his place Gulien would have been wishing for all that. But he said steadily, his Esse accented but clear, "I understand."

"I've word the sea-eagle came to shore three days ago, in the north, to the harbor by Addas. What does your prince hope to gain by this? He cannot possibly hope to take Carastind now; not without first taking Caras. What ally does he expect? Has he made common cause with Estenda against us? Or does he expect another of your Garamanaji princes to attack Caras from the sea while he comes down from the north? What does he intend?"

At his back Gulien was aware of Lord Paulin letting out what seemed a breath of protest, and at once realized he should not have provided plausible answers to the Tamaristan officer—now if the *karanat* said, *Oh yes, Prince Gajdosik has made alliance with Estenda,* how would Gulien know whether it was true or whether the man had simply seized on his own suggestion? But it was too late to catch back his words. He glared at the *karanat*.

Flinching from Gulien's anger, the Tamaristan officer lowered his gaze. He was shaking, fine tremors that at first Gulien had taken for the swaying of the lamps. A young man, injured and surely still in pain, Magistra Ilia's efforts notwithstanding, caught out in attempted deception by a trick that any child might have expected, explicitly responsible now for all his companions, helpless in the hands of enemies . . . Gulien might very easily have pitied him, except that he could not afford pity. He said, refusing to let himself feel ill and most certainly refusing the *karanat* time to think, "Well? Answer at once!"

"I . . ." The young officer looked aside, faltering.

Bending, Gulien seized his chin and forced his face up. He made his voice quiet, speaking only for the *karanat* to hear. "I've no intention of repeating any threats."

The *karanat* made a halfhearted effort to pull away, breath shuddering, then yielded to Gulien's grip and met his eyes again. "You say three days, yes? Then it does not matter what you do. You will be too late—"

Gulien didn't hit him, but the *karanat* flinched, evidently just from the look in his eyes. He said grudgingly, "My prince will take what remains of the Kieba's power. Then he will need no alliance, not with Estenda and not with his brothers."

Releasing him, Gulien straightened.

Behind him Lord Paulin said, "The young man is lying—or mistaken. Gajdosik can't do anything of the kind. It's not possible."

Thinking of the Kieba he'd met, Gulien decided he agreed. He asked the young Tamaristan officer in his sternest tone, "Is that the truth? Your prince thinks he can defeat the Kieba and steal her power. He actually believes that?" When he saw the karanat gather himself to refuse to answer, he added scornfully, "I don't think so. You *are* lying."

"It is not a lie! It was said. It was something he thought he might try. If he had no other choice. They said. It was said. I don't know! He would not say such things to me! But it has been three days, and it will be more before you could get there—four, five—so if my prince would do it, it will be done, and you cannot prevent it." The *karanat* drew a hard breath and straightened his shoulders, gathering the remnants of his pride.

Gulien frowned, because that much was certainly true—if Gajdosik had come to shore three days ago, then depending on how long it had taken him to gather the resources he'd need for a swift plunge inward toward the Kieba's mountain, he would surely have been there at least a day before anyone from Caras could possibly arrive. Maybe two. Maybe more.

The *karanat* glared at him, perhaps taking his frown for anger, perhaps even for a threat. "It is the truth! You should be glad! Prince Bherijda has the spirit of malice in him—and Prince Maranajdis is worse. *My* prince is an honorable man!"

"Oh, an honorable man!" Gulien eyed the Tamaristan. "The truth, is it?" he asked, deliberately testing the man's resolve. "Would it still be the truth if I ordered one of these men killed? Or if I ordered all of you questioned with fire and iron?"

These threats tempered the anger with fear, but the *karanat* still said stubbornly, "Whatever you do, you will see it is the truth, Madalin prince, but then it will be too late for you. But it is too late anyway."

"Yet this hardly seems likely," Paulin muttered.

But looking at the *karanat*, Gulien was almost certain the man was telling the truth. The part about timing, about days having passed, about it being too late for Gulien to interfere with whatever Gajdosik Garamanaj had intended . . . that had the feel of truth. The refusal to back down under imminent threat . . . that too had the feel of truth.

Beckoning to Paulin, ignoring Magistra Ilia's offended glare, Gulien walked out of the storeroom.

The Kieba's falcon had come to him—but that was yesterday. Gods remembered and forgotten, what he wouldn't have given to have it return now! Now he saw no way to give warning or ask for reassurance. He said grimly, "I'll go myself. Don't argue with me; what choice is there? *Oressa* is at the Kieba's mountain!"

"Am I arguing?" said Paulin, his round face carefully set in a neutral expression. "But I will ask: *Do* you believe the young man? He might well have lied. Though you were—your harshness took him by surprise, I think, Your Highness." He didn't say, *It took me by surprise*. He didn't have to say it. That was evident in the uncharacteristic caution in his tone.

Gulien didn't say, *Yes, it took me by surprise too*. He didn't want to think about what he might have done, might have had to do, if the Tamaristan officer had refused to answer him. He could see no way he could have just given up, but he wasn't Oressa, to think of some clever subterfuge. He would have had to carry through with some brutality. And he would have done it. He thought he would have. He folded his hands together to conceal a shameful tendency toward shakiness.

He said, "If he were lying, he chose a uniquely plausible tale, didn't he? What if Prince Gajdosik has some artifact that allows him to challenge the Kieba? If my father could defy her over Parianasaku's Capture, how can we know what artifacts Gajdosik might hold, or what they might allow him to do?"

"That's a concern, I suppose," Paulin admitted reluctantly. "But though it's also true we're discouragingly short of trustworthy officers, Your Highness, perhaps you might better send Beriad than leave Caras yourself."

"I might ask Beriad to deal with a Tamaristan incursion. Shall I also ask him to deal with the Kieba in my stead?" Paulin had no quick answer for this, and Gulien went on. "She has little partiality for my family just now, I fear, or for Carastind, though I hope that Oressa returning Parianasaku's artifact will cause her to look with more favor upon us. But I see no way to set this on another. I think the Kieba will at least speak with me, and I hope she will listen to me." Or if not the Kieba herself, then perhaps the kephalos, whose intentions or desires plainly crossed the Kieba's, at least to some extent. He didn't explain that, either; he had no way to explain it, since he didn't understand it himself.

"Well . . . well, one can hardly argue. Yes, very well. Though one may hope that if a Tamaristan company has gone inland, if it can be waylaid and destroyed, that's worthwhile on its own and might prevent any need to approach the Kieba. No, I'm not arguing, Your Highness. Likely enough the young man was right and it's too late to catch the Tamaristans short. But this Garamanaji prince can't actually break the Kieba's power. You don't believe that. You believe he will anger her, perhaps to all our peril."

Gulien opened a hand. He did think so. But it was worse than that. He said, "I don't believe he can steal anything of hers, not so long as she expects him. No. It's not possible. Not so long as the Kieba is in any way prepared for the arrival of enemies. But when I saw her, the Kieba was distracted. There is terrible plague elsewhere in the world."

In his memory—in something that was not quite his memory—a voice said again, *Elaru is burning.* He did not look at Paulin. "When I borrowed her golem—" But he didn't want to admit even to Lord Paulin he'd actually stolen the golem. With the kephalos's assistance, but now it only seemed to him that the kephalos was more mysterious, less know-able, less predictable than even the Kieba herself. If it was working in some way against the Kieba, if it had assisted Gulien against her, could he be sure it wouldn't also render such assistance to a Tamaristan prince? Especially if the Kieba's attention was turned elsewhere? Especially if Gulien was not there to protest?

"Or what if she decides she simply prefers Gajdosik Garamanaj to any Madalin?" he said out loud. "She as much as said she preferred him to my father."

"You do worry me, Your Highness," Paulin said grimly. "Go, by all means. How many men can we muster? We daren't strip Caras, no matter the threat this Tamaristan prince offers; who knows what may yet happen here? Well, we'll have to do what we can, and we may draw on private house guards as well as the general militia, I suppose. Mine, certainly." He hesitated, then added more quietly, "You had better not set authority solely into my hands—but I will ask you to give me some authority. Magister Toen . . . I can work with him, if you'll allow me to advise you, and some of the court would trust him more than me. Security on the tower . . . I'll see to that myself, if you'll allow it."

Gulien nodded. He knew he would have to. "Probably I'll find the Kieba in a good humor, Parianasaku's artifact in her hand, having tea with Oressa. She'll have fed Prince Gajdosik and all his men to her falcons or turned them into pillars of salt, and my greatest problem will be gain-ing her forgiveness for yet another intrusion against her privacy." Which might indeed be a problem, but he made his tone light.

"Let it be so," agreed Lord Paulin, with a grim little nod that suggested he wasn't fooled by any pretense of good humor.

CHAPTER 11

Obey all instructions instantly, the kephalos had told them. After what had happened, not even Gajdosik had been arrogant enough to test its warning.

The kephalos didn't answer Oressa when she spoke to it; it didn't answer any of them. Even when it finally occurred to her to take out Parianasaku's Capture and hold it up and ask to be allowed to return the Kieba's gift to the Kieba's hand, there was no response at all.

On the other hand, they were alive. She wondered if her name had mattered at all, or her brother's name, or the artifact she held. If Djerkest or Gajdosik had called out in surrender to the kephalos, would they be in this same situation? Or maybe imprisoned in lightless coffins deep in the earth, their deathless cries serving as an eternal warning for others, or however that story went. There was no way to tell now. Not even Prince Gajdosik seemed inclined to test the kephalos, even when its golems took them to a prison that seemed as secure as any lightless coffin.

It was a single room, though a big one, carved out of the ordinary red stone of the mountain. There was very little else to it. But water poured in a flat stream down the wall at the back, splashing into a wide, shallow pool, which was a welcome sight, and cushions lay piled to one side of the pool, which was far better than bare rock. The front wall was made of something that looked like glass, but one could apparently step right through it, as through the door into the mountain. Oressa was fairly certain that it would be more difficult to pass through in the other direction.

Gajdosik stepped through the glass wall and into the cell first. Laasat and the one remaining Tamaristan soldier followed their prince, but Oressa couldn't help but hesitate, despite the little golems surrounding her. "Please," said Gajdosik, seeing her reluctance. He half lifted a hand toward her, an urgent gesture. "Don't risk yourself, Your Highness. You need not fear me or mine. I promise you."

Oressa found she was far more afraid of the kephalos than of Prince Gajdosik. She stepped forward. She felt much safer once they were in the cell, which was ironic, but now at least she assumed the kephalos was no longer likely to kill them by *mistake*. She thought it would be humiliating to die by *accident* while waiting for the Kieba to realize they were here and make her own judgment. Her, Oressa hoped she might sway. She didn't dare try to argue with the kephalos, even if it would speak to her, which so far it still refused to do.

Gajdosik knelt down on the bare floor, gesturing his people down as well. He didn't quite look harmless even so, but he was clearly trying. "Please," he said to Oressa. "Come. Sit. Tell me—will you tell me what happened? I think you set a trap for me. Is that so?"

Oressa walked forward slowly and sat down with her back straight, facing Gajdosik. She said, "It's really the vault of plagues."

"Plagues," Gajdosik repeated. "*Plagues*. Forgotten *gods*."

"Her library and her tools, Gulien said. She uses the ones in the vault to find ways to cure new ones, or something. I don't know how that works. I was certain not even your magister could get in. Gulien said the kephalos said it was well defended. I thought . . . I thought the kephalos would have to guard it more carefully than anything, all the time, even when the Kieba isn't watching. Especially when she isn't watching. I couldn't think of anything else to do. I was afraid Magister Djerkest—" She stopped. After a moment she said, "He knew more than I thought. But I'm sorry for his death."

Gajdosik opened a hand, a gesture of concession. "You are not at fault for anything. I gave you no choice. All the choices were mine. So everything I have tried to do has come to this." There was a little pause. Then the prince said, "It stopped for you. For your name, or your brother's name. Or for the artifact you hold."

Oressa put a protective hand over her skirts where Parianasaku's Capture was tucked away, but Gajdosik made no move to take the medallion from her by force. Perhaps he feared that the Kieba might be offended if he did so, since Oressa had referred to it as the Kieba's gift when trying to get the kephalos to respond to her and Gajdosik had no way to guess that the gift had been given long ago and since regretted. She said cautiously, "Maybe. It might have been any of those things that stopped it, or something else. I don't know."

Gajdosik nodded. But he said, "Even so, Your Highness . . ." He nodded to Laasat, then to the one remaining soldier. "This is Laasat Jerant. That is Tamresk Kerenn. They are good men. Decent men. Perhaps you may find the Keppa regards your opinion. If this should be so, I hope you will speak for them."

Oressa stared at him. After a moment, she said, "Yes. But—"

"For them. If you will."

She hesitated a moment longer, then nodded slowly.

"Good. Thank you."

"Yes," she said awkwardly. "It probably won't help, you know. I'm trespassing here, too, almost as much as you are." She glanced uncomfortably around the cell, wanting to break the rather fraught pause that followed. "Do you suppose there's soap?"

There was no soap, and the kephalos did not answer her when she asked for it, but Oressa supposed they should be grateful for the pool. Clean water was much better than nothing. Though she would have liked privacy to wash, with or without soap. It was still only one room, after all, and there were no screens to block the pool from view.

"No one will intrude on your privacy," Gajdosik told Oressa.

He looked grim. He was ashamed, she understood, because he had brought her into this situation. He had been willing to threaten her himself, but this was apparently different. She found, to her surprise, that she believed he had never meant to carry out his threats and that she trusted his promise. "All right." She looked around the cell. No soap, no towels, no fresh clothing. She made a face. "If she'll see me at all, I'll have to face the Kieba in a wrinkled blouse and with my hair down. Well, I can always explain that this is all your fault."

The prince's mouth crooked with ironic humor. "That will even be true."

"It's always best to tell the truth," Oressa said virtuously.

So she washed quickly, and if anybody peeked, he was too subtle about it for her to catch him. Then she dressed again in the same clothes, which was not wonderful—she *longed* for Nasia to bustle in and start fussing about which dress she would like to wear for dinner. She hoped there would be some sort of dinner. The kephalos couldn't just starve prisoners, could it? Or they wouldn't ever last long enough for the Kieba to decide what to do with them.

After her bath, Oressa sat with her back to the pool while the men took their turn. *She* didn't peek, either, though she was very curious— Prince Gajdosik really was quite good-looking, though of course he couldn't match Kelian, but still. But she was pretty sure that if she tried to look, someone *would* catch her at it and then she would simply die of embarrassment, which would be a pity after surviving the kephalos. She combed her fingers through her hair and thought about what she might say to the Kieba when she finally got a chance. If she ever did.

Time stretched out and out, measureless without the sun to track across the sky or a dayglass to turn, but hours, surely. Food appeared, eventually: a whole low table set with bowls of mutton stew and plain round loaves of dark bread, heavy with amaranth. There was neither butter for the bread nor pepper sauce for the stew, but no one complained.

And still the Kieba did not come. The Tamaristans talked among themselves in Tamaj as they ate, and Oressa, mostly out of habit, pretended not to understand them. She learned no great secrets. Only that Prince Gajdosik worried about the rest of his men, which she would have known anyway. He was worried, for obvious reasons, about the company stationed below the Kieba's mountain, but also concerned about the rest, gathered, she learned, to the north of Caras, waiting for his return. Whether Gajdosik returned to them or not, it would be impossible for his people to go back across the Narrow Sea to Tamarist, apparently, though Oressa could not quite understand why his brother in Tamarist was so frightening and couldn't ask without giving herself away. But it gave her something else to worry about. Because if Prince Gajdosik's people could not return to Tamarist, then they must stay in Carastind, and wherever they went and whatever they did, they would be trouble. She saw that clearly. And she couldn't help but sympathize with Prince Gajdosik. She didn't *want* to, but she couldn't help it. In his place, she would be worried too, and for the same reasons. It was all very complicated.

She sighed.

Prince Gajdosik glanced at her, then jerked his head at Laasat, who lifted an eyebrow but clambered to his feet, beckoned to the soldier, gathered up the soiled bowls and spoons, and headed for the pool.

"I regret your presence here," Gajdosik told her, once his men were away. "But as you are not to blame for your trespass, surely the Keppa will not hold you at fault. I promise you, I will accept the responsibility for bringing you to this place. You will undoubtedly be allowed to return to your father's house."

Oressa thought this was in fact fairly likely, since after all she still had Parianasaku's Capture. She would return it to the Kieba, and the Kieba would surely accept her apology for leading the Tamaristans into her mountain and let her explain that Gulien should be allowed to rule Carastind, and then let her go home. Everything would be fine.

She sighed again, wishing she knew what was *happening* at home. Wishing she believed that Gulien had sent their father off to a desert retreat as she had suggested. She doubted her brother had done anything of the kind. It wasn't that Gulien was stupid, but when it came to their father, it sometimes seemed to her that he lacked *resolution*. Oressa longed to be at home, in her own rooms, with her own things around her—but not if her father was still looming over her whole world. Not if she still had to be afraid that he would shove Gulien aside and reclaim his throne and his crown and his right to command everyone's life as he saw fit, with nowhere any recourse—

"You *fear* to return to your home," Gajdosik said suddenly. Oressa jerked her head up, startled, and he gave her a crooked smile, more a twist of the mouth. "Or so I surmise," he said, a trifle apologetically. "Forgive me. I think I recognize this fear. I, too, fear to return to my home. My brother Maranajdis . . ." He shrugged, turning one hand palm upward in a gesture of resignation. "I think you are more fortunate in your brother. And yet you fear to return to your home?"

The Tamaristan prince was uncomfortably acute. Oressa didn't say anything for a long time. If he had pressed her, she would have refused to answer. But he only looked away, watching the water slide down the wall and run into the pool, flowing so smoothly it was almost soundless. Except for the faint splashing of the water where the other men lingered over cleaning the bowls, it was very quiet.

She said at last, "I suppose it doesn't matter if you know that my brother was supposed to depose my father. As the price of the Kieba's help. Because my father had offended her."

Gajdosik gave her a neutral little nod and waited for her to go on. Somehow his very neutrality made her want to explain. She said finally, "You don't understand about my father. You couldn't. Not even Gulien really understands."

Gajdosik nodded a second time, still wordlessly.

"My mother—" Oressa stopped. Then she began again, "She went to the dead gods' convent, you know. Where women go to suffer and atone for what happened to the gods, even though it wasn't their fault, so I don't know why they should; it's not like it does any good." Her voice had risen. She stopped again and took a hard breath.

Then she went on, much more quietly. "They hardly eat and they sleep on hard boards and . . . and, you know, I don't want to think about it." She glared at Gajdosik. "She didn't want to go there. If you asked anybody at home, they'd say my father didn't want her to go there either. They'd say he tried to persuade her to stay and she wouldn't. But they *don't know.*" She lowered her voice even more. "Where people could hear him, he said she should stay. He said, 'Poor Ledah, she feels the weight of the world so keenly.' Then when they were alone he told her, 'You've given me one son and that's all you've got in you; one heir is all very well, but prudence counsels a second lest disaster robs me of the first.' He said, 'Girls are valuable coin; possessing merely a single daughter too stringently limits my options.' He told her, 'A penitential attitude is becoming in a woman. I think you need to retire from the world, either you or that girl-brat you've given me.'" She stopped again.

"He said that *in front of you?*" Gajdosik sounded not only startled, but frankly horrified.

"He didn't know I was there. I was afraid of him already. I didn't understand exactly what he meant—I was only little—but I knew he'd just as soon have me out from underfoot until he was ready to sell me to some Illiana prince or Markand lordling." She glared at Gajdosik. "Or, worst of all, a Tamaristan prince."

Gajdosik spread a hand, yielding the point. "I would not have you believe my father was unkind to my mother."

"He kept her in a *cage!*"

"This is a very luxurious cage, with many woman servants and every fine thing. He would have been ashamed to speak to her as you say your father spoke to your mother. Had he seen fit to set her aside, he would have settled gifts on her that she might have returned to her family in honor. He would never have forced her into a . . . penitential house of remembrance and grief such as you describe."

Oressa shrugged angrily. "Well, I wish my father had just sent my mother back to her family. She died, you know. In that convent. When I was seven. They didn't tell me, but I heard . . . I heard things. Even then they didn't bring her back to inter her near her kin. Her family had been important, but they'd met reverses and by then my father didn't care if he offended them. He told Baramis it wasn't worth the bother and expense of a state funeral just to bring my mother back to Caras for internment. She wasn't worth the bother! That's what he said. And you know what?" Oressa gave Gajdosik a sideways smile. "That was actually funny, in a way. Because then his new queen died, too, and so my father didn't get a spare son after all, nor any more daughters, and he still had to pay for a big funeral. Wasn't that funny?"

"Not very funny, no."

Oressa, not really listening, went on. "Gulien—Gulien knows about our father, but not really. Anyway, it's different for him. He's male and our father's heir, so of course it's different. But he doesn't understand the way Father says just what he wants people to hear. People always lie, you know." She heard her own voice: bright and hard and brittle, but she didn't stop. "They say one thing to one person and something else to another person, but they lie all the time. Father's very good at that. He gets people to do what he wants. He says things and people believe him. You have to watch what he *does* to know what's true. Gulien knows that—but he's so honest himself, he doesn't really *know* it." She was distantly surprised that she had told Gajdosik those things—she'd never told anybody those things.

Maybe she told Gajdosik because he'd never known her father. Or because, buried within the Kieba's mountain, they were so far away from the real world that she could believe secrets would dissolve into the stone and be left behind. Or just because he *listened* to her. She didn't believe he could really understand, though. She shrugged and made herself smile. "So it's true I need to go home, to help Gulien hold the throne if our father tries to take it back. But it's also true I am a little bit afraid of getting back, in case . . ." She shrugged again. "Though I suppose the Kieba won't permit my father to reclaim the throne really, so there's nothing to worry about."

Gajdosik said nothing for a long moment. Then he met Oressa's eyes and said, "Your brother is fortunate in his sister. You will speak with the Keppa and return in triumph to Caras, and your city will rejoice."

Oressa found herself blushing. "Well, it's nice to think so." She couldn't believe she had said all that about her mother, about her father. She'd *never* told anyone all that.

Gajdosik might have seen this sudden uncertainty. He offered carefully, as though in exchange, "The queen's cage seemed the way of the world to me when I was a child. It seemed a place of safety and warmth. Later, when I was taken from the cage and not allowed to return to my mother, I saw that gilded bars could be cruel."

"You were taken away and not allowed to see your mother? Even though she was right there? How old were you?" Oressa had known about the gilded cage, but not about this part. That seemed even worse than having your mother sent away.

"I spoke with her through the mesh sometimes. I was twelve. In Tamarist, that is the age at which a prince becomes a man. It is . . . it is a shock, to leave the women's cage and come out into the world. Heirs used to be caged until they succeeded their fathers; did you know? All their lives until they succeeded to the throne."

Unlike her brother, Oressa had never studied history. She shook her head, trying to imagine this. "A prince would be kept in a cage until he was . . . twenty or thirty or forty, or even older if his father lived a long time? That doesn't seem like it would work very well."

"It worked rather badly," Gajdosik conceded. "Thus now princes are taken into the world when they are twelve. It is a difficult time for a boy. Exciting, but . . . lonely." Looking up, he gave her a sudden wary look, as though half expecting her to mock this sentiment.

Mockery was the last thing Oressa could imagine feeling. She suspected "lonely" was a severe understatement. At least she'd always had Gulien. All her life. When princes were rivals and expected their father to murder all but one of them, when girls were kept in gilded cages and their brothers had to leave their sisters and mothers behind . . . that was *terrible*.

The lights dimmed, and Laasat and the other soldier, Tamresk, came back. Oressa was almost glad. She didn't want to feel *sorry* for Gajdosik and for all his imagined brothers and sisters, and his mother, who lost each of her sons when he turned twelve.

Tamresk stacked the clean bowls and spoons on the table, which vanished. Fortunately the lights didn't go all the way out—forgotten *gods*, that would be *horrible*, trapped in the dark under the mountain. Tarod's stories about lightless cells in the stone came forcibly to mind again. But this wasn't so bad. They made pallets out of the cushions. The Tamaristans put theirs together in a row, and Oressa laid out hers over on the other side of the pool. She wondered what Gulien would say if he knew where she was spending this night. At least, she could imagine all too vividly what he would say.

She wished the Kieba would come. Though she was worried about Gajdosik. How ironic, to be worried about *Gajdosik*. He should have stayed on the other side of the Narrow Sea where he belonged, and then none of them would have anything to worry about . . . except his terrible brother Maranajdis would have killed him; she could hardly imagine the enmity that must lie between them. And his poor sisters, trapped in the women's cage. At least they were *safe*, but that did not seem enough to make up for their imprisonment. . . . Oressa drifted to sleep without knowing it, and if dreams of gilded cages or terrible spiders or grim, frightening kings troubled her sleep, she did not remember them.

She woke when the Kieba came.

The light brightened. That happened first. Oressa woke because of the light and sat up sharply, staring. The Kieba flicked suddenly into place outside the cell, between one instant and the next, and then Oressa stared in earnest.

The Kieba looked much older than Oressa had expected, and she wasn't at all beautiful, though to be fair Gulien had never said she was: Oressa had just assumed a woman who had once been a goddess must be beautiful. But the Kieba was too thin and fine-drawn for beauty. Her skin was pulled too tight over her bones, which were too sharp and angular and somehow just wrong. Her hands were too long, her fingers too bony. There was something wrong about the way she moved, too:

Every gesture she made was too quick, too abrupt. She didn't look at all like a normal woman, but she certainly didn't look like any goddess Oressa had ever imagined.

"Keppa," Gajdosik said. His voice was steady and clear. He had risen to his feet.

The Kieba turned her head and took one step toward him, a strange, sharp movement, and Oressa saw how Gajdosik hesitated just the tiniest instant before he stepped forward to face her, and she knew he was afraid. She didn't blame him for that at all. She was afraid too. She had thought she would be able to explain things, maybe argue for clemency for the Tamaristans as well as her brother, but the Kieba was different from anything she had expected. She wanted to say that she had Parianasaku's artifact and would be happy to return it, but now she was afraid to draw this terrifying woman's attention.

"Prince Gajdosik!" the Kieba said. There was a terrifying cold violence in her voice that made Oressa flinch.

Gajdosik did not flinch. He said, "Keppa. If I may—"

"How dare you?" said the Kieba. She moved sharply, aggressively, one step and then another, almost more like Gulien's spider-golem than a woman. She demanded, "Do you understand what it is you tried to do? Do you even *remotely* comprehend what it is you actually did?"

"Keppa," Gajdosik said again. "Forgive my stupidity—"

The Kieba lifted her hand and brought it down, as though to strike him, though she stood much too far away and on the other side of the glass wall. But there was a *crack*, and Gajdosik staggered, a thin, livid line like the cut of a whip appearing on his face. He lifted a hand, breath hissing out, stunned, and took the next blow across his arm and the back of his hand. Blood welled from the cut.

"Kieba!" Oressa cried, starting forward. Laasat and the Tamaristan soldier also rushed toward their prince.

"*No!*" Gajdosik said, not loudly, but with such intensity that everyone stopped. He said, in Tamaj, with that same awful intensity, "Laasat! *Keep the princess clear of it!*" Then he shielded his face with his arms and simply stood without moving while the Kieba beat him.

The Kieba's invisible whip cut like the worst kind of whip, the kind made of wire. It slashed through Gajdosik's shirt and left deep, narrow gashes across his back and shoulders and arms. Blood ran down and dripped on the floor and actually spattered into the air when the whip struck, which was awful. Oressa tried to put herself between Gajdosik and the Kieba, but Laasat caught her arm and held her back. The young soldier also tried to get to his prince, but Laasat seized his wrist, too, and then shook him when he struggled, until the young man yielded— he was weeping, Oressa saw. Laasat was not, but his hard, set expression was worse than tears.

Gajdosik had bowed forward under the Kieba's punishment. He was still on his feet somehow. Oressa wished he would fall. She thought maybe the Kieba would stop if he fell. But maybe she wouldn't; maybe she would beat him until he died. Oressa knew people *could* die of whipping. He was not screaming, but the thin, harsh sounds he made at each blow were terrible. Laasat flinched as each blow fell, but then Oressa realized she was doing the same thing. She was weeping too, and she hadn't at first realized that, either. She pretended to sag against Laasat and then suddenly jerked free of his hold and darted forward.

She didn't know what she meant to do. She had no idea what she meant to do or say, but she held her hands out toward the Kieba, pleading, "Stop, stop!" Her voice broke, and she gasped against a sob and cried, "Kieba, it's wrong—" And the Kieba's vicious, invisible whip slashed across the palms of both her hands. Though Gajdosik had taken each blow nearly in silence, Oressa was too shocked to do the same. She cried out, a sharp, high scream that echoed and reechoed between the walls of stone and glass.

The Kieba stopped, staring at her.

Oressa hunched forward over her injured hands. Blood ran through her finger and dripped to the floor. She felt faint with shock and pain.

"Oressa Madalin," said the flat, inexpressive voice of the kephalos, like it was answering a question or making a statement. "She possesses no apparent predisposition. However, she is affiliated with ancillary Gulien Madalin, who has entered memory and established a secondary identity. Though she holds no key of her own, she currently possesses Eirankan's Key."

There was no sign that the Kieba heard any of this. She made an inarticulate sound of rage, raising her hand to strike again. Oressa flinched and gasped a wordless protest, but the kephalos said, "Cease." And again, in the same blank, empty tone, "Cease."

And the Kieba flung up a hand in a violent, unreadable gesture, whirled, took a step away from the cell, and vanished.

"Gods dead and forgotten!" Laasat said, and leaped forward to support Gajdosik, who collapsed slowly to his hands and knees.

Oressa also let herself sag to the floor. She cradled her injured hands in front of her, gasping. She felt dizzy and sick and her vision seemed to come and go, but worse were the awful, pain-filled sounds behind her. She ought to think about what had just happened, think about how to approach the Kieba next time she appeared—if she appeared—but she felt blank and stupid. Her palms hurt. Nothing had ever hurt her like this. The welts were awful, white along the edges, seeping blood in the middle. She could hardly bear to look at the wounds. But Gajdosik had been hurt much worse. She could not imagine what his men could do for him, with nothing but cold water to work with. She thought he was probably going to die. Whatever he had done or tried to do—and yes, true, Oressa could not exactly pretend Gajdosik had been an innocent man—but still, it seemed terrible that he should die now and that the Kieba of Carastind should have deliberately tortured him to death.

The young soldier, Tamresk Kerenn, touched Oressa's shoulder, and she jumped and flinched and then realized he'd said her name, only she hadn't heard him. He was very pale. He said in strongly accented Esse, "Your Highness, you must let me . . . I will fix your hands a little. And the— the prince will see you. He will not—he insists he must speak with you."

He would refuse to rest until he did, Oressa understood from the soldier's tone. She did not want to see Gajdosik at all, not now, not like this. She swallowed and nodded.

"You stopped the Keppa," added the soldier. "Thank you."

"The kephalos stopped her," Oressa said, and realized from her own blank tone that she might still be in shock herself. She let Tamresk help her to her feet, let him guide her toward the pool. The water was shockingly cold against her wounds, first stinging ferociously and then numbing the worst of the pain. After a moment, feeling less like she might faint, Oressa managed to sit up straight and then to stand. The welts were not bleeding any longer, and she had begun to understand the limits of the pain and believe that she could stand it. She still couldn't bear to look at her palms, though, and held them away from her skirts, afraid of the touch of even the softest cloth.

Gajdosik had suffered far worse. He was lying facedown across a pallet of cushions. Laasat, sitting beside him, looked almost as blank and stunned as Oressa felt. He had draped the ruins of the prince's shirt across more cushions to hide the worst of Gajdosik's injuries. Oressa was grateful for that. She didn't want to see what had been done to him. She dropped to her knees so he would not have to try to look up at her and focused on his face. He was ashen, the whip cut shocking across his face, his startling blue eyes brilliant with pain and resolve. He whispered, "Oressa, good," and tried to push himself up, but she and Laasat both said, "Don't!" in the same sharp tone, and he stopped. He said, his voice gritty with pain, "Your Highness."

Oressa blinked at the formality. Then she straightened her shoulders and answered, "Your Highness." Then she said, which she hadn't meant to, "You shouldn't say anything important until you're better—"

Prince Gajdosik shook his head, a tiny gesture that nevertheless made his breath catch. He shut his eyes, but only for a second. He whispered, "Can't wait." And then, in a stronger tone, "Princess Oressa. Your Highness. I have three thousand men. On ships. Meant for half that. Not enough water, not enough . . . They'll have to come into harbor. In the north."

"Up by our border with Estenda, yes," Oressa said, to spare him the need to explain. "Up near Addas. I know."

"Yes," whispered Gajdosik. He should stop trying to talk to her; Oressa could hardly stand to watch him. But then, gathering his strength, he said much more clearly, "I doubt I'll leave this place. But you might. I know . . . I know we have been enemies. But you have to take my men into your hand. They can't go home. Maranajdis would kill them all. But if they stay on this side of the Narrow Sea, your brother will destroy them. Or Bherijda will, and that would—that would be worse." He stopped, shut his eyes, drew a breath, began again. "Your brother will need those men. You have to make him see—" He stopped, a shudder taking him. His face whitened, and he set his jaw hard against making a sound.

"Don't talk," Oressa said quickly. "Please, don't. Look, I'll do both parts. You'll say, 'Gulien will need men even more than your father would have, not only soldiers to strengthen Carastind but also men who can't possibly be your father's partisans, men who depend on him for everything and owe loyalty to no one else.' And I'll say, 'Yes, that's true, but the people of Carastind will hate them, and if Gulien makes foreigners the heart of his palace guard nobody will trust them but him and nobody will trust him, either, and it will be even worse.' And then you'll say, 'Your brother can find some way to show your people that he doesn't favor his new foreign soldiers too much. He can choose officers from his own people. He must have some people he trusts.' I'll say, 'But the ordinary people will still despise them,' and you'll say, 'They'll all marry Carastindin girls and become Carastindin themselves, and they can pay taxes at twice the common rate for two generations to show how grateful they are for the chance, and everybody else in Caras can pay a tenth less taxes, and then they'll be happy enough to make room for any number of Tamaristan soldiers, won't they?' And then I'll say, 'Well, yes, that's true. That would probably work.'" Oressa lifted her eyebrows expectantly.

Gajdosik's mouth was still tight, but he was smiling thinly. "Yes," he said. "Yes. Forgotten gods, what a queen you would . . ." He stopped, flinching and then catching his breath against the pain. He hadn't meant to say that last part out loud, Oressa saw.

She said, more gently than she'd intended, "That would have been different."

"I know." Gajdosik took a shallow breath. "I know. Couldn't have you . . . over the body of your brother. Doesn't matter. Oressa. Your Highness. You have to take my men. Promise me—"

Oressa knew exactly what he meant. She was sure, too, that he knew just how big a thing he was asking. Because it *was* big. Taking several thousand Tamaristan soldiers into her hand . . . That wasn't subtle or secretive or something you could do obliquely, without anybody exactly noticing. That was the kind of thing that would force you to stand right up in front of everybody and declare *I have the right to make huge decisions that change everything.* When she thought about it that way, Oressa honestly didn't know whether she could do it.

She imagined her father's expression if she came back to Caras leading a force of three thousand foreign soldiers. He would be . . . what? Furious, offended, outraged. Impressed?

Not that his opinion mattered. She was sure it wouldn't matter. Gulien wouldn't have let their father reclaim his power, not when there was so much at stake. Her brother *knew* how important it was to keep power away from their father, after all. He'd met the Kieba too.

He hadn't told her how terrifying the Kieba was. She had had no idea. Maybe the Kieba wouldn't let any of them go. Oressa could imagine *that* more easily than she could imagine facing down her father. But Gajdosik was still looking at her, with something too much like trust for her to refuse. At last she said, "I'll try."

Gajdosik managed a tiny nod. He whispered, "Good," and then, more strongly, in command: "Laasat."

Without a word, his officer knelt, took the prince's injured right hand in his, and gently worked off the ring he wore on his third finger. It was made of twisted copper and steel wire, set with the Garamanaj sigil. The sigil was worked in steel to show that Gajdosik was a legitimate

Garamanaji prince, set with amethysts to show the house was royal. The braided copper border showed that he had never been acknowledged as heir.

Laasat, his face set, offered this ring to Oressa, flat on his palm. He said, "Your Highness, wear this. Show it to any of the prince's men and they will know you. I mean, they will know he made you his heir. I will help you as much as I can. If he dies, I am your man."

"He won't die," said Oressa. She looked at the ring for a long moment. It was such a small thing, and yet she was afraid of it, afraid of what it meant. Which was stupid. And anyway, Gajdosik was still *looking* at her. Quickly, before she could think too much about it, she held out her left hand. It was too big to fit any of her fingers, but Laasat slid it onto her left thumb, careful of her welted palm. The ring felt cold and hard and unbreakable against her skin. Somehow its weight was more vivid even than the pain from the Kieba's whip.

Gajdosik's mouth twisted. He whispered, his voice husky, "Laasat will tell you the names of my captains and officers. They will be loyal if you give them the chance. Trust them. They are good men. I swear you can trust them."

"I will," said Oressa. Her throat ached with the effort he was making. "I promise you, if you can't care for your people, then I will."

"Yes," said Gajdosik. He closed his eyes, letting go of his resolve at last.

Oressa stood up slowly. She said to Laasat, "I'll try. I'll try to get you all out."

Laasat also got to his feet. He nodded. "Yes, I know you will," he said. And then as they both moved aside, he added, "Forgotten gods, I might have shot you."

That first day, he meant, when she had been clinging to the wall of the palace and he had not known who she was. Oressa said tartly, "Worrying over what didn't happen? I'd think you'd have enough worries right here and now." She looked down at Gajdosik, then quickly away, not wanting to see too much. "The kephalos stopped her. I wonder if it would give us medicine, physician's tools—Laasat, you can stitch wounds?"

"Not like those," Laasat said quietly. "Not so many, and some down to the bone."

"Well, you'll have to try!" Oressa snapped, then flinched violently back as a black rod fell suddenly out of the air in front of her. It was Laasat who caught it, purely reflexively, and then almost dropped it, but snatched it up quickly in his other hand. He held it carefully, not exactly as though it was fragile, but as though it was precious. It was about two hand lengths long, made of twisted black iron, with a thread of black crystal spiraling around it from one end to the other. From the way Laasat held it, Oressa knew it must be important and valuable, but she had no idea what it was until she remembered Gulien telling her about the pain touching Ysiddro's door had caused him and about the Kieba's caduceus. Then she held out her hands eagerly, palms up.

And Laasat knew what the caduceus was too, because without a word he traced a fingertip down the line of the crystal, from one end of the rod to the other and back again. Then he grasped her left wrist firmly and drew the tip of the rod quickly across the whip cut that split her palm. She flinched and gasped but didn't let herself pull away, and then she watched, fascinated, as the vicious welt closed to a thin red line. The cut still ached, but it was a better ache, as from an injury days old and nearly healed.

Still without a word, Laasat used the rod on her right hand as well. Then he straightened and walked back toward Gajdosik. He didn't run, but he walked fast.

Laasat thought the Kieba sending Oressa the caduceus was a sign that she couldn't be too angry with them. Oressa didn't argue, but she suspected that the kephalos rather than the Kieba had sent the caduceus. Even if it had, she didn't know what to expect from either of them now. Gulien hadn't been sure what the kephalos was or what its relationship with the Kieba was, but Oressa remembered that flat, emotionless voice commanding *Cease, cease,* and the Kieba's inarticulate gesture of frustration and fury. She didn't know which frightened her more: the immortal woman who had once been a god—or at least a servant of the gods, if the Tamaristans were right—or the mysterious kephalos that spoke elliptically of keys and memory and identity and seemed to command everything within this mountain. Even, possibly, sometimes the Kieba herself. She wished she knew what it *was.*

Time passed, more than one day, judging from the dimming of the lights. The hours dragged, heavy with both boredom and tension. At least it was reassuringly clear now that Gajdosik would not die, though he couldn't yet stand without help. He suffered a good deal of pain still, Oressa thought, even though Laasat used the caduceus on him twice more. Her own hands still ached a little. She tried not to imagine how Gajdosik must feel.

She waited for the prince to ask for his ring back, but he did not. That was a measure, she supposed, of his continuing pessimism. Or his clear judgment. One was difficult to tell from the other, under the circumstances. She made no comment about the ring. She had been Prince Gajdosik's enemy, but things were more complicated now. She wondered what would happen when—if—the Kieba let them all go. Preferably soon, before everything happened without them. She hoped Kelian and the other guardsmen were all right, trapped among Tamaristan soldiers, who must be terribly worried by this time.

She was also worried about Gulien. By now he must have realized not only where she had gone—naturally he would have figured that out very quickly—but also that something had gone wrong. She hated to think of her brother riding unwarned into Gajdosik's Tamaristan soldiers, as she had, or possibly worse, coming up the mountain after her. She wished she knew what was happening at home.

She also wished she knew how long the Kieba meant to keep them imprisoned within her mountain. She supposed they all wondered that, though nobody said anything about it out loud. Food appeared at intervals: loaves of bread, along with sharp white cheese and ripe pears. It was all a great deal better than nothing. And soap, appeared, too, and even fresh clothing: a startlingly beautiful Carastindin court dress of dusty gold and russet for Oressa and what she supposed was proper Tamaristan dress for the others. Oressa wished she knew if this portended a formal audience with the Kieba and wondered whether she should hope for that.

Laasat said he wasn't in a hurry. He said he hoped time would take the edge off the Kieba's temper. Oressa doubted he quite meant this, but she appreciated his reassuring air of calm patience. Tamresk, hardly older than she was, turned out to know a great many Tamaristan children's stories and a really startling number of rude barracks songs, which seemed a peculiar combination until he shyly explained that he was the eldest of seven children and that all four of his uncles had been soldiers.

Prince Gajdosik seldom spoke. He was very grim and silent now. Pain or fear or helplessness had turned his attention inward. Oressa found, unexpectedly, that she missed his confident arrogance. She found herself watching him without meaning to, her gaze resting on him while he slept or watched the water flow down the wall. She couldn't tell what he was thinking. But she was fairly certain he *was* thinking—that he hadn't simply given up. His was the quiet of waiting, not the silence of despair.

CHAPTER 12

Gulien hadn't know what he should expect to find when he arrived once more at the base of the Kieba's mountain.

He had brought half a company of mounted militia, brought them as fast as he could, and so they arrived as dusk approached, barely forty hours after leaving Caras. He had thought—hoped—that the Kieba herself might meet them. He had feared she might be impatient and annoyed at his return before his year had run out; he had hoped she might prove utterly dismissive of any possible danger to herself from a Tamaristan threat. Nothing of that would have surprised him. But he could see no sign of her, not so much as a larger-than-ordinary hare or mountain fox.

If not the Kieba, then he had hoped to hear the disembodied voice of the kephalos, offering uninterpretable comments about affiliation and identity. That would not have surprised him, either, and he had hoped the kephalos might prove easier to deal with. Several times during the bone-achingly fast ride from Caras, he'd glimpsed a falcon overhead and thought—hoped—that the kephalos was watching, alert and aware of everything that moved in the drylands. The idea was reassuring, though also, in another way, discomforting.

Or he wouldn't have been surprised to find one or more of the great spiderlike war golems patrolling the Kieba's boundaries, stalking along her wall, warning away trespassers who might threaten to intrude on her privacy. That, too, would have been both reassuring and discomforting.

Most of all, he had hoped to find his sister, having delivered Parianasaku's Capture and charmed the Kieba, cheerfully coaxing the kephalos to demonstrate how its golems could explode boulders and trying to persuade it to let her have half a dozen as a permanent guard for Caras. He could quite clearly picture Oressa engaged in just that sort of activity, ridiculous as he suspected the hope would prove to be.

And, of course, he had far more than half expected to find a considerable number of Tamaristan soldiers bivouacked at the foot of the Kieba's mountain. He had even been prepared to find disturbing evidence that the Kieba had already dealt with such an intrusion, prepared as well to beg her pardon for his own trespass with so many men.

Unfortunately, though the Tamaristan soldiers were indeed present, that was the only part of his expectations that was met, for he did not see the Kieba, nor any sign that she had even noticed either the Tamaristan intrusion or his own. Though he looked, he could glimpse none of the great war golems, nor his sister, but Tamaristan soldiers there were in plenty.

Gulien had thought carefully about how many men Prince Gajdosik might have brought with him. In and out as quickly as possible, Gulien was almost certain that was the Tamaristan prince's intention. The prince and his men must be mounted on stolen horses; surely it could not be easy to steal mounts and remounts for a great many men at such short notice—though that was good country for horses, up by Addas.

He had thought also about the Kieba's own defenses, which must make any numbers of soldiers irrelevant; and about artifacts, so wholly unpredictable; and so he had decided on half a company of his own because he had hoped it would be enough and was all he thought Caras could spare—and very nearly all the horses in Caras fit for a fast drylands journey too.

Now that they had arrived, however, he saw that he had been too optimistic on several counts, because it was immediately obvious that his own company was facing at least even numbers, possibly worse. Wherever Prince Gajdosik had found the horses, however hard he had driven his men, this was at least a full company, and moreover, the Tamaristan soldiers already held defensible positions in the main farmhouses and outbuildings clustered at the foot of the mountain. Standing up in his stirrups, Gulien stared across the river and through the shade of the overarching cottonwoods toward the nearest farmhouse, trying to figure out what to do.

"We can withdraw and send for reinforcements," said the senior officer of his own militia company, a captain named Aran whom Gulien hardly knew. "But if you wish to bring that force to battle, what I suggest is, we can fall back before they realize we're here, send the crossbowmen wide around the mountain, then at dawn have our arquebusiers make a noisy advance across the river and the crossbowmen move in from their rear. If we're quick enough—or not, curse ill luck and the enemy's good sense!"

"Too late," Gulien agreed, for he, too, could hear the shouts of the enemy, faint with distance, and see the rapid response to those shouts. Plainly it had just become impossible to try any such maneuver as his captain had suggested. On the other hand . . . "It may be just as well, as they may have my sister prisoner. And our people who came with her, and of course these farmers whose homes they've occupied. Bringing the Tamaristans to immediate battle under these circumstances would not be my first choice."

"Your Highness is quite correct that hostages complicate matters," agreed Captain Aran. "Though we don't know that's the situation, either. Kelian might have realized what they were riding into and gotten Her Highness and our people away; we don't know. It'll be interesting to see if they send a man to parley."

"We'll hope they do. Or if they attack, can we do better than hold this position?" Gulien asked. "If they would come against us here, they must ford the river and come up the bank." The river wasn't much of an obstacle, but enough, surely, to hamper an enemy. "Or if they refuse to advance . . ." He paused, having little idea what might be done if the Tamaristans refused to leave their current position. He quite clearly recalled the writings of his great-great-great-great-grandfather Ges Madalin, who had rebelled against the authority of the then king of Greater Estenda and forced Estenda to recognize Carastind as a free and independent country. Ges had had a good deal to say about the stupidity of attacking a fortified position and had been of the opinion that a commander who had no choice but to do so had better have either surprise or greatly superior numbers. True, Ges had been writing before the invention of cannon. But since Gulien had no cannons either, that hardly signified.

"They'd be fools to leave their positions, twice fools to attack across the river," Captain Aran agreed, not very happily. "If I were their commander, I'd stand fast and make us come to them right across those wheat fields. If they've got arquebuses and the sense to fire in volley, they'd cut us to pieces—and if they've got nothing but crossbows, they'd still cut us to pieces, only at slightly closer range. Though in either case our own arquebuses could at least reduce visibility. We might do something with that—put up a lot of smoke and use that as a distraction while we send in a small team to try to get Her Highness clear. If she's there." But he didn't sound very enthusiastic about this idea.

"Yes," Gulien acknowledged distractedly, both the thought and the reluctance. He could see perfectly well all the problems with either carrying the battle to the Tamaristans or sitting still for parley. But he wasn't certain he could dare stand still and just wait for the Tamaristan prince to finish whatever he had come to do—to use some artifact to attack the Kieba while she was distracted, in the worst case. Or to persuade the Kieba to throw down the Madalin falcon and raise up the sea-eagle in its place. That would be almost as bad and, Gulien feared, all too possible.

Was it possible he had been in time at least to pin Prince Gajdosik down on this side of the wall? That might not be quite so bad. But then Gulien could just imagine Gajdosik bringing his sister out as a hostage, just as he had before, and demanding whatever concessions he thought he could force Gulien to accede to.

It was insupportable. Yet obviously he dared not allow the Tamaristan prince a free hand, on this side of the wall or most especially on the other.

He said, rather through his teeth, "Very well, then. We'll send a man for parley; that will at least guarantee a pause, I hope. Meanwhile, I'll cross the Kieba's wall myself and go up the mountain. With luck, that Tamaristan bastard hasn't found a way into her mountain at all—I can hardly see how he could have come here so very much before us, and without leave from the kephalos he may well not have managed to find the way, no matter what artifact he might hold. So we will hope he has not gained leave from the kephalos." He only hoped the kephalos would still speak to *him*. But he said firmly, trying to sound as though he had no doubts at all, "I'll find the Kieba and speak with her and then . . . then we'll see. You, hold here and just wait. Just wait, and stop the Tamaristans from any precipitous action, and we'll see how matters look after I've had a chance to speak with the Kieba."

"Yes, Your Highness, and yet you must not—" Captain Aran began, not very happily.

Gulien lifted a hand, checking him. "What else can we do?"

"Yes, but—" repeated Aran, and pointed toward the Kieba's mountain. "It seems to me, Your Highness, that the Kieba may now refuse to permit anyone to go up. I'm sure *that* is not as tales describe her wall."

Gulien raised his eyebrows, peering past the cottonwoods and through the dazzle of the sun. Then he frankly stared, unable to understand how he had not seen the change at once, even distracted as he had been by the presence of the Tamaristans. The Kieba's wall, obvious even from this distance, had plainly at least trebled in height since he had last seen it. It now also glittered forbiddingly all along the top. From here Gulien could not make out what the top surface had been lined with, but he could imagine well enough: razor-edged shards of steel or broken glass, or perhaps most likely of all, knife-sharp fragments of crystal.

Where previously the Kieba's wall had been merely a warning, it was now a naked threat.

"Is that a response to my intrusion, I wonder?" he murmured. "Or to these Tamaristans?" Or to some other factor, but he did not believe that. He hoped for the latter, but remembering the Kieba's anger at Madalin defiance, he would not have lain odds against the former.

A glance toward the farmhouses showed the Tamaristan company holding its position, unsurprisingly. Since the Tamaristans seemed unlikely to move, Gulien hardly hesitated before saying, "Hold the company here. They can water their horses by turns, but until we have a better idea what we're facing here, they had better stay ready for action." Then he nudged his own horse forward. The horse balked a bit at the low bank but finally jumped down in an awkward little hop, splashed across the river, and surged up the gentler slope on the opposite side. He was aware, behind him, of Aran sending a sergeant and half a dozen men after him, but he paid no attention. All his attention was on the newly forbidding wall.

The wall was all still red local stone, but its outer surface was smoother now—not smooth as plaster, but no longer so rough as to afford good holds for a man's hands nor rests for his feet. And he had guessed right, for those were indeed shards of black crystal set forbiddingly into the narrow top of the wall. Dismounting, Gulien tossed his horse's reins to the sergeant and walked forward to stand in the wall's shadow, tilting his head back to stare up at it. Where before it might have been five feet or so, now he thought it must be at least twelve.

Of course it would not actually be difficult to get over the wall. A man could very well stand on a horse's back, or be lifted up by another man. A blanket could be thrown across the sharp-edged materials at the top. But all that would be difficult enough to make a would-be trespasser think twice were he at all wise. Gulien had not quite decided whether *he* was wise or not. He could see no hare nor fox nor mountain cat anywhere about on this side of the wall, but who knew what might be waiting on the other? Stepping back a bit, he called out, "Kephalos! Kephalos?"

For some moments, he thought there would be no response. Then a shrill cry above made him step back again and lift an arm, and a falcon—of course it would be a falcon—dropped sharply out of the sky to perch on his wrist.

Gulien lowered his arm and looked at the falcon, eye to eye. This one looked more like a real bird, with eyes more like a normal falcon's eyes, golden and round-pupiled, but it was heavy for its size and it stared into his face with a coldness that was nothing like a real falcon's innocent ferocity.

"Kephalos," he said to it, not quite a question.

The little falcon clicked its beak, and the kephalos said—speaking through the bird or from the empty air, he could not quite tell—"Gulien Madalin."

Gulien let his breath out, inexpressively relieved that it would speak to him. He wanted to ask about everything at once, and this made it hard to ask anything at all. "The wall—," he began, but changed his mind and started over. "The Kieba—"

"The Kieba has no preference," stated the kephalos.

Thrown off his balance, Gulien hesitated. "No preference—" *About what*, he meant to ask, but the kephalos interrupted him with the same cold indifference.

"*I* have a preference. Where there are rival claimants, I must have a preference. When you come to the trial, I prefer that you succeed. Your predisposition must be reinforced, Gulien Madalin. Your secondary identity must be established." And, before Gulien could demand to know what *any* of that meant, the falcon's grip tightened on his wrist, its talons piercing his skin so that blood beaded up and ran down from the wounds.

With a considerable effort, Gulien suppressed his reaction—he made no sound other than an involuntary indrawn breath, nor any move to knock the bird-golem away. The earlier wounds had closed cleanly, with no sign of wound-fever; he didn't understand what the kephalos meant to achieve by dealing such injuries, but he would bear it without complaint if it would only answer his questions. So he asked, striving to keep his tone reasonable, "Claimants to what? What rivals? Do you mean Prince Gajdosik?" Or, appalling thought, did it mean Oressa? He demanded, "Where *is* Oressa? Is my sister well?"

But if the kephalos answered, Gulien didn't hear it. Light bloomed suddenly behind his eyes, silent flowers of lightning, robbing him of ordinary sight, oversetting his balance. He flung out a hand to catch himself, but it seemed to him that he was falling, except he did not seem able to feel the ground beneath him. He seemed to hear shouting, dimly, and thought first of the Tamaristans and then thought it might be his own voice. Then he realized how alarmed his own people must be if he had shouted or seemed to have fallen into a fit, and he wished to reassure them but seemed unable to frame words. Or thoughts.

His vision had shattered into a tumbling kaleidoscope of images—his thoughts seemed to have shattered as well. He *remembered* the kephalos, remembered mastering its splintering vision. He remembered fierce triumph—he had won some victory, wrung it out of a flood of dire defeat, but he did not know what the victory had been or what the defeat had comprised. It had not been his own victory; he knew that suddenly; nor was it his own defeat. But though the memories were not clear, the ferocity of feeling was overpowering, and Gulien flung himself away. He did not know what he did, but jolting away from all the phantasmagoria, he found himself falling into welcome darkness, out of the busting light, gone.

He opened his eyes to darkness and lay still for some time, blinking into the blind dark, not quite thinking of anything. But gradually he became aware that the darkness was not absolute. An oil lamp was lit, though its baffles had been drawn, dimming its light to hardly more than candle-glow. He could see canvas overhead, rippling slightly in some unfelt breeze. . . . He was in a tent. Because he had left Caras and come . . . to the Kieba's mountain, yes. Following Oressa. Yes.

There had been Tamaristans. That came gradually clear to him, his own people on the bank of the river and Prince Gajdosik's Tamaristans sheltering in the farmhouses and barns of the small settlement. . . . Had there been battle? Had he been injured? He did not remember battle, nor injury. Although his wrist stung.

Memory returned—the Kieba's wall, the falcon—and his breath hissed. He lurched up.

A hand caught his shoulder, support and reassurance rather than restraint. "Easy, now," murmured a half-familiar voice. "You're all right. Or leastwise I figure you're all right. Say something, lad—Your Highness, I mean. You know your name, and my name, and where you are?" The man opened one of the lamp's baffles to let a little more light into the tent.

"Sergeant . . . Mattin," Gulien murmured. He felt steadier, though he touched his forehead gingerly with his fingertips. His head ached. Had he fallen? Or was this some remnant of whatever the kephalos had done to him? "I was talking to the kephalos. To its falcon. What—how long—" He tried to collect himself. "What's happened, Sergeant?"

"Captain'll be right glad you're awake," the sergeant murmured, kindly not adding, *And not babbling.* "Here's tea if you want it. Do you good, it will." He didn't wait for Gulien's nod, but put a mug into his hands and went on. "Nothing much has happened as matters. The Kieba's falcon spoke to you; you recall that much. You called out something, not in Esse—nonsense it sounded. Do you remember that? No? Well, a minute after that, you went down like you'd been shot. Took ten years off my life—off all our lives, I guess. But you'd taken no injury a mortal man could find, so the captain, he said we'd wait and see if you just woke up natural—this'n was at dusk, and if it's yet midnight, it's not much more, so you see you weren't down long, Your Highness."

That didn't sound nearly as bad as Gulien had feared. And the tea, astringent through the sweetness of sugar, seemed to be clearing his head. Whatever the kephalos had done to him, it seemed to have passed off. "The Tamaristans?"

"They haven't moved; we haven't moved. We're bivouacked in place, across the river from the mountain, and them Tamaristans are still where we left 'em as far as we know, in them farmhouses over the way. We've got sentries out, of course. Been quiet all the night so far. We're all just waiting on the dawn, I expect, them and us both, and herself up the mountain, as may be. You want to get some proper rest.

Likely that's the best use you can make of what's left of the night."

Gulien drew a breath, let it out, and leaned back slowly. "Aran?"

"The captain'll be glad to hear you're up and making sense, Your Highness. I'll see he gets that word, but I much doubt he'll find anything so urgent he has to put it before you this minute—unless it's *you* as has got something *he* needs to hear right this moment?"

Gulien shook his head. He hoped not. He couldn't think of anything, but all his thoughts still seemed sluggish.

"Good. Then go to sleep," said the sergeant kindly, no doubt seeing something of this on Gulien's face. "Just you rest, Your Highness, and we'll see what's what in the morning."

It seemed good advice. Certainly it could not be reasonable to rush around madly, alarming all his people, when he had, after all, no idea what to do. In the morning . . . in the morning surely he would feel sharper-witted. Gulien let himself be coaxed down and closed his eyes, though he opened them again long enough to say, "Leave the lamp. And wake me an hour before dawn—if the Tamaristans actually are waiting for dawn, let's not let them get before us, Sergeant."

"That we won't," the man promised, then patted him on the shoulder and reset the lamp's baffle to dim the light again.

The hour before dawn seemed to arrive in moments, but Gulien did feel much more himself when Sergeant Mattin gripped his shoulder to wake him. This time there was not only tea, but a basin of hot water and a bit of soap, and amaranth porridge with honey and dried apples in it. Captain Aran brought the porridge, handed the bowl to Gulien, and waved the sergeant out, himself dropping with a grunt to sit cross-legged on the floor of the tent, since they'd traveled too light to have even camp stools. "They're stirring over there, too," the captain told Gulien. "Not drawing up or anything, but getting on their feet, I expect, same as us. The wall's still there. No change to it. All night we've had reports of the odd fox and hare and owl, but the Kieba hasn't strolled down her mountain to call for you by name." He eyed Gulien sharply, but didn't ask, *Got your wits*

together? Or, *What did the Kieba do to you, and can we still trust you?*
Gulien imagined that both questions were in the captain's mind.

He nodded. "One hardly knows whether to find the Kieba's silence
reassuring or disturbing. But the Tamaristans may not know which,
either. Or they may know far more than we do. What I hope for this morning is a parley with whoever's in command over there—Gajdosik or one
of his officers, as may be. Before anything else, I want to know what they
know and where Oressa is."

"You can't put yourself in their hands, Your Highness—"

"Of course not, Captain. We'll see what acceptable arrangements can
be made. A neutral location, a few men. You may tell me whom you'd
like to send with the proposal." He thought of the reassuring solidity of
the sergeant and added, "Mattin, maybe, if you can spare him for the task."
Gulien finished the porridge, set the bowl aside, and stood up, not quite
able to straighten in the confines of the tent.

Outdoors was better. Gulien stretched gratefully, listening to the
low rippling sound of the river, the murmur of his people, the quiet shift
and stamp of the horses over in their picket lines. The predawn breeze
was soft, not yet carrying the fierce heat of the day. The stars spread
overhead. The moon, not quite full, lay pale and translucent, low by the
eastern horizon, where the dawn lent a pearly tint to the east beyond
the dark bulk of the Kieba's mountain.

"A peaceful morning," Gulien said to Aran. "May it continue so."

Captain Aran grunted noncommittally, meaning he doubted the like-
lihood of this. But he said, "Parley's a good notion, Your Highness. You're
right that we need to know what's toward. Got a whole lot of questions
stacking up, don't we, and maybe they do as well. What I'd suggest is, we
propose a couple of men each, meeting dab in the middle of that pasture
over there." He nodded across the river, where the pasture in question
was beginning to show silvery in the dawn light. "Both sides can see
the whole area plain, and it'd take quite a shot to hit anyone there from
either their position or ours, whether they've got arquebusiers or crossbowmen or both."

Gulien nodded, not much interested in these details. Somewhere not far away, he heard the rippling high-pitched call of the tiny desert owl, answered by the sharp *kek-kek-kek* of a falcon. He tensed, more than half expecting a bird-golem to snap down at him like a crossbow bolt out of the brightening morning. But there was nothing. Perhaps it had been a real owl and a real falcon, trading places as night gave way to day.

"Do you think—," he began.

"Well, now," Captain Aran interrupted him. "Begging your pardon, but it looks like maybe you're not the only one to think of parley, Your Highness."

Gulien followed the captain's nod and saw a single Tamaristan soldier, not obviously armed, riding slowly from the direction of the farmhouses toward the river and the Carastindin force. His own men were falling silent all along the river's edge as they became aware that something was happening. Gulien could hear sounds of arquebuses being primed and crossbows cocked, and the short tones of sergeants ordering both readiness and—undoubtedly equally important, under the circumstances—restraint.

"Well. It's true, one man alone doesn't seem likely to be anything but a request for parley," Gulien murmured. "How convenient."

"Could be it's too convenient," muttered the captain. "You oughtn't let that man close to you, Your Highness. Who knows what he might do? Especially if he realizes who you are."

But Gulien knew he needed to hear the Tamaristan emissary himself. "Let him come," he ordered. "He doesn't seem to be armed. Your men can make certain he hasn't a hidden knife—that's only prudent— but let him come. He may lie, of course, but I very much want to hear what he has to say." He raised his voice slightly so the nearest soldiers could hear. "I have full faith in the ability of your men to protect me, Captain Aran."

The captain sighed, but he made no further objection, and Gulien raised one hand in a gesture for the Tamaristan emissary to approach. The man, who had drawn rein and waited some distance from the river, obeyed that summons immediately. As he drew nearer to the opposite bank, it became possible to see that he was a young man, probably a few years younger than Gulien, wearing the badge of a *karanat*. He wore no sword and carried neither arquebus nor crossbow. In his upraised hand, he held a green, leafy twig that appeared to have been hastily cut from a pear tree.

The young man rode forward steadily until he reached the opposite bank of the river, ignoring Gulien's crossbowmen and, at so short a distance almost as dangerously accurate, his arquebusiers. But the *karanat* did not even glance at the leveled weapons. He drew his horse to a halt, studied Gulien with some intensity, and at last called across the small remaining distance, "Is that His Highness Gulien Madalin? Will you parley, Your Highness?" He spoke Esse clearly enough, though with a strong accent.

Gulien called back, "If you would parley, you may approach!"

The young *karanat* bowed slightly in the saddle. Then he touched the reins, encouraging his horse to step into the river. Gulien was aware of the nervous shift of soldiers all around him. He put up a hand to stop any precipitous action, saying out loud, just in case any of his people were not paying attention, "No, let him come! Let him come."

Here in this place, the river, wide as it was, could hardly be called more than a creek, though in the middle it was belly deep for the horse. The Tamaristan *karanat* ignored the water lapping at his boots, leaned forward to help his horse to lunge up the shallow bank, drew rein not twenty feet from Gulien, dismounted in one smooth movement, and dropped his reins to trail in the sandy mud. The horse sidled a step away, toward a nearby patch of grass.

The young man, ignoring the drawn Carastindin swords, walked straight toward Gulien, stopped a few feet away, and bowed respectfully. "Your Highness," he said. His accent seemed less harsh now that he was no longer shouting across the width of the river.

Gulien studied him. "Do you speak for Prince Gajdosik? Where is my sister, Her Highness Oressa Madalin?"

"Your Highness," repeated the *karanat*, bowing a second time. Then, straightening, he went on. "Two days ago—three, now—our prince Gajdosik Garamanaj and Her Highness Oressa Madalin cross the wall of the Keppa and climb her mountain. They have not return, Your Highness, and we are very concern. You see the wall of the Keppa." His Esse was quite understandable, though his verbs somewhat clumsy. As he finished, he turned to indicate the wall, where it ran north and west of the nearby fields.

Frowning, Gulien nodded. "Indeed. The wall is much altered from what I had expected. Did that happen before or after your prince went up onto the mountain?"

"The night after they go up. Went up," the young man corrected himself. "It was short first; then it became tall, as you see. We do not dare cross that wall. We think, better to wait. But three days now and, as I say, we are very concern." He paused, studying Gulien's face. Then he went on. "You are know the Keppa. She gave you her *autajma* to use. If a man climb her wall and go up, maybe you—"

"Wait!" interrupted Captain Aran. "Look there!" He pointed.

At once, turning his head, Gulien saw what his officer had seen: two figures making their way down the near slopes of the mountain.

CHAPTER 13

Another day crept past and once more Oressa and the others laid out their cushions to make pallets. She always put hers on the far side of the pool, of course, while Laasat and Tamresk laid theirs out near their prince. Oressa slept badly, dreaming in shattered fragments of Gulien and her father, of Prince Gajdosik and Kelian.

She heard the kephalos speaking her name. She was dreaming—she was riding a war golem through an empty city of broken stone. The stones were spattered with blood, and she knew it was Gajdosik's blood: She had killed him. She looked for him to tell him she was sorry and found his statue in the Hall of Remembrance among the others, only he had great stone wings like the god who had fallen from the roof of the palace. Shadows lay across his white stone face, and she realized suddenly that it was not Gajdosik at all, but Ysiddro, and the statue was not made of stone, but of glass. The glass rippled like water, and in a moment spiders of steel and crystal would shatter her from the inside. The goddess turned her cold glass face toward Oressa and said, "Oressa Madalin!" Only it was the flat, neutral voice of the kephalos, and Oressa woke.

She sat up, her heart pounding. On the other side of the pool, Tamresk was on his feet. Laasat was standing protectively over Prince Gajdosik, who was moving stiffly to get up.

"Oressa Madalin," the kephalos said again.

Her mouth was dry. She swallowed and rubbed the back of her hand across her mouth. Then she said, "Yes." She was relieved to find that her voice sounded almost normal.

"The Kieba sends for you," stated the kephalos. "Follow Ysiddre's stairway."

Prince Gajdosik came forward to grip her shoulder with forceful confidence, a gesture he might have used when sending a young soldier on an important mission. He looked into her face. "You'll do well," he told her quietly, as though he had no doubt of it. "You've cleverness and nerve to spare. Remember you hold my ring. My people are in your hands. I trust them to you, Your Highness. Their fate is more important to me than my own."

Oressa nodded, because she knew that. She wished no one was depending on her. She wished this audience was over. She wished she was home with Gulien. But she did not know what she should wish for Gajdosik. She met his eyes and smiled with deliberate confidence, then turned and walked to the glass wall, and through it in a wash of heat.

Ysiddre's statue and her white door were easy to find, even in the disorienting Hall of Remembrance. The door glowed like pearl in the goddess's moonlight, its amethyst veins glittering. Ysiddro's statue and door was almost entirely hidden by shadows. Oressa tried not to look at that dark statue because she was afraid that if she did she might lose her nerve. She pushed open Ysiddre's door and began her slow ascent of the white marble stairway. She seemed to climb the stairs for a long time, and then between one step and the next, dry heat folded around her, and she stepped forward into cool air, and there were no stairs, but only a small, round chamber carved out of solid gray crystal without doors or windows. A dais was raised up from the floor to one side; before the dais stood a plain chair. Both dais and chair were also made of crystal. She recognized all this, of course, from Gulien's description.

No one was in the room except her.

Oressa drew a breath and said cautiously, "Kephalos?"

"Oressa Madalin," said the flat, familiar voice. "Your primary identity is recognized. You hold no key, no predisposition, no affiliation, no aspect, no position." It fell silent.

"That's unfortunate," Oressa ventured.

"It is unfortunate," stated the kephalos, but exactly what it meant by its agreement, Oressa could not tell. She said nothing, and shortly it went on. "The Kieba's identity has stabilized. She will speak to you. You will speak for Gajdosik Garamanaj. His primary identity is recognized. He has possessed a key, but his predisposition is uncertain and must be tried. You will establish this necessity."

"I will willingly speak to the Kieba on behalf of Prince Gajdosik," Oressa said carefully. "Though I'm not sure why she should listen to me. But, if I may ask, what does, ah, trying someone's predisposition entail? And who decides whether someone . . . passes this trial? The Kieba? Or you?" She hesitated, then asked, "What are you?"

"I am crystallized memory," answered the kephalos. "No decision is required: Gajdosik Garamanaj will prove predisposed to the living crystal or he will not. He will prove compatible with an acceptable secondary identity or he will not. You are Oressa Madalin, descendant of Oren Madalin, whose inclination toward a predisposition was given unto his descendants. However, you have not been sufficiently exposed to living crystal, and thus your incipient predisposition remains inchoate. However, as you acted to protect the greatest danger that abides in the mountain, it is possible the Kieba may favor you and choose to renew her regard for the Madalin line. In this case, you will speak for Gajdosik Garamanaj."

Most of this seemed fairly promising, if opaque. Oressa began to frame another question, about what would happen if somebody had a useful predisposition and what would happen if not, and what was it a predisposition *toward*, anyway? But before she could ask, heat rose up around her and then folded away again, and not at all to Oressa's surprise, the Kieba was suddenly present, seated in the chair. She did not look quite the same; she seemed neither as thin nor as old nor as angry. Oressa was relieved. She tried to hide everything she was thinking behind the bland, docile expression she had learned for court functions, bowed her head, and waited for the Kieba to speak first.

"Oressa Madalin," said the Kieba. Her expression was unreadable but at least not angry. She held her hand out, palm up, moving with that strange, birdlike quickness, and commanded, "Let me see your hands."

Stepping forward, Oressa wordlessly held out her hands, palms up. The Kieba took her right hand, tracing the whip mark with her thumb. It was pale and thin, well healed.

"I am sorry for this," the Kieba stated, releasing Oressa's hand and meeting her eyes. "It was a mistake to go there while I was still having difficulty maintaining my identity and my aspect. I was angry, and I misjudged. I am sorry for it."

For a moment Oressa only stared at her. She found, to her surprise, that she was no longer afraid of the Kieba. She almost felt sorry for her, and wasn't certain why she should feel that way. It was disorienting. She found herself off-balance, rather as though she had jumped down from a height and discovered only when she hit the ground that it had really been too far to jump. She said at last, "All right. I do think you were unjust to Prince Gajdosik. He might have a predisposition, you know. It would be hard to find out about that if you had killed him. But the caduceus helped. Thank you for sending it."

The Kieba did not deny sending the caduceus, but she didn't acknowledge Oressa's thanks either. She tapped the arm of her chair with her long fingers, one of the most ordinary, human gestures Oressa had yet seen her make. But she said, "I was not unjust. Gajdosik's interruption came at an awkward moment, and I could not respond to his threat and yet maintain control of myself and the kephalos and the situation in Elaru. Once I regained control, it was too late to save the city, too late for any measures but a firebreak. I was justly angry."

Oressa stared at her. "A firebreak? You don't mean—I mean, the plague you were working on, in that other land, Gontai, you did fix it. Didn't you?"

"No," the Kieba said flatly. "I lost control of my work and was unable to regain it adequately. Then I was temporarily . . . I was discommoded and unable to return to my work immediately. I commanded the kephalos to burn a wide firebreak around the affected region in order to control the contagion. Everyone in Elaru will most likely die, though some small handful may be saved, and I hope that I may at least prevent the loss of any other city in Gontai."

Oressa didn't know what to say. So many people. Thousands of people, no doubt. A whole city, everyone dead. That was too big and awful an idea to think about, yet she couldn't help thinking about it. She didn't know Elaru, but she found herself visualizing Caras dead, everyone dead, even the carrion birds crumpled and limp in the streets. That was worse than anything Prince Gajdosik or any of his people had ever thought of doing. She shivered.

No wonder the Kieba had been so angry.

"It's my fault," she admitted. "I set Djerkest up so he would try to get into the vault of plagues. I knew you would stop him—I mean, I was *sure* you would stop him—and you did, but I didn't *realize*—" Her voice rose, and she cut off the last word before she embarrassed herself by crying like a child.

"Oressa Madalin. *You* did not come to this mountain of kept memory in order to cast me down and steal my power. I have been aware that the magisters of Tamarist have recently striven to block my awareness of their activities, but I was otherwise engaged and never sufficiently concerned. Clearly they have had very specific reason to wish me to look elsewhere."

Oressa shook her head. "No, but I did help them find the way into the mountain. They might never have found it if I hadn't told them what to look for. At least they might not have found it so fast. So that *is* my fault. I'm sorry. I knew it might be a mistake, but I didn't know what else to do. I didn't realize that Djerkest would be able to get the kephalos to recognize him, not until I saw he had the same kind of crystal Gulien's falcon is made of and realized that your whole mountain is made of that kind of crystal on the inside. *Then* I knew I'd probably made a terrible mistake, only I couldn't think of anything to do except try to get them to open your—" She found herself lowering her voice involuntarily to a near whisper. "Your vault of plagues. But that interrupted you, didn't you? So I ruined what you were doing in that city. Elaru. I'm *sorry*, Kieba. I didn't mean to do anything like that."

"Well," said the Kieba, and was quiet for a moment, absolutely still in her chair, more still than any mortal woman. Then she blinked and frowned at Oressa, seeming almost normal again. "You did well, in fact, Oressa Madalin. If the Tamaristan magister had found me just then, with all my attention elsewhere, he would have found me vulnerable. He would have tried to destroy me, I believe, in order to steal whatever part of my power he could recognize. He would have failed, I think. But if he had destroyed me . . . If he *had*, Oressa Madalin, I have no suitable heir at the moment. Certainly no Tamaristan magister would be suitable, even if he had realized what he had done. *That* would have precipitated true disaster. Not merely for Elaru."

Oressa stared back at her. She wanted to believe she'd done the right thing, or a right thing, or at least not a terrible thing. But she wasn't sure. She said numbly, "I didn't know. Only I was afraid of what he might do and what might happen."

"Rightly so," said the Kieba. "I had time to burn the firebreak, at least." She paused. After a moment she added, with a lack of emotion or emphasis that under the circumstances Oressa found disturbing, "The fault is not yours. The fault lies with your father, who sent the plague to Elaru, and with your brother, who disturbed my peace while I first worked to contain it, and with my kephalos, who allowed him to take a weapon away from this place, and of course with Gajdosik Garamanaj, who saw this weapon and desired others of his own."

"Oh no!" Oressa said immediately. "Gulien was right to borrow your golem, and the kephalos was right to help him. *You* should have helped Gulien when he asked you, and then Gajdosik and all his people would have been cast back into the sea and forced to go back to Tamarist!" And died there, maybe—him and all his people, given what he'd said of

Maranajdis. The idea was more disturbing than she had expected, and she faltered and fell silent.

The Kieba's eyebrows rose. "You disapprove so strongly of Gajdosik? You think he would make so poor a king for Carastind?"

Oressa blinked, trying to think of some reasonable, intelligent response to this question.

"Gajdosik would have done well enough by Carastind, I believe," the Kieba added.

"Well, but Gulien—" But Oressa cut that off and turned instead to the Kieba. "Listen, Kieba, you won't really punish my brother for taking your golem, will you? I mean, the kephalos offered it to him! He'd be a good king, Kieba. Really, he would. What you said about a year, you can change your mind about that, can't you? And Gajdosik—you've punished Gajdosik enough, but it's not right to give him Carastind—"

"Is *any* of this yours to decide?"

"Everybody has to decide about things like that!"

The Kieba looked faintly taken aback, the most human expression Oressa thought she had yet shown. She said at last, "Well, perhaps you are right. Perhaps every person must judge for herself what is just. But I have my own necessities. Your preferences do not figure highly in my decisions, Oressa Madalin."

Oressa took a quick breath and nodded. "I'm sure. What will you do, then?" She took Parianasaku's Capture out of her pocket and held it out. "Look. My brother *did* send you—"

"Eirankan's Key," said the Kieba, frowning. She took the medallion from Oressa and turned it over. All its colors brightened under her touch, the crystalline lines on its face broadening and shifting.

Oressa stared at her in dismay. *Now* she remembered that the kephalos had said something about somebody's key. That she had somebody's key and not a key of her own. She said, already knowing the answer, "This isn't Parianasaku's Capture?"

"It is not," murmured the Kieba. "Similar, in certain respects. Allied, in a fundamental sense. Osir Madalin's possession of this item may well explain how he came to apply Parianasaku's artifact to a broader use than intended, despite what should have been adequate safeguards." She frowned. "I wonder how long Osir Madalin has had Eirankan's Key in his possession."

"Gulien *meant* to give you the right artifact," Oressa protested. "I'm sure he *meant* to."

The Kieba set the medallion down on the arm of her chair with a sharp little click. It seemed to melt into the chair, becoming to all appearances a colorful flaw in the crystal. "Of course he did. I don't doubt it. Thus we find that error is almost as greatly to be feared as deliberate malice."

"You won't blame my brother!"

"In a year—well, a little less, now—I will decide what to do with Gulien Madalin. I will need the true Capture immediately, however." The Kieba tapped her fingers gently on the arm of her chair. "As for Gajdosik . . . I will question him shortly and then decide what to do with him. You maintain he may have a predisposition."

"Well, I—"

The kephalos, speaking for the first time in all this, said out of the air. "Kieba."

The Kieba held perfectly still for an instant. Then she said, "Kephalos. I surmise that you believe Gajdosik Garamanaj may have a useful predisposition."

"His associate possessed a key," the kephalos stated.

"Indeed. Indeed. I had forgotten," said the Kieba, and turned her head with what seemed an oddly studied precision to gaze over Oressa's shoulder. "Gajdosik Garamanaj."

Oressa turned quickly and found Prince Gajdosik, Laasat, and Tamresk standing in the doorway. She had not heard them approach and found that she wasn't even certain the doorway had been there a moment earlier. She frowned in quick concern, seeing how Laasat and Tamresk each had a hand unobtrusively under one of Gajdosik's elbows.

But at once Prince Gajdosik drew himself up and stepped forward ahead of his men. His quick glance took in Oressa and the Kieba and the room but revealed nothing of his thoughts. He moved stiffly, but he didn't stumble or fall. He laid a hand briefly on Oressa's arm as he passed her, in what seemed a casual gesture, but for that one moment he actually put quite a lot of his weight on her. Oressa had not realized how weak he still was, but then there were all those stairs—evidently almost too many for him. She stiffened her back unobtrusively to support him and tried not to let any of her nervousness show on her face.

Taking his hand from her arm, Gajdosik made it one more step toward the Kieba's chair before sinking down to one knee. He didn't actually collapse as he knelt, but his mouth tightened with the effort. Oressa thought he barely made it down and guessed he might not be able to get to his feet again without help. He looked the Kieba in the face for an instant, then bowed his head and said, his voice just a little taut, "Keppa. I beg you will hold all the fault to be mine alone and refrain from punishing men whose only fault lay in their loyalty to me."

The Kieba tilted her head, one of those odd, sharp, birdlike movements. "Choosing to serve the wrong lord often carries serious consequences. Your men followed you into my mountain of memory. No doubt they believed you to be in the right. No doubt you believed so yourself, Gajdosik Garamanaj. Yet the desire to do what is right unfortunately affords no guarantee against doing what is wrong."

Gajdosik listened to her carefully. Then he answered, "We make mistakes, being merely human and mortal. And so we must all hope that in your greater wisdom you will be generous to forgive us, O Keppa."

"Indeed," the Kieba said dryly. "Prettily said. Laasat Jerant!"

The Tamaristan officer flinched. Then he bowed carefully. "Keppa."

"Take your young soldier and go," the Kieba commanded him. "Leave my mountain. Take command of your prince's men waiting below. Wait there with them. I will decide in my own time what I shall do with you and with them. Do no violence to the people of Carastind; they are under my protection. Do not depart without leave. Do not on any account break my privacy a second time. Is that clear?"

Laasat bowed a second time, wordlessly, gathered up the younger

soldier with a glance, and took a step backward. They retreated without a word. Tamresk cast a worried look over his shoulder at the prince.
Laasat did not look back at all.

Once they were gone Prince Gajdosik said quietly, "Forgive all my
men their offenses, O Keppa; set their offenses against me. Allow my
people to withdraw from your precincts—"

"Where shall they go?" asked the Kieba. "To the north to join
your main force? And from there, where? Shall they give themselves to
Bherijda? Or go back across the Narrow Sea to face Maranajdis? Would
he welcome them?"

Gajdosik lifted his head at last. "Send them to Caras, O Keppa. Allow
Oressa Madalin to return to her home. Give all my people into her hand.
Let them become people of Carastind."

Oressa put in quickly, "I would take them, Kieba. That's a good solution, for his people and for mine. You should give all of Prince Gajdosik's
men to me, because it's the right thing to do, and trying to do the right
thing may not be any guarantee, but it's still our best defense against
doing what is wrong!"

The Kieba smiled, a thin, ironic expression. "They are yours, then. I
trust you will find something useful to do with them. Keep the prince's
ring. If you give it away, I will regard that as a sign you no longer wish
to hold those men in your hand. Then I or the kephalos will dispose of
them as we see fit. Do you understand?"

Oressa closed her left hand into a fist and put her right over it, a protective gesture. "Yes. I understand." She didn't look at Gajdosik, who
held very still, as though afraid to draw the Kieba's attention, or maybe
just afraid that he might collapse if he tried to move. But some of the
strain went out of his shoulders at Oressa's assent.

"I will send you out to them," the Kieba said to Oressa. "Soon. You
will inform your brother that though I do not object to taking possession
of the item he has sent me, it is not the Capture."

"I'll tell him," Oressa promised.

"Indeed," the Kieba said in a dry tone. She turned to Gajdosik. "Do you understand, Gajdosik Garamanaj, that I spend all my effort destroying and controlling the plagues that were loosed by the death of the gods? Plagues that can burn out of control—or, worse, smolder out of my sight, hidden in the blood of men as fire hides within coals? Plagues recently made both more virulent and less predictable by Osir Madalin's inappropriate use of Parianasaku's Capture."

Gajdosik said quietly, "I understand."

"I have been forced to destroy hundreds of men in the day just past in order to burn a firebreak around Elaru in Gontai. Very possibly everyone in the city will die because of your actions. Everyone who leaves the city must assuredly die, for I cannot allow the plague there to scatter across the land. If I miss even one, if I allow the plague to get out into the world, it might burn all across Gontai. It might even reach to Tamarist and then cross the Narrow Sea to this continent also. Do you remotely comprehend what that would mean? That is what you have done in challenging me in the wrong place and at the wrong moment."

"I am sorry, Keppa. I didn't know."

"That does not excuse you. I should send you to Gontai yourself, command you to bury all the dead in the lands around Elaru with your own hands. Only all those folk are ash and smoke now. They will not even lie in graves."

Gajdosik attempted no answer.

The Kieba regarded the Tamaristan prince silently for another long moment and then said, "However, it seems you may possess a valuable predisposition. We shall ascertain. Sit. Here." Rising, she indicated the crystal chair with a minimal lift of one hand.

Prince Gajdosik gazed at the chair for a long moment, as though it meant much more to him than it did to Oressa—as though it wasn't a chair at all, but something else, something dangerous. A weapon, or something worse than a weapon. He turned his head to look at the Kieba and said, his voice strained, "I protest nothing. But must the princess witness this?"

"You may shortly be grateful for her witness, Gajdosik Garamanaj.

But I think you mistake me. What do you believe I mean to do to you?"

"Maranajdis," said Prince Gajdosik, his voice low. "My brother Maranajdis has a chair like that one, only made of iron as well as crystal. . . ." He shut his eyes, as though to shut out the memory of that sight. He shuddered suddenly. Oressa moved impulsively to put a hand on his shoulder. Gajdosik opened his eyes and reached up to grip her hand hard.

The Kieba frowned. "Indeed. For what purpose does your brother employ this artifact?"

Gajdosik took a slow breath and met her eyes. "To destroy his enemies. To destroy their minds. Or, not their minds, but their will. Their volition. To turn them into his slaves. I've seen him do it. It is . . . unspeakable."

The Kieba regarded him curiously. She said after a moment, "I had not known. I have only lately become aware of how much Tamarist's magisters have hidden from me." She paused and then added, "But, Prince Gajdosik, I am assuredly not Maranajdis. This is not your brother's chair. It is not your destruction I intend. If you are destroyed here, it will not be in that way. Do I need to lie to you about this?"

"No," Gajdosik acknowledged quietly. "No."

"No. I am telling you the truth. The kephalos will determine your predisposition, if such you possess. But the trial will do you no substantial harm. Now, will you sit?"

Gajdosik took one breath and another. Then he got to his feet. Oressa helped, with a discreet hand beneath his elbow. He gave her a little nod, acknowledging the assistance, or maybe the irony. Then he was still for a moment, gathering his strength or his nerve. At last, without looking at her or at the Kieba, he walked to the indicated chair and lowered himself to sit with slow, deliberate movements. He curled his fingers around the ends of the carved finials on the otherwise plain arms and looked up to meet the Kieba's inhuman, remorseless gaze.

Needles of black crystal, and white crystal, and water-bright crystal grew suddenly out of the arms of the chair, piercing Gajdosik's hands and wrists. The prince's eyes widened and his head went back, but he didn't jerk away. Oressa flinched on his behalf, looking quickly at the Kieba, but the Kieba's face was blank. Unreadable.

Gajdosik closed his eyes and opened them again. His eyes moved as though he looked at things invisible to Oressa. His face had gone taut and strained, and she guessed that whatever he saw, those visions were not pleasant. But other than that he did not move.

Then the tension ran out of him, and he slumped in the chair, gasping.

"The predisposition is inadequate," stated the flat voice of the kephalos. "No secondary identity can be established."

Oressa had no idea whether this was good or bad and looked anxiously at the Kieba, trying to judge her response. Her smooth face was very hard to read.

"Unfortunate," said the Kieba, but not as though she cared greatly one way or the other. She said to Gajdosik, her tone abrupt and indifferent, "Tell me about your brother's things of power. You have seen him use remnants of the gods' tools, you say. Explain what you have seen."

Gajdosik had now leaned his head against the back of the chair. His eyes were open but glazed. He looked a bit like a man who had had too much wine at a banquet. Only it wasn't precisely like that, either. Oressa's experience with drunken men was limited, but in that limited experience, drunken men usually looked more witless and less strained than Gajdosik.

"There are needles in the chair," he said. His voice was low, a little unsteady, but clear, not a whisper. "Like these. They pierce a man's neck and hands. The blood comes down from the wounds, and the chair drinks the blood and turns red as blood, and there's a sound like serpents hissing. It swallows his mind, but not his memories. . . . He'll remember his wife; he'll call her by name, but he won't care for her; he'll strangle her if Maranajdis commands it. He won't care—"

"Again," commanded the Kieba. "Recall this in more detail. Describe the carving on the chair, describe the needles."

Oressa realized, listening to Gajdosik, that this must be one of the things that the Kieba's chair did: No one could have remembered so much detail about such small things. It was interesting and no doubt useful, but also rather disturbing. Or maybe it was just this Maranajdis who was disturbing. She listened to Gajdosik describe his brother's chair as though it were in front of him, as though he watched, right now, the destruction of one of his brother's enemies. Sometimes he spoke in Tamaj, but though he slurred his words a little, Oressa understood most of what he said.

"Ghemast Bhakrajda," murmured Gajdosik, naming the man his brother had made strangle his own wife. "He is one of our father's men. He is old and clever, and he never favored Maranajdis. Brave but stupid, to let Maranajdis guess. I could have taken Bhakrajda for mine; he would have brought me the whole east and half the north. I might have taken the throne myself, but Maranajdis got him first. I couldn't protect him. I tried. I did try." Prince Gajdosik's voice shook. "His blood feeds the chair, his mind . . . His face is the same, but there is nothing left behind his eyes. No one will dare defy Maranajdis *now*. I thought *I*—but it's too late now."

Oressa felt ill. As far as she could tell, however, the Kieba felt nothing at all. She said in that same indifferent tone, "This is Shakanatu's Throne. I can see how it might be turned to such a use. What other fragments of the old magic does Maranajdis possess?"

"I don't know," murmured Gajdosik. "None of us know. Not even Djerkest knows. He says Maranajdis must have acquired powerful artifacts and by that taken up the aspect of a god. Ininoreh maybe, or maybe Tolturantis. One of the violent gods—or one of the shadowed goddesses, Toromah or Gusanara. He's too powerful. I've lost men. Maranajdis will destroy anyone he knows is mine. . . ."

"Do your other brothers possess artifacts? Have they also raised up aspects?"

"Bherijda, he's got something; I'm sure he does. He killed Kedje; I'm sure that was his hand. Poor Kedje; he blew away on the wind, gray dust on the wind. . . ."

"Tonkaïan's Resolve?" The Kieba's tone had sharpened. "Is it possible *that* is what your brother Bherijda holds?"

"I don't . . . He hates me, and how can I fight him now? I have to get out. I have to get my people away from Tamarist. . . ." His face tightened, his voice trailing off again as he was absorbed by memory.

The Kieba, frowning, began to ask something else, but Oressa stepped forward impulsively and asked, "So you'll come to Carastind. Is that what you'll do? Come to Carastind and seize power there?"

"Carastind is weak," whispered Gajdosik. "That plague this spring weakened them; there's opportunity in that. Besides, Carastind's princess is the right age; she's the key. If I can take the princess, she'll bring me her whole country. Maranajdis will win Tamarist, but Bherijda's the one who will follow me across the Narrow Sea. I have to take Carastind first, or Bherijda will close his hand on it. Carastind will yield to me readily enough once the people realize Bherijda's their only other option. I can find some powerful artifact, force Bherijda back to Tamarist to fight Maranajdis. That will give me a few years to establish myself in Carastind, find a way to counter them both. . . ."

This was all more disturbing than Oressa had expected. She bit her lip, then prompted, "But it didn't work, did it?"

Gajdosik answered, his voice dull. "No. It didn't work. The Keppa may be dead, as Djerkest insists. She must be dead at last, for if not, we have no chance. But the young Carastindin prince got hold of one of the Keppa's tools." Blinking, Gajdosik lifted his head, squinting at the Kieba as though dimly aware something about this wasn't quite right.

"Did he?" murmured the Kieba, lifting her eyebrows. "But did he take up an abandoned tool, or was he given it? Do you truly believe the Keppa is dead? If you are mistaken and she yet lives, surely it must be dangerous to intrude upon her?"

Gajdosik shook his head. "Not . . . not as it once was. Our magisters, what they found . . . Maranajdis . . . and Bherijda . . . Bherijda *wants* to find the Keppa still living. He thinks he can take her power whole, rival even Maranajdis. He can't be allowed. . . . But if he's wrong . . . If Djerkest is right and she is dead at last, following the gods she always served . . . He must be right about that, or surely the Carastindin prince would never have been able to take up her autajma, which she ever guarded closely." Gajdosik turned his head, blinking at Oressa. He said earnestly, "It's too much old magic loose in the world. Got to be careful. Disaster and opportunity. I've got to get the Keppa's power myself, or Bherijda will take it, and we'll be crushed between him and Maranajdis. But we didn't expect anyone in Carastind to find fragments of the old gods' magic. Or use what they found. Ignorant as pigs. Always been too afraid of the Keppa to study the old magic. . . ."

"Yet they may have been wise, to fear the Keppa's power," suggested the Kieba.

"Maybe, maybe. Doesn't matter now, no choice . . . We've lost too much, Djerkest has to get me something I can use." Gajdosik leaned forward, blinking, his voice gathering intensity. "He has to. I have to have it. If that Carastindin prince can use the Keppa's magic, Djerkest can. If we can only get something to counter Bherijda and Maranajdis, I might take Tamarist after all, eventually, if I can use Carastind to strengthen my position. Gods dead and forgotten, let me only defeat Maranajdis and Bherijda and I do not even *care* who might take the throne; let Ajei have it, or Emarast would do better by Tamarist, if he lives. . . ."

He slid into rapid Tamaj, a harsh whisper, hard for Oressa to follow. "But then that went wrong, too," she suggested in Esse.

"It all went wrong," Gajdosik agreed wearily, following her into the same language. "I've lost . . . everything." He leaned his head back again and shut his eyes. "Poor Djerkest, not his fault, I should have guessed. . . . Of course the girl would lay a trap if she could; she's a clever one. . . . Stupid, blind, overconfident . . . Nothing I can do now. I've got nothing left. Maybe she'll try to protect my people. She might . . . might care to do that. . . . She's kind, I think. Best I can do . . . Can't do anything else. . . ."

Oressa found that she was biting her lip. She'd been fascinated by this chance to question Gajdosik, but this exhausted despair was not something she had been prepared for. She shot a look at the Kieba, then moved to lay a hand on Gajdosik's shoulder. The exhaustion in the prince's face eased a little. Oressa looked again at the Kieba, wishing now just for this to be over.

The Kieba did not move or speak. But the needles drew back into the arms of the chair. Gajdosik, freed, leaned slowly forward, dropping his face into his hands. He didn't make a sound, but fine tremors went through his body. Oressa rather helplessly patted his shoulder and wished Laasat were here. The Tamaristan prince did not seem exactly unconscious, but not really conscious either.

A golem shifted in the doorway: one of the small war golems. It entered, its steel-and-glass claws clicking on the darker crystal of the floor. It closed its claws around Gajdosik's arms and hips, lifting him gently. Gajdosik did not fight the golem, but he flinched and shuddered, his breath hissing.

"Wait!" Oressa said sharply.

"It will only take him to a quiet room where he may rest," the Kieba told her. "You may go with him. The kephalos will have left all his recent memories uncertain. He will need a friend he trusts to tell him what is true. You must take care with what you say, however, as he will believe anything you tell him."

"Oh. *Oh*. But then Laasat—" But Oressa paused, realizing how little Prince Gajdosik would wish any man of his, even Laasat, to see him in such a defenseless state. How little he would want *her* to see him like that. But perhaps even she was better than one of his men. She discovered she was biting her lip again and made herself stop. Then she hurried after the golem, which had not paused to wait for her, fearing lest it take Gajdosik away and leave her behind.

CHAPTER 14

Gulien leaned forward, squinting at the two figures making their way down the mountain, and then sat back; he was almost certain that both of those people were men and both wearing Tamaristan uniforms. He was entirely certain neither was his sister. If that Tamaristan bastard had taken her up onto the Kieba's mountain and *lost* her there . . . If the Kieba had let Gajdosik go but kept his sister . . . He had better not run too far ahead of his actual knowledge, but it was hard. Gathering his reins, Gulien turned his horse sharply and rode along the bank of the river toward the mountain, weaving between the cottonwoods and then sending his horse splashing into the river where it was shallowest.

His company jolted into startled movement, though Aran quickly sorted that out, detailing a handful of soldiers to follow Gulien and the rest to stay where they were and also gesturing the Tamaristan *karanat* to stop when the other made to follow. Over his shoulder, Gulien snapped, "Bring him," without slowing down. Over among the farmhouses, there was confused motion among the other Tamaristans. Gulien ignored them, other than one glance to be sure they were not showing any signs of forming up for attack.

The glass shards on top of the wall, broken into needles and splinters, presented a considerable obstacle. Gulien would just be able to see over the wall if he stood up on the back of his horse, but even if he could clamber onto the top of that wall, those blades of glass would probably go right through boot leather, and he didn't even want to imagine what they would do to one's naked hands. Besides that, the top surface of the wall was no longer broad enough for a man to stand upon it comfortably. It was no more than three fingers across, if that.

"Throw a saddle across the top," he said tersely to Aran when the captain, tense and exasperated, came up to him. To the *karanat*, whom several of his men guarded, he said, "I'd have said that neither of those men is Prince Gajdosik. Can you confirm that?"

"Yes," answered the young man, after mounting his horse and standing in the saddle to see. "That is *Addat* Laasat Jerant, who accompany my prince, and Tamresk Kerenn, one who also accompany him. There were others."

"*And* my sister," snapped Gulien.

At his tone, the Tamaristan prudently dropped to the ground and then to one knee. "Yes, Your Highness."

Quite unfairly, Gulien demanded, "Then *where is she*?" But, of course, though he flinched, the *karanat* could not answer. Gulien found himself drumming his fingers nervously on his horse's saddle and made himself stop. He snapped, "Oh, get up," at the *karanat*, and stood up in his own saddle to study the approaching men. The progress of the two men down the slope of the mountain seemed painfully slow. The Tamaristan company, until now drawn up in formation near the farmhouse, began a slow advance across the fields.

"Your Highness," began Captain Aran, indicating this movement.

"I know," Gulien said. "I think their commander means to make it plain that he won't allow us to take those men prisoner." He turned to the *karanat*. "You, go back to your commander and make it clear that *I* insist on speaking to your *addat* first."

"We and you can both speak to our *addat* at the same time, maybe, Your Highness," suggested the *karanat*. "We all wish to hear what has happen. We shall not do fighting."

"Do battle," Gulien corrected automatically, then realized how ridiculous it was to correct a foreigner's phrasing under such fraught circumstances.

But the Tamaristan only said, "As you say, Your Highness. We shall not do battle. We must learn what has happen."

Gulien gave a curt nod.

The *addat* and the other man had both paused for a moment when they saw that Gulien's people as well as their own waited for them. But they did not hesitate for more than a moment. Then the *addat* turned to come down the mountain more directly toward Gulien's position. He seemed slightly familiar; Gulien wondered if he had been present during that confrontation with Prince Gajdosik at the harbor of Caras but could not clearly recall. He had not really looked at anyone there besides the Tamaristan prince and his own sister. The man was older, with a reassuring air of steadiness even under these circumstances. He allowed his companion to offer a bent knee for a step and cupped hands. As the *addat* was boosted up, he caught hold of the near stirrup of the saddle and carefully placed a hand among the glassy shards of crystal on top of the wall.

At Gulien's gesture, one of his own men held the near stirrup firmly against the *addat's* weight, and almost at once the man had got a knee on the saddle and rose carefully to stand on top of the wall. He considered the men gathered in their disparate groups, Tamaristan and Carastindin. Then he said to Gulien, in a loud, clear voice, in very good Esse, "Your Highness, let us have a truce between our peoples. Until dusk, let us say, and then we may set other terms if we choose."

Gulien began, "My sister—"

"I will tell you. I will tell you everything. Your Highness, it is my *intention* to tell you everything. But let us avoid unfortunate confusion." He raised his voice again, turning slightly toward his own people. "Let us have a clear truce. Until dusk, a truce!"

Because he had to acknowledge that this was a practical idea, Gulien gestured assent. But he said sharply, "You will remain my—guest, *Addat* Laasat Jerant, regardless of what else we may decide."

"I agree," the *addat* said immediately. "My people will also agree." Turning, he felt for the near stirrup with one foot, lowered himself carefully belly down, and reached down to the man on the other side of the wall. A few moments of scrambling effort ensued, and then both Tamaristan soldiers had successfully descended to the near side of the wall. Neither was armed, even with a dagger, as was quickly ascertained.

"Well?" Gulien demanded.

"Yes," said the *addat*. "Her Highness is well and safe, I believe, Your Highness." He glanced at the *karanat*, then returned his gaze to Gulien and continued in excellent Esse. "I do not believe the Keppa is ill-disposed toward Her Highness. She was well when I last saw her, only half an hour since. It is my prince who has offended the Keppa. It is my prince and my people who await her judgment. My prince remains within her mountain, and I do not know what she will do with him." The young *karanat* drew a breath, and the *addat* turned to him and said, with some force, still in Esse, "There is indeed reason for concern. But there must be no panic nor hasty action." He turned at once back to Gulien and said, in exactly the same level tone, "*We* are not to intrude upon the Keppa's privacy, Your Highness. But I think you might."

"Is that your advice?" Gulien asked sharply.

"I would far rather have my prince in your hands than in hers."

Gulien did not know how to answer this. He thought the Tamaristan *addat* was speaking honestly, but he did not know how to weigh the risks of any course of action; and there seemed altogether too many courses of action possible.

As though guessing something of his confusion, the *addat* asked him, "What terms would you demand from me and my men, if you would go speak to the Keppa and make the effort to reclaim my prince from her hands?" He did not wait for an answer, but went on immediately. "I propose these terms: More than truce, I will offer my parole and that of all these men." He nodded toward the Tamaristan company. "Until you return or my prince returns or Her Highness returns, whoever shall come down the mountain first."

"Your *parole*, is it? Until you choose to resume your war against Carastind?"

"We will disarm, if you wish, Your Highness. I trust Your Highness will extend honorable treatment to all these men."

The *karanat* said urgently, "*Sir—*" He went on in Tamaj, too quick and fierce for Gulien to catch more than a few words.

Addat Laasat raised his hand, stemming this protest, and answered, in the same language, but far more slowly and clearly and with a glance at Gulien for permission to speak Tamaj rather than Esse. "All your objections, I understand. Djerkest is dead. He was gravely mistaken regarding the Keppa's vigor. It is now impossible for us to oppose the Keppa. The other men are dead. Our prince is himself in great peril. Even now he is attempting to set himself between the Keppa's wrath and all of us."

The younger man began another, even more fervent protest. Again the *addat* cut him off, with greater force, though he continued to speak carefully and clearly. "Yes, I agree with you! I am sure we all agree. I believe the Kieba favors Gulien Madalin over our prince. I see no better way to intervene for our prince than to ask the Carastindin prince to do so on our behalf, in return for all our people swearing to his service."

Gulien raised his eyebrows.

Seeing that Gulien understood what he was saying, the *addat* met his eyes and inclined his head, though he continued speaking ostensibly to the junior officer. "I agree this is not a good plan. I believe it is the best we can do. We have been strictly enjoined against intruding against the Keppa's privacy, and if we must swear to a foreign prince's service to earn a place on this side of the Narrow Sea, then we will do that. Our prince would not wish to spend our blood fighting when he cannot win—and he has already given us into Oressa Madalin's hands." Then he said in Esse, directly to Gulien, "We will swear to you, Your Highness, as long as Prince Gajdosik confirms the oath on our behalf, which I think he will do, if the Kieba opens her hand. I hope she will do that if you intervene on his behalf, Your Highness."

"But—" The *karanat* gestured up the mountain. "We—I—"

Addat Laasat said firmly, "If you attempt to scale that wall, I will borrow a Carastindin weapon and shoot you down myself."

The *karanat* drew himself up. Then, perhaps reading his superior's resolve, seemed to shrink a bit where he stood. "Yes," he said, yielding. He looked from Laasat to Gulien. "Yes," he said again, bowed his head, and stepped back.

"Your prince set you all into my sister's hands," Gulien said, to be sure he'd heard that correctly.

"He did, Your Highness. I witnessed the moment."

Gulien thought about this. Finally he said, "You will disarm your men first. Then I will go up to find the Kieba." He gestured to his own people that they should let the *addat* go, and hoped he was not wrong. He felt torn in all directions and tried not to show his impatience. His father would never have let anyone see him hesitate. But then, his father would never have been indecisive in the first place. He would weigh all his options and decide in half a heartbeat, and no matter what came of his actions, no one would ever see him irresolute or regretful.

Gulien should be more like that. He tried to reach a firm conclusion. He should go up the mountain. Maybe. Probably. The moment he decided, he found himself uncertain. That was no good. No, he *would* go. He had nearly promised he would, anyway. Though it was plain that he couldn't simply rush away over the wall and up the mountain until he made sure he wouldn't be risking a pitched battle behind him. He glanced uneasily over at the Tamaristan company. The *addat* had plainly started an argument. Gulien wondered who would win. He bet on the *addat*.

Though as far as that went, he had only the *addat's* word for what had passed between the Kieba and Prince Gajdosik and Oressa. But he could not quite imagine the man making up that story. Though after Gulien had stolen the Kieba's golem . . . What if he had offended her so badly that she handed Carastind over to Prince Gajdosik after all?

Gulien looked doubtfully up at the high, narrow wall, its top glittering with shards of glass, and could not decide what course to take. The other wall had almost seemed to *invite* approach, compared to this forbidding wall.

But Oressa was within the mountain. What if *she* offended the Kieba? It seemed all too likely that she might. She never had been afraid of anyone in her life, except their father. Gulien looked from the wall to the Tamaristan company, at least a dozen men arguing now, and back to the wall. He hated to think of trying to get over it, even with the saddle to guard his hands and knees against the glass. He would probably jump down on the other side and sprain his ankle, and then what? *Crawl* up the mountain? Very princely.

Reaching out, he laid his hand against the rough red sandstone of the wall, warm in the late-afternoon sunlight, and wished that all of this was *over* and everything *decided*, with no more need of doubts and hesitation and—

The sandstone crumbled out from beneath his palm. Gulien jerked back, reining his normally placid horse back so sharply that the startled animal pinned its ears and crow-hopped. He barely noticed, even though he had to grab the pommel to avoid a fall. All his attention was on the wall, which was turning to sand right before his eyes, a three- or four-foot width pouring away in a shower of grit and red dust. Shards of glass tumbled, glittering in the light, shattering when they hit the hard ground underfoot.

Gulien stared at the wall for one more long moment, while all around him men exclaimed and pointed. The gap was about as wide as a doorway.

If the other wall had been a stern warning and the new wall a blatant threat, what was this?

He looked around. The Tamaristans had stopped arguing and turned to stare. Laasat Jerant said something forceful—he was too far away for Gulien to catch anything but the tone, but it did not seem now that any of his people were inclined to dispute with him.

Gulien took a deep breath. Then he said, "Captain Aran. Please see that the Tamaristan soldiers are all disarmed and taken under loose guard. I don't think they'll make trouble for us. To ensure this, you will see to it that our people leave them alone. Is that clear?"

"Yes, Your Highness," Aran agreed, though rather unhappily. "But,

Your Highness, what if . . . ?" He stopped there, apparently unable to frame a coherent objection.

Gulien suspected he knew how the other man felt, but he did not see what he could do except pretend to a confidence he did not entirely feel. Swinging down off his horse, he handed the reins to the nearest man and walked through the gap in the wall, stepping carefully to avoid the still-sharp blades of black glass. Then he strode up the mountain. He did not look back.

The door into the mountain was much as Gulien remembered it. He did not need a guide this time, remembering the way with a peculiar vividness, as though he had come this way many times and not merely once before. It took less time than he had expected to find that blank red face of stone with the lightning-jag of crystal running through it, and he felt no uncertainty about the way. He put out a hand to guard his face in case the stone was solid, but he knew it would not be. Heat washed up around him as he stepped forward into the stone, and then the heat died away and Gulien was standing once more in the enormous, echoing Tomb of the Gods.

No one spoke, not even the kephalos. Gulien did not speak either, feeling oddly as though it would not be fitting. All the statues seemed somehow to be in shadow this time, from the nearest, which loomed over him, to the farthest, which were barely visible. Except Ysiddre's statue. The goat-headed goddess glimmered like the moon captured in a pool of water. Her door was standing open, moonlight shining along her stairway of amethyst-threaded white marble; the new moon carved above the door's lintel was etched with light.

In contrast, the shadows of the hall lay over Ysiddro so thickly he could hardly make her out. He remembered Ysiddro's door as black marble with veins of white and smoke-gray. Now it was a dull, flat black, starred with a network of fine fractures, like glass cracked in fire. The doorknob was simply missing. The full moon she held in her right hand was dull pewter, the crescent moon she held in her left hand powdery black.

Gulien shuddered, though he did not entirely know why. He did know that he would not have touched that black door for anything.

But it was the other goddess's doorway he needed anyway. He walked forward and started boldly up her white stairway. The air seemed cold for one step and then colder again with the next and the next, with a biting chill foreign to Carastind. He did not remember whether he had noticed anything of the kind on his earlier ascent of these stairs, yet the cold also seemed familiar, as though he had come this way a thousand times. Each step was carved a little bit too deeply for comfort, as though made for someone taller than any mortal man. That, too, seemed somehow familiar, like the cold and the silence and the misty light through which he climbed.

He came at length, as he had known he would, through a veil of heat, to the small chamber that had been carved out of the gray crystal, with its single chair of the same crystal. Beyond the chair, on the dais, lay a woman in a plain white shroud that left only her head uncovered. It was the Kieba, and she was dead.

No—no; he saw almost at once, after that first moment of horror, that this was not the Kieba. This was some other woman, like but unlike: older and thinner than the woman he had met, her eyes sunken, her bones stark beneath her skin.

Then Gulien blinked, and as though his vision had suddenly snapped into focus, he once more recognized the Kieba. He took a step back, baffled and beginning to be frightened, unable to understand why she had changed in his eyes—why his perception of her had changed and then changed back. Of course it was the Kieba. He had no idea why he had thought anything else, and he hurried forward, dropped to one knee, and touched her throat, feeling for a pulse. Her skin was cool, and he could find no heartbeat.

"Gulien Madalin," said a familiar, inexpressive voice. "Welcome. Your primary identity is recognized. Your secondary identity is: Manian Semai. Your affiliation is: to the Kieba. Your principal aspect is: undefined.

Your subsidiary aspect is: undefined. Your position is: ancillary."

Straightening, Gulien looked around, though he knew he would not see the bodiless kephalos. He hardly knew what to ask first—about the Kieba, about what had happened to her, about his sister, about Prince Gajdosik. He opened his mouth, shut it again, took a breath, and asked, "Kephalos, what did you do to me last night, and what am I supposed to do now? Where is Oressa? Where is Prince Gajdosik, and what has happened to the Kieba?"

"Nothing has happened to the Kieba," said the Kieba herself, opening her eyes and sitting up. Gulien, his breath hissing out in startlement, stumbled back a step, caught himself, and tried to reclaim something like dignity, though he didn't know how well he managed this.

"At least, not recently," added the Kieba, rising neatly to her feet. "I am not entirely myself, but I will do." The white shroud fell in smooth draperies around her, revealed now to be nothing more deathly than a simple long dress. She regarded him with every appearance of cool interest. "Gulien Madalin. So the kephalos has guided you to establish a secondary identity."

"It seemed best," stated the kephalos without emphasis. "Rival claimants are dangerous."

"I know your opinion," the Kieba said indifferently. "Manian Semai, is it, whose memories you have brought forward for this Madalin prince? I remember Manian." Her colorless eyes turned away from Gulien as she seemed to lose interest in him, her gaze growing abstracted. "Manian," she repeated. "Yes."

"I don't understand," Gulien said quietly, bowing slightly to try to recapture the Kieba's attention without angering her. "Who is Manian Semai? What has the kephalos done to me? What rival claimants exist, and what is to be claimed?" He hesitated and then asked, "Where is Oressa? Perhaps her fate is a small thing to you, Kieba, but it matters to me. Please, will you tell me what has happened to her?"

"Oressa," murmured the Kieba. "Oressa Madalin. She has no predisposition."

Gulien refused to be diverted. "Yes, but where *is* she? Is she well? What have you done with Prince Gajdosik? His people are very much concerned for his fate. So am I, as I would prefer not to have random Garamanaji princes wandering about Carastind."

"Your sister is perfectly well. So is Gajdosik Garamanaj," the Kieba said. "In a moment I—"

"You must return to Elaru," stated the kephalos.

The Kieba paused, her head tilting in a strange, quick movement, curiously nonhuman, as all her movements were just a little bit wrong. "Must I? Perhaps you are right," she conceded. "I do not believe anything of Elaru will prove salvageable, but it is true the firebreak must be widened and maintained."

"Nevertheless, it is also important to enhance the young prince's secondary identity and aspects and formally establish his claim."

The Kieba's voice sharpened. "Oh, unquestionably. We could hardly disagree."

"Will you tell me what that *means*?" demanded Gulien, then made himself add in a more conciliatory tone, "Please."

"Explanations rapidly become superfluous," snapped the Kieba, and walked away, back into the other room. She turned when she reached the chair and gazed expectantly at Gulien.

"Tell me what you plan to do with my sister, and I will obey you."

The Kieba tilted her head, considering him. "Oressa Madalin," she said after a pause, as though it had taken her a moment to remember whom he meant. "Well. I do not intend to do anything with Oressa. She is with Gajdosik Garamanaj, who requires her stability."

Her *stability*. Gulien wanted to ask whether they were talking about the same person, but the Kieba was going on: "He is no direct use to me, as he possesses no adequate predisposition. I will send him away."

"And Oressa doesn't have a predisposition either."

"No. She never held a key, I surmise. The key was yours."

"Ah." Gulien hesitated. "So you will release Oressa. And Prince Gajdosik. And me? Kieba, I have to—listen, you cannot simply turn

Gajdosik and his men loose in Carastind. I've gained the advantage over them now. I'm grateful to you for that, but now you must permit me to protect Carastind against such foreign aggressors—"

"We are not concerned for Gajdosik Garamanaj or his men."

"Kieba, you may have no need to be concerned, but I must admit I am not so sanguine!" Inspiration seized him and he added, trying to sound confident, "Besides, you gave me a year. That's what you told me: one year."

"Did I?" said the Kieba vaguely. "I did. Yes. We remember that. I remember that. I thought it best to allow your secondary identity to manifest gently, over the course of many months. The kephalos, it appears, does not agree." Her gaze sharpened. "To be sure, the entire question was predicated on the return to my hand of Parianasaku's Capture. That artifact has not yet been returned, young prince."

"But—"

"The artifact that was placed in my hand was another. You must acquire Parianasaku's Capture and return it to me. I require it most urgently."

"That was the wrong artifact?" But Gulien knew this was true. Of course his father had given him the wrong artifact. Of course Osir Madalin would do just that. And Gulien had only known that the artifact he was given was awake and alive and never questioned but that it was the right one.

"Indeed," said the kephalos. "However—"

The Kieba raised an impatient hand. "Yes, we understand: We cannot pursue Parianasaku's Capture instantly. Very well. *After* Gulien Madalin's claim has been reinforced and his principal aspect defined." She studied Gulien, then gestured decisively to the crystalline chair. When he didn't move in answer to this unvoiced command, she added more sharply, "I understand your reluctance. But while it is not strictly necessary that you do this of your own will, I believe it is in every way preferable."

Gulien could see that she wouldn't permit him to refuse, so how could anything he did be of his own will? Yet in another way, he understood what she meant. It wasn't exactly about having choices. It was more about how you met the only choice you had.

She had promised to release Oressa. She had more or less promised that. Hadn't she?

"Gulien," the Kieba said, patient but relentless.

Gulien took a step forward. Then he paused. "What will this do? Will you tell me that? What will this do to me? Is it like what the kephalos has done to me—twice—when it drew my blood? What does it mean, to define an aspect and establish a claim? How long will this take? Will this be—will this be like the other time?"

"I would hardly be able to define your experience." The Kieba tapped the back of the chair again. "Enough questions. You will find many of the answers here, Gulien Madalin. Come."

Seeing no way to protest further, and since it was plainly no use to demand answers, Gulien walked forward, hesitated for the length of one breath, and sat down in the chair.

The needles pierced his wrists and hands. It hurt for only a moment. Then he shut his eyes and fell into a thin, cold darkness. Strange, broken fragments of images and thoughts and emotions sleeted through his mind, sharp and glittering as shards of crystal.

CHAPTER 15

Oressa sat beside a narrow couch in a narrow room, watching Prince Gajdosik sleep. The walls were red stone, but draped with fine cloth in shades of blue and rose and cream; the couch and her chair were of dark, polished wood and lined with cushions in the same shades. The chamber was cluttered with small tables and chests, also of polished wood. A pitcher of water and several cups rested on one table, of normal earthenware, glazed a rich brown. All the ordinary furnishings and gentle colors were a welcome change from gray crystal. Oressa thought she would be just as happy if she never in her whole life saw another piece of smoky crystal or jade or soapstone or anything remotely like them.

Gajdosik lay on the couch, fully clothed. Oressa had tossed a blue-and-rose coverlet over him for good measure and now just sat, more or less patiently, waiting for him to wake up. He didn't seem as though he ever would. He lay very still; more still, she thought, than a man lost in any natural sleep. Though she was not very accustomed to watching men sleep.

In a way it was like something out of a story: a prince trapped in a timeless sleep, waiting for a princess to awaken him. Gajdosik could quite well have belonged in that kind of story, with his foreign good looks. In a story, they would fall in love and somehow resolve all their differences and live happily ever after.

Oressa could almost imagine exactly how that story would go.

It would have been funny, except that it wasn't. She could imagine what her father would say if he could see her here, watching over a foreign prince while he slept.

Well, no, she really couldn't imagine what her father would say. She didn't want to imagine it, in fact. Gulien . . . Gulien would probably be as horrified as their father, but he would also laugh, seeing how ridiculous a situation she'd gotten herself into. She was fairly sure he would see the funny side of it. She hoped he would. If he were here.

She hoped her brother was all right. She ought to have asked the Kieba. Surely the Kieba would know what was happening in Caras.

Gajdosik's eyes slitted open. Sometimes that happened. Then he would close his eyes again and lapse back into sleep, or unconsciousness, or whatever. Oressa tried not to be impatient.

Then he blinked and turned his head, and Oressa caught her breath, leaning forward. He *was* awake.

All his memories would be uncertain, the Kieba had said. He would need her to tell him what was true. He'd have to *trust* her to tell him. She knew now that he had courage in sufficient measure to face even that, but she flinched from even trying to imagine such vulnerability.

Gajdosik drew a breath. His eyes were wide with confusion, which was, Oressa thought, possibly turning into fear. Rising, she touched his shoulder. "You're—" She stopped, because she couldn't say, *You're all right,* or even, *You'll be all right.* She didn't dare make any such promise. She said instead, "What do you remember? Do you remember the Kieba?"

Gajdosik's eyebrows drew together. He tried to sit up, a painful effort. Oressa stuffed a silk cushion behind him and patted his arm, trying to look reassuring rather than worried. She asked again, "What do you remember?"

"I . . . ," Gajdosik whispered. "I don't know. . . ." His breathing quickened, and he put a hand up to cover his eyes, a helpless, defensive gesture.

"I'll tell you the truth," Oressa promised him, though she knew it was reckless and perhaps irresponsible to make any such commitment.

She patted his arm again. "You can trust me to tell you the truth—I won't ever lie to you. Or," she added, "if I do, I'll *tell* you I'm lying, all right?"

Gajdosik husked a laugh. "Oressa Madalin. I remember *you*."

"I'll tell you the truth," she promised again. "Can you trust me for that?"

He nodded faintly. "What did I tell the Kieba? She asked me . . . I don't remember. Did I tell her . . . ? What did I tell her?"

Oressa said gently, "You told her everything, I think. All your plans."

He turned his face away.

"But you gave me your ring." She held out her hand to show him. "Do you remember? The Kieba told me that as long as I wear it, she'll recognize my claim to all your men. Do you remember that? I promised you I would protect your people, and I *will*."

She would, too; she knew that suddenly. Even if it made Gulien angry. Even if she had to face the whole court in Caras and make them *all* accept what she'd done, and that was a frightening idea because she'd never in her life stepped out in the open to argue with people. Getting her way had always meant a nudge here and there, a threat delivered obliquely, a promise made in silence, with just a significant look at exactly the right moment.

But she had known when she'd accepted Gajdosik's ring that in order to protect his people, she would have to come out of the shadows. She tried now to pretend the idea of it didn't frighten her at all. All the time she knew it was just a pretense, but . . . she could do it. She was deeply grateful that though she might have to argue with Gulien and everyone else at court, she would not have to face her father with any of this. If there had been any living gods to pray to, she would have prayed she would never need to face her father again for anything. If she had to stand against *him* on behalf of Gajdosik's men . . . she wasn't certain she could do it.

"I remember," Gajdosik said quietly, not noticing her sudden silence. He leaned his head back against the arm of the couch and shut his eyes.

Oressa blinked, took a breath, and asked at last, "Are you . . . ? Are you well? There's water. Are you thirsty?" Her voice sounded stiff and strange to her ears. She took another breath and moved to pour him a cup without waiting for an answer. Then, even when he opened his eyes and sat forward, she had to help him steady it.

If he wondered what the Kieba meant to do with him, he did not say so; nor did he ask Oressa what she meant to do with his men. That wasn't chance, she knew. His mute passivity worried her. She guessed it came from the knowledge of failure, from loss and grief and shame, and she didn't know what to do about any of that. Before she had thought him insufferably arrogant. But now that his pride had been broken, she found she liked that even less. But she did not know what she could do or say to mend what had been broken.

There was a sound at the door. Oressa whirled around, but Gajdosik had to brace himself up with a hand that still trembled. She moved to steady him, trying to be unobtrusive about it.

But to her astonishment, it was her brother, Gulien, who rapped briskly on the doorframe and then opened the door. First Oressa was overjoyed to see him, but then she was horrified, for so many different reasons she could hardly number them. There were bruised circles under her brother's eyes, and he looked older, somehow. Well, she felt about a hundred years older herself. Gods dead and forgotten, it seemed *years* ago that she'd hidden under her father's chair and heard Gajdosik's name linked to hers for the very first time, and it had been hardly more than a week. Though a *very long* week.

Now, unwillingly distracted from her *ordinary* and *reasonable* worries by a completely different and unexpected set of fears, she demanded, "Gulien! What are *you* doing here? I'm so glad to see you, but you didn't have to *come after me yourself.* Gulien, honestly, you're so—so—"

"Dependable? Reliable?" Gulien was smiling, but to Oressa his expression looked a little forced. "I was worried about you. Among so many other reasons. You little fool. The things you get yourself into!"

Oressa wanted to shake him. "Yes, but how could you leave Caras? What did you do about Father?"

"Caras is fine! Father wasn't giving me problems. *You* were the one I was worried about!" He gave Gajdosik a hard look. "When I got word that His Highness had led a thrust inland toward the Kieba's mountain, well, what did you expect me to do, Oressa? Whom else should I have sent, knowing the Kieba might get involved—that we might have to *depend* on her to save us all? Especially knowing *you* were here, you little sneak! I left Beriad in charge of the guard and Paulin and Toen in charge of everything else."

Magister Toen was all right. Over-dignified, but also meticulous and diligent. Oressa liked him, but she had to admit he wasn't very quick-witted. No wonder Gulien had also appointed Paulin. . . .

"I know you don't like Lord Paulin," Gulien added. "But I trust him. And Magister Toen is steadfast; everyone knows that. He gave me his word, and he'll reassure anyone who wavers. They were the best choice, Oressa. I'm not worried about Caras, not unless some *other* disaster strikes." His tone was not quite assured on that last, as he plainly didn't entirely rule this out. But he added, far more firmly, "I was worried about *you*. And about His Highness."

Gajdosik lowered his gaze, making no attempt to answer this.

"Paulin and Toen together aren't half a match for our father," Oressa muttered. But she couldn't say her brother shouldn't have worried. That was too obviously untrue. She was sorry now that she'd shouted. Gulien looked *terrible*. "Are you all right?" she asked him, trying not to sound too anxious about it. "Have you seen the Kieba, or spoken to the kephalos, or . . . ?" She stopped, not knowing quite what she saw in her brother's face.

"Yes," Gulien said. There was something in his tone that said, *I don't want to talk about it*. He frowned at Gajdosik. "And you, Your Highness? Can you get up? Can you walk, do you think? The Kieba is willing to open her hand, but can you walk down from this mountain on your own legs?"

"She's letting us go!" exclaimed Oressa. "All of us? She did say she would. She *almost* said so. Anyway, that's wonderful! Now?" She barely restrained herself from pushing past her brother and out the door right then, but was held by her brother's upraised hand and, somehow, by Gajdosik's silent stillness. He had made it to his feet, though he was gripping the back of the couch for support. He was not looking at Oressa. She thought his attention was mainly on Gulien and on keeping himself upright.

"It seems so, yes," said Gulien. Though he was speaking to Oressa, his steady gaze was still fixed on Gajdosik. "I believe there are several matters that she depends on us to resolve. For example, we must find some useful way to deal with any adventuring Tamaristans who persistently disregard Carastind's sovereign borders and the Kieba's privacy."

Prince Gajdosik sank to one knee, carefully, steadying himself against the couch. Bowing his head, he said quietly, "Your Highness. I'm grateful you have won our freedom from this mountain. I acknowledge that I and my men are in your hands. You will do with me as you will, but I ask you to be generous with my people."

It was a powerful, arresting moment.

Oressa cleared her throat before either of the men could take it too seriously. "Well," she said in her blandest tone, "actually, Gulien, Prince Gajdosik and all his men are in *my* hands." She held up her left hand, showing her brother the ring Gajdosik had given her. "The Kieba gave them all to me herself and told me to find some practical use for them." She smiled brightly at Gulien. She wasn't certain the Kieba had meant to include Prince Gajdosik himself in that responsibility, but she didn't say so. It was always better not to raise subtle questions. It worked better to simply assume that everyone naturally intended to cooperate and see what happened. She had learned that from watching her father. Though of course *he* had no need to smile when he did it.

Gulien rubbed his forehead, as though he might be developing a headache. "Oressa—"

"Well, we can certainly find a practical use for them, can't we?" Oressa asked, sweetly reasonable. "Especially if any other Tamaristan princes have similar ideas, which I gather they might. Gajdosik's brother Maranajdis sounds especially unpleasant." She didn't glance at Gajdosik, from whom she had gathered that information. She was uncomfortable thinking about those grim moments with the Kieba and that horrible chair. Imagining how Gajdosik felt about it was excruciating enough without *looking* at him.

Her brother rubbed his forehead again without answering. Then he said impatiently to Gajdosik, "Get up, Your Highness. You do put us to more trouble. Not to mention—" But he hesitated then and visibly changed what he'd been about to say, snapping instead, "Why couldn't you just have taken your ships back across the Narrow Sea and left us alone? You know, parts of the palace are *still* collapsing whenever there's a hard breeze."

Gajdosik got slowly to his feet. Even Oressa couldn't tell how much of that deliberation was due to lingering weakness and how much to pride. He met Gulien's hard stare—that was certainly pride, and could not have been easy. "Your Highness, I thought I had no need to ask for charity. I thought I could take everything. I was wrong. If you are now good enough to offer my people sanctuary, I would be most grateful."

"Would you, indeed?"

"Gulien, the other Garamanaji princes are the real threat," Oressa put in. "They really are. Prince Gajdosik can't take his people back to Tamarist. He *really* can't," she added earnestly, at the skeptical tilt of her brother's head.

"Well," Gulien said to Gajdosik, "next time, when you find yourself pressed over-hard by your enemies, could you possibly just *ask* for sanctuary? As you have discovered, it's not comfortable for any of us, being forced to beg the Kieba's aid or pardon."

Gajdosik bowed his head silently.

"About the three thousand others who've landed in the north," Oressa said brightly.

"Yes," Gulien said grimly, glaring at Gajdosik. "I'd heard about that. Three thousand, is it? That's more than I'd have expected."

"But it's not too many, honestly, Gulien! Only you'd better let me send for them. We can use them, especially considering Prince Gajdosik's brothers. Unless the Kieba does something about them, which I suppose she might, but I don't think we'd better *count* on her help."

"I would be most grateful if you would offer all my people sanctuary," Prince Gajdosik repeated.

That humble tone didn't suit him at all, Oressa decided. When *she* sounded meek and docile, she was just trying to get her own way. She was afraid it wasn't like that for Gajdosik. She *hated* to hear him like that, so she said sharply, reminding him as well as Gulien, "All those men are mine! Unless you want to explain to the Kieba why they're not? Because *I* don't plan to." She lifted her eyebrows, staring at her brother, trying to look confident. "Three thousand definitely isn't too many if there's more trouble from Tamaristan princes, or even if there isn't! They'll be an asset to Carastind. I'm sure they will. The moment I get a chance, I'm going to send Laasat—or somebody—" She hoped Laasat and young Tamresk were all right, but went on. "Somebody to tell them all what's happened and that they're mine now and that they'd better come down to Caras again, this time peacefully."

"Indeed," Prince Gajdosik said, still with that quiet, deferential manner. He glanced at Gulien. "If Your Highness will permit, I would also suggest that one or more of your Carastindin officers go as well. To prevent misunderstandings between our peoples."

"Oh, is that what you suggest?"

"*I* think it's a good idea," Oressa said firmly. She wished Gulien would be nicer, and she wished Gajdosik would stop deferring to Gulien that way, which was ridiculous, because of course Gajdosik *ought* to be deferential and respectful and everything because he had *lost*, after all. But she still hated it.

Though, if Gulien decided to view things one way, then any men under her authority really did belong to him, because he was king— almost king, and that might change in a year, yes, but for now she was just his sister, which could be very awkward, if there was any argument. Much better if there wasn't any argument from anybody, especially not Gulien himself. So Oressa said, assuming her most confident manner,

"Gulien, Caras may have been peaceful and calm when you left, but *I* think you could really use three thousand Tamaristan soldiers who *never* owed any loyalty to our father. Don't you?"

"My men will obey you," Prince Gajdosik said to Gulien. "They will be loyal to Her Highness. Give them a place in your country and in your service, please, Your Highness, whatever disposition you make of me."

Oressa didn't wait to see what response her brother would make. She snapped, "Prince Gajdosik, your people are going to need you more than ever! You know they never expected you to surrender them to anybody, so you'd better be prepared to handle that!"

Gajdosik didn't answer, but Oressa nodded as though she was satisfied and said to Gulien, "Well? You said we were permitted to leave, and obviously there's a great deal to do. So can we leave now?"

"Yes," said Gulien. He glanced at her and ran a distracted hand through his hair. "Nearly. The Kieba does want to speak to you both first, I believe."

Oressa found herself trading a wary glance with Gajdosik. It occurred to her how strange it was that Gajdosik had somehow become something like her ally in this, above even Gulien. These shared days within the Kieba's mountain . . . Oressa had been frightened every moment. She longed to get back to the outside world. She longed to go *home*. But somehow the thought of leaving this place and stepping back into her expected role of Carastind's princess and Gulien's sister . . . Somehow that thought was not altogether a pleasant one, either. She didn't understand that.

And she was worried about Gajdosik. He hadn't flinched at the Kieba's summons, but the tension of his shoulders and the set of his jaw made it obvious to Oressa that he was afraid. She didn't blame him. She was frightened, too, of whatever last-moment warning or threat or punishment the Kieba might have in mind. And she was angry. The anger and the fear were on Gajdosik's behalf, she realized, not on her own. Which was ridiculous, because he might not be exactly an enemy anymore, but he was hardly a *friend*.

Oressa took a deep breath and put all those feelings away, deliberately smoothing her expression into a calm, attentive mask. *Meek*, she told herself. *Meek and polite and accommodating*. She'd worn that mask all her life. How hard could it be to wear it now?

Gajdosik, she saw, had now put on a quiet, attentive expression of his own. He asked no questions, didn't even look at either Oressa or Gulien, but only opened a hand in a silent acceptance of Gulien's authority.

CHAPTER 16

Gulien knew just where he was within the mountain, exactly where the Kieba now stood, and precisely which way he must lead the others in order to go to her. He knew which doorways were simple doorways and which might permit a man to step right across half a mile of solid rock or carry him from the top to the bottom of the mountain.

All this surety was reassuring in a way. In another way, of course, it was thoroughly disturbing.

Gulien did *not* know what the Kieba would do if he instead guided his sister and the Tamaristan prince toward the outside world. That, his unwelcome memory didn't tell him. He could guess that she wouldn't permit any such cowardly retreat, but he didn't *know*. He was almost grateful for that ignorance—no, he *was* grateful for it. It made him feel more himself, for he could hardly fail to realize that all his assurance with the geometry of the mountain came from foreign memory. From what the kephalos called his secondary identity, a frightening phrase as he began to understand what it meant. He understood now, at least a little, about memory and identity and the way the former informed the latter. He understood it too well. Better than he wished. Not as thoroughly as he feared he would be compelled to discover.

He had lived in this mountain once. Only it hadn't been him, of course, though he remembered it. Or . . . he didn't remember it, not really, except in his knowledge of the mountain's architecture and in scattered bits and flashes that came like bubbles of light around the edges of his own proper memory.

He knew to whom those disturbing flashes of light belonged. They belonged to that other man. Manian Sinai, whom the kephalos insisted was his *secondary identity*. A fraught phrase, considering that the kephalos seemed to consider Gulien's own identity hardly more justifiably his own than that of this other long-dead man.

It was made of memory, this mountain. Crystallized memory. Gulien knew that, or remembered it. *Part* of him remembered it, indistinctly. He remembered Manian Sinai's life, but vaguely and in fragments, somewhat in the way he remembered his own earliest childhood.

Then he'd found the key to memory . . . That, he remembered very well, though with greater understanding now. He'd been twelve, and Oressa not quite eight, and she'd found the way through the secret panel into the hidden crawlspace of the highest attics, and he had followed. And then, crawling back out, he had put his knee down hard on that fragment of dark gray crystal, smooth and almost greasy to the touch, that at the time he hadn't recognized. He'd only known that he'd liked it. He remembered that. He'd liked the way it felt in his hand, and had never guessed the pebble he'd eventually had carved into a Madalin falcon and strung on a gold chain was actually a fragment of memory. Not even when it had brought him strange, vivid dreams of lands he didn't know, of gods whose names he didn't recognize, of a voice that murmured in his ear and told him stories of the long-vanished past.

So all that time Gulien had held a tiny splinter of the Kieba's power. And his father had never known, nor had Gulien himself ever guessed, until desperation brought him to the Kieba's mountain and the kephalos said, *Your key is accepted*.

At the time he had only found that convenient. Now he knew that the kephalos had also found it convenient. Though even now he did not know exactly what might arise from that happenstance.

If it had actually been happenstance, a Madalin chancing to find a fragment of crystallized memory. Though Gulien hardly saw how that moment in the crawlspace could have been orchestrated by the kephalos or anyone else.

The crystal had been so small, of course, and it just hadn't ever struck him as looking like any obvious kind of artifact. But it had been potent enough to wake his predisposition, especially when he took up other artifacts such as Eirankan's Key; that seemed inarguable. He was hardly able to tell, even yet, whether that had been on balance a good thing or a bad. Though he was glad he was the one who had taken up the bit of crystal and not Oressa. That he and not his sister had been the one to wear Eirankan's Key until his father discovered how to wake it and took it back and used it in turn to wake the Capture.

Yes, better it had been him. Gulien could all too easily imagine how his sister would feel, finding herself subject to the incomprehensible machinations of the kephalos. He glanced down at Oressa affectionately. She would have hated it far more than he.

He didn't need to take his sister or the Tamaristan prince far, not in terms of the number of steps required, just along a short hallway and down three steps and into a kind of glass-roofed atrium through which poured the honey-gold light of midmorning. In another way, that short journey encompassed two-thirds of the width of the mountain and brought them from a chamber very near the summit about halfway down its height. Of course, neither of them knew that. Gulien could not fail to know it.

As they came into the atrium, Oressa tipped her face up to the light. Gulien smiled at her. His little sister had taken no harm of her sojourn within the Kieba's mountain. She wanted real sunlight and the hot wind against her face. Soon she would have those things. In that assurance, he could almost forget the way he had himself been snared into the Kieba's purpose.

Gulien stood aside to let Oressa go before him into a plain, stark room that was entirely empty. She looked around in evident unease, but the walls were ordinary walls of red sandstone, not soapy gray crystal, which she must find encouraging. Or, well, perhaps she didn't realize;

but at least *Gulien* found this room reassuring. And there weren't any crystalline chairs, for which he was even more grateful.

Almost better than the lack of crystal was the wide window set into the far wall, which let them see out into the empty sky and over the drylands that stretched away to the horizon. Gulien looked out, trying to see his men and the Tamaristan company, wishing to assure himself that everything out there was calm and that no disaster would be waiting at the foot of the mountain. But the angle was wrong, and he could see nothing but the empty drylands.

"Well, there's a sight," said Oressa, going to the window and pressing her hands against it. "Soon we'll be out there, right, Gulien? The Kieba's going to let us all go and not imprison anyone in a lightless cell for a hundred years. Isn't that right?"

Despite himself, Gulien laughed. "Oh, you've heard that story too?"

His sister smiled back, though there was a shadow behind her smile. But before she could answer or Gulien could reassure her, the Kieba was suddenly present.

She hadn't been, and then she was.

Gulien found that despite the suddenness of her arrival, he wasn't surprised by it. Prince Gajdosik stepped back, however, and Oressa flinched violently and then pretended she hadn't. Gulien put a reassuring hand on her back, and she leaned against him gratefully.

Gulien thought the Kieba looked calm, though reserved. Forbidding, maybe. But not angry. Not frightening. Not really *frightening*. He nodded to her in polite acknowledgment.

The Kieba returned Gulien's nod and then considered Gajdosik. He bowed his head and stood very still, waiting.

But the Kieba only said, "I am concerned about your brothers. About the artifacts they may have gathered into their hands. I am aware now that your brother Maranajdis makes use of Shakanatu's Throne. This troubles me, but not urgently, so long as he stays on the other side of the Narrow Sea. I am more concerned that your other brother, Bherijda, may have taken an artifact called Tonkaïan's Resolve into his hand. I am glad to have warning of the possibility, and as you have brought this warning to me, I forgive your trespass."

Prince Gajdosik let out a slow breath and bowed, without speaking.

The Kieba nodded graciously. She went on. "But even so, I have no time now for such matters. At this moment I am compelled to devote my attention to Elaru and the surrounding area. When I am able, however, I will see to removing all such fragments of gods' tools from your brothers' keeping. I should have little difficulty doing so, if they have only what I have thus far surmised they hold. I shall hope they hold nothing else."

"I am glad to know it, Keppa," Prince Gajdosik said in a low voice. "And I hope your surmise is correct. Yet Bherijda has trained as a magister. He would not—I do not believe he would have come to Carastind save that he hopes, as did my—as did Djerkest Manajarist—to take for his own the power of—of the mountain. Yet plainly any such attempt must fail in the face of your strength, Keppa."

"Yes." Then the Kieba was silent, her expression blank and abstracted.

"Does Bherijda Garamanaj possess a key?" inquired the kephalos, making Gulien twitch. "Has Bherijda Garamanaj established a position or a secondary identity?"

"This I do not know," Prince Gajdosik admitted.

"Does he possess a fragment of crystal?" asked Gulien, putting the matter in terms he thought more likely to be understood. "Or possibly it might seem like black glass."

Gajdosik considered this. "I believe he must surely possess a piece of black glass, such as the magisters of Tamarist use to make their farsight mirrors. These are used to capture images and memories."

"Such an item might possibly constitute a key," said the Kieba. Her expression did not change at first, but after a pause she frowned faintly, as though discovering that this possibility displeased her.

Gajdosik moved forward half a step and said, a faint urgency coming into his tone, "Bherijda is my enemy and the enemy of my people."

The Kieba looked at him blankly, but Gulien understood his prudence.

He said quietly, "The Kieba is hardly likely to mistake one Garamanaji prince for another. You challenged her, but you acknowledge you have been defeated—you do acknowledge that, do you not?"

"I can hardly do otherwise," the Tamaristan prince said, rather dryly.

"Then so long as you don't again make yourself her enemy, you need have no fear. Not of the Kieba." Gulien gave the Tamaristan prince a stern look.

"*Gulien*," Oressa said, and hit him on the arm. "Stop it."

The Kieba, ignoring this exchange, said thoughtfully, "If Bherijda has had a key for any length of time, it will certainly have infused itself into his blood and flesh, as yours has done, Gulien."

Oressa said, "Wait, wait! Into his *blood*?"

"The living crystal does sometimes show such an inclination. Such is the nature of keys," the Kieba said indifferently. "That is one reason among many that mortal men should leave such artifacts to me." Her gaze sharpened. "Gulien Madalin, though I am pleased to have recovered Eirankan's Key, I expect you to recover for me Parianasaku's Capture. I require you should do so. I urgently require this."

"Yes," agreed Gulien. "Of course, Kieba. I'm ashamed I allowed my father to pass off a lesser artifact in its stead. I won't permit that a second time, I promise you." He was determined that he wouldn't, though he knew it would require him to go through with the formal coronation and depose his father once and for all. The thought appalled him, but . . . not so much as it might have done a day ago.

Oressa said, "Yes, but, Gulien! Living crystal? In your blood?" She stared at Gulien and then at the Kieba. "What will that do to him? What *is* it doing to him?"

"This establishes the necessary predisposition," agreed the Kieba, still without much apparent interest, and went on, speaking to Gulien. "Parianasaku's Capture may appear as a medallion or a disk, a mirror or a rod. It might appear as a jewel or a set of jewels. It will be fairly small. It will have lines of crystal through it."

"Oh yes, good, something small with *lines* through it!" said Oressa.

"That will certainly narrow it down. Will *that* get into Gulien's blood?"

The Kieba shrugged, a tiny not-quite-human gesture. "Perhaps. It is, after all, attuned to the Madalin bloodline. But this is unimportant. Your brother's predisposition is already firmly established." She said to Gulien, seeming to dismiss Oressa completely, "Recover this artifact for me, Gulien Madalin. I am certain you understand the necessity."

"Yes," Gulien agreed, and rubbed his forehead, trying not to remember anything too strange about Parianasaku's artifact. He had a crashing headache, but surely that was only natural and did not presage anything more. Or anything stranger, or less tolerable. His sister was peering at him anxiously, and he patted her shoulder. "It's all right," he said, this hardly seeming the time or place to explain anything complicated or difficult. Especially as he himself still knew hardly anything.

"Then you must go. You may all go. Gulien Madalin, I still hope to give you a year. It is better to allow your secondary identity to settle. When it comes time to establish your affinity and take up your aspect, I will summon you. But I shall hope to give you that year."

Gulien shook Oressa slightly to stop her from demanding explanations or assurances. "Yes," he said, acknowledging the Kieba's claim. "A year, to see to Carastind's safety and prosperity." That had been the bargain, generous on her part, and he would not protest now, even with the splinters of foreign memory pressing on the back of his mind. He wanted, very badly, to get out of this mountain, out into the hot sunlight, and deal with ordinary problems and ordinary men.

The Kieba glanced around. "Kephalos?"

"Yes," it said, and across the room the window blurred and reshaped itself into a door.

CHAPTER 17

Oressa's first thought on seeing the new, taller wall was: Well, that's a statement. Then she saw the gap where her brother had, so Gulien explained, touched it and made it crumble to dust. She wondered if the Kieba had done that, or the kephalos, or if the wall's compliance with his wishes came from having crystal dissolved in his blood. She gave her brother a sideways glance, but he looked no different to her. Except for fine-drawn exhaustion. Was *that* the result of having crystal in his blood? She felt exhausted herself, and surely *she* didn't have . . . She stared down at her own hands suspiciously, but if anything had dissolved into her blood and flesh, she couldn't tell. Looking up again, she caught Prince Gajdosik's eyes on her face and knew that he knew what she'd been thinking. The weary, wry twist of his mouth might have been meant as a reassuring smile. He was tired, too. Though as far as she knew, *he* didn't have anything dissolved in his blood. She looked anxiously at Gulien, but he still looked just the same: tired, older, worried, but himself.

But the Kieba was going to summon him back to her in a year. So he could *establish his affinity* and *take up his aspect*. Oressa should have made the Kieba explain what that meant. She should get Gulien to explain it now, except he looked so tired. And she was fairly sure he wouldn't tell her any of the Kieba's secrets anyway, in case it was dangerous for her to know . . . whatever.

At least Gajdosik's people didn't seem to have fought with her brother's men. That would have been just one thing too many, when everyone was tired and worried and scared already.

From up here on the slope on the Kieba's side of the wall, Oressa could see Laasat standing beside a guard captain she knew slightly, a Captain Aran—a good man, though young for his rank. Oressa approved.

Kelian stood with Aran and Laasat. That was reassuring, too. Of the three men, Laasat looked by far the most tired and tight-drawn. Oressa certainly understood that. She waved discreetly at them all, but particularly at Laasat, to assure him that his prince was all right. Some of the strain in his face and stance eased, as though he trusted her reassurance.

The rest of the Tamaristan company was standing in orderly ranks near the wall. Nobody was actually guarding them, but they weren't armed—Laasat wasn't armed either, Oressa saw. The Tamaristans had clearly yielded to the Carastindin guardsmen. Laasat came forward a step when he saw them, but he stopped when Aran put out a forbidding hand.

Gulien led the way to the gap in the wall and stood back to let the others pass through before him, with a murmured warning about the shards of glass. Prince Gajdosik, expressionless, stepped through the gap first, brushing some of the sand and glass out of the way with his boot. Then, still without expression, he turned to offer Oressa his hand. She had refused his help over the wall on the way up the mountain, she recalled. That seemed like a very long time ago. This time she took his hand, even though she did not need his help. She touched the wall when she stepped through it, wonderingly. It felt like ordinary sandstone to her. It certainly didn't crumble away beneath her fingers.

Gulien came through last. Oressa half expected the wall to rebuild itself behind him, but nothing happened. Perhaps later. She did not feel very much inclined to stay here and watch.

She said instead, glancing from Gulien to Gajdosik and back again, "I think Laasat and some of our people should leave now, at once, to find Prince Gajdosik's other people." She looked around and added, pleased, "Oh, Sergeant Mattin can go—he's very sensible—and his squad. That's plenty enough to make sure there isn't any trouble. And I think the rest of us should start back for Caras immediately. I mean, there's no reason to linger here, is there? At least," she added, studying her brother anxiously. "Do you need to rest, Gulien? Gaj—Your Highness, do you think you could ride immediately? Because I think we need to get back to Caras right away, and get the Kieba's artifact from Father as soon as possible." She didn't add a warning that Gulien should probably watch out in case that, too, should "get into his blood." That didn't seem like a helpful thing to dwell on, even if she couldn't seem to help but dwell on it herself.

"I agree," her brother said, glancing at Gajdosik.

"I would far rather ride immediately than linger in the shadow of this mountain," the Tamaristan prince said. He spoke quietly but with considerable force. "Prince Gulien, into your hands I give my men. We shall not dispute your orders."

Oressa wondered how long that would last. She said prudently, with a meaningful look at Gulien, "Prince Gajdosik, you won't regret your trust in my brother."

"We shall endeavor to assure so," Gulien agreed, and turned to Captain Aran. The lieutenant had come up to hover anxiously, trailing Kelian and Laasat and half a dozen other men. "We will ride at once. The Tamaristans as well."

Nevertheless, it turned out they couldn't really start back *immediately*, because although Gulien and Gajdosik both insisted on courteous behavior from their respective men, the lingering dislike and suspicion slowed everything down. Gulien hesitated over whether to rearm the Tamaristan soldiers. Aran and Kelian both expressed horror at the possibility, but Gulien impatiently asked who exactly was going to carry that many extra swords and other weapons. Gajdosik politely refused to press him on the matter. Everything seemed to drag on and on. Oressa tried to push everyone along with the pure force of her own impatience, not very effectively.

But she, already mounted and hovering around the edges of the company, was the one who spotted the Carastindin messenger arrive. She saw the dust first: a plume of red dust over the road, so she knew someone was riding fast, and she might not be used to the desert, but even she knew that nobody would race his horse in the heat of the day without a very good reason. She called to Gulien and pointed, and everyone else turned, too, so everyone was waiting when the messenger rode out of the hot light of the lowering sun, crossed the river without letting his exhausted horse pause, and came toward Gulien, who had stepped out in front of the company.

It was Fellin, a man Oressa knew: a palace guardsman, no longer young, reasonably honest, sensible unless he was too far in his cups. He swung down from the saddle, staggering before he managed a bow. His horse dropped its head and blew, nostrils wide and red. Gulien waved impatiently for someone to come care for the animal and said, "Well, man? What's happened?" But Fellin was coughing from the dust and couldn't answer immediately. Gulien put his hand out and someone put a water flask into it, which he held out to the stricken man.

Oressa thought she already knew what news Fellin carried: Gulien had left Caras, and of course their father had immediately taken the throne back himself. Of course he had. She waited in dread to hear the man say so, and it was almost worse because she had known all the time that Father—

"Scorpion," Fellin said in a hoarse voice, and coughed, bent over, his hands on his knees.

Oressa blinked, baffled, but Prince Gajdosik, standing behind Gulien, brought his head up sharply.

"Ships," Fellin added. He drank from the flask, coughed, drank again, and straightened at last. Then he stared from Gulien to Gajdosik, seeming at last to notice the Tamaristan prince. He turned back to Gulien, clearly uncertain.

"Go on! We're all friends here!" said Oressa, who had swung down from her own horse and come to join them.

Gulien gave her a quelling glance, but nodded to Fellin.

"Your Highness," the man said. "Ships, Your Highness, Tamaristan ships, five of 'em. They came into the harbor almost as soon as you rode out, banners out bold as you please, a black scorpion on a green ground."

"Bherijda," Gajdosik said quietly to Gulien. "My brother Bherijda. That is his banner. He is not a man you would wish to hold power over your people."

Fellin shot another uneasy look at Gajdosik. "Bhera-something, that's right. That's what people said. He came in with maybe a couple thousand men, maybe more. I guess nobody's sure, but a lot. Only His Majesty—" Fellin stumbled over the title "—that is, your father, Your Highness, he went down to the harbor—"

"Beriad let him out?" Gulien exclaimed.

"I expect it was Toen," said Oressa. "Once he saw those banners, he'd go straight up to Father to ask for advice. Gulien, you know he would, and Father could talk him into anything." And without Gulien there, she didn't say, Lord Paulin obviously hadn't been able to stop him either. Nobody had been able to stop him. Of course they hadn't. She bit her tongue hard with the effort not to say so.

The guardsman said anxiously, "I don't know, Your Highness. Only His Majesty went down to the harbor and met that Tamaristan prince, Bher-whatever, met him right there under a parley flag, and I guess they worked something out, 'cause we got orders to stand aside, and they went up to the palace, your father and the foreign prince. And him with all his men, which they're lodging in barracks and in town, and we're to stay off the streets and not quarrel with 'em, and now either the scorpion prince is your father's guest or else your father is maybe his prisoner right in his own palace. Nobody knows which."

"You can't *tell?*" Oressa found this difficult to believe.

"Well, Your Highness, the orders to leave those scorpion soldiers free of Caras, some people are saying that means your father doesn't dare fight them. Only other people are saying His Majesty and the scorpion prince are allies now—"

"Impossible!" snapped Kelian, who had just come up and was listening.

"It seems unlikely," Gulien allowed.

"Certainly unfortunate, if it's true," muttered Gajdosik. "Bherijda has this artifact, this Tonkaïan's Resolve. Though Bherijda is neither a pleasant nor an honorable person, if the artifact is sufficiently powerful, your father might have had no practical choice but to accommodate him."

"Well, Father is certainly nothing if not *practical*," Oressa observed bitingly. "On the other hand, Gulien, if Father didn't give you the right artifact, then he's still got Parian's Thing, so if he found out about Bherijda's artifact, *he* might have proposed that they work together." He would have his own plan beyond any promise he had made, she was sure, but she knew her father could have persuaded that other Tamaristan prince of anything.

Gajdosik said in a low voice, "That is possible. Bherijda's attention would assuredly be captured by such a suggestion, if he believed an alliance would lead to certain victory against the Keppa."

Gulien scrubbed a hand across his face, nodding. "It might even be true. It would certainly be nice if the Kieba would now stride down from her mountain and sweep all her enemies away into the sea."

"Why wouldn't she, if they're her enemies too?" Oressa said with sudden enthusiasm at this splendid picture. "We should ask her to do exactly that." She thought about this and added prudently, "I mean, Gulien, *you* could ask her. You could ask her for half a dozen of those spiders, the big ones. Why wouldn't she agree? It's not like we'd be asking for help just for ourselves, after all."

"No, that won't work," said Gulien, as automatically as though he were explaining that dropped stones fell instead of floating. "Parianasaku's Capture blocks the kephalos, captures its influence, and prevents it from speaking to its accessories."

"What?" Oressa said blankly.

Her brother blinked, blinked again, rubbed his shadowed eyes, and said after a moment, "I'm not . . . I don't entirely know what I mean, actually. But I know it's true. It's part of why the Kieba can't just take Parianasaku's

Capture from Father: because it works against the kephalos. Or it can."

"It didn't before." Oressa objected.

"It did, though," Gulien said. "I realize that now. I . . . remember it." He sounded tired.

He *remembered* it. Oressa studied her brother uneasily, thinking about artifacts that got into someone's blood. She wanted to ask what he meant, but at the same time she was afraid to ask.

"Also, we know the Kieba must be concerned with the city in Gontai," Gajdosik said quietly. "Elaru."

Gulien rubbed his face again. "It's more than that. Worse than that. I don't know . . ." His voice trailed off.

Gajdosik waited a moment in case he would say something else. Then he said, "For whatever reason, then, it seems unwise to depend upon assistance from that quarter."

"Of course not," Oressa said, resigned. That would be too easy, of course. She asked Fellin, "But so far there hasn't actually been battle in Caras?"

The guardsman lifted his hands in an uncertain shrug. "Well, Your Highness, not as when I rode out. We don't any of us exactly know *what* it is with His Majesty and the scorpion prince, see, but His Highness brought the Kieba in on our side before, didn't you? So I said I'd come after you and tell you how it is."

"Yes," said Gulien. "Well done. Very well done, and I promise you, I won't forget it." He rested a hand on the guardsman's shoulder for a moment, then beckoned for someone to bring another water flask. "Rest," he told the man. "I'm not quite certain what we shall do, but we may have questions. Sit here, in the shade, and catch your breath."

"We don't know anything, not really. That's the problem, Your Highness," Kelian said to Gulien, ignoring Fellin, who stepped aside gratefully to sink down in the shade of a cottonwood. "We don't know what Prince Bherijda intends or what your father's thinking. If he's possibly already managing things with this Prince Bherijda, we don't want to get in his way—"

Oressa stared at the guard captain. "But you heard what Prince Gajdosik said! Bherijda's not honorable. What if he's fooled him"—that didn't seem likely—"or what if he's actually keeping Father prisoner and using him as a puppet to keep the city quiet? Should we get in *his* way, do you think? Or what if they've made common cause to attack the Kieba?"

"Your Highness, if your father is possibly in close negotiation with a foreign enemy, this must be a dangerous time to complicate matters! You can't doubt your father's cleverness or strength of will, and the Kieba can't be trusted to come to our aid. We all agree on that! She'll do what suits *her*, and never mind Carastind! Look how she refused to defend us against Prince Gajdosik, just out of pique because the king wouldn't give up that artifact, one that's belonged to the Madalin kings for hundreds of years!"

"It's not like that," Oressa began.

"It's exactly like that!" said Kelian condescendingly, as though he spoke to a child.

"We all know at least that her priorities aren't the same as ours," Gulien put in hastily.

"Exactly, Your Highness, and since that's so, much better to make peace with your father either way!" declared Kelian. "If the king has indeed reached some accommodation with Prince Bherijda, we can even take advantage of that—"

"What, you think we should look around for a Carastindin princess for Bherijda to marry?" Oressa asked him.

"Your Highness!" Kelian exclaimed, embarrassed now, and angry.

Gulien made a conciliatory calm-down gesture. "Oressa, no one's suggesting—"

"No woman of honor would consent to such a marriage; nor would any brother wish such a match on his sister," said Gajdosik with some force. "But in a city filled with confusion, where no one knows ally from enemy, a small force, effectively used, might accomplish a great deal." He was not quite looking at any of them, but went on in a quieter tone. "It is in fact quite possible that no matter who's in control of the city at the moment, we could retake the palace, capture both my brother and your father, and reclaim control of Caras." Though he didn't raise his voice, he spoke with such certainty that his words fell like shards of ice into the heated confusion.

This time the silence lingered.

"We couldn't," Gulien said at last, but not with conviction.

"If Prince Gajdosik says we could, then I'm sure we could!" Oressa declared. "Gulien, do you really want to gamble that Father's still in control, and not Bherijda? If we don't do anything, we might be handing everything to Bherijda, but if you come back and throw Bherijda's scorpion soldiers back into the sea, *nobody* will want any other king but you and we'll be able to depose Father again, permanently this time, get the Kieba's artifact back for her, *and* get rid of Bherijda all at once! Gulien, Father doesn't *have* to have everything his way! Not this time!"

Kelian said, "Oressa—Your Highness—"

Prince Gajdosik said flatly, "Her Highness's judgment is, as always, acute. I consider it extremely unlikely that Osir Madalin retains control of Caras. The telling detail is not the presence of my brother's soldiers in the city, but the orders issued to your own to stay off the streets. That is not an order given by a king who is free to act as he will."

"Exactly!" said Oressa.

Kelian started to answer, a sharp response judging by his expression, but Gulien held up a hand abruptly and cut him off. There was a pause, while Gulien looked at Oressa and then at Gajdosik and then, for a long time, at nothing: the dust hazing the air, the sweep of an eagle through the empty sky.

At last Gulien turned back to them. He met Gajdosik's eyes and asked in a clear, low voice, "Prince Gajdosik, if I wish to take your officers and men into battle, will they take orders from mine?" He paused and then asked even more quietly, "Will you take orders from me?"

Gajdosik drew breath to answer, but Oressa said swiftly, before he could, "No, Gulien. It has to be the other way around!"

Everyone stared at her. Mostly they just looked shocked. Prince Gajdosik, too, stared at her. He had paled. Oressa did not know why. His expression was no longer exactly neutral, but it was impossible to read.

"It's obvious, isn't it?" she said. "Well, it *is!* I mean, you have to decide what to do, Gulien, but when it comes to actually putting this plan into motion, well, which of us has had recent successful experience invading and conquering Caras with a small force of Tamaristan soldiers? Well?"

Gulien began, "Oressa—"

Oressa said firmly, "Prince Gajdosik's men are ours. They're allies, or at least they're not enemies. If there's fighting, they'll be on our side. I mean, there aren't exactly any other sides they can possibly be on anymore. Not only does Gajdosik have a lot more men, but his are experienced soldiers. They've done this before. Ours are mostly city guardsmen, not even militia, and they may be good, but that isn't the same! That means the question is, will *our* people take orders from *his*? And I think they will, to save Caras."

Kelian started to make a sharp rejoinder, but Gulien again put up a hand to stop him. Gulien looked at Kelian and then at Oressa and finally turned once more to Gajdosik. He began to say something but then visibly changed his mind. Oressa could see he truly did not know what to do.

Then the Tamaristan prince dropped to one knee. He said formally, "Your Highness, if you will permit me tactical command during this crisis, I swear to you I will do my best to serve your interests and the interests of your country."

"Prince Gajdosik—"

"Your Highness. In this crisis, your goals and mine align precisely. I would prefer to see you king of Carastind rather than your father. Above all I do not want my brother to take power here. A divided command will not serve. I will take your orders if I must. But I beg you will command your people to take mine." Gajdosik bowed his head and waited. His hands, folded across his knee, were open and relaxed, but the muscles in his back and neck were taut.

"Gulien!" said Oressa. She wanted to remind them both that all the Tamaristan soldiers were hers anyway. Only she knew it wouldn't help. It didn't even matter whether it was true or not: What mattered was what kind of alliance Gulien and Prince Gajdosik worked out between them, and if they couldn't work something out, then they might as well send to her father or Bherijda or whoever currently held Caras, asking for terms. It wasn't fair. It didn't even make *sense* except if you were a man, but she knew it was true. She waited, all but holding her breath.

"Your Highness," Gulien said at last. "For the duration of this crisis, please do me the favor of assuming tactical command."

Gajdosik's head came up. Rising smoothly to his feet, he swung around and stared back over their mixed company with focused intensity, clearly already assigning each man to a plan he held in his mind. Well, Oressa realized, that was ridiculous. Nobody could possibly have come up with a plan as fast as that—

"We have several advantages," Prince Gajdosik said crisply. "Surprise may well be one of them. We won't depend on it, but we'll certainly encourage it. Juranda," he said to one of his own people, "give the men a ten-minute warning: We'll ride out at once. Rearm our people and make sure everyone has a full water flask. You, Fellin, how far from here to the next farm with a good well?"

"Uh . . ." The man was taken aback, but rallied quickly. "Not far— there's a farm less than an hour's ride on. Um, m'lord."

"We'll fill the flasks again there," Gajdosik said to his officer, and waved the man away. He went on to Gulien. "We do need to send men north to the rest of my people. Some of my men, and some of yours, also, Your Highness. They must explain what's passed here and bring my people to Caras."

"Impossible!" snapped Kelian. "Men in a mixed company will spend so much time brawling with one another, they won't notice if half a thousand scorpion soldiers meet them on the way!"

"Mattin won't brawl, or allow his people to quarrel with the Tamaristans," Oressa said sharply, with a glance for the sergeant, who came forward a step in acknowledgment and gave them all a stolid little nod. It was indeed impossible to imagine the sergeant allowing any nonsense of that sort, and though Kelian opened his mouth to argue, he obviously couldn't find the words because he shut it again without speaking.

"Fellin can go with them, too," Oressa said, beckoning to the man. "That'll be an easier ride, at least at first, and he can explain in more detail just what's been happening in Caras. *He* won't brawl with Gajdosik's man, either. Or, at least, if he doesn't keep his mind on business," she added warningly, "I'll tell his wife the *real* truth about that summer he spent in Little Caras."

Fellin winced. Kelian looked taken aback. Gulien cast his eyes heavenward and sighed. Gajdosik lifted an eyebrow and nearly smiled.

"And Laasat can go," Oressa added, ignoring them all. "And a handful of Tamaristans so our peoples can start getting used to each other."

"That will do," agreed Gajdosik. He went on, speaking to Gulien. "Though we won't deliberately send word to Caras, I'd ordinarily expect news of our coming to run before us right to the palace doors. Some word certainly will, but with the immense confusion of recent days, it should be impossible for anyone to know what to believe." He turned to Kelian. "Take down Prince Gulien's banners," he ordered.

"Your Highness—" Kelian looked at Gulien.

"Do as he says," Gulien snapped, and glanced at Oressa as the man reluctantly left to carry out his orders. It was a faintly accusing glance. Oressa shrugged apologetically. Who'd have thought *Kelian* would be so halfhearted about everything? How could she not have noticed this about him before? It was hard to believe she'd ever thought running off to marry him would be a good idea. She was glad she hadn't tried it: He'd have been impossible to get *moving*.

"If he doesn't accept our decision, we'll be forced to replace him," said Gajdosik, adding to Gulien, "But it would be best to keep a stable chain of command if we can. Ah, good, Umank, there you are. Find some green cloth and tack together a decent copy of my brother's scorpion. Yes, you must do it while we ride; you shall have to contrive—the banners needn't fool a close examination."

"Well, *that's* good," said the officer he addressed, and hurried away.

"Now—" Gajdosik reached out absently to accept his horse's rein as someone brought the animal up, and swung into the saddle. All his earlier weakness seemed to have passed off, or he had set it aside by a sheer effort of will. "Now, Gulien," he went on. "Once we get to Caras, we'll find half our battle already fought. Our enemies might ardently desire to keep track of men entering and leaving the city, but the task is impossible. No one will have a clear idea who should be where or be able to distinguish strangers from citizens."

"You . . . We'll go straight in, then?" Gulien asked. He must have noticed, as Oressa had, that Prince Gajdosik was now addressing him simply by name, but he didn't comment. He seemed, more than anything, relieved at Gajdosik's confidence. Oressa certainly found the Tamaristan prince a pleasure to watch, now that he was moving again. She had a buoyant hope that Gajdosik and her brother really *would* be able to work together. She found herself believing that they *could* defeat her father—compared to him she barely remembered Gajdosik's brother— and that even now everything might work out. And surely neither Gulien nor Gajdosik would be able to turn against each other after *this*.

"The objective now, as it has always been, is control of the palace and of certain important persons. Long-term physical control of the city must be impossible for Bherijda for exactly the same reason it would have been impossible for me: He can't have enough men. His position depends on controlling Osir, or else he must depend on your father's goodwill."

Oressa made a scornful sound at the idea that anyone could possibly depend on her father's goodwill. She nudged her horse into a faster gait to keep up with the two men.

"Now," Gajdosik went on, ignoring her, "my brother will be dangerous and his men may prove an obstacle, but it's possible your father's supporters will also prove intractable. Gulien, I believe we can get past Bherijda and take control of the palace, but you must have some clear idea how you will then counter your father's influence. You must consider this as we ride."

Gulien nodded. They splashed across the shallow river, riding into the westering sun. It wouldn't be so very long until dark, but Oressa guessed they wouldn't stop before they got to Terand and maybe not then. At least the moon was nearly full. She asked, fascinated by Gajdosik's swift decisions, "Yes, and about taking the palace?"

"We'll divide our forces," Gajdosik said briskly. "I hate to do it, because we haven't enough men even if we all stay together, but we've no choice. Gulien, once we get close to Caras, I'm going to want a small group of Carastindin men to carry your banner toward the main gates. They'll offer Bherijda misleading information, or Osir if necessary. Or both. These must be loyal men, but they needn't number more than half a dozen." His eyes glinted with sudden humor, though he didn't smile. "It would be best if they've a taste for practical jokes. Perhaps Her Highness can suggest suitable men."

"Of course," Oressa assured him. She took a deep breath, gathered her nerve, and added, "I can do better: *I'll* go with them. No, listen, it's a good idea! Whoever's at the gates will know me; if I'm there, it won't occur to anybody there's a trick. I can make Bherijda believe anything you want—I can even make Father believe anything you want." She hesitated, finding herself less confident about that than she'd expected once she put it into words. "Well," she said, "I think I can, anyway! As long as he doesn't have reason to be suspicious. Anyway, I'll have a better chance than anybody else. I'll say Gulien's still in the Kieba's mountain. I'll say she's teaching him to use remnants of god-magic; *that'll* drop a hawk among the pigeons—"

"This is all completely out of the question," Gulien declared.

"We can't possibly risk you!" Gajdosik said at the same moment.

Oressa half wanted to say, *Oh, all right, then, never mind.* Instead, she gave them both a scornful glare, pretending she wasn't in the least worried, because she knew she was right. "What perfect nonsense. *Nobody* will hurt me on purpose: I'm a valuable commodity, remember?"

"Indeed," said Gajdosik grimly. "You will therefore immediately ride back to that farm below the Kieba's mountain and *stay there.*"

"A much better idea!" agreed Gulien.

"No, it isn't! It's ridiculous," declared Oressa. "I'm no use to anybody if I'm stuck hiding on some *farm*, and you know it, too, O great tactician Your Highness Gajdosik! You know I'm right, and if you try to leave me behind, I'll follow you; and you can't spare men to guard me either, so don't make threats you don't intend to carry out!"

"Your Highness," Gajdosik said sharply, "you promised to obey my orders."

Oressa raised her eyebrows. "I most certainly did not, Your Highness. Gulien promised to have our *men* obey your orders. Besides, if you get to be tactical commander, hadn't you better think tactically?"

Pressed beyond patience, Gajdosik reined his horse to a halt so suddenly that it nearly reared. He snapped, with no pretense of civility at all, "Fool of a woman, you are not going to put yourself into my brother's hands! You are indeed valuable! Even if Bherijda doesn't realize Gulien is in the city, he will know quite well he can use you to establish his own claim to Carastind!"

Gulien's mouth crooked, not without sympathy. He advised Gajdosik, "It's not that you're wrong, but you'll find it's very little use to tell Oressa what she may and may not do. Or she'd hardly be here with us now, would she?"

"But it certainly worked out for the best, didn't it? Your Highness, I won't be a hostage," Oressa assured Gajdosik, deliberately blithe. "That's exactly what Bherijda will think, I'm sure. He'll lock me up somewhere, no doubt, but I'll get out whenever I want. Gulien, tell him."

There was a pause. Gulien very clearly thought about not telling Gajdosik anything of the sort, and Oressa gave her brother a warning stare, meaning that she really would follow them if they tried to leave her behind. That must have been clear, because at last he said, reluctantly, "Oressa knows the palace better than anyone. All the hidden doors and things that Bherijda can't possibly know about."

"Hidden doors?" asked Kelian, riding nearby. "Really?"

"Secret doors and passages are everywhere in the palace. There's nowhere Bherijda can lock me up," Oressa declared.

Gajdosik gave Oressa a long look, perhaps remembering how his men had caught her in the first place.

"Besides, you really do need me to do this, and you know it. It might be different if you had days to arrange things, but you don't, and we have to have things go right the first time because there won't be a second chance. There's no point in arguing. You must know you'll have to agree with me at the end."

Gajdosik, who had opened his mouth, closed it again without speaking.

"Good, then," said Oressa. She started her horse moving again, compelling the men to come after her or be left behind. She pretended to be satisfied and brave and not the least bit uncertain. "That's settled, then," she declared. "Meanwhile, I guess you'll get in through the broken places in the wall, sneak around to the west, and then come up from the harbor flying scorpion and eagle banners? That's a good idea because you're right—absolutely *nobody* will know for sure who you are or that you're not really Bherijda's or Maranajdis's men. Well, except for Bherijda, I guess, but I'm sure you have something figured out for when you get that far."

Oressa knew she was right, but after the arguing stopped and she started thinking about riding boldly up to the gates and announcing herself to Bherijda's soldiers, she started getting nervous again. She almost wanted Gulien or Gajdosik to pick up the argument again and this time win. Only they couldn't, because she really *was* right and they really *did* need her to play her role exactly the way she'd said.

But it got more frightening to think about as they got closer to Caras. They stopped only when they absolutely had to, so their second dawn on the road found them not so very far away from Caras. Oressa had never been so tired or sore in her life, except then she started thinking about facing Gajdosik's brother and her own father, and that made her so nervous she could ignore her stiffness and exhaustion.

Gajdosik mostly rode aside with Gulien, talking to him about the rest of the plan where Oressa couldn't hear. He said flatly, daring her to change her mind, that this was because if she was going to be a hostage even briefly, she had better know as little as possible. She rolled her eyes with exaggerated scorn to show him she knew he was trying to scare her and, pretending she felt not the faintest flicker of nervousness or doubt, dropped back to ride with the small group of Carastindin soldiers she'd chosen to join her in the deception. Kelian, too, because he had insisted on joining her: Oressa guessed he must have decided he had to protect her, and maybe he'd even begun to like the plan. She'd chosen four other men: Maki and Kevan, and Big Fellin, who was naturally a much smaller man than the other Fellin, and Evad, who was famous for brawling in taverns without ever getting caught starting the fights.

"It's my innocent looks," he said, gesturing to indicate his much-battered brawler's face, and they all laughed, even Kelian, though he was still inclined to be a little stiff.

"Everybody needs to look as innocent as Evad," Oressa emphasized. "We've all been to the Kieba's mountain, and Gulien's still there, and we never saw the faintest glimpse of Prince Gajdosik or any Tamaristan, and we have no idea what's been happening in Caras—I guess that's even true—but as long as the Kieba doesn't object, it's fine with us!"

"We're shocked, *shocked* to find Prince Bherijda in the city," put in Big Fellin, who really did have a love for sly jokes. "But if King Osir thinks allying with Bherijda is a good idea, well, anything the king supports, we're all for it."

"Exactly!" said Oressa. She gave Big Fellin a sidelong glance, thinking that maybe this would all work perfectly after all.

Then they came around a curve of the road and looked down the long slope of the drylands that ran down toward the sea, and there was Caras before them, and the gates with the merciless sun shining on the wrecked wall beyond, and all at once Oressa wasn't tired at *all*, and everything seemed suddenly to be moving much too fast.

"Be *careful*," Gulien told her before she took her little group away from the main company. His tone made it clear he knew this was hopeless advice. He added, trying to smile, "Stay off roofs if people start blowing things up!"

"You worry too much! I never fall," Oressa told her brother with a bravado she tried hard to really feel. She added in a whisper, leaning from the saddle to embrace him, "You'll be doing the hard part. You be careful too."

"You don't even know what we'll be doing!" Gulien said in mock outrage. "Unless you've been sneaking around, listening where you shouldn't!"

"No, but I can guess." She let him go and straightened. "Be careful—be safe—I'll see you in the palace." She blinked hard and didn't wail, *It's not* fair. *We've done* so much. *Why can't we just go home and have everything be* over?

"Your Highness," said Prince Gajdosik, his tone unreadable.

Oressa turned to him. To her surprise, she was almost as afraid for him as for her brother. She wished there were living gods she could pray to for their safety. She said sharply, "You be careful too! If anything happens to you, I don't want to have to tell Laasat!"

"No," said Gajdosik, and just looked at her for a long moment. He said at last, "Fortune favor you, Your Highness, and attend your efforts."

"All of ours, I hope!" said Oressa, and turned her horse away hastily before she could change her mind. She was sure they didn't stand and watch her ride away, because that would be a stupid waste of time. She didn't look back, either, because she didn't want to see the distance between them widen.

The main gates were heavy, made of the whole trunks of huge trees imported from northern Illian. The logs had been smoothed, polished, bound with brass, and magicked against breaking or burning. They were still in fine shape. The wall to the left of the gates had been magicked too, but not with the same care or strength, apparently, because it lay in shattered ruins for thirty feet. With a hole like that, there wasn't much point in closing the gates, which stood wide open. There were soldiers watching people come and go—not many people. Admittedly, Oressa had never been down to the main gates at dusk in her life, but she suspected the presence of those soldiers inhibited normal Carastind traffic. Even from a distance, it was clear the soldiers were Tamaristan.

"What would I do if I came back to Caras and saw soldiers like those at the gates and hadn't had any advance warning?" Oressa asked Big Fellin.

The man shrugged. "Depends how confident you are of the Kieba's support and, you know, *active* goodwill."

Oressa thought about it. "Let's say I'm pretty sure," she decided at last.

"Then if you want to ride straight up to them and demand to know what's going on and who's their lord and who told them to watch the gates, we could do that, Your Highness. That'd be reasonable—if we had the Kieba at our backs. Too bad we don't have one of those spider things," he added wistfully. "Then it'd be *easy*."

"If we had a spider thing, we wouldn't need subterfuge." Oressa wished very much they *did* have a spider thing and *didn't* need subterfuge, but since they didn't and did and the whole point was to get the soldiers to take her to the palace so she could create a huge misleading fuss, she added, "But we'll pretend the rest of it is all true and ride straight up to them, just like you said. Remember we don't know anything—but we're confident the Kieba supports us. And remember we're not supposed to fight. We're *supposed* to get captured, although I guess if we can talk those men or Bherijda himself into surrendering, that'd be all right too."

All the men grinned, though Maki, the youngest, looked nervous, and Evad looked like he wished they *could* fight rather than meekly surrender.

"All right," said Oressa. She put on her most confident princess manner and nudged her horse into a fast trot, straight at the Tamaristan soldiers.

And it should have worked. It was going to work—it *was* working: The soldiers were startled, wary of their apparent confidence, impressed by Oressa's royal outrage when their captain dared lay a hand on her horse's rein. Everything was *fine*. Until they actually came to the palace and were immediately escorted to the pink atrium, where her father, with an air of never having lost control of events for even a moment, received them.

Prince Bherijda stood beside her father, like an ally or even a friend, but King Osir hadn't changed at all. He looked exactly the same: cool and uninvolved and perfectly immovable. Seeing him now, Oressa found it almost incredible that she'd ever thought Gulien could take their father's place in Caras or in this palace. She found herself believing that the age could turn and the Kieba vanish into time and that her father would *still* be right here, still compelling the world to work exactly the way he wanted it to by the sheer ruthless force of his will.

Except that Prince Bherijda leaned casually on the back of her father's chair, which no one ever did, and it was he who gestured for his soldiers to release Oressa's men and stand back. Oressa didn't know how he dared treat her father so dismissively, but then the Tamaristan prince did seem arrogant.

Prince Bherijda was younger than she'd expected. He looked like he was only about her own age, twenty or so, though she knew he was several years older than that. He was dark, like Gajdosik, and like his brother, he had blue eyes, though his were a paler color. There was something about the angle of the cheekbones that was the same, but the resemblance wasn't strong. Oressa decided at last that the difference lay more in how the two men presented themselves. Gajdosik was all brilliant energy; when he did something, he put everything he had into it.

Bherijda wasn't like that at all. He was shorter and plumper than his brother, but that wasn't why he looked languid and uninvolved. That was all deliberate affectation. He wore a cloisonné scorpion medallion, green and black, pinned at his throat. Oressa recognized that. But he also wore some kind of amulet on a chain around his neck: a flat, round medallion of gray crystal as broad as a man's hand. Runes sparkled on its face, as though light was shining out from inside it. Oressa had no idea what that was, except she was immediately sure it was a thing of power, a fragment of some dead god's tool. She could tell Bherijda was proud of it by the way he lifted a hand to trace its runes when he noticed her looking at it. She was immediately afraid of it.

Prince Bherijda stroked his thumb across his medallion again and smiled at Oressa, and that wasn't real either. He smiled like he was hiding horrible thoughts behind his smile. Gajdosik only ever smiled when he really was amused or pleased about something. Bherijda's smile was a lie straight through. Oressa hated him instantly.

"So this is your lovely daughter," Bherijda murmured. "One gathers she has been visiting the neighbors."

The Tamaristan prince spoke Esse very well, with even less of an accent than Gajdosik, but Oressa loathed his voice—too smooth and too *nice*. Ignoring him, she said to her father, pretending to be confused rather than frightened, "I guess a Tamaristan ally might be useful, but I don't know whether the Kieba will like it—"

"The Kieba has declared herself my enemy," Oressa's father said flatly. "Fortunately, this is not an insupportable difficulty." *He* wasn't wearing an amulet or medallion or anything: Oressa looked for one, thinking of the artifact the Kieba wanted, but she could see nothing. Her father wasn't even wearing any rings or anything like that. But then he said that about being the Kieba's enemy. She was sure he was. She was sure he meant to *use* Bherijda against the Kieba somehow, even if the Tamaristan prince wasn't smart enough to realize it.

Oressa longed to say *Prince Gajdosik didn't think he'd meet any insupportable difficulties either and look what happened to him*, but of course she couldn't. She meekly lowered her gaze. She felt like she'd never even left the palace or gone to the Kieba's mountain. She felt like nothing of that had ever happened, and her father was exactly the same, and she was, and the only thing that mattered was appeasing him and slipping out of his sight.

But that wasn't what she was supposed to do at all.

She started to say something about the Kieba and about Gulien, she hardly knew what, something plausible, only Kelian moved first. He took one step forward, toward Oressa's father, dropped to one knee, and said, "Sire, I fear your daughter has fallen in with dangerous factions. She's deceiving you. It's not her fault, I'm sure. Prince Gajdosik has magicked both Princess Oressa and your son, and he's bringing up a force of men from the harbor right now, meaning to destroy Prince Bherijda and overthrow you, sire. I think Gajdosik means to murder Prince Gulien and marry Oressa by force—"

"What are you *saying*?" cried Oressa, outraged and horrified. She had never thought Kelian was an *idiot*, and now he came out with *this*?

"What, indeed?" murmured her father, his tone rather blank. He stared at Oressa.

Prince Bherijda, straightening out of his indolent pose, snapped his finger for his soldiers to secure her few men. Oressa gestured for them not to fight. They had never meant to fight. They hadn't prepared for battle, and besides, Bherijda's men had taken all their swords. None of her men had more than a boot knife, and now, when she longed for a way out, there *was* no way.

"We must apprehend my brother!" said Bherijda.

Kelian said urgently, "Prince Gulien is with him, and they're carrying scorpion banners and the eagle banners of the Garamanaji—"

"Did you hear?" Bherijda snapped, speaking to an officer of his, a tough-looking man who straightened to attention and waited for orders. Decisiveness was a trait Bherijda unfortunately but very clearly shared with his brother, because he said, without a trace of his previous indolence, "I want my brother alive. Is that clear? Not the men; kill them all, but don't on any account harm Gajdosik! He will surrender if you promise to spare his men—make any threats, any promises, but take him safely. Is that clear?"

Oressa's father stood up slowly. Though he should have appeared powerless in this room filled with Bherijda's soldiers, he nevertheless drew all eyes. He said in a cool, level voice, "If *my* son is harmed in this, Prince Bherijda, I'll have *your* brother's head for it."

Bherijda gave him an astonished look but said smoothly, "Of course we shall take all possible care," and added to his men, "See to that as well." Then he smiled at Oressa and said, "And see Her Highness to her rooms. I'm sure she is exhausted if she's had to deal with my brother."

Oressa gritted her teeth, trying to decide if Bherijda had meant that the way it sounded.

"Her Highness claims she knows all the secret doors in the palace and swears she can get out of any room in which she's imprisoned," Kelian put in quickly.

"Secret doors?" said Prince Bherijda, his eyebrows rising.

"*Does* she?" murmured her father, gazing at Oressa with sharpening interest.

Oressa said nothing. There did not seem to be anything left to say.

CHAPTER 18

The dusty streets of Caras, crowded on both sides by the rickety frames of market stalls and by the blank whitewashed plaster walls of shops, seemed at once familiar and strange to Gulien. The colorful awnings of the shops had all been taken down; the market stalls stood forsaken and quiet; even the public fountain at the edge of the Crescent bathhouse was deserted. Or not quite deserted, Gulien saw: An old man had come to the fountain with a clay jug, but he had withdrawn softly into the recessed doorway of the bathhouse at their approach.

It should have been a young woman at the fountain, not an old man. It was girls and young women who fetched water for their families, lingered at the fountains to meet their friends, and bought sesame cakes and sweet ices and brittle amaranth candy from the venders who crowded about to take advantage of their custom. Today there were no young women, no venders calling their wares. Only one old man and a grim silence.

"They do think we're your brother's men," Gulien said to Prince Gajdosik. He had not thought the hastily made scorpion banners looked very convincing. The man who had made them had not had very much green cloth to work with; each long banner was a different shade, and one banner had been pieced together out of three different kinds of cloth. The black scorpions looked hardly more persuasive: neither painted nor embroidered, but simply cut out of black cloth and pinned onto the banners. The pins glittered in the sunlight, to Gulien's unvoiced dismay. No real banner would be stuck through with metal pins.

But Prince Gajdosik had seemed satisfied. "People see what they believe they should see," he had said, and as they had found their way through a broken place in the wall, he had gestured the standard-bearers to take their places with those false scorpions.

Now the Tamaristan prince answered only, "So long as Bherijda thinks so too, for just long enough."

"And as long as we're not ambushed by my own people," Gulien agreed. Privately he was almost disappointed that the people of Caras did not try to hinder the Tamaristan invaders—though he had to acknowledge that their king's apparent acquiescence to this invasion must be disheartening.

He did not believe for one moment that his father had actually yielded Caras to any Tamaristan prince. But that his father would go to considerable lengths to make Prince Bherijda believe that he had—he could believe that. Osir Madalin would like nothing more than to arrange things so that in the end Bherijda, no matter his advantages of conventional arms or magical artifacts, would find himself utterly outmaneuvered and defeated. Then Osir would calmly go about restoring Caras and erasing all signs that any upstart Tamaristan princes had ever interfered with his city or his country. Gulien believed that.

After that his father would take whatever artifact he had captured from Prince Bherijda—this Tonkaïan's Resolve—and go on to pursue a war with the Kieba, a war that would lead to utter disaster for him if he lost and possibly to worse disaster for the entire world if he won. Gulien believed that too.

He almost remembered Bherijda's artifact, a fragmentary and discomfiting memory of sun-shot power that left earth and trees and stones and people slumping slowly into formless gray ash, bitter ash that blew away on a cold wind. Tonkaïan's Resolve. Tonkaïan had been one of the shadowed goddesses, beautiful and terrible. Her aspect had been destruction-and-remaking. Part of Gulien seemed to half remember this fragment of her power, wicked and dangerous, that spawned plagues of dissolution. It had been part of something greater once, something that had been used for creation rather than merely destruction, but now it was only a fragment and could not be used for any good purpose.

Frowning, Gulien pressed the tips of his fingers against his eyes for a moment, trying to remember. All he could see was the red darkness behind his eyelids. He had never read Tonkaïan's name in any of his books. He was almost sure he hadn't. That wasn't *his* memory. It was the *other* memory, the memory embedded in the kephalos, shattered images and knife-sharp splinters of urgent emotion carried out of the past. They came to him more compellingly now that he marched through Caras at the head of a foreign—largely foreign—troop, his own men and Gajdosik's at his back. He almost seemed to be somewhere else, someone else. He felt as though the familiar city somehow echoed with the voices of the dead.

Maybe Bherijda's artifact called up those voices. Maybe Tonkaïan's Resolve preserved the voices of everyone it destroyed, held them forever in crystalline memory. . . . He could almost envision what that might be like. He shuddered.

"Forgotten *gods*," Gajdosik swore suddenly. "We can't get through *this*! Which way should we go now?"

Gulien looked around, blinking, embarrassed to find he had let his wits wander. He tried to drag his attention out of the fragmentary past and back to the immediate present. They had come, he saw, to Camian's Way, a good, broad road that should have led straight to the palace. But Gajdosik was right: No one could get through Camian's Way here. The whole width of the street, for as far as Gulien could see—admittedly not very far, through all the clutter—was blocked with overturned wagons, immense barrels and kegs, and broken stone hauled from the breached wall or perhaps from the shattered wing of the palace. Enough men working hard could clear the way, given enough time and given peace to work. But the brightly painted houses and dun-colored apartment buildings and whitewashed shops along this part of the street were tall and thick walled, with narrow windows to keep out the heat. There were no windows at street level, and furtive movement at the higher windows suggested that no Tamaristan company could count on peacefully clearing that tangled barricade out of their way.

Gulien found himself rather more cheered than otherwise by this evidence of his people's disinclination to accept the invader's presence in their city, even if it was inconvenient just at the moment. He thought, briefly, of striding forward and calling out his name, shouting up to those watchers in the windows to tell them who he was and gain their support. But no. There would be no way to stop his name going forward and out, carried by brave men who thought they could rally to him and take back their city. Then Prince Bherijda would be forewarned of their coming. He shook his head. There were tools that could have worked here, tools that could clear the street in moments. Tonkaïan's Resolve, of course and, all gods dead and forgotten, he did not want to think of that artifact waking in Caras. But other tools, not so dangerous. Gulien almost knew what they were, almost remembered the names of the gods who had made them or used them.

"Gulien!" snapped Gajdosik. "Which way should we go?"

"Oh—" Gulien flinched and looked around. "Yes, back that way a quarter mile and we can cut around toward the Pengolian Square. That's far too wide to barricade. From there we can take Culver's Lane, or even go straight through the park. That might be better—"

"We're taking too cursed much time as it is," muttered Gajdosik. "Yes, I remember the King's Park from the maps. It's got its own wall, isn't that so? Well, we'll see how that looks when we get there." And he lifted a hand to signal the retreat.

A thrown rock, rough-edged and heavy enough to kill a man, smashed down a handbreadth away as Gulien turned, and a pottery jug followed it as he stepped quickly sideways. Prince Gajdosik ducked and cursed. Gulien, also ducking, resisted the urge to wave approval of the thrower's spirit, if not his aim. But he was glad the people in those buildings didn't have crossbows.

The King's Park did indeed have its own surrounding wall, separating its fountains and raked sand and gravel pathways from the rest of the city. Its wall was intact, which turned out to be awkward, as they met another Tamaristan company—a real Tamaristan company of arquebusiers— just as they reached the park, so that they had to decide what to do: keep up their own pretense or fight right there, with their backs against the park's wall and no way to break away if the fighting went badly. The other company was right across Pengolian Square, so they were a fair distance away, but to Gulien the difference between the real scorpion banners and their own makeshift banners was immediately and glaringly obvious.

"Scorpions everywhere!" growled Gajdosik, which wasn't actually true, as this was the first such company they'd seen since entering the city. It was an undersized company, hardly better than a half company, no more than eighty men or so, but that was far too many to brush out of the way.

The scorpion soldiers were on foot, but so were they all: Gajdosik had known his brother's men would be on foot, and so of course if they would seem to be scorpion soldiers themselves, they must leave their horses behind. And so they had. Now Gulien, at least, regretted that decision. Horses were difficult to manage in narrow streets, but if they'd all been mounted, he'd have been confident they could take on eighty of Bherijda's men and win handily. But even so . . . He muttered, "We're not close enough to the palace yet. If we fight now—"

"I know," said Gajdosik grimly "Let's hope they're sun-blind, under firm orders to be somewhere else, *and* too busy swaggering to pay attention to what's under their noses." He signaled for his standard-bearers to dip their banners in salute and stepped up the pace to a fast march.

Gulien looked uneasily over his shoulder. "They haven't stopped."

"They haven't stopped *yet*," snapped Gajdosik. *He* didn't turn his head. Gawking around would be thoroughly out of character for the commander of a military detachment, Gulien presumed.

Gulien said, "We'll be around the corner and out of their sight in just a—" Then he cut that off, squinted, and said tensely, "They're turning toward us."

Gajdosik still didn't turn to look. "All of them, or just the commander's aide?"

"Looks like all of them."

Gajdosik snapped his fingers, and one of his men hurried up.

"Go tell their commander some tale," Gajdosik ordered the man. "Something plausible—special orders. We've heard that Prince Gulien is in hiding somewhere—" He glanced impatiently at Gulien, who said immediately, "Below the town house north of the next square over that way, in the cellars or near their cistern—that should seem plausible."

"Tell them that," Gajdosik ordered. "Five ships, my brother brought. That commander can't know every man. Make up a name. Sound confident and he may believe you. Slow him down for us, Marakat."

"Sir," said the man, without flinching, turned on his heel, and strode away.

Gulien couldn't restrain himself from staring after the man. It seemed unlikely to him that the other commander would believe Marakat's story; it seemed far more likely that Gajdosik had just sacrificed him. No doubt that had been the only thing to do. He said nothing. There seemed nothing to say.

Following the park's wall took them around a corner and out of sight of Pengolian Square. Though Gulien listened, he could hear no angry shouts behind them. Maybe . . . maybe they would get away with this deception for just a little bit longer. For just long enough.

Around the park, and then they turned onto another broad street, this one showing signs of a halfhearted attempt at a barricade, but all the debris had been cleared out of the way and the people here had not, evidently, tried again. They were very near the palace now; no doubt the scorpion presence was heavier here and resistance more difficult. Especially with the militia and the palace guard ordered to stay in barracks.

There was no sign of pillage or recent burning. The shops were closed, the shopkeepers absent from the streets, but the shops were intact, and Gulien hoped that the shopkeepers were also intact. There had been no sign of that kind of damage anywhere in Caras, no bodies in the streets, no slaughtered animals or smoldering, broken homes or screaming women. Whatever bargain Gulien's father had made with Prince Bherijda, it had done that much, at least. The only damage Gulien could see had plainly happened days ago, during Gajdosik's own abortive attempt to take the city.

Gulien could imagine so much worse. Images flickered through his mind's eye, unfocused and distant: another city plundered and burned, Esai, the Flower of the East, the Painted City, its splendid domed towers broken, the trees of its beautiful gardens cut down and burned, the decapitated heads of its people piled up into a mountain, sightless eyes staring, dead mouths gaping, crows and black kites and carrion vultures overhead, a thin stream of refugees stumbling away from the vast column of black smoke rising behind them. He had known the danger, they had known the danger. The tattooed barbarians of the plains had always threatened the settled peoples of the east, but he had believed, they had believed, he had believed Esai strong enough to hold, but they had been wrong, he had been inexcusably wrong—

"Gulien!" snapped Gajdosik, and Gulien flinched, shuddering and blinking, glad to be recalled from *that* memory into a clearer awareness of himself. Esai's destruction had been terrible enough that even this present moment was better—even marching through Caras disguised as the enemy.

Then he saw the Tamaristan soldiers drawn up before them in front of the palace, waiting for them. Or waiting for something—Gulien looked at Gajdosik's grim expression and knew the other man's impression was identical to his own. He wasn't certain that he wouldn't have preferred to stay lost in a distant memory, no matter how terrible.

"This is a trap," Gajdosik snapped, confirming Gulien's fears. "They were waiting for us." He indicated the road to their right, also blocked by Tamaristan soldiers, and said bitingly, "And the other company is coming up from our rear. This is a trap, and we've walked straight into it. They were expecting us."

Gulien said, instantly afraid for her, "Oressa." What had his sister walked into?

"She wouldn't have betrayed us, of course." Gajdosik sounded gratifyingly certain of it. "She'd have told some clever tale as though it were truer than the sky and made my cursed brother believe every word. But *something* gave us away from the start—from before we even entered the city—or they'd never have put all this together in time. I wouldn't have thought Bherijda so perceptive."

"My father," said Gulien. "He might have realized what we were doing." He felt sick. He should have known that his father would be ahead of them from the beginning, every step of the way. But he had not thought of coming against anything like this. Now he did not know what to do. He said, "We can't fight that many."

"We can. We would all die, but we could certainly fight. It's not what they're after, though, or they wouldn't be holding their positions; they'd be advancing. On the other hand, this is your city, not theirs, and your people are plainly not resigned to my brother's presence here. If we cast down our black scorpions and raised up *your* banner, Prince Gulien, what would your people do?"

"Against all those soldiers?" At least three hundred, Gulien thought, maybe closer to four. And if Bherijda had known they were coming, he would have covered at least the western approach to the palace as well; he would be able to pull men off that approach and reinforce his men here.

Worse, Gulien had no idea what his father might do, or might have done already. If he was truly allied with Bherijda—not impossible if he thought his Tamaristan ally was his key to destroying the Kieba and taking her power—he would use Bherijda and then when a convenient moment arrived slide a knife into his back so smoothly the Tamaristan prince would never feel it go in. And he would not thank Gulien for interfering.

Only that would leave the Kieba dead or cast down, and after that, no matter what Osir Madalin believed . . . After that, most likely the world would end, as one artifact after another spawned plagues that could not be stopped. Someday the world might be able to stand on its own without the Kieba. But Gulien knew that this was not that day.

He should have done something to make sure his father could not possibly reclaim his power in Caras. He should have done *something* to make sure no other Tamaristan force could possibly get a foothold in the city. The harbor cannons—he ought to have made sure they were reset where they could do some good. He should have had the walls repaired. All gods dead and forgotten, how could he have let any of this *happen*?

He said, "We *have* to fight."

"We can't win," Gajdosik said impatiently. "Unless the city rises. Will Caras rise? If you raise up your banner, will her people rally to you to throw back Bherijda's men? Will they do it when they can plainly see you're allied with me? They'd have to be blind to mistake my people for Carastindin, no matter what banner we raise up."

"I don't . . . I don't know." Gulien was sinkingly certain the people of Caras would not rally. Not fast enough. Not if his father ordered the militia and guard to support Prince Bherijda. Some of the men of Caras would not obey that order, but others would, and the confusion would be Bherijda's ally.

Gajdosik must have seen something of this in his face, because he gave a short, sharp nod and said, "Then our choices are unfortunately limited."

"Look," said Gulien, indicating one man who was coming forward alone. "They're requesting parley."

"Of course they are," snapped Gajdosik. He cast a swift, hunted look around at the streets, empty except for Bherijda's men and their own company, and at the town houses and shops that lined the streets.

Gulien followed his example, looking hopelessly for options. He could not find any. Here, close to the palace, where the wealthy merchants and highborn courtiers lived, the narrow windows of those houses and shops were covered by dark wooden shutters, intricately carved and polished to a high glossy finish. But all the shutters were closed. The whitewashed plaster of the walls was blindingly white in the intense afternoon sun, blank and faceless as the sky. Gulien could not guess what the people inside were thinking or might be prepared to do. He couldn't guess whether anyone recognized him. Probably they did not. He had, after all, intended to be taken for a Tamaristan officer, at least from a distance.

If he raised a banner—if he raised the Madalin falcon—how many of the people in those town houses would believe it, and of those, how many would respond quickly enough? And how many militia or guardsmen could possibly be concealed behind those blank white walls and carved shutters?

Time. They needed time. Delay had been their enemy when they had thought themselves disguised and unknown, but Prince Gajdosik was right: Now delay was their ally. Gulien said, "We have to keep them talking."

"Yes," Gajdosik said tersely.

But this proved impossible. The man, a Tamaristan *addat* with the black scorpion device on his shoulder, demanded just one thing: immediate surrender. He called both Gulien and Gajdosik by name and declared that surrender would purchase the lives of all their men, that defiance would cost all their lives, and that when the sun had moved a finger's width across the sky—about ten minutes—he must have their decision or order the attack. From this ultimatum, he would not be swayed.

"Who rules here?" Gajdosik asked Gulien in a low voice, because they had agreed that Gulien must be the one to represent himself to Bherijda's officer. "Can your father be trusted to keep his word? My brother cannot."

"I cannot believe your brother has outmaneuvered my father," Gulien muttered back. Then, turning to the scorpion *addat*, he raised his voice and asked plainly, "In whose name do you speak? Whose command do you convey? Is this the command of your prince Bherijda Garamanaj, or of my father Osir Madalin?"

"Indeed, Prince Gulien, my prince and His Majesty Osir Madalin speak with one voice, and this is an order both give," declared the man. "They are allies and friends, with a common purpose and a single voice."

Gulien refrained from any comment about people who thought they spoke with one voice with Osir Madalin. He said instead, "Of course we cannot doubt your word; nor do we doubt it. As this is my father's command, let a man of his come forward to demand obedience in his name."

"Alas, my orders are strict—"

Without lowering his voice, Gulien stated, "If no man of the falcon badge can be found within one finger's width of the sun's course across the sky, then we must after all question your understanding of the situation within Caras and believe that Osir Madalin must be your prince's prisoner and not his ally." He looked to one side and the other, deliberately, wondering how many of his own people listened and now perhaps waited for the Tamaristan *addat's* answer.

In a low tone Gajdosik said, "Well thought; and now if a man of undoubted loyalty to your father is produced?"

Gulien shrugged minutely. "Have any useful tactical ideas occurred to you?"

"Alas!" called Bherijda's *addat.* "My orders are clear, and the sun is halfway through its finger width now! You must decide what you will do, Prince Gulien! But I give you my word that His Majesty supports my prince!"

"Now would be a good time for tactical inspiration," Gulien pointed out.

"I have one tactical idea," Gajdosik muttered grimly. "Agree to everything, get that bastard to think we're yielding, and then a fast, concentrated effort to break through their lines, right there in front of us, where they've got space to retreat. If that fool had met us in the street we'd have no chance, but we might break past them up there in the palace courtyard. So, get past them and get into the palace, take Bherijda and your father both exactly as we planned, and then we can argue out the rest from a position of strength."

This plan sounded startlingly plausible laid out like that. Gulien had not expected it, and wasted half a second staring at Prince Gajdosik. Then he said, "Very well. I agree." And then he stepped forward and called out loudly, "Very well. We agree!" And, spreading his hands in token of surrender, he started forward to do his part, distracting Bherijda's man while Gajdosik got the rest of this effort organized.

He was aware, distantly, that they all might die in the next moments, that he might die. No doubt that would interfere with the Kieba's plans. And Oressa would be upset. He hoped she was all right. He hoped nothing had happened to her and that whatever came now, nothing would happen to her. His father might be upset, too. It was hard to decide exactly what Osir Madalin would do if his heir was killed by this new ally of his.

He drew a breath to call out something, some agreement, some capitulation that might, if he said just the right thing, lull their enemy for half a heartbeat. *Oressa* would be able to pull this off. She would sound perfectly meek and sincere while she lied through her teeth—she was a lot more like their father than she wanted to think.

Then the paving stones of the courtyard began to dissolve before his feet, and he leaped back, astonished and horrified.

It was Tonkaïan's Resolve. It was Bherijda Garamanaj with some terrible fragment of Tonkaïan's Resolve, and nothing Gulien possessed or knew or called upon could possibly match it. There was nothing he could do. They had lost.

CHAPTER 19

Oressa was not, after all, allowed to go to her room and have a bath, though she begged in her very best helpless-princess manner. She was all dusty from the road and anybody could see she *had* to have a bath, but oh no, she was compelled to stay in the pink atrium with Prince Bherijda, and worse, her father. This was infuriating, because if only she'd gotten to her room, she could very easily have gotten out again and then she could have raced down the hill and found Gulien and Gajdosik and warned them.

Instead, she was forced to sit in a heavy chair carved of pink stone and just watch as her father and Bherijda laid their own plans. Bherijda's scorpion soldiers would come in and mutter to their horrible prince, and he would speak to her father, and the soldiers would go out again, and it was perfectly infuriating because her chair was against the far wall, too distant for her to overhear what was said. Even worse, whenever there weren't soldiers hurrying in and then out again, Bherijda amused himself asking her about the secret doors and hidden passages in the palace, and her father didn't stop him. Although Oressa pretended that Kelian had made all that up, she knew neither of them believed her.

"*Is* there a secret door in this very room?" asked Bherijda, not for the first time. He was evidently bored because none of his soldiers had come in for several minutes. He looked rather as though if Oressa's father hadn't been there he might have started fingering the pink crystal roses carved into the corners of the ceiling or tossing the rugs aside to examine the tiles.

Oressa didn't know how she was ever going to recover her meek, dutiful image. She'd been so foolish, claiming publicly that she could get out of any room in the palace—she'd had to explain that to Gajdosik, yes, but she'd been such a fool to let everybody else hear her boast. She did her best to look confused and stupid instead of frightened and furious, but had no confidence she was managing it.

Her father said calmly, "I fear the palace is not quite so rife with secret doors and panels as Kelian seems to have inferred."

"How very disappointing," said Bherijda. He was almost pouting, like a little boy who wasn't getting his own way. "I do love secret passages."

Another soldier came in, no, two soldiers—one of Bherijda's men, accompanied by Erren and Kelian. Oressa tried hard to look young and helpless and not as though she was contemplating ways to murder Kelian.

"They're headed toward the King's Park!" Erren announced, loudly enough for Oressa to hear him. Her father fixed his guard captain with a thoughtful look, and Erren flushed, hurried forward, and muttered in a lower voice that Oressa could not overhear. She tried not to roll her eyes and instead gave her father a pleading look. "Please, sire, I don't feel well. *Please* may I retire?"

Her father answered dryly, "I fear that just at the moment, a hysterical princess dashing about the palace with romantic ideas about daring adventure and dramatic rescues might prove inconvenient." He pronounced every word of this statement with deliberate care, studying Oressa's face. She bit her lip, fixed her gaze on the floor, and tried not to shiver. She had always been afraid of drawing her father's close attention. Now that she finally had caught his eye, she knew she hadn't been afraid of it *enough*.

Her father added, "Oressa, I wish very much to hear every detail of your visit to the Kieba's mountain. However . . ." He glanced at Prince Bherijda.

"Yes, yes." Bherijda sounded a little petulant. "I'll see to everything."

But I need you to keep the Keppa and all her magic out of my way."

"Indeed," murmured her father. He gave Oressa one more thoughtful glance, then turned that same thoughtful gaze on the nearest of the scorpion soldiers. The man blanched, which indicated to Oressa that he was not entirely imperceptive, and bowed in acknowledgment of the unspoken order to keep Oressa both safe and secure. Then Osir beckoned to his men, and he and Bherijda and Erren and Kelian all went out, undoubtedly to see to the final arrangements they'd made to trap Gulien and Gajdosik.

But not all of the scorpion soldiers left. Naturally. Two of them stayed in the room, guarding her, including the man her father had clearly assigned to that duty with his single wordless glance.

On the other hand, that glance *had* been wordless. If the men didn't actually have *specific* orders . . . Oressa glared at them. Then she stood up, tossed her head—she wished she'd had that bath, because a beautiful dress and clean hair dripping with pearls added a lot to haughty flouncing—and declared, "I *am* going to my room." She started arrogantly toward the door, as though confident Bherijda's soldiers wouldn't dare stop her.

But the man did stop her. He went further: he chained her to her chair. Oressa hadn't expected that at all. She didn't see how she *could* have expected anything so outrageous. The chain, hurriedly brought by the other soldier, was a pretty, ladylike example of the metalsmith's art, its snug-fitting manacle made to look like a bracelet of pearls and copper, copper wire twisted decoratively around the slender steel links of the chain. This was disturbing: Who went to the trouble of making a *pretty* chain? Was it so common in Tamarist to chain up highborn ladies that every army carried a selection of chains made up to look like jewelry? Maybe it was. She could believe it. Or did only Prince Bherijda travel with such things in his luggage?

"There," the one soldier said to the other in lower-class Tamaj, his accent unfamiliar enough Oressa had to concentrate hard to understand him. "That'd make certain. Best take no chances with this'n. She's been let have notions, you can see. Too easy with their daughters by half, them Carastindi, but any fool can see that Madalin king tain't the kind to get on the wrong side of."

"Our prince's got him wound up," said the other man, but uneasily.

"Best take no chances," repeated the first obdurately. "Anyway, His Highness tain't want the princess getting off on her own, neither, not sen he's got her trained proper."

"*Hst!*" said the other man, glancing around uneasily. "Not so loud."

"Ah, no one's here, and them don't speak Tamaj any list," said the first man, but he fell silent anyway.

Oressa lowered her eyes, concealed her rage and fear, and composed herself to wait.

The minutes dragged interminably, but it was not actually very long before Prince Bherijda returned.

Oressa knew immediately that he'd caught Gulien and Gajdosik. She knew before he said anything. She knew before her brother and Gajdosik were brought in. She knew by the malice and satisfaction in Bherijda's face. Even so, when he smiled at her triumphantly, she straightened her shoulders and blinked back in a show of meek bafflement.

Prince Bherijda settled himself in her father's chair and fussily straightened the lace on his sleeves. Then he waved his hand in a deliberately lordly, condescending gesture, and his men brought in first his brother and then hers.

Neither her brother nor Gajdosik had been seriously hurt; that much was immediately obvious, so Oressa's first terror was assuaged immediately. They were both on their feet, and she could see no obviously dangerous wounds and only little smears of blood here and there. Of course, Bherijda had wanted Gajdosik taken alive, and her father had ordered the same care for Gulien, but things happen in battle. Oressa's relief was so great that she actually felt light-headed; she had to close her eyes and concentrate on her breathing or she would have swayed or fainted or burst into tears. She couldn't afford to do anything so ridiculous, because everything else was awful.

Her brother and Gajdosik had both been bound, which wasn't surprising, exactly, but still insulting because they were, after all, princes. They each stood between two soldiers, so one had to wonder what the point of the bonds was, except to shame them. Which, Oressa thought, was perfectly in character for a man who would chain up girls.

Most alarming, though she looked for them, she couldn't see any Carastindin people anywhere in evidence. Only Bherijda and his men.

Gulien looked furious and haughty, which Oressa knew meant he was afraid. So was she.

But Gajdosik looked worse than Gulien. He might not be badly hurt, but his face was bruised and his mouth swollen, and his hands were cut, and plainly some of his fingers were broken. But Oressa had seen him frightened, and he didn't look frightened now. He looked murderously angry.

Bherijda, in contrast, was clearly very pleased with himself. He leaned back in her father's chair, his elbows propped on its carved arms, smiling, satisfied as a well-fed kitchen cat and, Oressa was sure, twice as cruel when he had someone in his claws. She wanted to seem helpless and ineffectual so when she actually did something useful, she'd take Bherijda and his men by surprise, except chained as she was, she couldn't think of anything to do. Nevertheless, she jumped to her feet and took several steps forward, clutching her hands together and trying to look nervous and modest and not like she wanted to spit in Bherijda's face. "Please," she said pleadingly. "You won't hurt my brother? Please don't hurt Gulien," as though the choice was entirely Bherijda's and her father had never made any threat.

Bherijda preened—of course he was the kind of man who liked to have girls plead with him. *That* wasn't a surprise at all. "As you see," he said, smiling, "your brother is quite well. Indeed, I have little interest in *him*." He turned and faced the bound men, smiling deliberately at Gajdosik.

Oressa was standing quite close to one of the scorpion soldiers now. She might have snatched the knife from his belt and stabbed Bherijda, except she was fairly certain the chain wouldn't give her enough length to reach the prince. She wasn't precisely certain how best to stab a man, but how hard could it be? She might have made her best guess about it, except for the chain.

"What shall I do with you?" Bherijda murmured in Tamaj. He was looking at Gajdosik, but his voice was so low that Oressa wondered if he might really be speaking to himself rather than to his brother. He was still smiling, but it was a tight, wary smile with no humor in it. He said more loudly, to the soldiers, "Strip him."

The soldiers hesitated. Probably they were reluctant because Gajdosik was a prince, but Oressa thought maybe they were also just plain afraid of him, even though he was bound and unarmed and they were all big, strong men. She thought their hesitation was a measure of the rage that radiated from Gajdosik, invisible but potent, like heat radiating from sun-heated stone.

Gajdosik didn't move or take his eyes from Bherijda's face. He asked in a low, tight voice, also in Tamaj, "Does your new ally know you make so free with your sworn word, brother?"

For a long moment Oressa couldn't figure out what he meant. It was Gulien's expression that told her. She abruptly remembered that Bherijda had ordered his men both to *Make any threat or promises you must* and *Kill all his men.* He'd given orders very like that, anyway, and Oressa had thought he'd meant, *Kill the men if you must,* but instead he had meant exactly what he had said. She closed her own eyes for a moment, swallowing. A whole company of Gajdosik's men. And Gulien's men: them, too, probably. The Kieba had spared them all, but Oressa was certain Bherijda hadn't.

Oressa hadn't known all of the men, but she'd known some of them. Tamresk, who had been with them inside the Kieba's mountain—he'd come through so much, and now Gajdosik's own brother had killed him out of spite. All those men. Bherijda might have, must have promised to spare them if the two princes surrendered, because how else could he have taken them alive? But then he had slaughtered them all anyway. Oressa didn't *know* it, but she was sure.

"I beg your pardon. Did you mean to make a joke?" Bherijda asked, his tone smooth and amused, and repeated, more sharply, "I said, strip him."

This time the soldiers obeyed, drawing knives to cut Gajdosik's shirt off his body. Gajdosik made no undignified attempt to resist them, but before they were quite finished with the shirt, Bherijda put up a hand to signal them back. His eyebrows had gone up. He walked around Gajdosik in a slow circle, studying the whip marks, red and angry against Gajdosik's dark skin. Then he came back around to face him and asked, "Who did that?"

Gajdosik answered tonelessly, without elaboration, "The Keppa."

Gulien looked appalled. Oressa hadn't even remembered that he might not know about that—it had never occurred to her to tell him about it. She hadn't wanted to think about it at all. When he glanced at her, she shrugged, meaning, *Yes, sorry, I forgot, but who wants to talk about something like that anyway?*

Bherijda's eyebrows went up again higher, but he didn't look appalled at all, only surprised and doubtful. He said, "Well, I understand that she might feel the urge, but the marks seem months old."

"She provided a caduceus," said Gajdosik, still in that flat tone. The word "caduceus" was the same in Tamaj as in Esse, apparently, which Oressa hadn't realized.

"Did she?" Bherijda walked around him again, then traced one of the whip marks with a fingertip. Another. "Why do this and then allow you the use of a caduceus?" Bherijda wondered aloud. Then, when there was no answer, "It's a good idea, though. After all, that allows one to do it again." He paused, perhaps to allow Gajdosik to respond. When Gajdosik did not answer, he added regretfully, "Though I have no caduceus, unfortunately."

Oressa was glad to hear it, under the circumstances.

"I do have this, however." Bherijda went over to a side table and came back with a riding whip, which he tapped lightly into the palm of his hand. He was smiling again.

Gajdosik curled his lip. "Yes," he said, speaking with slow deliberation. "I remember that whip."

Bherijda stopped smiling. Stepping to the side, he brought the whip slashing down across his brother's back, once, twice, and a third time, so fast Oressa couldn't even gasp. The welts were narrow, puffy, red edged with white, not as vicious as the gashes made by a wire whip, but awful enough.

Gajdosik barely flinched, though his face tightened. He didn't make a sound. Of course he didn't; if he hadn't cried out when the Kieba beat him, he would hardly scream now for his horrible brother. Bherijda raised the crop again, and Oressa cried, "Don't! Don't!" before she even knew she was going to make a sound, and Bherijda smiled at her and brought the crop down again, and Oressa screamed. Then she kept on screaming. She was appalled that it had taken her so long to think of the possibilities inherent in really loud screaming, but she put her whole heart into it now. She screamed as loudly as she could, as fast as she could draw breath. She backed away from a soldier who tried to grab her, and kept screaming.

"Enough! Quiet! Be quiet!" Bherijda shouted at her, first in Tamaj and then in Esse. Oressa ignored him. He had jumped like a startled cat at Oressa's first scream—everybody had—and now waved another soldier after her, but Oressa dodged that one, too, except the chain limited how far she could back up, and he caught her after all. She kept screaming. Her throat hurt. She didn't care. The man put his hand over her mouth, and she bit him, hard, jerking her head to the side, trying to take a real piece out of his hand, and the man yelled and jerked away, and Gajdosik shouted, but Oressa couldn't understand him, and then Bherijda hit her across the face with the riding whip.

Oressa hadn't seen the blow coming; she hadn't even known Bherijda had run up close to her. The blow stung first, and then itched suddenly and fiercely—and then the pain blazed up, like a brilliant light flashing through the dark, like a line of fire laid suddenly across her cheek. Her screams cut off abruptly. This wasn't a deliberate choice;

she was too shocked to scream. She touched her face with trembling fingers, staring at Bherijda. He wasn't smiling now. He was panting and furious.

But it didn't matter. Because the door was abruptly flung back so hard it crashed against the wall, and her father stood there, tall and grim, silhouetted against the light.

Then he stepped forward, and the light came across his face so they could all see his cool, disinterested expression. He didn't say a word. No one did. The silence in the room felt as deep as a desert night.

The king glanced briefly around the room, taking in his son, bound; Gajdosik, half naked, new welts overlying the old marks of the Kieba's whip; and the soldiers, all Tamaristan. Finally he turned to gaze thoughtfully at Oressa, with the welt across her face, and at Bherijda where he stood near her, with the riding whip still in his hand.

Bherijda began, "I—"

The king lifted an eyebrow, and Bherijda stopped.

Still without a word, Osir crossed the room. He glanced at the chain that led from the pretty little manacle around Oressa's wrist to the heavy chair. Then he put a hand under Oressa's chin and tilted her face to the side, inspecting the welt across her cheek. Then he turned at last to look at Bherijda with withering contempt. Oressa was fascinated to see Bherijda flush dull red under that dispassionate regard, like a boy called out for some shameful misbehavior.

Reaching out, her father took the riding whip out of Bherijda's hand and dropped it disdainfully on the floor, shaking his fingers as though he had touched something disgusting. The Tamaristan prince made no move to stop him and said absolutely nothing.

The king walked forward, treading deliberately on the discarded whip, and went to Gulien. He studied his son for a moment, then said over his shoulder, his voice cool and flat, "No doubt, Prince Bherijda, you intended momentarily to inform me of my son's arrival." He held up a hand, checking Bherijda's tentative response, and went on, with no more emphasis. "I see, of course, that you were distracted by other matters of greater consequence." He turned to face Bherijda, lifting an eyebrow again in detached inquiry.

"I—"Bherijda stopped.

"Yes?" said the king, in a tone that really meant *Don't you think you've dug this hole deep enough?* When Bherijda fell silent, the king added calmly, "I am so very gratified that you have recovered my son. Unharmed, I see." He ran a thumb thoughtfully across Gulien's bonds and then held out his hand toward the nearest soldier. After a moment the soldier realized what he wanted and warily put a knife into his waiting hand.

The king cut Gulien's bonds without a word, and without a word Gulien sank down to kneel at his feet. "Yes," said the king in a very dry tone. "I should think so." He paused, studying his son for a long moment. Then he touched Gulien on the shoulder, granting him permission to stand.

Finally he turned to Gajdosik, who met his eyes for a moment and then consciously bowed his head.

"I have heard," murmured the king, "that you have magicked my son and my daughter, making them into your slaves."

"No," Gajdosik answered quietly. "That is not true."

"No," said the king. "I thought it seemed unlikely." He paused, studying his prisoner. He said, not taking his eyes from Gajdosik's face, "Prince Bherijda, this prisoner is far too valuable to permit accidents to befall him." He put no special stress on the word "accidents," but merely went on. "I am certain you will permit my most experienced guardsmen to keep your brother safe under their eyes."

Bherijda made no answer.

"Yes," murmured the king. He crooked a finger at Gajdosik, *Come.* Then he laid a hand on Gulien's arm and turned his head to gaze at Oressa. His eyes lingered on the manacle around her wrist until one of the soldiers hurriedly unlocked it, and at last the king tilted his head toward the door.

Oressa had never in her life been so glad to accompany her father anywhere.

CHAPTER 20

Osir Madalin took all three of them to his own rooms—the tower apartment. This alone would have made it plain to Gulien, if he hadn't already guessed it, that his father felt vulnerable and in need of greater security than the ground-level apartment could provide. So would the increased number of guardsmen at the foot of the stairs and again on the landing directly outside the apartment. Gulien knew all the men they passed slightly and believed them competent and loyal to the king and was both pleased his father had men he could trust about him and disheartened to see none of the guardsmen he had himself promoted.

The king personally conducted them through the apartment to the largest sitting room. The room held several chairs. Osir took one of these, swung it around, dropped into it, rested his elbows on its arms, tented his hands, and gazed at them over his steepled fingers. No one else had the temerity to even look at a chair.

The king studied Oressa's face. He said, in a tone of cool inquiry, "Your screams appear somewhat disproportionate to your injury."

"Oh," said Oressa, plainly startled, lifting a hand to her face and wincing. Her cheek must hurt quite a lot. That was obvious, but Gulien thought she had almost forgotten the injury for these few moments. Plainly the pain had now been recalled to the forefront of her mind. The welt certainly looked ugly enough: It ran from just above her lip almost to her ear, a vivid red line bordered by puffy white edges. But Gulien's sympathy was at least half for his sister's nervousness. Oressa sounded perfectly stupid, as she almost always did around their father.

Under their father's patient regard, Oressa opened and closed her mouth, ducking her head in apparent confusion. Finally she whispered, "I hoped you would hear. Or someone. I didn't know what Bherijda was going to do, but I thought . . . I thought he might do too much. I thought someone might hear, and they would tell you, and I thought . . . I hoped you would come."

The king's eyebrows rose. "That was . . . clever."

Her father had never thought Oressa clever in her life, so far as Gulien knew. His sister dropped her gaze, flushing nervously.

"In fact, though I am certain half the palace staff heard you quite clearly, it was Lord Paulin who came to inform me," added their father, with no change in his tone. "You seem to have persuaded him, at least, that there was some urgency. I believe he actually ran all the way to this residence. Fortunately his heart did not burst from the exertion."

Gulien, too, was surprised that Paulin had had such an effort in him, but he was particularly gratified that the older man had had the sheer nerve to face the king for anything after supporting Gulien. He hoped that his father hadn't been hard on Paulin but did not dare ask. Oressa glanced up, opened her mouth, shut it again, and looked down dumbly.

The king, his expression thoughtful, turned his attention to Gulien, who immediately dropped his gaze, feeling his face heat. He knew he had lost his father's good opinion, and now he had no idea what to say. What *could* he possibly say? That he'd thrown his support to the Kieba? His father already knew that. That he had now changed his mind and would loyally support the king in everything? His father would never believe that; nor did Gulien think he could bring himself to lie to him. That regardless of anything else, he would certainly support him against Bherijda? His father must know that, but it wasn't yet clear whether he and Prince Bherijda were enemies or, to some degree, allies.

In the end Gulien said nothing. After a moment he went to his knees, trying to make the gesture look respectful rather than desperate.

"Yes," said the king coldly. "You should indeed beg my pardon. I will permit you to do so shortly. I may grant it."

"Sire," Gulien answered in a low tone, not daring to meet his father's eyes.

At last the king turned his head to regard Gajdosik. His expression was distant, cool, unreadable.

Gajdosik stared back, not in the least cowed. He was still bound, still half naked, still a prisoner. Even so, he managed to look every bit a prince. Gulien might have been envious of the other man's self-possession, except he knew at least half of it was an act and the other half arose mostly from the Tamaristan prince's lack of acquaintance with Osir Madalin.

The king said softly, "If not for your brother's obvious enmity and the fact that his magisters have laid claim to the larger and more convenient cells for their . . . work, I would chain you in the dungeon below this palace. However, that appears impractical."

Gajdosik lowered his gaze briefly, then once more looked the king in the face. He stood quietly, but the earlier passivity Gulien had seen in him when he'd found him in the Kieba's mountain, was completely lacking. So was the leashed, murderous rage he had shown when faced with his brother. This was a man, Gulien thought, who had met reverses but still hoped to overcome them. He stood with patient composure, waiting to see what he might yet do to wrestle difficult circumstances around to his own advantage. Gulien doubted he could have done as well in a similar position.

"Kedmes!" called the king.

The brawny man, bodyguard more than servant, appeared instantly at the inner door of the apartment. He took in the scene instantly, his expression unchanging. If there was a certain masked satisfaction in his hooded eyes when he glanced at Gulien, on his knees before his father, Gulien could not honestly blame him for it.

To Gajdosik, the king said briefly, "Bathe. Dress. Kedmes will provide clothing for you, as what's left of yours hardly seems salvageable. Your fingers appear to be broken. He will set them. Kedmes."

The servant straightened attentively. "Sire?"

"Prince Gajdosik is my prisoner, not my guest. Have him carefully attended. If he gives you the least trouble, inform me. Send for a chain from the prison. Two chains. The short ones. And . . . hmmm. Perhaps you might obtain the long light one with which Prince Bherijda saw fit to adorn the pink atrium. Have the heavy chains installed"—the king moved a dismissive hand—"somewhere in this apartment. Somewhere not too inconvenient, if possible. The smaller sitting room, perhaps. The light chain can go in the adjoining chamber."

"Sire," acknowledged Kedmes, and looked expectantly at Gajdosik, who bowed to the king with precise formality and followed his servant without a word.

"Now," said the king. He leaned back in his chair and stared at Gulien. "My son."

Gulien lifted his head, though he did not otherwise move.

"Start at the beginning," said the king, "And go on to the end. I would particularly like to hear about the Kieba."

Gulien took a breath. He described, in a few brief words, his first encounter with the woman who had been a goddess and was still something more than, or other than, mortal. He hesitated before recounting, in the most toneless voice he could manage, the Kieba's response to his plea for her intervention—her condemnation of his father, her desire for the return of the god-artifact she had called Parianasaku's Capture.

The king's mouth tightened slightly. "The Capture. Yes." He drew circles on the arm of his chair gently with the tip of one finger. It was impossible for Gulien to guess what he might be thinking. He murmured, "It is seldom advisable to seek the Kieba's intervention. An artifact constantly in the keeping of the Madalin kings is ever so much more reliable. Perhaps you have learned this."

Gulien did not dare answer.

His father sighed, then asked, "And the second time you went to her mountain?"

Gulien had had this in the back of his mind the whole while, and now carefully outlined a second visit to the mountain that left out the kephalos, the falcon, his own collapse, or most particularly, any mention of memory or secondary identities or crystal that got into one's blood or anything of that kind. He described only finding Oressa and Gajdosik and then went on cautiously, "But before she permitted us to depart, the Kieba warned us that Prince Bherijda may have an artifact called Tonkaïan's Resolve and that the older Garamanaji prince, Maranajdis, may be misusing a still more powerful artifact called Shakanatu's Throne. I do not know what these artifacts may be, nor whether Parianasaku's Capture—which I know you still hold, sire—may protect Carastind against them. But the Kieba—"

This king lifted a finger, bringing this cautious, half-begun plea to a halt before Gulien could quite give it voice. "My son, enough. This continual refrain does you no credit."

Gulien met his eyes. "Am I your heir?" he asked. "If I am your heir, then surely all these things are very much my concern. One recalls many vivid tales concerning the artifacts left scattered across the world by the forgotten gods. Whatever you think of the Kieba, Bherijda Garamanaj hardly seems the sort of man one would wish to hold a powerful artifact—"

His father moved his hand again, sharply enough that Gulien closed his mouth almost involuntarily. Osir Madalin made no comment about Gulien's position as his heir, but asked instead, "And Prince Gajdosik? What sort of man is he? You seem to have made the man an ally of sorts. That, I did not anticipate. How did it come about?"

Gulien hesitated. Then he said, trying to keep any note of defiance out of his tone, "You may—you may scorn me for stepping into her shadow. But the Kieba set Prince Gajdosik into my hands. He yielded himself and his people to me." He didn't glance at Oressa—he could hardly imagine what their father would say if he admitted the Kieba had actually set Gajdosik and his men into *her* hands, but he could quite well imagine the incredulous lift of his father's eyebrows. He wouldn't do that to Oressa, so he said instead, "Then word came from Caras, and we thought—we all thought Bherijda ruled here. We believed you a prisoner, sire, and word of an alliance a mere ruse on Bherijda's part. I believed that. Prince Gajdosik thought we could take the palace and capture his brother, and—and—"

"And myself," said the king flatly. "And thus claim Parianasaku's artifact for your own after all. Yes. I see."

Gulien shook his head, adamant on this one point. "Not for my own. Never for my own, sire. I thought . . . Forgive me for saying yet once more that I thought it best to return this artifact to the Kieba. I still think it important to do that, sire, and wish you would do so—"

"My son, you know less than you believe of this matter. I shall shortly demonstrate, I hope, that we may claim the Kieba's power and assume her role and that the world will not end when we do so."

"Sire, I . . . I think perhaps you may have been hasty in assuming—"

"My son, enough."

Unable to defy that flat tone, Gulien lowered his head.

To his complete surprise Oressa took a small step forward and protested, "Father—"

Their father looked at her, and she stuttered to a halt, mute and helpless.

The king turned back to Gulien, by all appearances dismissing his daughter completely. "My son, you have been persuaded by a woman who in no way holds our best interests or the best interests of mortal men as her highest priority. Overawed by the Kieba's name and reputation, you have accepted her word and discarded mine. This is in some part understandable, but neither wise nor acceptable." The king paused. Then he said, his tone flat, "Now you may beg my pardon."

Gulien said immediately, sincerely, "I beg your pardon, sire."

The king set an elbow on the arm of his chair, rested his chin on the back of his hand, and was silent, considering. Gulien didn't move. He tried not even to breath. He half believed his father would refuse to grant his pardon; he would not have been surprised if the king had declared, *You are no longer my heir.* But Osir Madalin merely asked, "Tell me, my son: What shall I do with Prince Gajdosik Garamanaj?"

Gulien hadn't expected this. He did not know how to answer. He said at last, "He—I—he surrendered himself and all his men to me. He was due protection from me in return, and I failed him. You know Bherijda ordered all his men killed, even after he promised to spare them. Prince Gajdosik—sire, he has suffered enough."

"He has more men," murmured King Osir. "Thousands, I believe, provocatively landed in the north, near Addas."

"He put them in my hand," Gulien repeated, not even glancing at Oressa.

"Did he?" said the king, but not in a way that encouraged any answer.

The inner door of the apartment opened. Gajdosik came in, with Kedmes at his back. The clothing the Tamaristan prince had been given fit him. Two of his fingers had been splinted. His hand was still swollen; bruises still showed dusky on his face, but he looked much better. His wrists were bound again, however, this time with wide cuffs of leather linked by a short chain. *He is my prisoner*, King Osir had said, and Gajdosik was plainly meant to feel so.

Gajdosik's glance went to Gulien, still kneeling, and then to Oressa, and finally to their father. He walked slowly forward and bowed to King Osir, the precise degree proper for a foreign prince facing a king not his own. Then, straightening, he waited.

Osir paid no attention to Gajdosik, plainly meaning to let the Tamaristan prince wait, as Gajdosik had no choice but to do. Instead he said, "My son, come," and rose, gesturing for Gulien to accompany him, and led the way farther into the apartment.

Without a word, with only a quick glance for his sister—Gulien hoped he didn't look too desperate—he got to his feet and followed their father.

The bathing room was small but well appointed, with the servants already pouring clean water into the basin. Towels and fresh clothing had already been laid out, Gulien's own, brought from his own apartment.

The king tilted his head toward the basin and leaned his hip against the edge of the table that held the soaps and towels, regarding Gulien dispassionately. "Bathe," he ordered briefly. "And tell me now what you declined to tell me in your sister's presence. Did that Tamaristan prince dishonor Oressa?"

Gulien, his shirt half off, briefly froze, his memory stuttering over the fact that he had found his sister and Prince Gajdosik waiting for him together within the Kieba's mountain . . . that they had been unchaperoned there for days, with none of Oressa's women about her, no Carastindin folk at all, only the Tamaristan prince and his people.

But almost at once he remembered Prince Gajdosik's dismay at the accusation Gulien had leveled at him at their very first meeting, the painful dignity with which the Tamaristan prince had presented himself to Gulien on their second meeting within the Kieba's mountain, and the quiet self-possession with which Gajdosik had begged generosity for his people. The man Gulien had faced on those occasions had been defeated, but he had not been *guilty*.

The man he had ridden beside from the mountain to Caras, the man who had faced without flinching the Kieba's cool displeasure and Prince Bherijda's spite and King Osir's cold authority—Gulien found he could not believe any such offense of that man.

Besides . . . no. No. There had been nothing of that kind of offense in Oressa's manner. Instead she'd spoken up for Gajdosik, argued with him, even *teased* him as though he were a friend.

Gulien dropped his shirt in a heap beside the basin, faced his father, and said in his most decisive tone, "I think that is impossible, sir."

The king studied him. "You cannot think it necessary to protect your sister by concealing any such matter from me . . . no? Very well." He gave a slight nod, provisionally accepting this judgment. "Then, taking the matter from the other side, has that weak-witted girl conceived some romantic notion about the Tamaristan?"

Gulien snorted. "Oressa? Hardly. Besides, I can't see that she'd have had time, even had the circumstances been conducive to romance, which I very much doubt."

His father lifted an eyebrow. "In my experience, foolish infatuation seldom requires long acquaintance. Rather the reverse. Shared danger is certainly conducive to romance. I gather you think Oressa unlikely to be subject to such foolishness."

He added this last with faint incredulity, so that Gulien, goaded, answered a little more forcefully than he would have intended. "Most unlikely, yes. You have always held Oressa too lightly."

"Clean yourself up," Osir ordered, dispassionate as always. He didn't argue. He seldom argued. That was one reason it was so difficult to change his mind about anything. But Gulien thought his father now seemed . . . a little thoughtful, perhaps.

Stripping off his remaining clothing, Gulien lowered himself into the warm water, hissing slightly. He had no memory of taking any particular blow during that last hopeless struggle when both he and Prince Gajdosik had tried so hard to stop Bherijda from murdering Gajdosik's men, but plainly he had taken more than one. Only the odd contusion, for Bherijda's people had obviously been ordered to be careful of his life and health, but he felt every bruise now.

"Your pendant," his father said, shifting suddenly a step closer to the basin. "The Kieba gave you that?"

Startled, Gulien moved a hand involuntarily to protect the crystalline falcon on its chain, realized it, and made himself drop his hand. "No, sir. I've had it for many years. I found it when I was a boy." He didn't explain where he'd found the bit of crystal, or that it had seemed to give him dreams even as a child, or that the kephalos had called it a key, or that it had somehow gotten into his blood and predisposed him to the kephalos's purpose. He couldn't guess what of that his father might already know, but he hardly saw how any of it would be safe to put into words now.

Osir studied the falcon for a long moment. He asked at last, "Would it harm you to put it aside?"

Gulien shook his head, not in denial, but faintly incredulous of the question, of his father's obvious awareness that the crystal was no natural stone. And if Osir had seen this pendant years ago, would he have known even then that his son had somehow come upon a broken shard from an artifact, or a fragment of the kephalos, or anyway a bit of crystal that was in some manner uncanny? Gulien guessed now that this must be so. If his father *had* seen it, recognized it, taken it away immediately . . . Gulien could hardly imagine. Except that everything would be very different.

He said, almost gently, "I don't think it matters anymore. I think it's too late. I don't think it would make any difference at all whether I put it aside or swallowed it whole." In fact, he knew —some part of him knew, some echo of memory that wasn't his—that this was true.

Perhaps hearing this certainty, perhaps knowing from his own studies that this was true, Osir nodded, frowning. "Does your sister wear a similar pendant?"

"No, sir." Again Gulien was quite certain. If his sister had ever come upon a shard of the Kieba's crystal, then she, too, would have possessed a predisposition.

This, too, Osir seemed to accept. But, startling Gulien, his father asked abruptly, "I gather that you believe your sister cried out on purpose, in order to balk Bherijda's intentions? She was not merely overcome with hysterical terror?"

Gulien could not quite prevent himself from rolling his eyes. "Oh, indeed, hysterical terror. No, of course she did it on purpose." Accepting a servant's arm, he stood, carefully, and took the offered towel. No doubt it was ridiculously shallow to feel so much better merely for the chance to bathe and dress in fresh clothing, but he could not deny that he did feel less desperate. Though he was sufficiently stiff to be grateful for the servant's assistance with the shirt.

Then he looked up to meet the king's considering frown and suddenly wondered if perhaps he should have let his father go on thinking little of Oressa.

But no. Letting that go on had never served either his sister or their father well, however Oressa felt about it. Besides, Gulien and his sister were both in such dire standing with their father now, Gulien no longer cared whether the king realized how much he, Gulien, resented his treatment of Oressa. He met his father's eyes for a long beat before lowering his gaze.

After a moment the king said, "This way," and directed Gulien out again into the narrow hallway, not back the way they'd come, but toward the smaller sitting room.

This, despite its name, was a generous space. It held two groups of comfortable chairs beneath hanging porcelain lamps, a sideboard for chilled wine or other refreshments, wide murals on three walls, and a single large window that looked out onto a sheer drop to the gardens below. It also held, new just this hour, Gulien surmised, two of the short, heavy chains used to confine violent prisoners in the dungeon below the palace. The chains had been placed about ten feet from each other, about four feet from the floor, each flanked by a chair on one side and a low table on the other.

The king crossed the room to the chair by the farther chain and beckoned to his son.

Gulien didn't move. In that moment he couldn't have moved to save his life. "Sire—" Then his breath failed. He tried again. "Father—"

"My son," the king said, his tone flat, and beckoned a second time.

Gulien did not precisely disbelieve that his father would do this, but . . . he couldn't believe it. He felt sick. He felt as though he had been struck and was only now beginning to understand the severity of the blow.

He didn't know what his father saw in his face, but Osir made a slight movement, instantly checked, and said, "Gulien—" Then he cut that off and stood in silence for a long moment, his steady, dispassionate gaze on his son's face. Gulien was unable to read anything in his father's expression, but at last Osir said, not gently, but more mildly than Gulien would have expected, "I grant you pardon, my son. I have no intention of looking elsewhere for my heir."

Gulien took a breath as though it were the first he'd managed in an hour. "Then why . . . ?"

"Practical necessity." Osir beckoned a third time, this time with a curt impatience that required obedience.

Crossing the room seemed to take longer than any reasonable measure of time. Time enough for fury to kindle and burn high and wither to ash, for defiance to struggle to be born and die again, for shame to crush Gulien's heart. Gulien did not resist when his father took hold of his arm. He only said quietly, "Father. Please. This isn't necessary."

"You are mistaken," the king told him shortly, locking the chain. "I am unfortunately required to leave Caras. I trust my absence will be brief, but I would prefer to find Caras still mine when I return. Though I have pardoned you once, I do not wish to be compelled to do so a second time."

Unable to meet his father's eyes, Gulien dropped his gaze.

"Fortunately, Prince Bherijda will accompany me, which should remove the greatest chance of peril for both you and the city. However, I am not inclined to risk your wandering freely about the palace while I am gone. Particularly not as that foreigner's men will remain in occupation."

"In occupation?" Gulien asked sharply, bringing his gaze up again. "What bargain *have* you made with Bherijda?"

"A practical one. A temporary one. The game I am playing with Prince Bherijda has high stakes and a difficult board. I do not wish you to complicate the play, my son. While you are here in this apartment, my people can protect you and you cannot interfere with my intentions. I will therefore ensure that you remain here. Sit down, Gulien, and compose yourself."

Gulien sank into the only chair he could now reach. The chain was long enough to let him rest his arm on the arm of the chair. He could stand up, if he wished. He could reach the table. That was the extent of his free movement now.

"Be patient. Shortly you will have company in your detention," said the king, and in an unexpected gesture that Gulien did not know how to read, touched him lightly on the shoulder before leaving the room.

CHAPTER 21

Prince Gajdosik's demeanor was calm as they waited for Oressa's father to return, but Oressa could see the tension in his shoulders and back. That always gave away his uncertainty or fear, and when had Oressa learned to see through his mask of impassivity? She wished suddenly and intensely that for once Gajdosik should not be the one set at a disadvantage and forced into the role of a supplicant. But there was nothing she could do. She couldn't even talk to him, not with Kedmes leaning in the doorway, glowering watchfully.

Then her father's man glanced back over his shoulder and moved aside, and her father came back into the room.

Though Oressa had been unable to stop herself from flinching at his return, the king paid no attention to her at all. He looked Prince Gajdosik up and down, his expression impersonal but intent. Gajdosik met the king's eyes, not precisely with defiance, but with no sign of subservience.

After that first comprehensive examination, the king resumed his seat and said, "Prince Gajdosik, you are my prisoner. I expect you to show me appropriate humility."

Gajdosik hesitated a bare instant. Then he went to one knee and bowed his head.

"Your brother appears to hold you in some dislike," the king said to him.

Lifting his gaze again, Gajdosik shrugged. "We have never been friends. I used that very whip on him once, when we were both much younger. He had offended the sister of one of my men. It's rather a habit of his, unfortunately. I hadn't realized he'd kept the whip with an eye for . . . future possibilities."

"A long and silent grudge," said the king. "I see." He considered for a moment. Then he went on, without emphasis. "You would have been wiser to kill him, Prince Gajdosik, rather than leaving an enemy at your back. Now he is ascendant and you are, fortunately for you, my prisoner. I expect I shall receive a request or a demand that I return you to his keeping. What shall I say to him?"

"What you will," Gajdosik answered, his voice level. "I am your prisoner. Whatever you do, I have no recourse."

"What shall I say?" repeated the king patiently.

After a moment Gajdosik said, "Tell him that you will deliver me as a gift to our brother Prince Maranajdis. That thought will please Bherijda, should you wish to please him."

King Osir tapped the arm of his chair very gently with the tips of two fingers. "Interesting," he murmured.

"Or if you require some manner of barter with my brother, then offer me to him in exchange. You may bargain high, if you wish," Gajdosik added, his tone edged.

"Hmm."

"Or you might tell him that you will set me free, that I may remove my men from your northern coast and put them to use harassing Prince Maranajdis. That would be convenient for you, and there would be little risk that I will turn back against you now that Bherijda is your ally. I don't have the men to face you both together."

"I see," said the king. "Yes. Enough." The king considered his prisoner silently for some time. It was not a comforting silence. Boring and fraught at the same time. Oressa's cheek still stung, but now her back ached as well, and her knees. She shifted her weight gingerly from her toes to her heels and, after a little while, back again. It seemed to her she had been standing here in this room forever, nervous and uncomfortable, unable to leave or sit, afraid to do anything that would draw her father's attention to her. Her palace-honed sense of time, however, trained by innumerable court functions over the years, told her it had not even been an hour.

Gajdosik waited quietly, his head bowed. Oressa knew it was harder to kneel for a long time than to stand, but though he had to be as exhausted as she, he showed no sign of weariness. She wondered whether her father was deliberately drawing out this interview, maybe to test Gajdosik's patience. She wondered just how far that patience would last today, when the Tamaristan prince had already been pressed so hard.

But at last the king said, "Prince Gajdosik, tell me about the Kieba. In some detail, if you please."

Gajdosik lifted his head. He glanced at Oressa, but away again at once. She realized he was wondering what she might have already told her father. She wanted to say that she hadn't yet told any part of the story, that Gajdosik could say anything he wanted and she wouldn't contradict him, but of course she couldn't. She tried hard to keep her face set in the proper calm court-princess mask.

Gajdosik described, in brief, terse phrases, what had occurred inside the Kieba's mountain. He told the king about the savagery of the roused Kieba. He left out the vault of plagues and without exactly saying so made it sound as though the Kieba's servants had simply perceived a threat without Oressa having anything to do with what had happened. He described the Kieba's prison and, briefly, her appearance outside that prison, and what had come from that. He said nothing about the kephalos. It occurred to Oressa that Gulien had also left out any mention of the kephalos. She began to consider how she might cast her own story so as to do the same, because though she could not see any particular advantage to leaving out that part, it was obviously just as well to reserve as much as you could when you were questioned by an enemy.

Then Gajdosik described, succinctly but more or less truthfully, what questions the Kieba had asked him and what answers he had given, so far as he remembered, though he didn't mention the Kieba's chair.

"Then she sent us away, with firm advice to manage our own affairs ourselves," Gajdosik finished, and waited. He didn't glance at Oressa again. If she had already told her father everything, if she had been completely honest, well, Gajdosik hadn't actually *lied* at all. Though he had certainly left out quite a lot. Oressa kept her expression bland.

"Well?" her father said to her. "Is this account accurate?"

"Oh," said Oressa, surprised. She hadn't expected to be asked yet. "Yes, sire, I think so," she said promptly and confidently, because no one but she and Gajdosik knew what was true in that account or what had been left out, and she was sure neither of them would give anything away.

The king said to Gajdosik, his tone flat, "You alarmed the Kieba by your ill-considered attempt to steal her power. Now she will be on her guard. For that alone I should not only give you back to your brother but also provide him, if he is so inclined, with his choice of whips."

Gajdosik said nothing.

The king said, his tone even flatter and less expressive, "And you took my daughter with you into the Kieba's mountain. You offended the Kieba while my daughter was in your company, by all you knew drawing her into your calamity. For that," he said very softly, "I should wield the whip myself."

Gajdosik still did not answer, but this time he flinched and lowered his head.

"So Prince Gajdosik held you as his prisoner," Osir said to Oressa. "Did he offer you insult? Did he offend your honor?"

Gajdosik stiffened but did not otherwise react to this. But Oressa straightened in outrage, aware even at that moment that she was affronted on his behalf as well as her own and that this was not very sensible. But she said sharply, "No! Prince Gajdosik and all his men have been perfectly courteous! Not like *your* friend Bherijda!"

Her father tapped his fingers on the arm of his chair, not quite in an even rhythm. "Indeed," he murmured. But he seemed, a little to Oressa's surprise, to accept this as truth. He added, "Well, that is fortunate."

Fortunate. Of course. Her father certainly wouldn't his daughter's *value* compromised. Oressa clenched her teeth, not only furious but ashamed that Gajdosik should see her father treat her so.

Her father studied Gajdosik. His eyes were narrow, which could sometimes be a sign of temper, but his expression remained unreadable. After a moment he called, "Kedmes!"

The man came forward a step, bowing. "Sire."

Oressa's father got to his feet, grimacing a little. Oressa supposed he did not much care for having to move back into this high apartment with all the stairs to climb and hoped, vindictively, that his knees hurt him.

But the king did not pause. He beckoned to Oressa, said, "Come," curtly to Gajdosik, and led the way deeper into his apartment. Kedmes followed Gajdosik closely.

The king took them to the smaller sitting room. Gulien was already waiting there, seated in one of the chairs. He had bathed and changed his clothing, but he looked, if anything, worse for the opportunity: pale and stiff. He rose as their father came in, with a very small bow, and that was when Oressa noticed the chain. With an effort, she stifled her exclamation of dismay and anger, so that all that emerged was a throttled hiss. Her father glanced at her, his expression unchanged.

Kedmes traded Gajdosik's bonds for the other chain. The Tamaristan prince did not resist, but merely stood in his place, watching the king with strict patience.

The king paid no attention to him or to Gulien. "Oressa," he said shortly, and took her into the adjoining room, which was a small bedroom—obviously, by the feminine appointments, meant for a woman, on those occasions when Osir wanted a woman's discreet companionship. She guessed that there might be a hidden door between this bedroom and the king's. The thought that there might be a secret door between this room and her father's made her skin crawl, but she couldn't immediately spot any likely places for such a door, so maybe there wasn't one. The room was prettily appointed, its porcelain lamps and fixtures painted with birds and flowers, but it had no window.

And Bherijda's pretty chain had now been added to the room's ordinary amenities. The chain had been looped around one of the bedposts, which reached to the ceiling and, despite its ornate carving, looked discouragingly sturdy. Unlike the chains from the dungeon, this chain was slender, light, and at least fifteen feet long. Oressa would be able to move freely between the bedroom and the smaller sitting room. She knew her father could just as well have had a third chain brought from the dungeon for her, but she did not find it easy, at the moment, to be very grateful for this consideration.

Her father gazed at her, narrow-eyed. Then he picked up the decorative manacle and held out his hand expectantly.

Oressa gave him her left hand and waited, expressionless, while he closed the pretty, delicate-seeming manacle around her wrist and locked it with its little silver key. She didn't protest. She longed for him to be done with it if he was going to do it, and then to just go *away*.

Once the manacle was locked, however, her father tucked the key away and folded his hands behind his back, considering her. His gaze was steady and thoughtful—too thoughtful—the wrong kind of thoughtful, and Oressa realized that she had made a serious mistake. Impassivity had been all wrong. The girlish and none-too-intelligent daughter she'd always pretended to be would have cried and pleaded with him not to chain her up, begged to be allowed to go back to her own rooms, and promised to obey him. Instead, she had stood with her back straight and her eyes blank with secrets, and she had let herself look at him with the silent, concentrated hatred of a captive watching her enemy. And he had noticed it. He could hardly have missed it.

She had done everything wrong. She understood this all at once with a cold shock that was almost physical. *She*, unlike Gulien, had never knelt down and begged their father's pardon. It hadn't occurred to her, but it should have, and now it was too late. She shouldn't have waited with such painful endurance through those awful interviews in the other room. She should have cried and protested on Gulien's behalf and her own, passionately and without much coherence. Instead she had let her fear make her silent, and in her silence her father had seen that she hated him and was his enemy, and it was too late now to try to make him see something else. She dropped her gaze, not because she thought it would help, but because she didn't dare look him in the face.

Her father said in a level tone, "My daughter, you were foolish to trust Kelian."

Astonished, Oressa stared at him. She knew she should lower her eyes again. But she was angry as well as afraid, furious for Gulien's sake, and Gajdosik's, and even on her own behalf. And it was too late anyway. So she said instead, matching his tone, "I know that. If you trust Bherijda, then you're a fool as well—but you don't, of course. You've made him fear you. That could be worse."

Her father's eyebrows rose slightly. "It is a calculated risk. As is so much else we must do." He paused, considering her, and then added, "But you know that as well, do you not, my daughter? Gulien was correct. I have held you too lightly, and valued you, I think, too little."

Oressa didn't dare answer.

Her father turned and walked away without a word, back through the smaller sitting room and out, gone at last. She heard the door click shut behind him, took a long, shuddering breath, shrugged her shoulders to try to dismiss the tension that tightened all her muscles, and went back into the small sitting room, where at least she could join her brother and Prince Gajdosik in their captivity. If her father's people would leave them alone, she had some hope she might be able to do something about that even now.

So, not much later, while Gulien fretted over his inability to pace and Gajdosik pretended to be perfectly at his ease, Oressa perched on the windowsill in the smaller sitting room, her back half turned to the view, her legs tucked up under her dusty skirts. She was working delicately to break one of the decorative copper wires off the manacle that encircled her left wrist, bending it back and forth, back and forth. All the wires were so tightly enmeshed that she could bend her chosen wire only a tiny bit each time. More a wiggle than a real bend. The wire might take all afternoon and half the evening to break. If it broke.

"He won't keep us here long, not like *this*," Gulien said. He jerked his wrist against the limits of his chain. "It's unnecessary, it's insulting, it's offensive, and it's *completely improper*."

Oressa made a scornful sound, not looking up. "He'll probably decide he *loves* having us quiet and contained and keep us chained up until he dies of old age and you succeed him. The Tamaristans used to do that to their heirs. Did you know that? You probably did."

Gulien gave her a curious look, then glanced at Gajdosik, no doubt guessing where she had learned this tidbit. He said mildly, "Not a custom that worked out very well."

"I'm sure Father will believe that if *he* does it, it'll be different. Anyway, improper how? I have my own room, don't I? Unless it's Gajdosik's injured dignity that worries you."

"There are worse places to be chained," Gajdosik said dryly. He lounged in his chair, feet up on a small table and crossed at the ankles, head tilted back against the cushions, eyes mostly closed. He would have managed to look comfortable, except that he was also ashen pale. There were dark shadows under his eyes and lines at the corners of his mouth that Oressa was almost sure hadn't been there even a day ago. She didn't know whether she was seeing the effect of weariness or pain or grief or defeat, but she knew she was glad he wasn't chained in the dungeons beneath the palace, in his brother's power.

"Father wouldn't have brought me here unless he thought I wouldn't be safe in my rooms," Oressa added. "And he wouldn't have imprisoned Prince Gajdosik here unless he thought he wouldn't be safe in the dungeons, and he wouldn't have chained *you* at all unless he thought you wouldn't be safe anywhere else in the palace. Though I expect he's also just furious. It's a good punishment, especially if he wants to demonstrate his authority to you and everyone else, and *especially* if he doesn't want you doing anything or talking to anyone. *But*," she added, raising her voice slightly to stop her brother from interrupting her, "what *I* think is, punishment or not, he wouldn't have chained us all here together in his own apartment if he had enough men to guard us all separately."

Gulien clearly hadn't yet thought past his outrage and hurt pride to reach this obvious conclusion. He thought about it now. He said, "But it's not Bherijda he's afraid of—"

"Maybe it is, though. He *humiliated* Bherijda." That had been extremely satisfying, and Oressa paused for a heartbeat to savor the memory. Then she finished. "And now maybe he's afraid of what Bherijda might do to get back at him."

"King Osir has something my brother wants," said Gajdosik, not moving or opening his eyes. "Parianasaku's Capture, I presume. Plainly my brother believes your father can be persuaded to serve his ambition. But not, obviously, forced."

"No one can force Father to do anything," Oressa agreed. "But Father wants something from Bherijda, too, obviously, and plainly he can't force Bherijda to give it to him or do it for him, either, or he would. If they have each proven to the other that they must join together to attack the Kieba, that would explain everything."

"Father wouldn't . . . ," Gulien began, but his voice trailed off before he finished his sentence.

Oressa lifted her eyebrows at him. "Wouldn't destroy the Kieba and then use his artifact to make all the endless plagues his personal weapons? Of course he would."

Gulien shook his head stubbornly but said nothing.

She had always known her brother wanted to admire their father, that he wanted—even needed—their father to be a good man as well as a strong king. That was just part of Gulien's wanting everybody to be better than they were. That was a good thing about Gulien. Except in this one area. Because he just never *would* see the truth about their father.

Oressa had paused in her attempts to break the wire. She resumed bending the wire back and forth, though now she was thinking about the Kieba and her father and Bherijda and wondering how much time any of them had to do anything. Not that she could think of anything they could do, even if she could get free of Bherijda's pretty chain. The wire *was* getting easier to bend, though. Maybe it *would* break before the next age dawned.

Though she did not stop working with the wire, she said slowly, "Bherijda can't just take Parian-whoever's artifact. It's something that was given to the Madalin kings, and nobody can take it away, not even the Kieba herself, certainly not Bherijda. But he wants Father to give it to him, or use it for him. And, you know, one of the ways he might try to make him is with a hostage. I wonder . . . I wonder how sorry he is now that he let Father take us away from him?"

"King Osir surprised him, I imagine," murmured Gajdosik. He had closed his eyes. But his voice, though quiet, was edged with something hard and aggressive.

"If they fear each other," Gulien began, and then stopped and said instead, "Oressa, *what* are you doing?"

Oressa had finally broken the copper wire off the manacle, with a stifled hiss of triumph. Now, having slipped the wire into the manacle's lock, she was discovering that it really wasn't stiff enough to even feel anything properly, much less move the internal tumblers. "Nothing, probably," she admitted, probing gently. "I was never very good at this. And this wire isn't really . . ." She hissed again, this time in annoyance. She drew the wire out of the lock, bent it in half, and began to twist it to make a shorter, stiffer tool. It might be too thick that way, but the other way was hopeless.

"Oressa—" Her brother stopped.

"What?" Oressa looked up and found not only Gulien but even Gajdosik staring at her from their respective chairs. "I need something to do with my hands," she said defensively. She slipped her wire back into the tiny lock, closed her eyes, and began to feel again, delicately, for the internal shape of the lock and the slotted tumblers.

"What do you think we might do if you got that chain off?" asked Gulien. "I don't imagine it would do any good to find Kelian and try to persuade him to bring over the guard to our just and noble cause."

Oressa opened her eyes again so she could glare at her brother. "I've already *said* I'm sorry about Kelian! I will *always* be sorry about Kelian! I swear, Gulien, I *thought* he was loyal and I *thought* he was quick-witted—"

"I think possibly he is," said Gulien.

Oressa paused, staring at her brother. After a moment, she said, "Oh."

"He is, of course, loyal to your father the king," Gajdosik said. His lifted eyebrows made this a question.

"He lied to us," Oressa explained. "But Gulien thinks he lied to Father as well. Or why all that nonsense about romance and magic, that's what Gulien's wondering. He thinks Kelian is too smart to believe any of that, which would mean he's not Father's man at all. But whose, then?" she added doubtfully. "Bherijda's? Or I guess he might belong to Maranajdis, or one of the other Garamanaji princes."

"Whosoever the man may be, I assure you, he is not mine," Gajdosik said, his tone extremely dry.

"But you did have agents in Caras," said Gulien. "If one Tamaristan prince could have agents here, why not two? Why *not* Bherijda? Especially if he meant all along to come to Carastind and challenge the Kieba. It would explain everything—unless I'm missing something?" he asked Oressa.

"No," she said slowly. "No. It fits. It's possible. Everyone has spies, of course, and getting a man into the palace guard, anybody would be glad to manage that. I bet it *was* Bherijda." She was getting angrier and angrier as she thought about it. "We *should* have suspected Kelian. A man with no family or friends in the city? I mean, of course Erren checked his references, but Erren was always the sort to round off corners when he could get away with it, and Kelian seemed like such a find! Everybody liked him! *I* should have suspected him. But I actually *believed* that all those letters he sent north were written to his *mother*! Such a dutiful son! I'm sure!" She was disgusted and outraged, and she couldn't even get up and stamp her foot because Gajdosik was watching and he would think it was childish. She said, trying with only moderate success to flatten her tone and not shout, "I'm going to—I—I don't know, but he'd better not come near me next time I'm out on the roof or I'll *push him off.*"

Gulien chuckled, though she wasn't actually joking. But he also cautioned her, "It may not be true, you know. Maybe he really *was* writing to his mother. Maybe he really did believe Gajdosik used some kind of artifact to bewitch us both. But it's something to keep in mind, at least. And if Kelian might be a Tamaristan agent, who else might be? So, again, Oressa—what do you have in mind to *do*, if you get free?"

Oressa began to work the wire inside the lock again, shutting her eyes to make the task easier. "Well, I suppose Paulin isn't a traitor—but I don't trust him not to be Father's man. So we can't trust him, either. And if we can't trust anyone here, then we need to go somewhere else."

"North," said Gajdosik.

Oressa nodded.

"And find your men, and recruit them to our banner, whichever banner we decide is ours, and ride back to Caras and fight Bherijda to the bitter end," said Gulien. "And what about Father? Send him an ultimatum insisting he choose Bherijda's side or ours?"

"If we have a side," muttered Gajdosik. He sounded tired.

"Well, both Bherijda and our father are the Kieba's enemies," Oressa pointed out. "So she ought to be on our side."

"It's a risk. Another risk. I would like," Gulien said, with some intensity, "to free myself and you from these dead-gods-damned chains, even if for no other purpose than to stay right here and see what can be done once both Father and Bherijda are out of the city. We need to clear out the rest of the scorpion soldiers—and Bherijda's magisters—"

"*Oh* yes," agreed Oressa. She looked at her brother with respect. She hadn't expected him to be willing to defy their father again, at least not so directly and forcefully.

"Then if—when Father returns—he'll see—"

"What?" Now she glared at him. "A demonstration of filial loyalty? As if he'd be impressed!"

"Oressa, truly, you don't know Father as well as you think you do—"

Oressa made an unladylike sound.

"Oressa," Gulien said, this time in a tired, resigned tone that made her pause and look at him. He saw that he had her attention and said slowly, as though feeling for words that might make her actually listen, "Great-Grandfather killed our grandfather, you know."

Oressa stared at him, momentarily forgetting her efforts with the wire and the lock. "What?" And then, with instant suspicion, "Who told you that? Father?"

"He killed our grandfather *and* Uncle Mikel," said Gulien, ignoring this. "That's how Father became heir. Oh, Great-Grandfather didn't have them deliberately put to death. It was almost worse, in a way. He was just so . . . so *ineffectual*. Estenda set up this whole series of stupid little provocations, and Great-Grandfather just tried and tried to conciliate the merchant-princes. They got more aggressive and he kept trying to appease them, and of course the merchant-princes took all his efforts as weakness, so everything he did only made everything worse, until at last—"

"The Little War," Oressa said, frowning as she suddenly put things together. She had always known their grandfather had died in the Little War with Estenda. And their father's brother Mikel, too. But that was all so long ago. She hadn't even been born yet. She hadn't, she realized now, ever really thought of Grandfather Gerrel or Uncle Mikel as real people. She scowled at Gulien. *He* hadn't been born then, either.

"Father doesn't talk about it," Gulien said. "But Lord Paulin told me a little, and once you know what to look for, you can put the story together from the archives. Anyway, I just thought . . . I wanted you to know. Because I think that's why Father feels he has to, I don't know. Control everything. Get everything to happen just the way he wants. Because he just doesn't trust anybody else to do things *right*. Anyway—" He gave her an oddly anxious look. "I don't suppose it matters now."

Oressa stared at him for a long moment. "You're right!" she said at last. "It doesn't matter now. Anyway, I don't care!" But she wasn't sure whether this was the truth or not. She transferred her glare to the lock in her hand, because at least she knew exactly what she thought about *that*.

"I'll never get this dead-gods-damned—" But then she checked herself just as her brother said in a pained tone, "Don't swear, Oressa!" She had finally felt the wire slip neatly past the first tumbler. She scooped up and forward and a little around and lifted the second tumbler as well, and she held the wire steady, bent, closed her teeth gently around the manacle directly beside the lock, and pulled sideways.

The manacle snapped open.

Oressa looked up. "Well," she said, in her most blasé *of-course-I-did-it* tone, "yours should be easier. They're so much bigger."

But they weren't. The iron chains might be big and heavy and the manacles sized to match, but the actual locks weren't much bigger than the one on Oressa's little chain. Besides that, the tumblers were much stiffer and harder to catch and lift than the ones in her manacle. She only bent her wire, trying to shift the first tumbler in Gulien's manacle, and when she broke another wire off the manacle and twisted it around the first to stiffen it, the wire was too big.

"Oressa," Gulien said. "Oressa, it's all right. Of course it's hard to do, or they wouldn't use them in the dungeon cells, would they?"

"There's probably a magic on the locks," Gajdosik put in. "We make them so, in Tamarist. Princess, don't cry—"

"I'm not crying!" Oressa rubbed her hands angrily across her eyes, flinching as she accidently touched the welt across her cheek. It hurt, once she thought about it, and she was stiff from bending over Gulien's manacle, and she was desperately tired, and she had a headache, and she longed for own room and her own bed and Nasia to bring her hot brandied milk and warm pillows, and she was *not crying*. "Anyway," she said in a muffled voice, "it's my fault. I thought Kelian was so wonderful, and I decided I had to go to the gates myself and Kelian should go with me, and I should have got away to warn you only I couldn't. All your men were killed, weren't they? After everything else they came through, your own brother killed them—"

"None of us guessed about Kelian!" her brother said, and Gajdosik said very quietly, "After all we came through, my own brother would have killed me, except for you."

Oressa rubbed her eyes, sniffed, straightened her shoulders, and said with dignity, "And I was not crying, either."

"Of course not," Gulien agreed firmly. He and Gajdosik didn't look at each other, which Oressa appreciated.

"Anyway," Oressa said. She took her long chain with its empty manacle back into the other room so that Kedmes or a casual guard or even her father might think she was just not in the sitting room, rather than realizing she was gone. How much longer could it be before a guardsman or servant came in? She wondered if somebody would tell Nasia where she was, if maybe Nasia would come here herself, bent on performing her duties even under these circumstances. She *wished* Nasia would come and bring her clean clothing and run her a bath with scented soap . . . but not really. No. No, really, she wished she was away from here, that all three of them were away, and safe, and the Kieba was doing something to solve all their problems.

But it was perfectly obvious that no one was going to solve their problems except them. So she had better hurry. Only this was such a feminine room, it made her think there might be women's things in one of the drawers of the dressing table. She opened one drawer and then another, and found a clutter of embroidery things in the second drawer, including a pair of embroidery needles. If she weren't a fool, she'd have thought to look there first, but at least she'd thought of it now.

Gulien's manacle didn't want to yield even to a good, stiff needle. Oressa jabbed one of the needles against the floor to bend its tip into a tiny hook and then, working with her eyes closed, managed to catch the first tumbler with one needle and hold it with the second. Then the other tumbler, which was very stiff and hard to move, but she got it at last. Gulien jerked the manacle open so forcefully that she lost both needles, then apologized and helped her find them.

"It can't be much longer before— Oh, here, Oressa!" The second embroidery needle had flown under one of the other chairs, but he had found it at last by patting his way across the rug beneath the chairs. He dropped the needle into Oressa's palm and said again, "It can't be long now before someone comes."

Oressa was perfectly well aware of this. She'd wanted to get Gulien free if she could. He'd hated the chain so much. She was very glad she'd gotten his manacle open. But now she almost wished she'd worked on Gajdosik's first. *He* was the one in actual danger, and here he was, still chained up like a dog. And when she knelt beside his chair and began to work on the lock of his manacle, she found it even stiffer and harder to work with than Gulien's. Gajdosik showed no overt sign of impatience, but he gripped the other arm of his chair so tightly his knuckles were white.

Oressa promised him, "I'll get it—" But she hissed under her breath as the first tumbler started to move under her probing needle, but slipped.

In the hall outside the sitting room, booted footsteps suddenly echoed: Somebody had come into the hallway, and whoever he was, he was coming toward the sitting room.

Oressa jumped to her feet, took a nervous step toward the window, hesitated, started toward the other room instead, hesitated again—the footsteps went on by without pausing. She felt for a moment like she might faint right where she stood.

"Oressa—" Gulien reached for her hand.

Oressa took a step back, shaking her head. "I need to get out—I need to get away. The man could come back any time. *Anybody* could come at any time, and then what?" She looked again at the window.

"Oressa!" Gulien said sharply. "You *cannot possibly* go north *on your own.*"

"Someone has to!" Oressa pointed out. "If you can't get out, I can, and someone has to go to Prince Gajdosik's people, and this *is* all my fault anyway—"

"Oressa! Nothing is your fault!"

Oressa wasn't going to argue. She took a deep breath, lifted her chin, and walked firmly back into her private room. She began undoing the buttons on her dress—whyever did seamstresses have to put thousands of tiny little buttons on everything right where they were hardest to reach? She wished again for Nesia, but she got the last of the buttons at last and stripped off the tight, confining bodice and heavy skirts. Her shift left her arms bare and swirled lightly around her knees. Much better. She twisted her hair up and fixed it in place with an embroidery needle. Then she took a breath, raised her chin, and went back into the sitting room as she was, barefoot and in only her shift.

Gulien blinked. Gajdosik stared at her, went red, and whipped his gaze away.

"Sorry," Oressa said, trying not to laugh. "Well, no, actually, that was a lie." At Gulien's exclamation, she said virtuously, "What? I swore I'd tell him if I lied to him, you know!" But then she added to Gajdosik, much more sincerely, "You can look—a shift is almost as long as a servant girl's light dress, you know. I haven't given up on your manacle; just give me—"

There wasn't time. The booted footsteps sounded again, and this time the man stopped outside their door and the doorknob rattled.

Oressa darted to the window.

"You're not! It's six stories up!" Gajdosik exclaimed in an urgent whisper.

"It doesn't matter how high you are if you don't fall! And I never fall, not even when someone blows up the palace around me." Oressa put a foot on the windowsill, turned, bent her knees, pushed herself lightly backward, and dropped neatly off the windowsill. She felt madly alive and perfectly free. She knew she wouldn't fall.

She slapped the sill with both palms as she dropped, tucked herself inward, found the carved head of a falcon-headed goddess under her bare feet, turned, and stepped across empty air to the head of a snarling animal, something with sharp teeth and round eyes and swirls of carved hair. There was more carving on the palace walls the higher you went, gods and goddesses and monsters and all kinds of curlicues; builders always seemed to want to put all the big impressive pieces up high along the tops of walls, which was actually very helpful. It was just a matter of moving fast and never pausing, because there were plenty of hand- and footholds just as long as you didn't think about them. It was important to see without looking, to feel without thinking, to know just when a hard gust of wind would carry you that extra fraction of an inch.

Tower wall to lower tower roofs, then across to the sprawling eastern wing of the palace. None of that was difficult, but it took Oressa longer than it should have to work her way that far because she had to go around damaged parts of the palace. All the way, she could hear ordinary folk in the palace below, servants mostly, and court functionaries; guardsmen and Tamaristan soldiers—that was less welcome but not surprising. She heard masons and carpenters over on the damaged side of the palace. The courtyards and gardens were busy with ordinary comings and goings, plus the builders and the Tamaristan soldiers, but Oressa was confident no one would look up, and no one did.

She made her way toward her own rooms. Nobody should be there, except possibly Nasia, and she was sure her maid wouldn't give her away. Oressa knew exactly what she wanted: the kind of dress she could wear out in the city and not have people turn and stare—the kind she could climb in if she needed to. And she didn't have any money, but she could use some of her jewels to buy things—she tried to decide if beaten disks of gold would be better than pearls or the other way around.

But there were voices in her rooms. Men's voices. She paused, clinging to a not-very-comfortable perch above the window.

". . . come here anyway," complained one voice.

"I'll be sure and tell His Majesty you said so, shall I?" asked a second, nearer. Then the speaker put his head out the window and looked out.

Oressa froze, feeling her fingers cramp. . . . Her toes suddenly felt wrong on the stone, or maybe the stone itself suddenly felt as though it might crumble out from under her. She pressed her cheek against the wall and held her breath, staring downward until she suddenly thought that the pressure of her gaze might pull the man's attention upward—she just knew he was going to lift his head suddenly and meet her eyes.

But the man wasn't looking for her at all. He stared out and down, gazing after a column of departing men. Oressa, following his gaze, blinked: That was a lot of men. Her father had said he was leaving Caras, and yes, she could see the bronze and blue of the Madalin falcon at the head of the column. But he hadn't said he was taking with him all the able-bodied men left in the whole Caras militia. Maybe he needed them in case of trouble with Bherijda's men, because there were a lot of men marching under the scorpion banner, too, including at least half a dozen black-robed magisters.

She was sure her father had not only invited Bherijda to march east to challenge the Kieba, but also got him to take along lots of his men. That would get the scorpion soldiers out of Caras, which was good right there. The only question was, what clever thing did her father actually mean to do once he got to the Kieba's mountain? Oressa could imagine him setting up a battle between Bherijda and the Kieba and then staying out if it himself. Whoever won, he would be rid of at least one of his enemies, and he could claim that all the time he'd really been supporting whoever won. Actually, that sounded *exactly* like something her father would do.

On the other hand, he might truly believe he and Bherijda together might defeat the Kieba. Might *claim her power* and *assume her role*. He'd said that, or something very like it. Yes, he'd said, *We may claim the Kieba's power and assume her role, and the world will not end.*

She felt sinkingly certain that if her father truly believed he could destroy the Kieba, he must have very sound reasons for that belief. But she wasn't nearly so certain that the world wouldn't end if he achieved his ambition. If her father used Bherijda to destroy the Kieba . . . that would be a lot more dangerous than using the Kieba to rid himself of Bherijda.

That possibility lent a new urgency to her plan to seek out Gajdosik's men in the north. Though she knew her brother would need those men here, too. Except that if Gulien used Tamaristan soldiers to reestablish his authority in Caras and claim the throne, then people would say forever that he had used foreign soldiers to depose his own father, and Gulien would hate that.

It was all so complicated. Everything was so big and important. The only thing she knew for sure was that she needed to get out of the palace and out of Caras and away north and find Gajdosik's men. *Then* she would at least have the ability to *do* something. If she could decide what to do.

The watching man made a disgusted sound—at what, Oressa had no idea—and pulled his head back into the room. He said, "But you're right. She won't come here, not if she's trying to stay out of sight. She'll have more sense." He added, his tone admiring, "You heard she bit a chunk out of one bastard Tamaristan who laid hands on her? Blood all over the atrium, *I* heard. Too bad it wasn't His dead-gods-damned Tamaristan Highness himself."

"Maybe next time," said the first voice. "If there's a next time: *I* think King Osir plans to come back alone."

The man snorted and pulled his head back in the window. "I won't give you odds on that. But if Prince Bherijda *does* come back with him, two gets you three our little princess'll get ahold of a knife and cut His Highness's throat for him. And *I'll* drink a toast to her when she does it." His steps moved away from the window, his words growing muffled.

Oressa blinked hard and then turned her head and rubbed her eyes on her shoulder. She wasn't crying, and she wasn't shaking either, and she felt *perfectly fine*. She climbed, as silently as she could, into her room and tiptoed to her jewelry cabinet. She caught up a hasty handful of necklaces: one of thin hammered gold disks, one of silvery pearls, and one of garnets and black pearls strung on a gold chain. Then she found a clean dress, one without lace or fancy needlework, the kind she might have worn to go riding, with a hidden pocket in the bodice for her to hide the necklaces. And she needed slippers. . . . Surely she had a plain pair of slippers somewhere. Well, these with just a little fancy stitching on the toes would have to do.

It all made an unwieldy bundle. That was all right. She could fasten it around her waist with a narrow belt. She was afraid every moment the men would come back, but they didn't. Even so, she didn't dare linger in her room a second longer than necessary.

The aviary was an easy climb, one she'd done dozens of times. Her hands were shaking, though, and she stopped for a minute, clinging to a carved flourish, her feet resting on a ripple of brick and stone. Her fingertips hurt. She climbed carefully sideways and up, one familiar hand- and foothold after another, almost not paying attention because she was afraid of missing her grip if she thought too hard about what she was doing. The aviary was right above her, and she got a hand on the sill, ducked her head, and rolled in, not very gracefully.

The aviary, at least, was deserted by all but birds. Pigeons cooed and shuffled in the dimness, calming quickly from their momentary alarm at her clumsy entrance. There was a strong musky scent of guano and sawdust, but the pigeon keepers cleaned the aviary every day, for which Oressa was grateful. And, almost as welcome as solitude, there was a barrel of clean water in the corner.

The pigeons murmured and shifted and fluttered their wings, a peaceful sound that made Oressa feel safe. She pried the lid off the barrel and drank handfuls of the water. It was flat and stale, but she was very glad someone had gone to the effort of lugging it up the stairs. There were smocks hanging on hooks; she dabbed one in the water and cleaned herself up as best she could. Soap would have been nice, but one couldn't have everything. There were bins of cracked grain and unmilled amaranth but no loaves of old bread, which was even more of a shame than the lack of soap. Even so, Oressa didn't mean to leave the aviary for anything, not until it got dark. Now that she was safe—safer—she was desperately tired. Surely dusk could not be so very far away. She could nap right here in the aviary for an hour, even two, and then at night, in her clean dress, she could surely slip out into the city with no one the wiser

She longed for fresh air and open space and freedom, but she wasn't winged like the pigeons and she couldn't climb in the dark. She would go the other way, out the door and down the stairs, like a normal person. Soon. But not quite yet.

But when she woke, in the close dark with the pigeons shuffling gently around her and her face aching, she realized she had another problem. She put a hand to her cheek.

She had almost forgotten about the mark Bherijda's riding crop had left on her face. She remembered it now. The few hours of rest had helped. It must have helped, though she felt like she could crawl into a real bed and sleep for days. She was still tired, still aching from . . . everything. But her face hurt worst of all. She traced the line of the welt in the dark: swollen and tender. Bherijda's men might recognize her by it even if they didn't know her by sight. Could she avoid them as well as her father's men?

Oressa suddenly found herself too paralyzed with fear and uncertainty to move. She wanted to tuck herself down again among the pigeons and hide and wait for someone else to do something and solve everything. She wished Gulien were here. Her brother was *too* calm sometimes, but now there was hardly anyone she wanted more. Or she wished Gajdosik were here. *He* would have some ideas about what to do.

But hiding in the aviary among the pigeons for the rest of her life didn't seem like a very good plan.

In the end she took her hair down and arranged it as well as she could to fall across her cheek. If she kept her face down, she thought maybe the welt wouldn't be instantly obvious. There was no mirror, of course, so she couldn't be sure. But surely it was late enough that even the servants would mostly have gone to bed?

It was long past dusk, she found, when she finally left the aviary. Most of the lamps had been put out even in the servants' narrow hallways, which meant she had been right and all the late work was done. She wondered whether she might risk ducking into the kitchens just for a moment, but the kitchen staff would start the bread long before dawn and might already be mixing the dough, and anyway she thought maybe some of the potboys and scullions might actually sleep in the kitchens, under the tables or somewhere. She went the other way, keeping carefully to the servants' halls and stairs. After all her worry about her face, she met no one. She heard people several times, the booted tread of guardsmen or soldiers, but each time she was able to keep out of their way. Once she heard the murmur of voices, but though she paused to listen, she couldn't make out the words.

She slipped at last out of the palace into the starlit dark of the east courtyard. She thought there had to be guardsmen posted somewhere, but she didn't see them; she thought there might be Tamaristan soldiers, but she didn't see them, either. Creeping around drew attention, so she took a deep breath, lifted her chin, and walked straight across the courtyard to the gates. Nobody seemed to be watching. Maybe all of her father's and Bherijda's men were busy spying on one another and couldn't spare the time to actually guard the palace. She passed through the gates and darted through the shadows, away from the palace she knew so well and into the city she didn't know at all.

CHAPTER 22

Gulien, unable to even think of following his sister out the window, sent one swift, speaking look at Prince Gajdosik. Then, since he had no choice, he turned to face the door. He put his father's anger and disgust out of his mind, or he tried to. Surely this could not actually *be* his father returning. He'd said he was leaving Caras, leaving Bherijda's men in occupation. Of the palace, of Caras. But Bherijda himself was leaving as well; they might already be gone.

All this went through Gulien's mind in a single heartbeat. Straightening his shoulders, he folded his arms and fixed his thoughts firmly on the surety of his own rank and authority.

The door swung open.

Kedmes stepped in. But behind him, confounding all of Gulien's half-formed expectations, stood Lord Paulin Tegeres, and behind Paulin, some number of men all wearing, so far as Gulien could see, the fox badge of the Tegeres house.

Osir Madalin's burly servant could hardly be browbeaten or over-awed or least of all suborned. Kedmes took his orders and his tone only from the king and regarded the king's son, as nearly as Gulien could tell, as a boy of little account. When Gulien had usurped, or attempted to usurp, his father's authority, surely no man in Caras had resented it more than Kedmes.

On the other hand, Gulien was clearly not chained up like a dog.

And so far as Kedmes knew, only the king himself could have locked or unlocked the chain. Gulien saw the man's eyes go from Gulien to the chain and back again, his brows drawing together in bafflement.

"Well, well," Lord Paulin said, puffing slightly with a hasty climb up all the stairs. He also glanced at the chain and then at Gulien standing plainly unbound in the center of the room. "It seems our understanding of, ah, recent events, might have been less than entirely clear. We're relieved to see you, ah, in good health, aren't we, men?" He glanced over his shoulder at his men, who obediently murmured agreement.

"Of course. Thank you, my lord," Gulien said, and asked immediately before Kedmes could interrupt, "Has my father yet departed?"

"Ah yes, well, I believe His Majesty's company has probably just departed the forecourt."

Ah. And Paulin had clearly rushed up the tower stairs the moment they had gone, Gulien realized and reassessed the older man.

Paulin, still puffing, pressed a hand to his heart. But he said almost smoothly, "So I imagine they will be out of the city in mere moments. Though a swift-footed young person, unlike myself, might be able to bear a message to His Majesty for you, if that is what you wish." His tone on this was bland, but his gaze was shrewd.

"No, no, that should not be necessary," Gulien said, then added, with an eye to Kedmes, "I believe my father and I have a clear understanding of our necessary course of action." He wondered, rather desperately, what "course of action" this might plausibly be.

Kedmes began, "I will go—"

"I wouldn't put you to the trouble," Gulien assured him.

"Ah yes," agreed Lord Paulin. "That is, no, of course not. Rias." He addressed one of his own men. "I'm sure none of His Majesty's servants need trouble themselves to run messages; if anyone must, I'm sure you can find a fast young man among our own people. Good, good, yes, I was certain of it." His tone hearty, he turned back to Gulien. "Well, Your Highness, and what course of action might you—and your father, of course—have in mind, in this exigency? The palace is still occupied by upward of forty Tamaristan soldiers, I believe—and if there are less than two thousand out there in the city, there surely aren't less than a thousand, and even that's too many for us to easily be rid of them."

"Yes," Gulien said, and looked at Prince Gajdosik.

Gajdosik straightened and set his elbow on the arm of his chair, the iron chain clattering with the movement. He no longer appeared in the least weary or disheartened but filled with confidence and purpose.

This was an impression Gulien much admired and wished he knew how to emulate. He said, as decisively as he could, "Your Highness, if you have a suggestion, then by all means."

Gajdosik gave a grim nod. "Your Highness, as you have done me the honor to ask for my advice, I must agree that the first order of business, as your father has now succeeded in removing Bherijda from Caras, is to clear the city of my brother's remaining men. Though the soldiers are important, I must reiterate that Bherijda's magisters should be your primary concern."

Gulien cleared his throat, raised his chin, and said to Paulin, smoothly, he hoped, "Can you tell me how many Tamaristan magisters remain in the palace? In Caras, or anywhere nearby, for that matter. Do please assure me that Bherijda himself is out of the city."

Paulin began, "Indeed—" But Kedmes, shoving forward, demanded abruptly, "*Did* His Majesty free you? I don't believe it! Where is the princess?"

Gulien raised his eyebrows in assumed astonishment at this interruption. "Well, who else do you imagine could have?" Then he added, deliberately borrowing his father's flattest tone, "Oressa is exactly where she is supposed to be." He raised a finger, interrupting the other man's attempt to break in a second time. "Forgive me, Kedmes, but we have matters of greater urgency to address." Turning back to Lord Paulin, he asked, "My lord, you were saying?"

Kedmes glowered, but Lord Paulin smiled and said smoothly, "Your Highness, indeed, I was about to assure you that, as you hoped, Prince Bherijda departed the city with His Majesty."

"Good, good. And *did* Prince Bherijda take all of his magisters away with him?"

"Unfortunately not, Your Highness. At least four remain, in their . . . workshop. They have established themselves in the dungeons. One is not entirely certain what courses of action they may be pursuing, but one fears it may be difficult to come at them there. One fears that is precisely why they chose that location."

"I see," Gulien said, trying to sound thoughtful rather than worried or confounded. He couldn't restrain himself from looking at Gajdosik.

"Your Highness, allow me suggest once more that you free me," Gajdosik said. "Or—" He hesitated, and Gulien saw him reconsider what he would say. He did not glance at Lord Paulin, but he went on urgently. "Or leave me chained if you don't trust me; that's well enough. But allow me to advise you. You know I am Bherijda's enemy. I *will* help you throw down my brother's people."

"Your Highness—" began Lord Paulin.

"His Majesty—" said Kedmes at the same time, and they both stopped. Kedmes glared at Lord Paulin but had to give way. Paulin turned to Gulien and said firmly, "Your Highness, I think we have had enough of Tamaristan princes! I must advise against trading an alliance with one Tamaristan prince for another!"

"I cannot dispute your wisdom, Paulin, and yet Prince Gajdosik's advice has been useful to me, and will be again, I believe." Inspiration struck, and Gulien said to Kedmes, "Strike the chain, but leave the manacle." Then he said to Gajdosik, "Let the manacle you wear be a reminder to you, Your Highness, that you remain my prisoner and in my hands. But deal faithfully and honestly with me, and I swear I will deal generously with you and all your people."

"I agree," Gajdosik said instantly. "I give you my word, Your Highness." He turned to Lord Paulin. "You must also be aware, my lord, that Bherijda is my enemy, and I, his."

"I trust his word," Gulien put in, and waited, trying not to show his anxiety, to see what everyone would do. Ultimately, Kedmes was not important. Paulin was the key. And he had already made his decision. He must have done. That was why he had come up here to find Gulien, hard on the heels of Osir Madalin's departure from the palace. But asking him to take Gajdosik's word was something else again; Gulien knew that, too. He didn't think Paulin would change his mind now. But on the other hand, he had said perfectly plainly that a swift-footed man might still carry word to the king.

For a moment Gulien thought it might go either way. But then Paulin nodded abruptly and said to one of his men, "Well, you heard His Highness! Strike the Tamaristan prince's chain. Kedmes will show you where to find tools, or if you have to, go down to the smithy for a chisel or whatever. I'm sure you needn't put Kedmes or any of His Majesty's other servants to the trouble."

Gulien nodded as though he'd been perfectly confident all along that Paulin would yield. He asked, "Have those magisters any fragments of artifacts, do you know, and what do they have?"

"Unfortunately, Your Highness, I fear we have no idea."

"Well, it doesn't matter, as we will have to contrive regardless," Gulien declared. He was pleased to hear how confident his own voice sounded. "Whom can we rely on? Beriad?"

"His Majesty took the majority of the palace guard with him, of course, Your Highness, including Beriad. As he doubtless discussed with you, Your Highness, he left Erren in command of the remaining guard and the militia."

"Yes, of course." Erren, naturally. Gulien suspected that was going to be a problem. He said out loud, "I shall have to see Erren, of course. Immediately. Who else do we have?"

Erren was a problem. Gulien, remembering Oressa's opinion of him, was not surprised. He'd had one of Paulin's men bring Erren up to the tower, since this apartment was clearly as secure a place as any to lay plans and gather what paltry assets he could muster. But Erren clearly didn't believe the king had left Gulien to rule in his place, just as Kedmes hadn't believed it. Well, and Gulien knew perfectly well that Lord Paulin didn't believe it either.

Paulin had his men, and another lord, Beroen, offered men as well. But against the thousand or more scorpion soldiers left in Caras, Gulien knew he needed Erren's guardsmen as well. And he needed all of his people to take not only his orders, but Gajdosik's, and that was a sticking point for the whole lot of them.

And all the while he could feel time pressing at his back—he had no idea what the Kieba was facing, no idea where Oressa was, no idea what he could do about any of that.

So he lost his temper.

"I tell you all," he nearly shouted, "if I can't find guardsmen or militia to do this job, then I'll find shopkeepers and farmers, do you hear? The people of Camian's Way, shall we say! *Their* courage I don't doubt, nor their determination, nor their willingness to work with whatever they have to hand! If we'd thrown up barricades like theirs all through the approaches out of the harbor, Bherijda wouldn't have had everything his own way! Nor before that would we have needed the Kieba's help to give Gajdosik a fight! Our people are not cowards, and if they haven't swords, they'll use chair legs and butcher knives! With your help or without, we *will* drive Bherijda's murdering bastards back into the Narrow Sea! And if they haven't time to board their ships in their rush to get away, then *let them drown*!"

There was a stark pause. Then Lord Paulin ducked his head. "Forgive us, Your Highness. Of course you are correct. What are your orders?" And Erren, looking hunted, muttered that of course he hadn't meant, that is, naturally he would—

"Very well!" Gulien snapped. "Prince Gajdosik, your advice?"

Gajdosik inclined his head. "My brother's magisters must be our priority," he said, his quiet tone obviously a deliberate counterpoint to Gulien's fury. "We must break their power at once, a problem complicated by our lack of information about what artifacts they may currently hold. The actual garrison Bherijda left in Caras is not so important, though it is of course strategically desirable to recover control of the harbor, the city gates, and the main approaches to the palace. However, I—we—you can induce Bherijda's soldiers to surrender at your leisure, after the magisters have been brought down."

There was another little silence. Then one of Erren's men, a grizzled older man, said, speaking to Gulien and carefully ignoring Gajdosik, "They've set themselves up in the dungeons, Your Highness, which that'd be a good place for them, you might say, as His Majesty hadn't been using them for much else lately, only it's hard to come at 'em there, and worth every man we have if we try, even leaving aside those scorpion bastards, which important as they aren't." The guardsman gave Gajdosik a wary glance. "If they get started burning and murdering in the city, Your Highness, I don't know how we can stop 'em."

Gulien said to Gajdosik, "Well?"

"Powder," said Gajdosik immediately. "All you have left. Set charges directly over the magister's position. Your dungeons will make a fitting grave for them."

The same guardsman said heatedly, "That'd destroy half the palace! What's left of the palace!"

Gajdosik raised his voice slightly. "Time is our tightest constraint in this battle. You daren't act against my brother's men while his magisters may wield old magic against you, but the moment they're gone, it won't matter that Bherijda's garrison outnumbers our men—your men—three to one. Your palace is a necessary casualty. Tip it over on the board and press for the win."

The guardsman began, "This isn't a *game*—"

"*Enough!*" Gulien snapped, and the guardsman stopped. Gulien said more quietly, "Prince Gajdosik is correct in every particular. We will proceed exactly as he suggests. Dry powder, as much as we have. Who here knows exactly where those magisters are? All right, Mikke, find Magistra Lara; if anyone can help fix the best place to put the powder, she can." He hoped the man would be able to find Magistra Lara; the scholar-mathematician was surely the perfect person to bring down the palace neatly just where they wanted it to fall. Gulien went on. "I'm sure we all agree that if we must blow up half the palace, it would be better to blow up the correct half."

Everyone stared at Gulien, not moving immediately. Then Lord Paulin cleared his throat, clapped his hands together, and declared, "It's a good plan, Your Highness. It will work. My people will see to clearing our folk out of the palace." He looked around meaningfully, and his men scattered, suddenly industrious, followed quickly by everyone else.

"It *is* a good plan," Lord Paulin said to Gulien more quietly, not quite looking at Gajdosik.

Gulien rubbed his forehead. "It should be quick and decisive, at least. And I doubt Bherijda's people will have prepared for it. Several tons of stone dropped on their heads ought to discommode anyone, no matter what artifacts they may hold." He gave Prince Gajdosik a slight nod. "It's a good idea. I think it will work."

Gajdosik inclined his head. "I think it will. Though I don't know what Her Highness will say when she sees what I've done to your palace this time."

Gulien stared at him, then laughed. "Oh, *I* know exactly what Oressa will say!"

When she returned. Gulien wished he dared send a man after her. But he wasn't even certain she'd gone north; if she'd had a better idea, or what she considered a better idea, who knew what she would do or where she might go? If she was out in Caras, no one would find her.

Surely she was not up on the rooftops of the palace. Surely not. He had better send a man or two to look for her, quietly. Because the guardsman had been right about that much, at least: When they set the powder off, half the remaining palace was going to come down.

This proved, in the event, not to be quite true. In the event, the whole palace fell. Or nearly.

They set the powder up all through the ground floor of the east wing of the palace, above the upper dungeons, which was where the

Tamaristan magisters had set up their workroom. It took all night, which made Gulien nervous, but men could do only as much as they could do.

"They've got all these strange things," volunteered one of the kitchen girls, who had been brave enough to take a breakfast tray of meat pastries and amaranth cakes down to the magisters in order to ensure they knew for *certain* where the Tamaristan magisters actually were. "A thing shaped just like a cone of sugar, but three times the size and made of black glass, a piece of gray crystal shaped like a great beetle, and this strange thing"—she sketched it with her hands—"like a birdcage of gold wire, only just little, like this, and all filled up with a spiderweb, but that's gold too, only it's got a little red stone in the middle."

Even Gajdosik shrugged and spread his hands, wincing a little as he remembered his splinted fingers, but appearing to have no more idea than anyone else what any of the things might be. Gulien started to shrug and then blinked and shook his head, golden webs tangling in his memory. "Oh," he said. "Oh. Yrïenku's Net. We don't want them using that. No, we don't." He blinked again, rubbing his eyes, just as glad for once that the half-glimpsed memories refused to come clear. "That's in the upper dungeon too?"

"Yes, sir," agreed the girl anxiously. "I don't know what might be lower down 'cause I didn't go look, sir, seeing as I hadn't any reason to poke about. But the magisters were all in the upper dungeons, sir, like as four black crows."

"Good," Gulien told her. "Perfect. We'll drop the whole east wing on top of them." He and all his people were gathered in the kitchens, that being as far from the east wing as they could get without putting themselves in the way of the scorpion soldiers left in the palace. He looked at Gajdosik. "That's perfect, isn't it?"

"Your Highness, I think it is," Gajdosik answered formally.

"Then—" Gulien opened a hand.

Gajdosik turned briskly to their allies, to all appearances with the same confidence he might have had in his own men. "Mikke, Teras, let us be certain the stairway door up from the dungeons is barred, yes? It would be as well to make quite sure. Baris, Periane, this would be the time to distract Bherijda's men, as we discussed. Ready? Excellent, off you go. Tand, if you would begin your count for the upper fuses? You will light them exactly on the count of one hundred, yes? Run!" Then he took a lighted taper from the fire, inclined his head, and offered it to Gulien. "On a count of one hundred fifty, I believe? It is *your* palace, after all, Your Highness."

The palace came down beautifully, in the end. At first there was only a muffled *thump*, some shattering glass, and a surprisingly small puff of gray smoke at the windows on the first floor. Gulien, watching from a prudent distance, far across the courtyard, with Gajdosik and Lord Paulin and Erren and a handful of others, thought the whole scheme had failed.

Then there was a louder thump, and a grinding, crashing groan of stone against stone, and the second floor slowly collapsed into the first. And then the third floor collapsed inward as well. And then all the outer walls began to lean inward, gently at first so that Gulien thought he might be imagining the tilt, but then more dramatically until there was no doubt of it. *Then* the nearest wall swayed over a bit more and toppled, disappearing into the rising cloud of smoke and red dust, and then the whole inner wall of the north wing fell in, and in the end Gulien found, watching the dust swirl and settle, that he was quite, quite certain that Yrïenku's Net was not going to be a problem in the future, and his heart lifted even though he still had no clear memory of what it did or was or had been.

"If only Bherijda himself had been down there," Gajdosik muttered, and coughed. Soot streaked his face, all their faces, as the cloud of smoke and dust rolled across their position.

"One thing at a time," Gulien muttered back.

"Sir—" The kitchen girl's voice was urgent. "Sir—"

Gulien looked around, blinking, and then followed the direction of the girl's pointing hand, up into the billowing smoke that now obscured half the sky. Then he braced himself and flung up his arm just in time to receive a falcon that fell like a bolt of lightning out of the sky to light on his wrist.

This falcon could never have been mistaken for a natural bird. It flew like a bird and its talons pricked Gulien's skin like those of a real falcon, but its feathers seemed to have been spun out of steel and glass and it glared at Gulien out of eyes made of smoky gray crystal.

"How can you send so obvious a golem here?" Gulien demanded. "You said, you said *plainly* you could not—"

"Gulien Madalin," it said in the toneless voice of the kephalos. "Parianasaku's Capture has left Caras. Osir Madalin still holds it. Even now he brings it to the Kieba's mountain. Bherijda Garamanaj holds a fragment of Tonkaïan's Resolve. He brings this also to the Kieba's mountain. The Kieba is in peril. Your affiliation is to the Kieba. The Kieba requires you now. The mountain of kept memory requires its Kieba. You must establish your aspect and raise your position. Time is of the essence. You recall the place where Berakalan's door opens. Go there. I will open Berakalan's door from within the Tomb of the Gods, that you may come at once to the mountain."

Gulien stared wordlessly into the falcon's crystalline eyes. Its feathers ruffled in the hot wind, steel and silver and glass. The smoke and grit in the air dimmed its shine but could not make it appear like any natural bird. It did not speak again, but waited, with a patience as unnatural as its metallic feathers, for him to answer.

Looking up, Gulien found himself first meeting Prince Gajdosik's intense gaze, then glancing away at the little knot of his people gathered there.

"You can't leave Caras now!" protested Lord Paulin. "Your father's already left Caras. If you go too, then . . ." He spread his pudgy hands, letting the rest of his objection stand unspoken.

He hardly needed to complete his protest. Gulien knew he was right. A good few of Bherijda's scorpion soldiers must still be out there in the city somewhere, and for all he knew, yet another Garamanaji prince was just waiting for his chance. Prince Gajdosik's three thousand men were all too likely to march down from the north. They might arrive in an hour or a day, with or without having met Oressa, and then what? Or if they didn't, then Caras would fragment all on its own; Gulien could imagine it clearly. Lord Paulin would have his ideas about what to do, Lord Beroen quite different ideas. Magister Lorren would probably be dying to uncover the buried dungeons and get his hands on any surviving artifacts—luckily that would probably be impossible—and dead gods knew, if Magister Baramis hadn't accompanied Gulien's father in the first place, he would insist on going after him.

Gulien scrubbed his free hand over his face. Then he straightened, dropped his hand to his side, and looked directly into Prince Gajdosik's face.

"You must go, of course," the Tamaristan prince said flatly.

Everyone started to speak at once. Gulien put up a forbidding hand, and they all stopped, even Lord Paulin.

Prince Gajdosik said with the same flat certainty, "It is insupportable that Bherijda should lay his hand to the Kieba's power."

"It would be better if my father didn't, either," Gulien said, not quite to him, but to the whole small gathering. "He is the Kieba's enemy. But he's wrong. We need the Kieba. Not just us. Everyone. We dare not allow *any* of her enemies to cast her down." There was a slight pause. Not even Paulin said a word.

Gulien turned slightly to take in the ruined palace. Dust and smoke swirled slowly and heavily where the many-storied palace of the Madalin family had once stood. One might see a kind of metaphor in that, if one were so inclined.

He said to Gajdosik, "You remain my prisoner, Your Highness."

Prince Gajdosik inclined his head. "I acknowledge it, Your Highness. I do not dispute it."

Gulien nodded. "I gave you tactical command. You hold it still, Prince Gajdosik Garamanaj, and you must continue to hold it. Establish order in my city. That is my command. Clear out the rest of your brother's men. Protect Caras from all her enemies. I leave my city to you in trust,

Your Highness." He more than half expected someone—Lord Paulin or Erren or *someone*—to object. No one said a word.

"I will keep this trust," Prince Gajdosik said formally.

"I know you will," Gulien told him. "In this exigency, my people will support you." He looked at Lord Paulin and then Lord Beroen and then at Erren, collecting reluctant acknowledgment from one man and then the next and the next. Satisfied—as satisfied as possible under the circumstances— he started to turn, then swung back. "Cooperate with one another!" he ordered them all. "If the Kieba sends word to you here, then obey her word as well!"

"With a dedicated will, Your Highness," Gajdosik promised him.

Gulien nodded. He wanted to add, *And find Oressa.* But he didn't dare admit publicly he didn't know where she was. Besides, though Gajdosik would surely send someone after her, notwithstanding the most dedicated will in the world, he knew no one would find his sister if Oressa didn't want to be found.

He wanted to look for her himself. But he had no time. He knew that most clearly of all.

CHAPTER 23

Oressa had thought it might be exciting, being alone outside the palace, disguised as a common woman. In fact, it was awful. An ordinary night might have been different, but she had forgotten somehow that Caras was an occupied city—that Bherijda's men would be patrolling the streets and that at night, without lamps over doors and lanterns glowing in windows, the city would be terrifyingly dark. Almost no moonlight made its way down to light the narrow streets between the blank walls of the closed-up houses. Only the scorpion soldiers carried lanterns, which made them easier to avoid, but it was almost impossible to pick her way through the streets without a lantern of her own.

Not only that, but she found out the hard way that not all the scorpion soldiers traveled in a wave of light and noise. One small, quiet troop nearly caught her before she got properly away from the palace. Oressa tucked herself behind a feathery tamarisk in a heavy stone planter until they were past, then peeked cautiously after them until she lost them in the darkness.

There seemed a great many scorpion soldiers. Far more than she'd expected. She'd thought Bherijda had taken them all with him, but plainly he had left a good many behind. She supposed there was no reason to think Bherijda had brought fewer men across the Narrow Sea than Gajdosik. In that case, even if he'd taken a thousand men with him on the road toward the Kieba's mountain, he might have left thousands more in Caras. It certainly *seemed* like thousands, when one was attempting to sneak unobtrusively out of the city. She hoped, at least, that if so many men were out here in the city, then Gulien might have more freedom to act within the palace. But that was only a hope. What she *knew* was that at every turn she seemed to be surrounded by enemies.

Oressa also couldn't guess what her own people would do if she stumbled into them and asked for aid. Would they help her get away to the north? If she told them who she was, what then? Would they believe her, and if they did, would they expect her to lead them in some mad, defiant gesture? She rather liked the idea of a mad, defiant gesture, but not when she actually needed to get away and find Gajdosik's people. Besides, she wasn't quite certain how she could explain to her own people that she meant to get away in order to bring back a lot more Tamaristan soldiers. On the whole, it seemed better to slip away unobserved by anyone at all.

But the city seemed bigger and darker and far more frightening once she started trying to find her way through it alone and on foot. She simply hadn't realized how utterly strange it would be to sneak through an occupied city completely on her own.

But she would do it. She *would*. She would get out and get a horse somehow, ride north and find Gajdosik's men, and nothing would stop her.

Even if she had to wait till dawn to make her way through these streets, which seemed frustratingly inclined to tangle up into a maze. At least she had managed to pick her way a little farther from the palace and so felt a bit safer, but though she longed for light, she was afraid to stop without finding a better hiding place. If she could find a way to scramble up onto the rooftops . . . That way, once the sun came up, she could see where she *was*—

There was a faint, unexpected clatter, not very far away, as of someone stumbling over something in the dark, and someone hissed, "*Hsst!* Ox! Watch where you put your feet."

Oressa froze, not knowing whether to crouch down in the dark and hold still or bolt back the way she'd come. But those words had been in Esse; those weren't Bherijda's men. Running away blind seemed like a stupid idea; she'd surely trip or run into something. She thought again of the rooftops, but the nearest wall, when she ran her hand across it hopefully, was smooth, unbroken plaster. Even her breathing seemed loud to her.

"Someone's here," whispered a different voice. "Spread out, you lot."

Oressa guessed there were at least three or four men ahead of her. She began to edge away, back the way she'd come, gently, not too fast. She was listening so intently to the whispers that she ran right into someone else, someone big and sturdy but alarmingly quiet, who closed powerful arms around her before she could duck away. He had, she realized instantly, been waiting for her to be spooked back into him. They'd done that on purpose—flushed her just like a hare into a hunter's net.

There was no way she could get away. But she knew the man was Carastindin, not one of Bherijda's men. So Oressa didn't try to pull away. Instead, she said, in an icy, quiet voice, not whispering, "Don't we have enough trouble with all those scorpion soldiers without ambushing one another? Let me go."

"A girl!" exclaimed her captor. He did let her go, mostly, though he kept one broad hand wrapped around her arm. He patted her on the head with his other hand gently, as though he were reassuring a dog.

"Not safe out for a girl during daylight, never mind at night," muttered one of the other men, who seemed to be the leader. "What are you doing out here, girl?"

"Trying to get away from *them*," Oressa said truthfully. "But I think I'm lost."

"I think maybe you are," agreed the men, and laughed, a short, grim sound without a lot of humor to it.

Oressa could hardly see her captors, but she could hear them breathing. They smelled of olives and smoke and something else, burnt clay or something. She wondered who they were—potters, craftsmen? Militia, more than likely, whatever else they were. She asked tentatively, "Can you help me? I was trying to get to the north road. It's important I get away to the north. They might be looking for me—"

"Maybe, maybe," muttered the man. "Hush!"

For a long moment everyone stood very still, listening.

In the distance Oressa could hear some of the scorpion soldiers— loud, rhythmic, marching in step. The light from their lanterns dipped and swayed as they drew near. They were moving at an oblique angle, but she could tell they were going to come quite near.

She stirred anxiously, but before she could speak, the leader said to the big man holding her, in a low mutter, "We'll deal with *those*. You, get her to the other one, that guard officer from the palace. He's wanting to go north. He can escort her. Don't take all night about it, hear me? I need you here."

Oressa was cautiously delighted. This sounded perfect. A guardsman from the palace! She wasn't sure why a guardsman would be going north—perhaps to rally help from Addas, that might make sense. Or maybe to get a firsthand look at Gajdosik's men, bring back news about exactly where the Tamaristan force was and whether it was moving and how fast and in what direction. That seemed likely, in fact. Any intelligent man would want to know all about the sea-eagle, whether he hoped Gajdosik's men might be allies against Bherijda or feared they would be yet more enemies. Lord Paulin would know how important it was to have real information—or Lord Beroen might have sent a man.

Anyway, it must be someone she knew. Not Erren, surely, but someone with sense, someone like Beriad, who could guide her and help her, so she wouldn't have to try to do everything by herself. Beriad would be *perfect*.

But when the big man finally led her up to a dark building—that looked to Oressa exactly like every other building they had passed— and tapped a rapid sequence on the door, and the door opened into lantern-lit warmth and safety, it wasn't Beriad who turned sharply to see who had come in.

It was Kelian.

Oressa was torn between leaping back out the door into the dark city and stalking forward to slap him, but settled for a glare. "What are *you* doing here?"

Kelian seemed at least as startled to see Oressa as she was to see him, and not, apparently, much better pleased. He opened and closed his mouth several times, like a fish. When he finally got his breath and started to say something, she put her fists on her hips and stared at him, and he sputtered wordlessly.

"I don't want *his* help!" Oressa told the big man who had brought her here. He truly was enormous, now that she could see him properly: not much taller than Kelian, but twice his bulk, with blunt, heavy features and deep-set eyes. He looked strong enough to pick up a horse with one hand, and possibly the wagon it had been pulling with the other. He also looked confused.

Kelian began, "No, now, look—"

"What *are* you doing here?" Oressa interrupted him. "They said you were going north. That's why they thought you could escort me. Why would you be going north?" She hadn't even known there was a puzzle, but now pieces slotted into place one after another. She gave Kelian a narrow, considering look, and he paled. Then she was sure. Turning to the big man, she began, "Listen, he—"

Jumping forward, Kelian wrapped one arm around her shoulders and flattened his other hand across her mouth. "She's a traitor," he said to the big man. "She's working for *them*. She's one of the bunch that blew up the harbor cannons. She's trying to get out of the city to carry news to another detachment of Tamaristan soldiers. Good job bringing her to me! I'll take care of her now."

The big man grunted, an impressed sound, and glowered at Oressa. She tried to bite Kelian's hand, but the way he held her, it was surprisingly difficult. She tried to struggle, but he was taller and stronger and heavier than she was, and she couldn't budge him. He tightened his grip, and she began to think he might smother her, possibly by accident, and how stupid would that be? She stood still.

"You think your people've got horses ready yet?" Kelian asked, panting slightly. When the man nodded, he went on, still a little breathlessly. "Then I think I'll go right now. It's almost dawn anyway. No, I appreciate your concern, but haste is of the utmost importance! Your help has been invaluable, my friend, simply invaluable, and you may be sure I'll mention your name to the king! Let me have a bit of cloth for a gag, if you would. Can't have the girl crying out for help, all those Tamaristan friends of her . . . Excellent. Thank you, my friend. Now, if you could check outside—"

Kelian turned out to be unfortunately thorough and competent, now that he was acting on his own behalf and not pretending to be on her side—on Carastind's side. The horses had cloth-wrapped hooves and muffled bits, and the men who had brought them looked at Oressa in disgust and didn't question Kelian's decision to take her with him. Why would they question him? He really was a guardsman from the palace, and in her plain servant's dress, not one of them recognized her. Despite her furious lack of cooperation, the big man had no difficulty lifting her into the saddle of one of the horses. Kelian tied her wrists to the pommel and took her reins.

Oressa, finding no chance to get away as Kelian led her horse through the dark city, pretended to have given up. She knew he really was going north, and she knew he really was going to take her with him, and she knew he wasn't going to hurt her. Because—she had no proof, but she was sure she was right—he was a traitor himself. But he wasn't working for any Tamaristan prince. She was almost entirely certain he was working for Estenda.

Long ago, when the Kieba had first raised up her mountain in the heart of the drylands of what was then merely the least regarded of the sprawling provinces of Greater Estenda, Ges Madalin, Oressa's great-great-great-great-grandfather, had seized his chance to rebel. He had flung down the Estendan prince who ruled the province. With the

Kieba's favor, he had made the drylands into the free land of Carastind. Estenda, weakened and embarrassed, had ended up losing more than the southern drylands, because Markand, in the east, had also seized the opportunity to break away. Now Estenda ruled only the northern lands beyond the broken hills, and both Markand and Carastind made their own laws and trade agreements and paid tribute to no one.

Estenda had not, Oressa knew, ever quite resigned itself to its lesser role in the world. Its great king had been replaced by a clutter of merchant-princes who agreed about nothing, except about their right to rule the world—thus the Little War in which Oressa's grandfather had been killed. But the Kieba's presence in Carastind had prevented the Little War from becoming a great war.

But now one or another among Estenda's merchant-princes must be wondering whether the Kieba would again intervene for Carastind. If even Tamarist had guessed that she had quarreled with Osir Madalin, Estenda must have been nearly certain of it. So they had sent a man of theirs to find out the truth of that quarrel. Oressa could see now that Kelian must have been their spy all along. But he'd fooled her completely. How pleased Kelian must have been when Gulien had given him that artifact to carry to the Kieba! And how furious when Oressa had invited herself along, stopping him from bearing it instead to his master in Estenda.

Now he would take *her* to Estenda instead. However things worked out in Carastind, his master would no doubt be delighted to bargain with either her father or her brother or Gajdosik or Bherijda for her. How ironic, that *any* of them *would* bargain for her.

She was not going to let it happen.

But she could not immediately see any means of stopping Kelian from getting away with everything.

The sun was coming up at last, the interminable night giving way to a rose and peach dawn. The whitewashed homes of the city glowed apricot in the new day, the roof tiles a dark and ruddy red. Kelian had brought them through the maze of narrow streets where the houses and shops all ran together. They passed a dozen places where Oressa could easily have scrambled from her horse's saddle to the rooftops, and once up there, she knew she could keep away from a dozen pursuers forever, and never mind Kelian. But her hands were tied to the pommel, so that was impossible.

And now, as the alleys turned and twisted, she could catch glimpses of the wall. She wondered whether the north gates would be open or shut, and who would be guarding them if they were shut. She was fairly certain Kelian would have no trouble talking himself—and her— through those gates if they were held by her own people. It seemed strange to hope that they were guarded by Bherijda's men—in fact, she didn't hope for that, but then she hardly knew what to hope for instead. She twisted her hands gently against the thongs that bound her. They were tight, and a lockpick wouldn't help her now, even if she had a lockpick, which she didn't.

On the other hand, most of Kelian's attention was on the surrounding streets, not on Oressa, whose horse had to come behind his in the narrow alleys. From the moment they had started moving, she took every chance—as they crossed another street or an open square or paused to listen or to wait for someone unseen to pass by—to duck her head and work at getting the gag out of her mouth. That, she knew she could do—it was a little looser every time she jerked at it. Once she succeeded in getting the gag off, she could at least hope to call out. One chance, that was all she'd get, at best.

As soon as she got the gag off, she started using her teeth to try to get the cords off her wrists. At first it seemed hopeless. The knots were too tight, and she was certain that at any moment Kelian would see what she was doing. He did frequently glance over his shoulder at her, but he was distracted, and for the first part of the ride it was luckily too dark for him to see that the gag wasn't over her mouth anymore. Then, as the sun rose, the threat from scorpion soldiers became greater, so he had less attention to spare for her. And she made sure to keep quiet, so quiet that he might think she was too cowed to fight him. And she suspected he had never really taken her seriously anyway.

But then, she had not really taken him seriously either, or he would never have fooled her for so long. She had been remarkably stupid; she saw that now. Worse, she had very little hope now unless he was more foolish still.

They were approaching the wall now, and Kelian probably had seen whether the gates were open and whose banner flew over them, but Oressa didn't dare take time to look, because at last she almost had the thongs—at least one of the thongs—pulled free. She could hear people moving around, men, soldiers—boots ringing on the fitted stones of the north road entryway and thudding more softly on the packed earth of the ordinary streets. In a minute Kelian was going to turn his head and look at her, she could feel it—Oressa jerked the gag up with her still-bound hands and straightened in the saddle.

An instant later Kelian turned his head. Oressa glared at him above the loosened gag, and reassured, he turned back to study the gates.

This time, so did she, though she also twisted her left hand slowly and painfully back and forth, trying to pull her hand through the loosened loop of the thong.

The scorpion banner was flying there, she saw at once, but then she saw that the Madalin falcon was flying above the gates as well. Of course her father and Bherijda were still pretending to be *allies*. Who knew what their men thought of that, but at the moment *both* had men guarding the gates of the city. She should have expected that, but she hadn't. Four of her father's men, she saw, and four of Bherijda's, and couldn't she do something with that? Because even from this distance she could just *see* the radiating distrust between the two groups.

But it wasn't just the guards and soldiers at the gate: Ordinary people were lined up to leave Caras, especially families, which made sense if they had relatives out in the drylands with whom to take shelter while waiting to see what happened. She could also glimpse farmers waiting to enter, their wagons loaded with pears or grain or cages of chickens, which surprised her until she thought about it. But of course those pears wouldn't keep, so the farmers had to sell them or see them spoil. Besides, everyone in the city still had to eat, and if Bherijda's men frightened off the farmers, they would find themselves in serious trouble, so perhaps that made sense after all.

All those people also offered Oressa a chance. Kelian knew it, too, and studied her warily. She glowered back, trying to look like a young woman who was cowed and helpless but trying to look brave. It was a complicated role; she wasn't certain she pulled it off. She jerked at the thongs, pretending they were still secure. How did Kelian expect to explain her to the Carastindin guardsmen? Surely they would want to know what he was about, gagging and binding young women and dragging them about the countryside, even if they didn't recognize her.

He must have thought he could get away with it, though, because he squared his shoulders, lifted his chin, put on a confident expression like a mask, and nudged his horse toward the gates, tugging hers along.

People turned to stare as Kelian hauled her after him, using his horse to shoulder a way forward past the common folk. The people, respecting his uniform or his confidence, pressed back to give them space to go forward. The guardsmen and the scorpion soldiers turned too, hands on the hilts of their swords, all of them posturing at one another like feist dogs after the same bone, and the farmer who had just brought his wagon inside the walls took the chance of their distraction to urge his mule forward. The wagon rolled forward, and the soldiers stepped back to let it get out of their way, and suddenly, unexpectedly, the way was *completely clear* between Oressa and the north road.

She knew if she hesitated the moment would be lost, so she didn't let herself think. It was like leaping from a height—speed and balance and trusting the wind to carry you that last inch. She jerked her left hand out through the loosened thong, ignoring the burn as she scraped the back of her hand raw, snatched down the gag, whipped out the necklaces she'd hidden in her bodice, snapped the chain of gold disks, and flung all the glittering gold in a high, wide arc so that the disks scattered over the road. At the same time she lashed her horse with the pearl necklace, screaming.

The horse, already nervous because it had sensed her fear and fury, leaped straight into a dead gallop, jerking the reins out of Kelian's hand, pinning its ears back, and pointing its head straight at the open road. Oressa wrapped her hands in its mane, pearls scattering in her wake and rolling in the dust of the road. She wanted the reins, but as long as the horse bolted straight down the road, that was fine. When she managed a glance back, she wanted to laugh: Kelian, tangled in a brawl of furious soldiers and scrambling farmers, did not look likely to get clear of the gate anytime soon.

Oressa was small and light, and the horse was a good one. By the time he came after her, she hoped she would be so far ahead he would never catch up.

Much later, afraid of pushing the horse too hard in the heat of the day, Oressa dared stop at a farmhouse for a few minutes. She traded a pearl for a bucket of water for the horse and a dipperful for herself, and for a loaf of bread layered with roasted chicken and spicy mustard, and a comb. She would have liked to trade the horse for a fresh one, but the farm owned only draft mules, so that was no good. Oressa told the curious farmwife that her husband had hit her once too often and she was going back to her father's house in Addas, and the woman nodded and exclaimed and gave her salve for the whip mark on her cheek and listened carefully to the description of her "husband." Oressa took great pains to describe Kelian accurately.

"Just hope you didn't catch a baby, my dear," the woman told Oressa. "Your father *will* take you back, won't he?"

"Oh yes. He never wanted me to marry that man at all. He'll be so surprised to hear me admit he was right that he probably won't say a word of blame. And I'll never be fooled by a handsome face again," Oressa declared emphatically, and the farmwife nodded and said that was a lesson all girls needed to learn, and she had daughters herself, and if that man came by this farm, as was likely enough as farms were few this far from the city, well, she also had big strong sons who would be happy to tell him what they thought of men who beat their wives. And she gave Oressa a little knife to tuck in her pocket, in case she met the wrong kind of trouble before she made her way back to her family. The woman showed Oressa just the right way to stab a man to make sure he wouldn't get up again. That certainly seemed very practical. Oressa tucked the knife away in her skirt pocket and thanked the woman profusely.

When she left the farm, Kelian still had not shown up. Careful of the horse, Oressa rode gently all the rest of the day, and she told the same tale of a violent husband to the man at the public house where she spent the night. He believed it too, so apparently it was a good story, or maybe he just liked the look of the garnets she offered him in payment for the room and for food for herself and the horse. Certainly the man wasn't nearly as sympathetic as the woman at the farm. He did stir himself to say, "A young woman your age, alone on the road, you're asking for worse trouble than a husband who's a little rough! You should travel with someone. Them, maybe." He indicated a farmer and his sons. "I know 'em, and they're decent people. If you're smart you'll ask the old man tonight and be up bright and early tomorrow."

Oressa meekly thanked the man for his advice, and she was indeed up very early, although she was so tired that this time a whole night on a prickly straw mattress seemed the height of luxury. If she dreamed, she didn't remember her dreams on waking, and she was glad of that, because whenever she let herself think about anything, she only made herself afraid.

But she rode out alone because she didn't dare let herself be slowed down by the farmer's wagons. She thought it was five or six days to Addas, and she didn't know exactly where she might find Gajdosik's people.

But Oressa's recently acquired horse was really very good, and Oressa herself hardly a weight for him, and though twice a man or a couple of men tried to approach her, she let her horse gallop and got well away without waiting to see what they might want. She felt a little guilty about it. At least one of them looked concerned, not threatening, but you couldn't tell, really. Kelian had fooled her completely, after all. She hoped very much that he had stopped to ask about her at that farm with the woman who had the big, strong sons.

But she never reached Addas, because before noon the day after that, she met Gajdosik's Tamaristan soldiers instead.

First she began to pass ordinary people startled out of their homes by the Tamaristans. Some, seeing the column of foreign soldiers approaching, had ridden to carry warning to Caras, and those were the people she met. They warned everyone they passed, and Oressa saw how farm families drove their livestock away from the road, into the drylands. The women herded the cattle and goats; children drove carts loaded with chicken cages and such small belongings as their families owned. Most of the men saddled their horses and rode toward Caras.

Four different times someone stopped to urgently warn Oressa against riding north, and once an old man tried to get her to join his own family. "Those Tamaristan bastards aren't burning and looting, not so there's word of it come south, but they're soldiers and they're foreign and a pretty young woman like you doesn't need to meet men like that," the man said earnestly. "I'm sorry you've family in Addas, but there's nothing you can do for 'em except keep yourself safe and find 'em later. Now, don't tell me you'd be any trouble, child. We won't hardly notice another girl in among all the grandchildren."

Touched, Oressa thanked the old man and promised she would turn her horse off the road and ride through the drylands, well outside the sight of any soldiers on the road, but of course she didn't. She met the Tamaristan army an hour later. There were scouts out in front, which she hadn't expected, though of course she should have. She stayed on the road to meet them, though they weren't riding under any banner, so she just had to assume they belonged to Gajdosik. She wished the gods weren't all dead because she would have liked to pray to someone she trusted.

The scouts looked her over carefully, evidently seeing nothing to alarm them. One, a grizzled veteran with scars on his hands and only three fingers on his right hand, said in rough Esse, "Off the road, girl. Mens coming, lot of mens. Go over there and wait. No ones bother you." He pointed to a nearby farmhouse, now deserted.

Instead, Oressa showed him Gajdosik's ring.

It was a little like dropping a stone into a pool: a sudden noise that turned into silence, with ripples spreading out and out. The man, perfectly speechless, stared at the ring, then at her face, then at the ring again.

Oressa tried not to show what a tremendous relief this reaction was. "I want to see Laasat Jerant," she said firmly.

"Yes," said the man, still stunned. He waved the younger scout to ride out ahead again and escorted her himself.

Laasat rode at the forefront of the Tamaristan army, under the sea-eagle banner, with half a dozen other men and Sergeant Mattin and, to Oressa's surprise, two older women. She was surprised too at how grateful she was to find Laasat. She instantly felt safe. She hadn't realized how frightened she'd been until she saw Laasat at the head of Gajdosik's small army, and the fear went away. Not because it was really *her* army. That was just a polite fiction—wasn't that how people put it? But because it was Gajdosik's army, and she trusted that his were civilized people. For the first time since she'd gotten away from Kelian, she felt herself begin to relax.

The army itself didn't seem so small when you had a chance to look at it. It seemed to stretch back along the road for a long way. Nearly all the men marched on foot, at the pace of the mule wagons that kept to the left side of the road. There were women walking between and among those wagons. Not woman soldiers like there were said to be in distant Illian, and not the women that were politely referred to as camp followers. These Tamaristan women looked like they might be the soldiers' mothers and wives and little sisters. Ordinary civilized women in modest dresses, who looked tired and anxious but somehow like they belonged where they were.

Oressa almost asked Laasat, *Do you always go to war with your wives and your mothers?* But then she didn't ask, because she suddenly figured out the answer. She hadn't understood before that Gajdosik had come to Carastind not only with soldiers to conquer, but also with their families because he had meant from the first for them to build permanent lives here. She could see now that Gajdosik would do anything he had to, anything at all, to establish a place for them in Carastind. No wonder he had been willing to humble himself before Gulien once he had realized that force of arms couldn't get him what he wanted. She was awed by how determined he must have been before he even arrived on this side of the Narrow Sea. He hadn't known, couldn't have known, exactly what he would find here. But he had known his people had no option but to go forward.

Laasat didn't recognize Oressa as instantly as she had recognized him, but then she had expected to find him exactly where he was: at the head of Gajdosik's army. He hadn't expected to see her anywhere along the road. He looked first at the scout with an expression of weary resignation, as though wondering what new calamity the man had brought word of. Then he glanced past the scout at Oressa, blinked, looked at her again, lifted his eyes to contemplate the empty road beyond her, notably empty of any proper escort, and checked his people to wait for her. Once she'd come close enough, he said, "I expected to be met, Your Highness, but not by you and not like this. Tell me . . ." He hesitated.

"Prince Gajdosik was still alive when I left Caras," Oressa assured him quickly, and looked at Sergeant Mattin. "So was Gulien. That's the, um, good news."

"Ah." Laasat was silent for a moment, absorbing the implications of so qualified a reassurance, and of Oressa's arriving, unescorted, to meet them. Then he said, "I've bad news of my own, I fear. Who should go first?"

"Well . . . Let's hear your bad news first." She hoped that knowing what else had gone wrong might make it easier to decide what to do now. Gulien could probably use these men in Caras, so maybe she should split this force and send some men to help Gulien and only take some east with her. On the other hand, a lot of scorpion soldiers had gone east with her father and Bherijda, and she might need all these men to deal with them.

It was all very complicated now that it came to actually making decisions.

Laasat grimaced. "Another complication. Estenda apparently thinks the confusion in Carastind offers a wonderful chance to bite off a chunk of your north for themselves—"

"Oh, gods dead and forgotten, I know they do. Of course they didn't wait for Kelian," said Oressa, and rubbed her forehead.

"Kelian? Huh," muttered Sergeant Mattin.

"I know!" Oressa told him. "It's obvious *now!* But what's happening with Estenda?"

Laasat said, "We could have kept them pinned forever in those high-lands along the border, but unfortunately the militia commander in Addas doesn't trust us. He was quite prepared to throw his people against two enemies at once, for all your honorable sergeant could do—"

"Oh, forgotten *gods*," muttered Oressa.

"Yes. So we pulled our people out as quickly as we could, to relieve the commander's mind of the distraction. We've no idea what's happened in Addas since—though your militia might be holding yet; we haven't had a stream of refugees passing us on the road. And, ah," he asked cautiously, "your news, Your Highness?"

Oressa looked around. She was surrounded by Tamaristan officers she didn't know. They looked hard-faced and weary. Oressa swallowed, focused on Laasat, and told them all about Kelian and her father and Prince Bherijda, what she surmised had happened to the company of Tamaristan soldiers Gajdosik had taken into Caras, and what her father had done with Gulien and Gajdosik. She explained, not in detail, that she had gotten away and had thought she'd better come north to meet them so they would know everything. Then she added that she'd seen her father ride east with Bherijda, and since she'd freed Gulien, she thought maybe her brother could do something in Caras, especially with Gajdosik to help him. Then she stopped. She hardly dared look around again. So much news, and so much of it bad, and those were their friends and companions Bherijda had murdered, and she hadn't stopped it.

"Our prince needs us. We'll go on at our best speed," Laasat said at last. He glanced around at the rest. They were all nodding.

"No," said Oressa. Everyone stared at her. Oressa didn't blame them. It wasn't that she doubted her decision exactly. Only . . . it was such a *big* decision. Bigger and more important, maybe, than any other decision she'd ever made in her entire life. But she didn't have any choice except to stand up and make it, because nobody else here would—nobody else here even *could*. She was the *only one* who cared about Carastind and her brother, *and* about Gajdosik's people, *and* understood that the Kieba had to be defended first of all, before anything else. She shivered, remembering her father's cold certainty: *I shall demonstrate that we may claim the Kieba's power, and the world will not end.* Her father would never have gone east to challenge the Kieba unless he was certain he *could* challenge her.

It occurred to Oressa that this might be a little like being the Kieba, not just because everything was so big and so important, but because no one but her saw all the parts of it. The Kieba must feel like this *all the time*, only about everything. She shivered again. But she also fixed her mind on the Kieba's cool, ruthless purposefulness, so like her father's heartless determination to get everything exactly his way, and yet completely different. The Kieba, she thought, had shown her a whole different idea of what power was, or maybe . . . maybe a different idea of what power was *for*.

Only she didn't have time to think about this now. Because she had to make a choice *right now*, and she had to make it for all of them, and it had to be the right one. She lifted her chin and met Laasat's eyes. "I understand why you think you need to get to Gajdosik. But you're wrong. Caras isn't the biggest problem. Neither is whatever's going on in Addas. I might be able to make the militia commander there cooperate with you—"

"Nothing could make that man cooperate with us," muttered Sergeant Mattin.

"*But,*" Oressa said with some force, "the *biggest* problem is Bherijda and my father and what they might be planning to do when they get to the Kieba's mountain. Because I happen to know they took a lot of their soldiers and headed down the east road two days ago." Or was it three now? She could hardly tell, but it wasn't important; everything she said was still true.

"Ah," said Laasat.

"So," said Oressa, "I think Bherijda and my father *really can* threaten the Kieba, in which case, we should send a couple of messengers to Caras. They can try to get word to Gulien and Gajdosik about Addas. But *we* should go east. If we come in on the Kieba's side and defeat her enemies and wrap them up for her, she should be grateful, shouldn't she? And if they *can't* threaten her, then she might not even notice them, but we can still surprise them and defeat them, can't we? And then we won't have to worry about them coming suddenly back to Caras and interfering with my brother and your prince. Isn't that right?"

All the Tamaristans were looking at her with varying expressions of surprise, except for Laasat, who looked resigned instead. He said, but with an inflection that made it a question, "Your Highness, you can't think that Prince Bherijda can actually threaten the Keppa now that she's been forewarned by my own prince's attempt?"

"I *do* think maybe he can. Bherijda had magisters with him, lots of them, I saw them, and he has something else, some kind of artifact or a fragment of an artifact, and who knows what that might do? Besides, my father would never have gone east unless he thought he could not only challenge the Kieba, but *win*. And if he thinks he can, then I think so too."

"I believe last time she was distracted—"

"What makes you think she isn't still? From what she said, that plague she was worried about is still out there and she still needs to fix it, or else everybody in the world, almost, could die. Oh," Oressa added at his startled horror, "I suppose you weren't there when she explained that part. But it's true, or I guess it's true, and what if Bherijda's magisters know too much about the wrong things? They might be just like Djerkest, only worse. After all," she added, realizing as she said it that this too was true, "Bherijda *also* knows that the Kieba must be forewarned, and he still marched away east. Maybe he's stupid, I don't know, but my father isn't, and *he* also went east. We have to go east too."

CHAPTER 24

Gulien dreamed.

He dreamed of Elaru, white and red towers on three hills—white stone and red brick—large houses near the towers and then small, crowded homes farther out, then farms, broad pastures and fields, and beyond the fields, woodlots that rose up into the encircling hills. It had been a beautiful land and a handsome city. He glimpsed it as it had been and as it now was, images mingling and confusing.

The plague had destroyed Elaru. It was the worst kind: a mist of dusky purple and black that crept between the towers and among the houses and out into the farmlands. It clung to anything living that it touched, ate into the living tissues of beast or bird, person or plant. When it moved on, it left behind only bursting clouds of black and purple, dead wood and wisps of hair and downy feathers blowing on the wind. There were not many living people left in Elaru now, and Gulien could not help but be glad, because watching them die was unbearable. The people had died, along with their cattle and their dogs and the birds that built nests in the eaves of their houses and the slender trees that had lined their streets.

Fire destroyed the mist, so the people of Elaru had burned much of their own city, trying to protect some islands of safety. But their efforts had largely failed, because the mist could creep across charred ground and ash, and because sometimes a bird, caught by the mist and fleeing in terror, carried its corruption from one place into another before it died. So he had established his own firebreak—no, *he* hadn't; it had been the Kieba. He forgot who he was sometimes, memory and vision shifting behind his mind's eye. His sense of self had become fragile, scattered across ages of fragmentary memory.

This had been a green, gentle country, all this land. He remembered it, or some part of him remembered it; a thousand years of memory scattered in his mind, a thousand views of Elaru as a village and a town and an energetic, ambitious city, and then later, a quieter and more gracious city, after the capital of Gontai had been moved west toward the sea. Those weren't *his* memories, but he remembered them— more clearly if he dwelled on the visions that came to him. Sometimes he wanted to remember the past. Sometimes that seemed better than gazing down upon ruined Elaru now. His firebreak—the Kieba's encir-cling firebreak—a circle of char and ash five miles wide, surrounded the city. War golems stalked within that wide strip of land, burning anything living that tried to cross it, burning the creeping mist as well. The mist caught fire easily, burning in tiny vivid flickers. It had to burn. He, they, he, the Kieba, they had to burn it, had to keep the firebreak inviolate lest the plague escape to burn out across the land, across all of Gontai.

Every time the horror of it truly struck him, the vision broke and he found himself again, dazed and blinking, his own and other memories tangling in his mind. That happened again now, and Gulien came to himself, back in the Kieba's crystalline chair, its needles piercing his hands and wrists. He didn't feel them. Or only as a sensation of cold. The falcon of steel and glass perched on his shoulder. Its sharp talons pierced his skin through his shirt. That hurt. He was glad of the small pain. It helped him remember who he was.

Closing his eyes, he pressed his head back against the cold crystal of the chair. How many times had he dreamed and then lost the dream? How many times lost himself in the Kieba's memory and then staggered out of it, back into his own body and mind and self?

He would never manage the coolness of mind necessary to master the kephalos. It was impossible.

"You will learn to engage gently, watch unmoved, and accept calmly the memories and thoughts and visions the kephalos gives you," the Kieba had told him.

Gulien had followed the glittering falcon through Berakalan's door into the Tomb of the Gods and discovered at once he did not depend on the kephalos's guidance to find Ysiddre's door and her white stairway and the room carved out of crystalline memory at the heart of the mountain. He had remembered the way. It seemed . . . it *seemed* like his own memory. That was how far he had come, even then. He had come that way twice—had it been twice?—but he couldn't even tell whether that was his own memory or not. Sometimes it seemed to him he might have run up Ysiddre's stairway a hundred times before, or a thousand times.

But he had met the Kieba there. He was almost certain that part was his own memory. She had been standing absolutely still in the exact center of the room, her back to the chair, while all around her visions sleeted through the surrounding crystal: visions of the surrounding drylands and Caras, of the sea and mountains, of cities and landscapes Gulien did not recognize, or half recognized.

Trying to ignore the fragmentary images, he had said to the Kieba, "You sent for me. Because my father and Bherijda are coming, and they're a danger to you, and you need my help." It seemed unbelievable, put into plain words, but the Kieba had nodded, her expression absent, as though this was so obvious that most of her attention was still on other things.

"Parianasaku's Capture," the Kieba had murmured. "And Tonkaïan's Resolve. Yes. An awkward combination." She had looked at Gulien as though she was really looking at something else, something invisible in the air before him, or maybe something a thousand miles beyond him. "Yes," she said. "You must take Parianasaku's Capture and prevent Bherijda Garamanaj from achieving his ambition. Or if you cannot take the Capture, then you will have no choice but to master the kephalos and establish your identity and your aspect, defeating both Osir Madalin and Prince Bherijda that way. You are not ready to master the kephalos, but there is no time now for you to make yourself ready."

"I don't understand," Gulien had admitted to her. "I don't understand why you need me when you have so much power and knowledge and I have so little. But I'll do what I can to help."

She nodded, though still vaguely, as though she had hardly heard him. "Also, the plague in Elaru must be contained. There is no time for that, either. There is always time, but now all the seconds and minutes and days have run through our hands and there is no time left."

"Kieba," said the kephalos, flat and cold.

The Kieba had blinked, seeming to come to herself. "Yes." She had looked at Gulien then as though she saw him. "Gulien. Good." She indicated the crystalline chair. "You will establish your identity and define your principal aspect. You will attempt that now, while I remain able to guide and protect you. We must hope that there will be enough time for that; or, if there is not, then you must assuredly take Parianasaku's Capture from Osir Madalin. One or the other, without fail. Do you understand?"

That much Gulien thought he understand. Or at least he accepted that it was true. "I'll try, Kieba."

"Yes," she said. She nodded toward the chair.

It was a small, sharp little movement, almost birdlike—rather like the sharp way the glass-and-steel falcon moved, in fact—and Gulien, who was already moving to obey that gesture, blinked in surprise and stopped where he stood. A realization unfolded all at once: Intuition, suspicion, disbelief, and conviction all whipped through his mind between that one step and the next.

The Kieba, seeing him stop, tilted her head in that odd little gesture of hers, almost but not quite human, and Gulien exclaimed, "You're a golem!" Then he stood, shocked—by the idea, by the certainty he felt, by the sound of the declaration made out loud, and most of all by his own boldness, or maybe foolishness, in blurting it out like that.

The Kieba gazed at him, silent. She didn't look offended. She didn't look *surprised*. Or maybe she did look surprised, but it was the wrong kind of surprise—surprise that he should make that accusation, but not shock at the accusation itself. So he knew it was true. But he had already been certain. It explained everything. She had said it herself: *I am not entirely myself.* She had told him that. That had been clear enough, but he had not understood. Now that statement made perfect sense.

Gulien stared at the Kieba's eyes. They looked like real human eyes. Her face looked like a real human face—or very nearly. She *looked* like a real person. But he knew she wasn't. He said, "You told me. You almost told me. But I didn't understand."

"You do not understand yet, I think. It is true that this body is a golem, but it does not belong to the kephalos. I mastered the kephalos. This body belongs to me. I inhabit it. When I—she—when the woman I was began to die, the seat of my awareness, the source of my mastery, shifted to dwell primarily within this body."

"A temporary measure," stated the kephalos.

"Yes. Temporary," the Kieba conceded. "For the present I am able to inhabit this body primarily, but I must occasionally inhabit my living body. Thus my primary identity maintains coherence. Even after the death of my living body, my primary identity will be sustained for some time by long familiarity. But without the coherence of a living body, that cannot last."

"I see." Gulien hesitated. "How long . . .?"

"My living body will fail entirely within another year." The Kieba didn't sound very concerned about this, even when she added, "My primary identity will lose its coherence within another year after that. When that identity becomes incoherent, this body will become neither more nor less than any other golem."

So the kephalos could continue to use her golem body even after she was dead. All the way dead. That was truly horrible. Gulien didn't say so.

The kephalos stated, "The living body will fail, and I will then be left without a Kieba. This circumstance is forbidden. Multiple claimants exist. It is my prerogative to support a preferred candidate. I do not consider it probable that Bherijda Garamanaj will provide suitable material from which to make an appropriate Kieba."

"Ah." Gulien saw now why the kephalos had sent for him so urgently. He felt very cold, and gripped his hands together tightly. "You think, I gather, that *I* might provide suitable material."

"I believe it may prove so," the kephalos said, cold as ever. "In order to take up the Kieba's primary aspect, a claimant must possess a clear sense of responsibility to the larger world. In order to take up the Kieba's subsidiary aspect, a claimant must be prepared to wield power, yet without seeking power as a goal in itself. I do not consider Bherijda Garamanaj likely to possess these intrinsic qualities, Gulien Madalin. But I believe that you do."

Before Gulien could begin to frame an argument, the Kieba added, "Bherijda Garamanaj may not own the qualities desirable in a Kieba, but he may nevertheless possess the qualities necessary to master the kephalos. Were my own identity fully secure, I would be able to prevent him from making any attempt to establish himself as a claimant. But under these peculiar circumstances, Osir Madalin may be able to use Parianasaku's Capture to enclose my awareness and separate me from the kephalos. Then Bherijda Garamanaj will most likely have the capacity to destroy my primary awareness and identity. My primary identity no longer has sufficient resilience to withstand such an attack. Then I would not be able to prevent him from mastering the kephalos."

Gulien took a deep breath, trying to wrap his understanding around all this. He had always *known* his future. It had always been laid out for him, and now . . . Now he didn't know, except that what the Kieba wanted of him, what the kephalos wanted, was too much, too big, too strange. He asked helplessly, "But my father also seeks to master the kephalos. Is that what you believe? Maybe . . . maybe he would . . ."

"Osir Madalin is not a claimant," said the Kieba. "He merely seeks to destroy me. He has, I believe, little awareness of the kephalos as an entity. His intentions are simple to understand. However, I suspect Bherijda Garamanaj wishes to become a god."

"Bherijda wants to . . ." Gulien glanced from the Kieba to the chair, and around at the room with its thousands of flashing visions falling through its crystalline walls. "He can't do that, surely. Can he? Not even if he wins here—wins everything. The Kieba was never a goddess. Bherijda can't make himself into a god." He didn't ask it as a question. He was certain he was right. Those visions were memory, crystallized memory, and some of them—some of them he almost recognized.

"Certainly not," agreed the Kieba. "All the gods are dead."

Her eyes glinted—not human eyes after all; not quite. Gulien wondered how he had ever mistaken her for anything but a golem. Though not an ordinary golem. He believed that, too. He asked tentatively, "How many—how many Kiebas have there been, since the ending of the age of the gods?"

"Nine. I am the ninth. My name was Tanothlan. I was a woman of a land called Karanan, in Gontai. On my fifth birthday I was given a crystal shaped like a star, as all the women of my family were given crystals. I wore this fragment of living crystal all my life, but of all my sisters, the predisposition took firm root only in me. When the Kieba came for me, I left my family and my children and took up memory and duty. When she died, I took up also the primary aspect of Ysiddro, patron of healing and the living world, and the subsidiary aspect of Ysiddre, patron of memory, and left my name behind."

Gulien could almost remember that. Or something like that. He remembered a girl named Tanothlan, and then the young woman who had grown into that name, and then the older woman who had at last taken up the burden handed off to her, as it had been handed off from one Kieba to the next for . . . "Three thousand years," he murmured.

"Indeed. Five women came before me, and three men," agreed the Kieba. "Not so many over the course of three thousand years. We live a long time, those of us who succeed in mastering the kephalos. Though we are not generally expected to . . . linger, after our deaths. Manian

Sinai did not linger. There was no need. His successor was prepared to take up his affiliation and aspect and identity. You will remember them all, in time."

"Manian Sinai was the first Kieba."

"You remember. Yes. He was not a god. But he was more than a man. That is why his identity attracts you with its strength and coherence. More than one strong Kieba has drawn his secondary identity from the memories of Manian Sinai. So will you. That is already established."

The crystal that surrounded them suddenly clouded, all its images vanishing within a shimmering misty darkness. The Kieba did not appear concerned by this. She said absently, "I remember the gods. So do you. Or you will."

Gulien shook his head, not because he didn't believe this, but because— despite himself—he was not at all certain he wanted those memories. He almost thought he glimpsed something of the gods now, or had, or would. Time seemed to slide around him, and he took an abrupt step and set his hand against the crystalline wall to steady himself.

The Kieba took no notice. She said, still speaking as though to herself, "Once the gods were beautiful and terrible, so powerful they could reshape the world and walk amid the stars. Now they are gone into the eternal dark. But we remember. As we should. They deserve to be remembered. But the gods were difficult masters in those last years. When they discovered they had made a terrible error and would die of it, many of them became . . . capricious."

Gulien nodded, listening to her with his eyes closed. With his eyes closed, he almost thought he could glimpse the gods themselves. Beautiful and terrible. And dying. They had taken a long, long time to die. He whispered, "A terrible error. Yes."

"Yes. One of the gods made a mistake," the Kieba agreed. "Or perhaps one of them deliberately chose to destroy all the world. We do not remember. We remember that others tried to stop that destruction, but they could not. The best of them—Ysiddre, Eneolioir, Umadancu, most determinedly Ysiddro—when they finally knew they would fail and die, they made Manian Sinai into the first Kieba. He was not a god. But when they finished, he was not human. But he was human enough that he wished to protect the human people who were left in the world after the gods were gone."

Gulien almost thought he remembered something of this. The tale the Kieba was telling him slotted into a framework, familiar, recognizable. He knew how the tale ended. He knew what the Kieba was going to say. She was going to say—

"When the last of the gods died, their servants and slaves took what they could of their power. But they mishandled what they took. What in the hands of the gods had been useful became maleficent in the hands of mortal people," said the Kieba, as he had known she would.

"The plagues," Gulien said.

"Yes," agreed the Kieba. "Those were difficult years. Manian Sinai strove to contain the plagues, but it was a long task. Very many people died during that time, all but a few of the gods' servants, all but a scattered handful of men. A few survived in Gontai, a handful in what later became Tamarist. More here in this country, though it was not Carastind then. It had no name. But fewer plagues burned here in the drylands. That is why we set our mountain here. Some plagues could potentially endanger crystalline memory. Manian Sinai considered it best to establish the Kieba in a land where such plagues come seldom and lack virulence."

"*You* stopped the plagues. Or he did. The Kieba stopped them."

"The Kieba fought the plagues across all the world. Yes. Here as well. But the task was endless, and Manian Sinai was not immortal. He tried to make a woman from this country his heir, but that woman proved unable to master the kephalos. A man from Gontai failed as well. The woman who eventually succeeded was from the land that became Tamarist. And so one Kieba has passed the mastery of the kephalos to the next for three thousand years."

"Everybody thinks you—the Kieba—is immortal," Gulien murmured. "They think you used to be a goddess. But you never were, and not even the gods were *truly* immortal. And now nobody remembers you need to pass your power on to an heir. Or people who do, don't remember it properly. But Bherijda, at least, thinks he can take it."

The Kieba shrugged, a minimal movement. "The memories of men are short. I have been the Kieba for a long time, and so when men think of the Kieba, they think of me. But," she added, "I am failing, Gulien. I—the woman I remember being—I, she, I lost five possible heirs to age or mischance or failure. So in order to win time, she made this body, and at first all seemed well. But now her body is dying and her—my— identity, without a living body to anchor it, will fade soon after. Your predisposition is strong. The kephalos entered your blood and your dreams long ago and believes you possess the qualities it seeks for a claimant."

"I understand," Gulien said. He did. He was afraid, but he understood. He couldn't even be angry. Or he could, but there was no point to his anger. It wasn't anyone's fault that he'd picked up that bit of crystal as a boy, or that his family had been primed with possession of powerful artifacts so that he'd been able to dream in response to its prompting, or that the kephalos thought he had the right qualities for a Kieba. He pressed a hand against his eyes for a long moment, but the darkness behind his closed eyelids was not darkness, but waiting memory. Lowering his hand, he said, not expecting it to matter against the terrible urgency of the Kieba's need, "I don't want this. Even if I wanted it, I'm not ready. You *know* that."

"No," agreed the Kieba. "But you are my last chance to make an heir. I meant to give you a year. A year to establish your identity within the kephalos, a year to learn to encompass memory, a year to become accustomed to the idea of becoming the Kieba in my stead. But now there is no time."

Gulien shook his head, but he didn't know how to argue. He knew it was all true. He *remembered* that it was all true.

"To master the kephalos, you must establish your own identity within it. You must remember yourself amid the memories of three thousand years. The kephalos will try to take your memories and your identity and make you part of itself. It is crystallized memory, and so it will try to encompass your memory and your very self and hold it. That is what it does. It is a powerful tool, the heart of the Kieba's power, yet you must master it and not allow yourself to be mastered. You must encompass it and not allow yourself to be encompassed."

Dread was running through Gulien now, like ice. "I don't . . . I can't do this. I haven't agreed to any of this!"

"But you will. You have no choice—or if you believe you have a choice, then after all, you do not have the qualities the kephalos values. Gulien Madalin, in this exigency, when no one else can do this, will you try?"

Gulien shook his head. But he didn't say no.

"It is true you are not ready. But you must try. No one else can. So you will succeed."

"I will strive to prevent anyone from claiming the superior position save you or the current Kieba," stated the kephalos. "I will try to assist you."

This time Gulien nodded. Because the Kieba was right. He had no choice, not now, and he knew it.

The kephalos wasn't a person. He knew that now. It wasn't a person or a creature or, in a sense, real at all. It was in the crystal. It *was* the crystal. It was crystallized memory.

But it was *like* a person, in some ways. It did not precisely have a *self* of its own, or its own desires or intentions. Not as a person did. But Gulien knew, part of him knew, that it had its own kind of identity even so. If he had to do this . . . if he *had* to, then he was glad to have it as an ally.

It said, "I will present you with the clearest secondary identity possible. But you must take it and make it yours, while retaining throughout your own identity."

"You will learn to engage gently with memory that is not yours," the Kieba told him. "You must not allow it to move you. You must accept memory and vision that is not your own. Fear is your enemy, unless it is your own fear. So with anger. So with love. All strong emotion will shake you and make it harder to keep your balance in the ocean of memory. Do you understand?"

Gulien hadn't understood. He did now, much more so. He had discovered very quickly, once he took his place in the Kieba's chair, how one memory and vision dissolved into the next within the kephalos, and how each vision shattered when he lost that necessary indifference. He knew, too, without anyone precisely explaining it, that each breaking vision marked the point at which he would have failed to master the kephalos, if he'd actually been trying. The result was a horrifying exhibition of his own lack of ability.

If he tried and failed to master the kephalos, it would master him. He would lose himself in its flood of cold thoughts and three thousand years of memories.

He'd thought it difficult enough merely to be king of Carastind after his father. To deal with the fractious lords of Carastind and the acquisitive merchant-princes of Estenda and the aggressive Garamanaji princes. To marry an appropriate girl he'd hardly met and didn't know, and hope she lived—the memory of his two brief engagements had trailed at his heel, the deep understanding that death could take anyone. Anyone.

And now this. All his expectations turned awry, all the fears of his youth shown as paltry, and his own hand meant to be set between everyone he loved and the bitter death of the lingering plagues.

The sudden shift in his fortunes seemed both profoundly disorienting and yet almost expected, almost familiar. He thought now that he might have dreamed this, too. This moment. Or one very like it, so like it ancient experience blended with his own living experience . . . It was a most peculiar feeling.

A year. He had been meant to have a year to learn this. He had, if he had not lost track of real passing time, about one day.

So now he sat in the heart of the Keiba's mountain of crystallized memory, watched shards of present and past sleet through edged, shimmering darkness, and tried not to wish too fiercely for the past, for his own home, for everything to be back the way it was supposed to be, because whenever he did, the longing itself broke whatever vision he was trying to hold. Whenever this happened, the Kieba protected him. He knew she had somehow put herself between him and the kephalos; she was preventing it from taking his memory into itself. He could not prevent it, so she was doing it for him, while simultaneously working to contain the plague mist in Elaru. He could not have done that. He could not manage either to protect himself or to contain the plague, even though he *remembered* how to do both.

Except it wasn't him, it wasn't his memory, not quite. He couldn't quite encompass it; it lacked the integrity of a living person, but it was older and stronger and far deeper than he was; if he tried to take it into himself, he would lose himself in it. He couldn't do it. He was afraid to try.

Another vision formed, so that he seemed to look down through the eyes of a broad-winged eagle that soared in wide circles over the harbor of Caras. The kephalos showed him this, reminding him of his own identity. The kephalos was not his enemy. He knew this, too. It wanted him to succeed. But the ships in the harbor flew black-and-green scorpion banners, and he saw fighting in the streets, and he was afraid for his people. And then, shattered by his fear, the half-grasped images of Caras fragmented and dissolved and left him with nothing.

The kephalos did not understand fear, or desire, or love, or anything human. That was why the Kieba was necessary. But the woman who had been the Kieba was dead, and the golem into which she had put herself was almost but not quite what she had been. It—she—was losing her primary identity. He understood that. She herself now also barely remembered fear or desire or love or anything human. Those were all part of being human, and she was losing them all.

He was the only one here who knew what it was to be human, and he was not the Kieba, except in scattered, fragmentary memories. When the kephalos showed him his father riding at the forefront of a long column of soldiers, Carastindin and Tamaristan both, with Bherijda Garamanaj beside him . . . he cared too much. The vision broke into pieces in Gulien's mind and he could not hold it. The vision fractured again into a dozen other pathways, and he lost track of everything.

Terror shivered through him, and exhaustion. He was tired—tired of trying to keep his mind as open and calm as the kephalos demanded, bitterly tired of failing. He let the vision go, let everything go, and tried to scrape together some fundamental belief in his own identity. And suddenly he glimpsed Oressa, on a racing chestnut horse. She was somewhere on the road—he couldn't tell where—not in Caras but somewhere on the open road. She was leaning far forward, her eyes wide with excitement or fear. The horse flung itself through the morning sunlight, and Gulien, wrenched out of scattering memory, shouted, and the vision shattered, first Oressa and then the whole scene falling away in a shower of sharp-edged shards, glittering, opaque, and ungraspable.

Gulien jerked up sharply, his own eyes opening, the vision cascading around him. He jerked his hands away from the arms of the chair and lurched to his feet, ignoring the pain and the blood where the kephalos had withdrawn the needles not quite fast enough to accommodate his furious movement. His head pounded, and his vision—his own vision, he thought, but was not sure even of that—wavered and spun. He felt dizzy and sick. That last might just have been fear. He hardly understood what he'd seen, but he understood that Oressa was in trouble. And his father was getting closer, with that bastard Bherijda. And there was fighting in Caras, between the remaining scorpion soldiers and his own people.

He pressed both his hands over his eyes, trying to drive back the exhaustion and collect himself through a sheer effort of will. Gajdosik and Paulin between them could handle Caras. They would have to. He said, "Kieba—"

"There is time. There will be time," she told him.

She might have meant to sound reassuring. But he could hear, now that he knew to listen for it, the flat indifference behind her tone. He was afraid for her—afraid for them both. Afraid for them all. He said exhaustedly, "I can't . . . I can't not *care*."

"Yes," she said dispassionately. "That is part of your primary identity, and part of your principal aspect. But you must learn to set all that aside in order to allow the kephalos to support you. You will need the memories of ages past. You must learn to hold them beside your own memories so that they blend only along the . . . edges."

She paused, studying him, and Gulien wondered whether she remembered exhaustion and fear. Whether she remembered being not only human, but young and new to the crystallized memory of the kephalos. He suspected she had forgotten. He said, "I can't do this."

"You can. But there is time. Nothing will happen today. Perhaps not tomorrow." Turning, the Kieba put her hand out and opened a door that hadn't been there a moment ago. The stairway curled down through the reaches of the mountain—not Ysiddre's white stairway, but rough, red stone steps that twisted around and vanished into the welcoming sunlight of an ordinary morning.

"Go," said the Kieba. "Rest. Eat something. You are human; some of your distress comes from hunger. The kephalos will provide food. I will fortify this mountain and see what may yet be done to salvage something of Elaru. You, go. Eat and rest and think of nothing, remember nothing—fear nothing."

Gulien thought her advice to think of nothing would be impossible to follow. But he stumbled down the rough stairway and found himself in what seemed for all the world like an ordinary bedchamber, a room of comfortable dimensions, with walls of whitewashed plaster rather than glittering black glass, plain furniture of wood rather than stone or soapy gray crystal. A couch wide enough to serve as a bed rested below a wide window. Sunlight came in through a wide window, along with a warm breeze carrying the scents of hot stone and dust, dry grass and pine. The view through that window was of nothing but the slopes of the mountain and, beyond, the level drylands running out as far as the eye could see. Twenty feet away, sparrows, their breasts streaked with taupe and their wings barred with rust and brown, hopped and fluttered below a twisted pine. On a table beside the bed, a round loaf of bread rested on a cloth, beside it, a crock of honey and a bowl of stew redolent with beef and onions and turnips.

Gulien felt tension unknotting from his shoulders and back. Though he had not been aware of hunger, the smell of the stew and the bread woke his appetite, and he longed to eat and then stretch out on that couch and close his eyes and *not dream*. But he did not move at once toward the table. He said out loud, "Kephalos, where is Oressa? Is she safe?"

There was a slight pause. Then the kephalos answered. "Oressa Madalin rides north from Caras. She appears well."

"You have a falcon watching her? You've had one watching her all the time?" Gulien took a step toward the table and gripped the back of the ordinary chair drawn up to it. "Kephalos?"

"I am watching her now," the kephalos said. "I will protect her now. You are the preferred claimant, and I understand Oressa Madalin is important to you. Do not allow your mind or attention to be distracted from your own necessities."

Gulien subsided slowly into the chair and rested his hands on the table. His hands and wrists stung, though not badly. His skin was stippled with tiny dots and smears of blood. He had achieved that much: He could tear himself free of the kephalos's control fast enough to do himself an injury. Progress, of a sort. He opened and closed his hands slowly, aware of the flex of muscles and tendons beneath the skin. He was alive, and human, and himself. Still himself. He said, "You'll continue to protect her. To protect all my people. Gajdosik—gods." It was impossible. He was silent.

"For as long as practicable," said the kephalos. "Eat. Rest. When the Kieba sends for you, I will wake you. It is important that you return to the heart of the mountain of your own will."

"I know," Gulien said wearily. He did know that. Or something in him knew it. He picked up the loaf of bread and broke it in half in his hands. They *were* still his hands. He dipped a piece of the bread in the stew and ate it, shut his eyes, and thought about nothing.

The kephalos said, "Gulien. Gulien." It said his name a third time, no louder or more emphatically. "Gulien."

He did not so much wake as dream he was awake, dream he stood up and followed that summons. He walked through directionless light and warmth and into a haze that dimmed and then cleared to light again. Then he blinked, and he was awake. Or else the dream became more vivid; he was not entirely certain.

It was suddenly as though he were standing high on the slopes of the Kieba's mountain, with the high, bright sky above and, far below, the road running through tawny fields of wheat and pastures with goats and mules. But a thousand men were spilling out to either side of the road, and there were men among the farmhouse and the outbuildings. Men with torches and swords. The barn nearest the main house wasn't yet on fire, but a lot of the other outbuildings were, and one of the smaller houses and the closest fields. The flames were almost too pale to see in the brilliant light, but black smoke poured upward into the clear sky, and the scorpion banners whipped out to their full length in the fiery wind.

For a moment Gulien held perfectly still, too shocked to move. Then he knew he was awake, and he turned, shouting, "Kieba!"

He was not outside at all. He was in the heart of the mountain, surrounded by crystal, but all around him the crystal held the same vision of fire and violence. The Kieba was lying on the dais. She looked, as before, still as death. This time he knew she was not dead. He thought he knew that. He moved cautiously forward. "Kieba?"

"The Kieba's enemies wish to force her to show herself to them," stated the kephalos. "She cannot do so safely. Her primary identity cannot withstand challenge. Thus I am limiting her awareness to Gontai. I will not allow her to manifest herself here."

"You've trapped her in Gontai? In another golem body in Gontai? Kephalos, how am I supposed to do this without her? There was supposed to be time! I was supposed to have *time*!"

"She cannot assist you. Given the brevity of time available, I projected that further experience would be less useful than rest. You must be ready."

"I—you—can't *you* stop them, slow them down at least, give me more time to—to learn how to do this?" He turned helplessly back toward the chair, gestured toward it, a sharp wave of his hand. "To do *that*?"

"My defense is so far largely unsuccessful," it told him. Images whirled around Gulien, images of Elaru and, in the other room, of the drylands around the Kieba's mountain. He glimpsed a woman and several children hiding in the main house, several men in the nearest granary, others in one of the barns. Prince Bherijda stood high up on a wagon, the scorpion banner flying above him, watching everything with wide, excited eyes like a child watching a puppet show. A medallion at his throat instantly caught Gulien's eye. He knew, without knowing whose memory it was, that this was Tonkaïan's Resolve, at least a fragment of it, and far more dangerous than the fire.

Half a dozen black-clad magisters crowded around Bherijda's wagon, each holding a short, fat crystalline rod in one hand and a round black disk in the other. Two of the magisters knelt in the wagon, their heads down and their eyes closed. Blood dripped between their fingers where they held their rods.

To one side, a small company of Carastindin soldiers held their horses under tight control. They neither joined the destruction nor moved to prevent it. At their head, Osir Madalin, armed and armored like his soldiers, had not even drawn his sword. His hand rested on its hilt, but he merely watched, without expression, as the scorpion soldiers deliberately shot at the frantic goats in their pasture, clouds of white smoke from their arquebuses joining the black smoke from the burning buildings. Gulien knew that lack of expression. He knew his father was furious. But whether he was angry with Bherijda or the Kieba or these circumstances,

Gulien could not guess. His father must have Parianasaku's Capture with him, but Gulien could not see anything that might be the artifact.

Several men broke suddenly from the barn and ran toward the main house. Soldiers came after them, but one of the Kieba's falcons suddenly darted out of the smoke, metallic feathers blazing in the sunlight, talons flashing, faster and more agile and far more dangerous than any natural falcon, and the soldiers fell back. The farmers reached the house after all, and the falcon flung itself through the choking air, circling the house.

"The *falcon* is the only defense they have?" Gulien snapped at the kephalos.

"I am attempting to deploy adequate defensive measures," stated the kephalos. "I am prevented."

"Prevented!" said Gulien. He braced himself with his hands on the back of the chair, furious and sick.

"I am now receiving contradictory instructions. Two claimants other than you are striving for mastery."

"You can't let *Bherijda* claim *any* kind of position!"

"I am not to permit mastery to anyone other than the Kieba or you. I am aware that allowing these other claimants access would vitiate my primary purpose. I am attempting to prevent these claimants. Thus far Bherijda Garamanaj is not among the claimants."

The two magisters in the wagon, Gulien realized. They were trying *right now* to master the kephalos. They couldn't—he was certain they couldn't. Only he wasn't *that* certain, and what if they did?

The falcon flashed through the farmyard, too swift to shoot, too dangerous to ignore. It circled the wagon where the magisters worked, but apparently couldn't attack them. But it could attack the soldiers, and did: anyone with a torch, anyone who tried to approach the house. It cried out, too sharp and fierce for a *real* falcon; it wasn't a falcon's voice, but an inhuman voice with words in it—curses, in fact. Men shied from it, and Gulien thought they really had given up trying to enter or burn the house. At least for the moment.

But the golem's fierce defense wouldn't matter if either of those Tamaristan magisters mastered the kephalos. The black-clad magisters were an island of stillness amid the frenzy of the fire.

His father had done nothing at all to prevent the razing of the farm, but now he suddenly reined his horse across the path of scorpion soldiers who began to set fire arrows to their bows so they could fire the house. He stared their leader down. Gulien held his breath, but the Tamaristans gave way, glowering, and turned back to burn the pasture grasses instead and shoot the cows. His father, appearing entirely unmoved, turned to speak to one of his officers. Below, the scorpion banner flew against a sky hazed with smoke, and the magisters stood in a little circle with their crystalline rods clenched in their bloody hands.

"The enemy has breached the outer perimeter," the kephalos said tonelessly.

Gulien flinched and looked around. Bherijda's men were going to cross the wall and come up the mountain *now*, he realized. Bherijda himself, with Tonkaïan's Resolve. And his father would be with him, with Parianasaku's Capture. And each of those magisters had something, some fragment of crystal—one kind of key or another. For all he knew, one of those magisters or Prince Bherijda himself might have just as strong a predisposition as Gulien himself.

The kephalos hadn't stopped them. It couldn't stop them. His father would probably know just how to find and open the door into the Tomb of the Gods. Of course he would know. He knew more than that if he had learned to read the knowledge held in the interstices of Parianasaku's Capture. He would know the architecture of the mountain and the coded paths of the gods and more than likely how to step through the interstices between one place and another, which Gulien himself only barely remembered. He slapped his hand hard against the smooth, cool wall of the crystalline chamber and ordered fiercely, "Blank the walls! Don't show me *anything*!"

Immediately, all the images vanished. That made it easier for Gulien to think, easier to collect himself and reach for the calm he needed to work with the kephalos directly. He asked, striving for that calm, "If *I* take the mastery, if I can do it right now, I can stop *them* doing it, can't I? That's what you want, isn't it?"

"Yes, Gulien," said the kephalos, perfectly unmoved. "If you take the superior position, you will be able to deny it to other claimants. This is what you must do."

"But you're preventing the Kieba from returning her attention to this mountain. Without her protection, if I can't master you, then you can't prevent my identity from being subsumed within the span of kept memory."

"An accurate summation."

Gulien shut his eyes and took a breath. He was afraid. But if he was sure of one thing, it was that he had better not have a divided mind or heart when he tried to master the kephalos. And if he was certain of another, it was that he dared not allow Bherijda or his father to seize mastery of the kephalos or destroy the Kieba. What was left of the Kieba. The images of Elaru, the memories of a hundred thousand terrible plagues, rose up within him, and he shuddered.

"All right," Gulien whispered. He said again, out loud, "All right." He took a slow breath. Another. Calm. Calm. Stone-calm, mountain-calm, calm as though he'd turned himself into stone, into far-sight crystal, with eyes that saw everything and cared for nothing.

He knew he couldn't reach that kind of calm, the Kieba's calm. But he tried. Rubbing his wrists, breathing deeply, he started toward the terrible crystal chair that would carry him into the cold mind of the kephalos.

Two Tamaristan magisters appeared in the chamber, one and then the other, and although Gulien leaped toward the chair, one of the magisters lifted up his rod of metal and crystal, a sharp, aggressive movement, and Gulien was hurled to the side. He tried to catch himself with his arms against the crystalline wall, but had too little time even for that and found himself on his knees besides the Kieba's dais, shaking his head, struggling to regain his balance and get back to his feet. But one of the magisters had already hurried across the room and now stood running his hands over the back and arms of the chair, his expression rapt and intent, and the other, his expression triumphant, stood over the dais and the Kieba's abandoned golem body.

Then Prince Bherijda appeared, and after him, three soldiers, and Gulien's father last of all. Then it was too late to do anything. Gulien, on his feet, his hand flat against the wall for balance, ignored the soldiers with their drawn swords. He paid no attention to Prince Bherijda, either. He could not take his attention from his father.

For half a heartbeat he thought Osir was dismayed to find him here in the heart of the mountain. Then indifference closed over his father's face. The king raised his eyebrows, sardonic and unmoved and utterly in command of himself. Straightening and dropping his hands to his sides, Gulien faced his father's cool regard without a word.

"Well, here she is after all!" said Prince Bherijda, staring at the body on the dais. "The famous Kieba! She doesn't look very dangerous, does she? And what a surprise!" he added, with a malicious sideways glance at Osir. "His Highness Prince Gulien, here with the Kieba in her very mountain! You do seem to have some difficulty ruling your son. You should have left him to my people after all, it seems."

King Osir ignored him. He said to Gulien, in a tone suggesting mild surprise, "You left Caras? In whose hands?"

"*You* left Caras," Gulien snapped. "In the hands of *his* men." He indicated Bherijda with a contemptuous jerk of his head. "To what end? To come here and destroy the Kieba? Believe me, the Kieba *is* all that stands between the world and the lingering plagues—"

"My son, enough," Osir said with finality. At his tone, one of his soldiers came forward a warning step, clearly prepared to silence Gulien by force if necessary. Taking a hard breath, Gulien stopped and stood still, trying to calm himself. It was impossible, but he hoped at least for a reasonable pretense. The kephalos had not yet spoken to any of these people, so far as he knew, and as soon as he realized this he resolved not to mention the kephalos at all, though he couldn't see how keeping this silence could actually help.

Prince Bherijda said in an unctuous tone, quite obviously enjoying this situation, "A disloyal son should be put to death, my father always said."

"He would have known, certainly," Osir returned. "I, however, think that is not necessary and may prove inadvisable. My son is potentially valuable in any number of ways." Then, as Bherijda began to answer, he turned and gazed at him with an air of polite incredulity, lifting an eyebrow.

Prince Bherijda closed his mouth, staring at Osir in impotent fury. The fury made sense, but Gulien didn't understand the impotence, except that while the magisters belonged to Bherijda, somehow all of the soldiers who had come to this place were Carastindin. He didn't understand how his father had managed this, but he was becoming sure Bherijda hadn't done it that way on purpose. Gulien wished, suddenly and intensely, that Oressa were here. His sister might be safer where she was—she almost certainly was safer where she was, especially if she had found Gajdosik's people—but if she had been here, she would probably have thought of a way to pit their father against Bherijda and snatch some clever victory out of the resulting confusion.

Bherijda turned his back to King Osir and Gulien, a contemptuous gesture, but Gulien thought it was also a stupid thing for him to do. Maybe Bherijda thought he knew what Osir would do, but Gulien had no idea. He hoped his father would suddenly draw his sword and stab the Tamaristan prince. Osir wore a sword, exactly the kind of weapon a king should carry, with pearls on the scabbard and a big star ruby set in silver on the hilt. But he showed, unfortunately, no inclination to draw it.

Prince Bherijda gestured to his magisters, an impatient gesture. "Well? I don't think we wish to wait for her to wake up!"

The two men glanced at the Kieba's uninhabited body and then at each other. Then the younger of them swallowed, stepped toward the chair, and seated himself, moving slowly and deliberately. He set his hands over the ends of the arms of the chair, and the needles must have pierced his hands and wrists, for a thin rivulet of blood began to make its way slowly across the crystal, drops falling on the featureless floor.

The young magister's eyelids fluttered shut, and his body sagged in the chair. But his hands didn't relax their hold. Gulien watched him closely, almost imagining he could follow the dizzying flicker of multiplying vision and scattering awareness as the connection between the magister and the kephalos strengthened.

Bherijda and the other magister watched, too. Bherijda's expression was avid, but the tension in the other magister's face betrayed a deep unease. The magister was an older man with graying hair and lines deeply engraved around his mouth. He said suddenly to Gulien, "You have tried this?"

Gulien was almost as surprised as if a golem had spoken. He realized he had barely thought of the magisters as real people; he had almost thought of them as though they were golems belonging to Bherijda. Now he saw that the older man was afraid but determined, that he might have some idea what mastering the kephalos entailed and it frightened him. Gulien was almost sorry for the man, except he'd come here, after all, to attack the Kieba.

Prince Bherijda was staring at Gulien, too, intent on whatever answer he might make. *Everyone* was staring at him. After a tiny pause, he said, "I tried. I failed."

Plainly surprised, the magister said, "But you are still yourself. You haven't lost yourself in the crystal."

"The Kieba protected me," Gulien told him. "Who here will protect you?"

The magister began to answer, but then broke off as the younger magister in the chair suddenly gasped, his hands spasming and his back arching. He brought his head forward away from the back of the chair, but then slammed it back again, hard. The dull thump of the impact was unpleasant. The older magister leaped forward, eyes wide with alarm, to cushion his fellow's head with his hands.

"Well, there's another lost," said Bherijda, sounding mildly disgusted.

"Our protocols can't have been correct," the magister answered in a strained tone. "We've missed some important facet of the mastery protocols. Or we simply do not have the experience, or a sufficient pre-disposition, or . . ." He shook his head in baffled distress. His younger colleague was limp now, and quiet. Not dead, exactly. Or maybe he was, although his body still breathed. Gulien studied the body in some dismay, fairly certain that would have happened to him if he had tried to master the kephalos without the Kieba to protect him. It was worse, somehow, looking at a man who had only just now lost himself to the kephalos than merely experiencing it secondhand, through the mirror of old memory. It was strange to be almost grateful that her enemies had arrived and stopped him from risking that fate.

"Ah," Prince Bherijda said to Osir. "I see now that you were correct. Your son may indeed be of some use!" He turned to Gulien. "*You* have a predisposition, do you not? Excellent! Then you must certainly try again to master the Kieba's power. Perhaps this time you may succeed. Think of that! More likely you will elucidate some greater part of the mastery protocols as you fail, but then every failure teaches us how to go further. So you see, we are all grateful for your presence after all."

Gulien lifted his eyebrows, an expression he had borrowed, he realized, from his father. He said, consciously trying for his father's tone of cool contempt, "Or if I come too near actual mastery, you'll cut my throat. It's a clever plan, I suppose, if you're confident you can recognize the crucial moment."

"Oh, I can recognize it," Bherijda said with assurance. His sly gaze slid to Osir's face. "But naturally I would not cut your throat. Because the Kieba will doubtless wake to protect you. *That* would do as well—indeed, it would be best of all." He curled a hand around the artifact he wore on the chain around his neck and smiled. It was an ugly smile.

Osir, his eyes narrowing, actually appeared to be considering Bherijda's proposal. Fearing that his father might actually agree to this plan, Gulien said quickly and emphatically, "It won't work. She knows you're here—she's undoubtedly preparing to destroy you herself—"

"I believe that is unlikely," murmured his father.

"Or if she won't face you, she certainly won't for my sake!"

Osir did not shift his gaze from Gulien's face. "My son, why did you defy me and come to this place if not to ally yourself with the Kieba and against me? Why are you here in the heart of the Kieba's mountain, except that you have made yourself my enemy?"

"If you hadn't made yourself the Kieba's enemy, it wouldn't have come to this!"

"Treacherous whelp," said Bherijda, smiling. "I think—"

Osir gave him a mild, incredulous look, and Bherijda closed his mouth with a snap, stiffening in offense.

The older magister took the crystal rod away from his unconscious colleague and held it out to Gulien.

Gulien stared at him. To think he had felt sorry for the man only a moment before. He was appalled at the magister's callousness and his own cowardice, and at his father's betrayal, and at the whole situation. He wanted to back away, but all too obviously there was nowhere to retreat. The magister continued to hold the rod out as though he expected Gulien to yield and reach for it, and finally, after one more glance at his father, Gulien did—and threw it down, hard, against the edge of the dais. The magister, breath catching, leaped after the rod, but not fast enough.

But the rod, though it chimed like a dozen separate bells when it struck, did not break. It rebounded without the least sign of damage and rolled across the floor, the light catching and glittering from its needles.

Prince Bherijda, his mouth tight, stepped up and slapped Gulien across the face, hard, and tried to do it again. But one of the soldiers, scowling, forcefully blocked the prince's second blow, shoving Bherijda back a step.

In that moment, when everyone was distracted, King Osir, who had been watching all of this with an air of patient indifference, abruptly drew his sword with polished, smooth speed and brought it slashing down right through the neck of the Kieba's untenanted body. The head rolled away from the body, bloodless, the cut surface glistening like metallic clay, and fell off the dais. The ruby in the sword's hilt blazed, the star in its heart rising up, burning and huge, spinning in place, its rays raking through the air, reflected over and over in the crystalline walls that surrounded them.

Everyone ducked away from the expanding star of light and fire except Osir, who drew his other hand sharply across the edge of the blade close to the hilt and then laid his bloody palm against the burning ruby. Red light blazed between his fingers and then went out, and the star vanished, leaving them all in a dim, silent room with the Kieba's headless golem body limp and abandoned on the dais and her—its— head near the far wall.

In the shocked instant that followed, Gulien jerked himself free from the magister's grip. As though his movement released them all, Bherijda drew breath, took a step toward the Kieba's headless body, whirled toward King Osir, and said furiously, "Fool! That is only a golem! *Look* at it! That cannot be the seat of her power."

Osir kept his attention on the body of the golem. He said softly, "Perhaps it *is* the seat of her power."

"Never tell me you expected this! She put a golem here to draw our attention—she never intended to face us herself. How am I to master the Kieba if she is not *here*?" In his rage, he actually stamped his foot.

Osir shrugged. "I don't imagine you can." He held his cut hand loosely clenched. The ruby in the sword hilt now looked exactly like any big, impressive jewel. He was studying the body, his expression merely thoughtful.

Prince Bherijda said, *"You—"*

The kephalos interrupted suddenly and coldly. "The Kieba has died. The superior position has been vacated. Emergency conditions obtain. Ancillary positions are liable to promotion. Gulien Madalin—"

"She *died?* Her real body died too?" But Gulien understood: that blazing ruby in the hilt of his father's sword *was* Parianasaku's Capture. His father had used Parianasaku's artifact against the Kieba's golem body. He had captured her awareness, exactly as she had feared, and her living body, wherever it was, weakened and near death as it was, had not been able to sustain the shock. He said grimly to the kephalos, "All right, listen to me—"

But at the same time, Prince Bherijda exclaimed, "The superior position, vacated!" and turned quickly toward the chair. The runes on the face of Bherijda's medallion, Tonkaïan's Resolve, blazed to life, almost familiar, not to Gulien exactly, but to some half-held memory within him. They were old runes. That was an old artifact. Old and dangerous and now nearly awake.

"Hostile assumption of superior position disallowed," stated the kephalos. Around them, the black crystal walls and the dais, the ceiling, and the floor all filled with light and then cleared, becoming transparent as water. But Gulien stared in horror as the ruby in his father's sword once again filled with light too. Its star started to lift itself free of the ruby once more, slowly revolving as it brightened and lengthened. Osir held the sword up in both hands, increasingly hidden by the burning light of the ruby. All the light in the room seemed to bend toward the Capture. All the light and sound and *texture* in the world—

Suddenly everything seemed to be happening at once: The remaining Tamaristan magister caught up the crystalline rod, hesitated for the barest fraction of a second, and closed his hand down on the needles. Immediately the magister's eyes glazed over, and he swayed, but he didn't fall. At the same time, Bherijda, with a thin sound of terror, rushed forward, tore the medallion off its chain, slammed it flat against the back of the chair, and held it there while tracing its central rune with the tip of a finger. He had tilted his head back and squinted his eyes nearly shut, as though he was terrified to be so close either to the chair or to his own artifact.

Then King Osir slowly lowered his sword, the light of its star ebbing. Beginning around the tip of the sword and then rippling outward, the crystal slowly became opaque.

"Kephalos!" Gulien said urgently, and the kephalos began to answer, but fell silent before it uttered even a single word.

"Gods!" Bherijda breathed, his tone almost reverent, like a prayer. He pulled his medallion away from the chair and leaned on the chair himself, his expression dazed.

Then the magister groaned, and his face twisted. Gulien thought, vengefully satisfied, that at least the Kieba's enemy wouldn't long outlive her. There wouldn't be anything left of him except a kind of diffused awareness in the kephalos—except, it occurred to him, there wasn't anything left of the Kieba but that same kind of diffuse presence, and that was a disaster.

Then the magister's expression smoothed out. He smiled. His face was calm, and he was *smiling*. Gulien knew that he had, whatever the kephalos had said, managed to master the kephalos—or at least he must be close to doing so. Prince Bherijda thought so too. He stared at his magister, his face twisted with satisfied ambition as well as with fear, but he drew a knife from his boot and started forward, plainly meaning to cut his own magister's throat, stop him from taking the superior position. Then he would himself follow the pathway the man had mapped out.

Gulien understood all this as though Bherijda had painstakingly explained it to him, but he also thought it was too late. He thought the magister would take the mastery and claim the superior position, and that no one, not Bherijda nor Gulien nor the kephalos, would be able to stop him. Perhaps the Kieba might have, but her awareness must now exist only as scattered, diffused memories in the kephalos.

And *then* he realized, with a terror that mixed oddly with triumph, that this might not be true. Of course the Kieba's identity had *not* diffused into the kephalos. That was the whole *point* of Parianasaku's Capture.

And that being so, he saw there might yet be a way to defeat all the Kieba's enemies and save the Kieba herself. One way to save everything. Or everything that mattered. Fear ran through him, but distantly, as though the insight left little room for terror.

He said quickly, urgently, "Kephalos! *Do* you now contain the Kieba's memories?"

"No, Gulien," answered the kephalos, its tone as indifferent as ever, and stopped, answering only the question he'd actually asked.

If the Kieba's mind and awareness and memory hadn't yet dissolved into the kephalos, Gulien knew exactly where they must be. He knew Parianasaku's Capture—he *remembered* it, with a memory that couldn't be his but felt real and solid. Without pausing, without letting himself think, Gulien took three quick steps toward his father and snatched the sword out of his hands, heedless of the sharp blade and of his father's startled attempt to step back. Gulien brought one hand down hard upon the needles rising from the chair's arm and closed his other hand firmly over Parianasaku's Capture.

The room around him vanished. If his father tried to take back his sword, Gulien wasn't aware of it. If Bherijda did anything using Tonkaïan's Resolve, he didn't know it. He was aware only of the rushing clamor of memory and vision within the kephalos, among which his own identity was lost as one pebble among a multitude in a spring-flooded creek. In all the rushing flood of memory, there was only one point of stability.

Gulien's mind divided endlessly, pouring out like the thousand flooding streams brought by the spring rains. There was far too much; he couldn't begin to make sense of anything. It did not precisely hurt. But the multiplicity of vision was harder to endure than pain. He struggled to limit his vision. He knew—he remembered—that mastering the kephalos meant inhabiting its passionless, powerful mind so that he could encompass and understand everything at once. But he discovered immediately that he could not do anything of the kind. He had not been ready, and he was losing himself within the diffuse mind of the kephalos's. He could feel himself losing his sense of himself already.

So he let himself go. He gave himself up.

Parianasaku's Capture had not been made as a trap. It had been made as a haven. Even while Gulien's own awareness shredded in the storm of memory and vision, Parianasaku's Capture unfolded, like a coal blooming into flame or a bud bursting into flower, and the Kieba's awareness and identity, emerging whole and unharmed, caught his and enclosed his awareness within her own.

Gulien gave her his urgent knowledge of Bherijda, of the magister, of the beheaded body of her golem, of King Osir. He also gave her his own mind and identity, solidly anchored in his living body; all his frustrated anger from the past days; his terror; and his faith that she would use what he gave her to do what he couldn't.

Gulien's awareness somehow blurred and simultaneously clarified as the Kieba took what he offered her. The Kieba's awareness, in contrast, towered within and around his. The kephalos was like a thousand sparkling drops of water, but the Kieba was the flood tide that cast them into the air. Only she was really like an ocean that condensed itself into a cup, rushing inward from all directions. Gulien was the cup, and the Kieba poured herself into him and anchored herself in his mind and his awareness and his mortal body.

Bherijda's magister trembled on the edge of mastery; in another instant he would achieve it. But the kephalos denied him and denied him, and he sought a way around its denial, and so the instant of mastery stretched out and out. It seemed to Gulien that the Kieba had all the time in the world to close her awareness first around his own, sorting his memory and identity and self out from the flood. Then she encompassed the magister's awareness. And then—Gulien was almost aware of it as it happened—she anchored her awareness and identity in the magister's living body, cast his identity and consciousness and self out into the rushing flood of the kephalos, and simultaneously loosed her possession of Gulien's body and restored his own mind to its proper place.

In the same stretched instant, the kephalos, freed from all constraint, caught up Bherijda, along with Tonkaïan's Resolve; Osir Madalin with Parianasaku's Capture; all three soldiers; and even Gulien—everyone but the Kieba herself and the body of the magister, which she now possessed. It flung them all, in one wild surge of power, out of the mountain into the world under the open sky. And then it instantly slammed shut every connection between the world and the heart of its mountain and locked itself away within crystallized memory. Gulien, abandoned, utterly incapable of balance, took one blind step and fell, and would have sprawled helplessly on the sand except someone caught him. And even in that moment of abandoned confusion, part of him knew it was his father, and was comforted.

CHAPTER 25

Oressa thought at first that they had managed to catch Prince Bherijda unawares and pin him between the Kieba's mountain and her own— well, Gajdosik's—men. Her people outnumbered Bherijda's by so much that she even asked Laasat to have a man ride back to Caras to let Gulien know they'd arrived at the Kieba's mountain and what was happening, and Laasat agreed without hesitation, so she knew she was right and that they had already nearly won. Later she would surely be able to send another messenger to tell her brother that they'd won and everything was fine.

They had surprise on their side, and a lot more men than Bherijda had brought, and everything went perfectly. Laasat said that never happened, but it did this time, though Oressa was sorry to see Carastindin soldiers supporting Bherijda's and wished she could get them out of the way, and then realized that actually the Carastindin contingent did not appear to be very enthusiastic about fighting.

She looked for but did not find her father, but then her father was too practical to put himself in danger at the forefront of battle. He would be standing somewhere he could see the field of battle, murmuring quiet, effective orders to messengers who would in turn relay them to his officers . . . apparently orders to hold back. She wondered if her father had realized she was with Gajdosik's army, but didn't see how he could have. She, too, was at the rear, up on a horse where men could see her because Laasat said that put heart into the men, though she didn't know why it should, as she certainly wasn't in command. That was Laasat. Though probably even if her father knew she was here, it would make no difference to him.

Bherijda's soldiers had burned a lot of the farm and its lands. Dead mules lay in the farmyard and dead cows in the pastures, and the fields still smoldered. She hoped it hadn't been the Carastindin soldiers who had done that, though they must at least have stood aside and watched it done. At least no one had burned the main house, within which she hoped Tania and her whole big family sheltered—there were no people lying dead among the mules.

"Prince Bherijda will have hoped to draw out the Keppa," Laasat began.

"Yes, I know," Oressa said impatiently. She understood, because everyone had explained it, that Bherijda had meant not to kill the Kieba, but to defeat her and take her power for his own. Bherijda had trained as a magister, which Gajdosik never had. Gajdosik had meant just to make a place for himself in Carastind and had only been driven to the Kieba's mountain by desperation. But Bherijda had always intended to defeat and master the Kieba if he could. They had all those peculiar ideas about the Kieba in Tamarist, and Bherijda was obviously a pretty knowledgeable magister with at least one powerful artifact. Oressa was glad she had decided to come after him and had caught him before he could do anything. It served him right.

Then Laasat told her, which she should have realized before but hadn't, that Prince Bherijda wasn't with his men at all.

"He's already gone across the wall," Laasat said.

Oressa looked again for her father. She couldn't see him anywhere. She was aware of a sinking feeling right through her whole body. She said, "My father—" and stopped. She said finally, "I'm going up the mountain too, then. I'll find them. I'll—"

"No," said Laasat.

"Laasat—"

"No," said Laasat again, even more firmly. "Your Highness, no. In a very little while we will call for the surrender of Bherijda's men, and for that of your father's men also. We will offer terms. *You* will offer terms—Your Highness."

Oressa stared at him. She'd thought her important role was to bring Gajdosik's men here and then let them loose to defeat Bherijda's scorpion soldiers. She hadn't realized she had a role beyond that. Yet it was immediately obvious that Laasat was right and that if her father had crossed the Kieba's wall and not returned, then his men, especially, would probably yield to her. They probably wouldn't surrender to any Tamaristan officer. Especially if they were used to Tamaristans like Bherijda's barbaric scorpion soldiers, who burned farms and slaughtered mules. She began to say that she understood, only before she could, there was a strange hard explosive sound, as though someone had fired a cannon or set off a powder bomb. There was no actual explosion. Only grit and dust swirled in an abrupt eddy of hot air, and suddenly her father and Prince Bherijda and Gulien and a scant handful of Carastindin soldiers all staggered into shape on the slope of the mountain above the wall.

Oressa recognized her father first. Oddly, she recognized him before she even recognized Gulien. She didn't recognize her brother until he collapsed and their father caught him. Her father caught Gulien, broke his fall, and knelt down, easing Gulien to the gritty soil of the mountain. Oressa tried helplessly to decide whether her brother was alive or dead. Would her father have been so gentle with his—his body, if Gulien were dead? But she couldn't decide.

Then her father stood up again, looking, even from this distance, coldly furious. All three soldiers with him carried naked swords, but her father was the one who looked dangerous. Prince Bherijda stood all by himself, drawn up to his full height, his hands on his hips, like he was acting the role of a conqueror. But Osir Madalin, surveying the scene below with impatient disdain, was the one who looked like a king.

Below, the struggle had paused at the crashing explosion, and then the pause had lengthened as the Carastindin men recognized their king and Bherijda's men their prince. Gajdosik's men fell back, allowing the pause to linger, waiting to see what would happen. Oressa's father strode straight down the mountain. Bherijda hurried in the king's wake, plainly furious to be forced to trail behind like a servant. Gulien didn't move; he lay where their father had left him, limp in the fierce sun. Oressa wanted to run up the mountain and see for herself whether he was living or dead, but she was frozen in place, staring at her father. He had seen her too now, and he altered his direction so that he would come to the Kieba's wall just opposite her position.

Oressa didn't know what to do. She thought maybe she should call for the surrender of Bherijda's men, since hers—Gajdosik's—still had the advantage. She half wanted to call for the surrender of the Carastindin soldiers, too, only she tried to imagine her father allowing his soldiers to surrender to her, and she just couldn't. She tried to imagine herself defying him, ordering her men to take him prisoner, but her imagination stuttered to a halt. She wished fervently that Gajdosik himself were here. *He* would know what to do—and he wasn't afraid of her father.

But she knew she wasn't going to try to command Gajdosik's men to yield to her father either, especially with her father allied to Prince Bherijda. She *really* couldn't imagine them obeying any such command and suddenly realized Laasat was thinking the same thing, and that was why he had sounded so stifled. He was trying to think how to tell her that, whoever wore Gajdosik's ring and was nominally in command, he was now going to refuse any order she gave him unless that order was to capture her father and Bherijda and take them prisoner. Or would he demand their deaths? They were both enemies of his real prince.

He said again, "Your Highness—"

Oressa held up a hand. "Wait," she said sharply, and to her surprise Laasat fell silent.

Her father had come to the wall. Two of his soldiers made a step for him with their hands and lifted him to the top. He did not hurry to step down again, though more of his men ran to help him. Instead, he stood for a long moment, surveying the confusion and disorder of the recent battle.

His gaze came to rest at last on Oressa, and he stepped smoothly off the wall—his men were there to help him, and he stepped from the shoulder of one to the bent back of another and then to the ground. Prince Bherijda's men rushed to help their prince too, but Oressa's attention was locked on her father. He strode through the recently embattled men. Whichever banner they followed, they fell back and let him pass. He stopped a few steps away from her horse and stood for a long moment, his eyes on her face. Oressa could see nothing in his expression but his usual cool indifference. She waited, in an agony of impatience. He had to say something, to give her something she could respond to, so she would know what to do. But when he did not, at last she demanded, "Gulien isn't *dead*, is he? Tell me!"

Her father bent his head slightly, then met her gaze again. "Not dead. No. Ruined, possibly. He spoke a few words to me. They did not make sense. I do not quite know what the Kieba did to him. Or what Bherijda did."

"And you *left* him lying up there *by himself*!"

"Do you think he would be better brought down here, into the midst of all this?"

Oressa had to admit that her brother must surely be much safer where he was, alone on the slope of the mountain. But she said furiously, "If anything *has* happened to Gulien, it's *your fault!* I told you that you'd be a fool to ally yourself with Bherijda!"

"So you did," her father said, his tone quite neutral. "If this unfortunate chance determines that you must be my heir, my daughter, it's as well you are not stupid. Of course, I did not ally myself with the Tamaristan prince, whatever he might have believed. But nor did I expect your brother to complicate matters by coming here before me."

Oressa glared at him, still utterly furious, but no longer quite sure what she ought to blame her father *for*. He might not have known about the Kieba's special doors that let one step across the miles in a heartbeat, but *she* had forgotten about them, though Gulien had told her. She knew now, too late, that her brother had never forgotten about those doors. Or maybe the Kieba had reminded him, sent for him, required him to come here to her mountain. She stared helplessly up the mountain, wanting to run up and see for herself whether Gulien was all right, afraid of what she might discover. Her father thought her brother had been *ruined*. That sounded terrifying. It was true that Gulien was probably safer out of the way—

Then Prince Bherijda came up, panting, and stepped right in front of her father. Oressa was distantly amazed that he had the nerve to do anything of the kind, but her father only lifted a scornful eyebrow. Bherijda, ignoring the king, grabbed the reins of Oressa's horse. He said hoarsely, "Your Highness! What a surprise! And how convenient!"

Oressa stared down at him. She could see that he was consumed by a wholly unexpected self-satisfaction that was really frightening. She began, "You—the Kieba—" Bherijda tapped the carved disk on its chain around his neck. It had changed color, Oressa saw: It was now bloodred, shot through with thin black lines. And the carving in the middle had changed too: All the patterns were different. It should have looked like a different artifact entirely, and yet she could tell somehow that it was the same.

"All the mysteries of the ages—all the secrets of the gods!" said Bherijda, and laughed. He looked exalted—he looked drunk—he looked mad. Oressa wanted to back her horse away from him, but he still held her reins. He said, speaking fast and emphatically, "She thinks me defeated? She broke me free of her kephalos, but that was a *favor*! I thought I knew how to use my power before, but I knew *nothing*, and she doesn't even know she showed me herself! She thinks she cast me out of her dead-gods-damned mountain? I'll *level* that mountain—I'll do more than level it. I'll leave a pit so deep it will take blowing sand a thousand years to fill it! Ten thousand years!" Laughing again, Bherijda reached up to take her hand and told her, with horrifying satisfaction, "Carastind can join to Tamarist. We can have the wedding right here. There are plenty of witnesses—"

Leaning forward, Oressa slapped him across the face as hard as she could.

He let go of her hand and of her reins, his hand going to his cheek. He wasn't laughing anymore, Oressa saw with mingled terror and pleasure. He looked stunned. But behind the stunned expression, fury was gathering. Worse, light was also beginning to condense in his medallion: bloodred light struck through with streaks like flashes of black lightning. Oressa tightened the reins, backing her horse a step—another— then she kicked her right foot free of its stirrup, grabbed the pommel of her saddle, leaned dangerously out, and snatched for the medallion. She got it too, only it jerked like a live thing out of her hand, and rather than catching her balance and kicking her horse into a run as she had planned, she fell. She never fell, but this time she did, and the horse jolted forward without her.

Bherijda laughed, with malice rather than humor. He took a step toward her, his mouth twisting. He didn't say anything. He raised a hand as though raising a weapon, and the gritty soil beneath and around the medallion began to . . . dissolve. The medallion's red light shone through a growing haze as the very earth turned to fine dust.

Oressa knew she should run, but she couldn't move. The haze extended toward her, reaching with a horrifying kind of mindfulness. She knew Bherijda was directing it, and she knew she should run, but though she thought the haze moved slowly, she seemed to have no time at all to gather her wits and actually *do* anything.

Bherijda said something Oressa couldn't properly hear. He didn't speak in Esse nor in Tamaj, but in some language never meant for men. Black-streaked red fire crept through the air around him, and the medallion rose up to his hand, and the air glittered with dust, and she cowered as the dissolution slid toward her. She knew she was going to die. Everyone would die, even after they'd all tried so hard. Bherijda was going to kill her and defeat her father and then Gulien, and he would turn on the Kieba, and with his power, he would cast her down too. He was going to rule the world. She couldn't make a sound.

"Unacceptable," said her father flatly. Drawing his sword, he took one long step sideways, putting himself between Oressa and the dissolution that reached for her. The star ruby on the hilt of the sword blazed to sudden vivid life.

Oressa's eyes widened. A small object with lines through it. She had seen that star ruby a thousand times at least, but she would never in a thousand years have realized it was an artifact. Now it seemed to spin itself outward, away from the sword, crimson light dyeing her father and the sandy earth and the very air the color of blood. It was Parianasaku's Capture, and whatever the artifact was and whatever her father had been doing with it, Oressa was suddenly, ferociously glad he had it after all. She glared at Bherijda triumphantly, no longer in the least afraid of the glittering haze spreading outward from *his* artifact.

Her father did not look frightened or angry. His lips were thin and straight. But he met Oressa's eyes, and for just a moment she almost thought she saw the faintest trace of humor in the lift of one eyebrow.

Then Bherijda's artifact's dissolution took both Osir Madalin and Parianasaku's Capture, and both the king and his artifact crumbled to dust. Oressa's father did not even have time to look surprised or annoyed. The crimson light was gone as though it had never been. The dust blew away on the wind. The haze was gone too, leaving a hole in the world through which a different and more natural wind blew. Oressa stared through empty space at Bherijda and felt just as empty and blank as the space where her father had been. She felt as though the very air had disappeared and left her smothering, as though the world itself shuddered underfoot.

Bherijda only looked mildly disappointed. "Not exactly as I remember," he muttered in Tamaj, speaking to himself or to the air. He turned the now quiescent medallion over in his hand, staring down at it.

There was a sudden, hard, explosive sound, and everyone turned to stare up at the mountain. Oressa turned with the rest, though even that small movement felt strange. She had never really imagined there could be a time without her father in it, and now she found there was a moment, and another after that, and she was standing in it. The world hadn't stopped after all. Time somehow proceeded forward unchecked along its ordinary course, carrying them all with it. Prince Bherijda was still here, and the confusion of men, and beyond them the mountain and the burning crops.

The Kieba stood high on the mountain, beside Gulien. She bent briefly to touch Gulien's shoulder before she strode down the slope of the mountain toward Bherijda, and Oressa almost found that she liked her for that, even if the Kieba was frightening and unpredictable and far too powerful.

"You see what you have done!" Bherijda called up to the Kieba. He was smiling again. His hand was resting on his medallion. Red light gathered in it, and he shouted, "I *remember* this! And you were never a god! Why should *you* have such pretty toys?" And he laughed.

The Kieba did not answer. She walked swiftly toward them. Her wall tumbled down before she reached it, though no hand touched it. The stones clattered over one another and rolled out of her path, and she walked across the line where it had stood as though there had never been a barrier there. She wore no medallion such as Bherijda had. She appeared to possess no tool of that kind. But the steel falcon flew out of the smoke haze and perched on her shoulder, mantling its wings and hissing.

"You may have your kephalos, and much may it profit you," sneered Bherijda. He stroked his medallion with the tips of his fingers.

"Prince Bherijda, you have been and are and will be a fool, and I see no help for it," answered the Kieba dispassionately. "Tonkaïan's Resolve was never meant for the hands of men. Have you not realized even yet what becomes of the tools of gods when men attempt to wield them? And the use to which you mean to put that one is worse. You wish unrivaled power—unrivaled indeed—but do you not know what will happen to the world without my ceaseless efforts to preserve it? Against just such tools as you hold, misused by just such hands as yours?"

"The generous Keppa! The selfless Keppa! The only fit *keeper* for the gods' power!" Bherijda mocked her. "A tale for children, a tale to keep *men* cowering like children in the dark, while all the time *you* have kept the gods' power very close, have you not—but not unfailingly. *I* have my own power now, and you know it, or you would never have left the place of your strength to come after me. But nothing you do will avail you now."

The Kieba did not deny this. She said nothing, so that Oressa realized that Bherijda was actually *right*. That was impossible, because the Kieba was supposed to defeat him and rescue them all, or why had she come out of her mountain? Except that now Oressa thought maybe she had come out to challenge Bherijda in the hope that she could face him before he learned to use that artifact. And that was no use. Because whatever he'd done or seen or learned inside the Kieba's mountain, he had already mastered it.

Bherijda laughed again, black lightning flickering through the red light that surrounded him, and Oressa, furious and terrified and grieving and outraged by Bherijda's petty *smallness* even as he reached after a power no mortal man should hold, snatched the farmwife's little knife from her pocket, stepped forward, and thrust it into Bherijda's back, low, aiming for the kidney, exactly as the woman had told her.

Bherijda gasped. The Kieba stepped swiftly forward, moving more quickly and abruptly than any ordinary woman, and caught his medallion as he dropped it. The artifact shattered to dust in her hands, scattering on a hot wind that blew up out of nowhere. The red light stretched out in all directions, wavering and suddenly thin, though black lightning still hummed through it. But the Kieba, with a coolly satisfied nod, held up her hands, empty now, and the wind died, and the light went out.

Bherijda collapsed to his knees and then rolled over sideways. He was still gasping, which was awful, but his eyes were fixed and staring, and even as Oressa hesitated, torn between stabbing Bherijda again and just backing out of the way and begging anyone else to finish him off, his breath suddenly choked him and he coughed and died. Oressa stared at him, hardly able to believe he was dead, not knowing what she should feel or think or do.

"Well done," said the Kieba, and Oressa looked up quickly. The Kieba did not look kind, but she did not look angry either. She looked, in an indefinable way, grieved. She nodded toward Bherijda's body and said, "I will take that. It may yet contain the seeds of a plague, which though now inert might someday give rise to terrible peril."

Oressa nodded shakily. She didn't even want to imagine what that haze would do to a city if it were ever released without direction. She didn't say the first thing that came into her head, which was that the Kieba could certainly take Bherijda's body and do anything she wanted with it, as long as Oressa herself never had to see it again. She said instead merely, "Thank you."

"The debt lies, unexpectedly, entirely in the other direction," the Kieba said. "If your family required redemption in my eyes, then you and your brother have redeemed it, Oressa Madalin. Call upon me, if you wish." She tossed her falcon into the air and turned to go.

"Wait!" said Oressa, but bit her lip when the Kieba turned back because she was afraid to ask. But she did ask at last, because she had to. "What . . . what *about* Gulien? My father said he was . . . he wasn't making sense." She glanced up the mountain, toward her brother. She could see now that her worst fears had not been realized: Gulien was sitting up. She had been so afraid he might have died after all. She was still so afraid he might have been seriously hurt by whatever had happened. Gulien was sitting up, but the *way* he was sitting, with his head in his hands, that didn't look good. She looked furiously at the Kieba. "He's all right, isn't he? He *is* all right?"

"He poured himself out like a stream into the ocean to protect me," the Kieba told her. "Truly, he offered me more than you realize. An anchor to life. Fortunately, his gift allowed me an opportunity to find an alternative anchor. I put him back as well as I could. But one cannot do as he did and remain unchanged."

"But . . ." Oressa was bewildered. "But what did he *do*?"

"He poured himself out," repeated the Kieba, not without sympathy. "I poured him back into himself. Time and patience may complete what I have begun. Or complete it *enough*. You understand me?"

"Yes. Maybe. I think so." Oressa found her eyes stinging. "I think I understand enough."

"Good." The Kieba looked around and frowned. "You must see to your brother. You, first. Try to recall him to himself. I have a great deal to do here, urgently so. I will come back, however. As soon as I may."

She walked away without another word. Oressa stared after her for a second. Then she went up the mountain to find Gulien. She walked at first, but by the time she had crossed the remnants of the Kieba's wall, she was running.

CHAPTER 26

He sat on a bench at a table, in an unfamiliar house, in a warm kitchen, surrounded by people who came and went. He was aware of this, but only tangentially, around the edges of his awareness. Someone talked to him, trying and trying to get him to answer her. She patted his hands and his face. He half recognized her, but his recognition was like his awareness of his surroundings and of himself: distant and without context. Her voice came and went, seeming first close and then far away. Sometimes he understood a word or two, but more often he did not even recognize the language she spoke.

When she folded his hand around a cup of hot tea, he lifted the cup automatically but then paused, struck by the sight of his hand. It was thin and brown, strong but bony. Two of the nails were broken. He did not recognize this hand. Though the fingers opened and closed in response to his will, the hand seemed as foreign and strange as the kitchen, as the young woman who had pressed the cup on him, as the language she spoke. Yet he did not know what hand he had expected to see lifting the cup. He wanted to speak to her, but when he spoke, his own words felt unfamiliar on his tongue, and the young woman looked at him in astonishment and he faltered.

Others came in and went out again. Sometimes he almost knew who they were, but more often he did not. It occurred to him that he ought to care about the uncertainty of his memory, but he did not remember why. The young woman . . . he knew her. He thought he should. Her eyes were wide and dark, her strong-boned face tight with long strain and new anxiety. Her name was . . . Her name was . . . He thought he knew and tried to hold it, but it slipped away from him. He ought to know things. He ought to know everything. When he reached after memory it should *be* there, safe and clear. But everything was uncertain, and familiarity came and went in the world according to no pattern he recognized.

Then at last Tanothlan opened the door and came into the kitchen, leaving the door open behind her. The sun glowed low and red over her shoulder. The breeze that came in with her smelled of smoke and dust and blood, of hot earth and horses, and more distantly of the river and cool shade. It was all familiar, but not as familiar as Tanothlan.

He knew her at once, with a welcome surety. She wore a golem, but it did not mask her to his eyes. He knew her in any guise. . . . He had known her all her life. . . . He had put a crystalline key into her young hand and set the kephalos loose in her living blood. He remembered that.

Then he shuddered, the memory sliding away, uncertain once more. Tanothlan seemed to shift between young and old as he stared at her, at once a child and an old woman . . . but she met his eyes, and he knew her. He *did* know her, and he knew the kephalos that rested behind her eyes and looked back at him as she did. She settled in his vision, then, to the woman he knew. Had known. Knew. Time shifted around him dizzyingly. He rose, clumsy, not understanding why he should be clumsy. Perhaps he had been injured, but he did not remember it. He gripped the table with his hands. For a moment he recognized those hands, and then he didn't.

"Gulien," said Tanothlan. She came close and looked into his eyes and said again, "Gulien!"

Gulien blinked. That was his name. He knew it; he knew himself. The world swung around him, and settled. And then shifted again, so that he tightened his grip on the table with hands that now seemed half his and only half foreign.

"You are frightening your sister," Tanothlan told him.

Gulien blinked again, reaching for memory, for knowledge, for clarity. But there was no clarity, and memory fractured as he reached after it.

"*Not* through the kephalos," Tanothlan said severely. "Let that go, Gulien. Listen to me. Let it go. Let it wait. This is not the time." She paused, looking at him with a hard focus. Then she repeated, "Let it go, I say! Your memory of having mastered it is not your own; your memory misleads you. You have lost the surety of your self. You know perfectly well that you must not touch the kephalos again until you regain that surety."

For a moment that made no sense. Then it did. Memory cracked and shifted. . . . He wanted to reach after solidity, but there *was* nothing solid within reach.

"Gulien!" said Tanothlan. "You *will* remember who you are."

She sounded very certain. Gulien clung to her certainty, since he had none of his own. He pressed his hands over his face, then held them out and stared at them. They were *his* hands. Too young and too bony as they were, he claimed them, tried to recognize them, reached after any memory that knew them as his. He swayed, but caught himself before he fell. Memory came momentarily into focus, then scattered again. He said in a voice he almost recognized as his, "Help me. Tanothlan. I don't know what's real."

"Everything you remember is real," Tanothlan promised him. "But not everything you remember is your own memory. Your name is Gulien. You have few years of your own to remember; thus you find older memories compelling, though they are not rightfully yours. But those memories are fragmentary. Yours are whole. Your name is Gulien. Look around you. Look! That is your sister, Oressa. You remember her."

He looked, and thought he did. Oressa—of course, Oressa. Her expression was urgent; she needed him to be all right. He knew her. She was part of his own life. His memories began to settle into place, becoming at last distinct from other memories that had never been his. He closed his eyes, shuddering, then looked back at the Kieba. Tanothlan. He knew that Tanothlan had become the Kieba and lost her own name. He *remembered* that. He remembered her as a child, as a girl, as a woman; he remembered her as an ancillary, learning to raise up her aspect . . . or part of him remembered that. But now he remembered being Gulien, too, who had not even been born until the Kieba, *this* Kieba, was already old. Yet the memories of his own life, short as it had been so far, carried a deeper sense of reality than his . . . other memories.

"I was in Gontai," he said. "I was in Kansai, when the white city burned under the red mist and died. But that wasn't me, was it?"

"No," the Kieba said gently. "Though it is a true memory, it is not yours."

"It was you. It's your memory. I was . . . before that . . . I defeated the poison rain in Gerranan. That wasn't me, either. But I remember . . . Luenuthlas challenged me while I was distracted, as Bherijda challenged you. He found an aspect of Ininoreh and raised the attribute of fire. . . . Who was I then?"

"That was Manian Semai. You remember him clearly, I know."

Gulien laughed, a desperate little sound. He *remembered* that his name was Manian Semai. Had been. Was. No. *Had been.*

The Kieba said gently, "You have most of your own memory, Gulien. In time you will learn to sort out the memories that are rightfully yours from those that you have . . . acquired. I believe you will. I wish I could tell you I am certain. I am not certain. Gulien, I do not believe that anyone ever did before what you did for me."

Those memories, too, were confused. He slid backward and forward in time, trying to remember . . . then shook his head violently and asked, in his confusion, "What . . . what did I do?"

"You remember. King Osir struck against me, against this body, and succeeded, in one sense. Parianasaku's Capture took in the whole of my remaining self and closed around me. In my absence, Magister Ghemat mastered the kephalos. He tried to reduce me to disembodied memory, but I was held safe by Parianasaku's artifact. Then you opened it and released me. Only I had no living body to serve as my anchor, so I could not reestablish my identity. So you gave me the use of your living mind and body. Thus I regained the surety of self necessary to resume mastery of the kephalos and defeat all illegitimate claimants. You remember all this."

Gulien nodded slightly. He did. Yes. That wasn't his other memory, Manian's memory. That was his. He did remember. He shuddered, not sure whether he would have done it if he'd known it would lead to this confusion of memory and identity.

"Then I inhabited Magister Ghemat's mind and body, since I needed a living anchor and he was available. My awareness is not here." The Kieba touched the breast of the golem body she wore. "It is in the living body of Ghemat."

Gulien nodded. He thought that he should have found that horrifying, that perhaps he soon *would* find it horrifying, but horror seemed beyond him at the moment. And after all, Magister Ghemat had tried to destroy the Kieba.

She added gravely, "This is a temporary measure, for his identity will struggle to reestablish itself, and as the living body is rightfully his, eventually it will succeed. But by this exigency you will gain time, Gulien. You must have time in yourself. In your self. This will give you that time." The Kieba touched his shoulder and waited for him to look at her. "I did not even lose the thread of my work in Gontai. You gave me that chance, Gulien."

Gulien was fiercely glad of that, and knew that the fierceness came from Manian, who had for centuries owned the duty of stopping plagues. But he was almost sure that some of the gladness was his own, too. He took a slow breath and straightened his shoulders. "I'm—it's all right. I know who I am. I think I do." He took another breath. "I *do* know who I am."

"Yes," said the Kieba. She lowered her hand and stepped back. "You will recover your self, in time. In time you may try once more to master the kephalos. When you do, I think you will succeed."

Gulien shook his head, not in disbelief or refusal, but because he could hardly imagine the clear surety of self that mastery of the kephalos required . . . and yet he could *remember* exactly that. From several points of view.

"While we wait for you to recover, I think we might investigate the recent work of Tamaristan magisters. I surmise they have learned too much and understood too little."

Gulien felt almost amused by the idea of challenging the magisters of Tamarist. The amusement was because of Manian, he realized. The Kieba said he was like Manian Semai, but that wasn't exactly true. Manian would have *enjoyed* challenging the gathered opposition of the Tamaristan magisters. Gulien shook his head and didn't even know if he meant the gesture for the Kieba or for the part of his memory and mind that rightfully belonged to Manian.

"Gulien?" asked the Kieba.

"I don't—I can't—I don't think you can trust me to help you with that. With anything. I'm not *him*!"

"No. You are yourself . . . plus a little. I think I can very well trust you with everything. Not immediately, of course. But as your memories settle and your primary and secondary identities become established and reach a balance."

Gulien shook his head again, but again, it was not exactly disagreement.

"I might well guess the names of some of the artifacts the Tamaristan magisters have found. But so might you, I think."

"Yes . . ." Gulien was struck by the unsettling feeling that this might be true. He almost thought he knew how he might pull their teeth, figuratively speaking. As long as they were using the artifacts he thought they were. He could have named them out: half a dozen lingering artifacts that Maranajdis might have used to defeat all his brothers and establish his own power in Tamarist.

This knowledge was most uncomfortable.

"So," said the Kieba, watching him closely. "A year, perhaps, until Magister Ghemat recovers ascendency within his mind and body. A little more, a little less. That will be time enough, Gulien."

Gulien took a deep breath. "All right. All right. Maybe..." He took another breath, pressing his hands to his eyes, trying to remember who he was and sort through memories that were his and not his. Then he dropped his hands in sudden realization. "Carastind," he said.

"You are not now fit to be king of Carastind; nor can Carastind wait without a king while you recover yourself. Your memory will not be sufficiently your own for some time. And it does not matter, anyway. You cannot be your father's heir, because you must be my heir."

"No. No, I know that. I see that. But—" He turned to Oressa. "Father—"

She was pale, but she said immediately, "I'm sorry, Gulien."

Gulien stared at her. He understood, but he said nothing because he did not want to understand. To him, at this moment, it seemed one loss too many.

"Father died stopping Bherijda," his sister told him, her voice soft. "He died protecting me. I don't know . . . I think he meant to destroy Bherijda, but surely he didn't know . . . Except Bherijda's artifact was stronger than Parianasaku's Capture. But Father saved me, and then I killed Bherijda, and the Kieba turned Bherijda's artifact to dust. . . ."

Gulien rubbed his face. He could hardly believe their father was truly gone. Even more completely gone than to any ordinary death, if he had been destroyed by Tonkaïan's Resolve. He said slowly, "I doubt Father thought his artifact the stronger. He would never . . . He would never have let Bherijda balk him, never have let him have the victory. And after all, you were his daughter."

"He hated me!"

"You hated him," Gulien said wearily. "You never understood each other. He wasn't . . . fond. But you were his. He would never have let Bherijda hurt you, especially not after . . . after what happened to me. And I think he might have realized, finally, that you were as much a Madalin as he. Only better at hiding what you were."

"Maybe," Oressa said, in a tone that said she didn't believe any of this for a moment but wasn't going to argue.

"He was a good king. Until the end."

"Well, *right* at the end, he was a good king," Oressa admitted reluctantly. "He did stop Bherijda. But *you* would be a good king too. Better than him."

"No. Not anymore."

Oressa hesitated. Then she said, not arguing, "I think I followed most of what the Kieba said. So I think I understand. It's all right, Gulien. It is. Or it will be. You never wanted to be king anyway. Not really. But I don't know what to do without you. They won't accept me as queen regnant. Well, some people might, but . . . I don't know. This isn't Illian, where queens rule alone."

Gulien unexpectedly found himself smiling. He took his sister's hands in his. "Oressa. You will find a solution. You always do, and it's always clever. Go back to Caras. Straighten everything out. By the time you do that, you'll know what to do next."

"Ha," said Oressa, pleased but not convinced. "You're sure you won't come? For just a little while, maybe?"

Gulien flinched at the thought. "I can't."

"In time you will find yourself able to walk even the streets of your youth where people knew you," the Kieba promised him. Then, as though satisfied that everything was settled, she turned to the farming family that owned this house and this farm. Both the man and his wife were present—the man big and steady and quiet, his wife worried but not, so far as Gulien could see, very much frightened by any of her uncommon visitors.

The Kieba told them, "I have put right what I can. I have provided good timber and stone and golems to rebuild what has been torn down. Though I do not know whether you will wish to stay now in the shadow of my mountain."

"Shall we expect your enemies to come again?" the farmer asked grimly. He squared his shoulders and faced her directly. And the farmwife asked, not in the least frightened of the Kieba, "Shall we expect our children to be crushed between you and your enemies?"

The Kieba sighed. "I failed your trust," she admitted. "I did not know I had enemies who had discovered enough of the old gods' power to challenge me and yet not enough of the gods' wisdom to know why they should not. It was my duty to know, but I did not. I assure you, I will not be taken unaware a second time."

The farmer gave her a hard stare, plainly not convinced.

"It wasn't her fault," Gulien told the man. "It truly wasn't. Their power built swiftly, with the discovery of only a mere handful of artifacts. One can't predict such things."

The farmer's expression shifted from closed toward uncertain, though he still looked angry.

"It was my fault," said the Kieba. "I should have been paying attention to the magisters of Tamarist."

"There are always magisters, or men like them. You can't spend every moment watching for the dead gods' tools to reappear in the hands of men. I know that. So do you."

The Kieba shrugged, not quite a concession. She said to the farmer and his wife, "May you and yours flourish, whether you stay here or go elsewhere. If you stay, you will be most welcome. I like to see your family prosper here by my mountain. You remind me of the wide world and of my life before I became the Kieba of the mountain of memory."

Then she said to Oressa, "I owe you a debt too, Princess Oressa, and I would offer you my help now, to reclaim Caras and establish peace throughout Carastind—but I think you will not need it."

Oressa looked half reassured by this and half wary. She gave a little nod. The Kieba returned it gravely. Then she turned and walked swiftly away, out the door and away, toward her mountain.

Gulien followed her. He remembered to look back, but by that time he could not see his sister plainly, nor any details of the life he was leaving behind.

CHAPTER 27

Only after the Kieba was gone did Oressa realize that really they had better get on with their own business. Which was to leave. And leave Gulien behind. That seemed unbearable, but plainly it was the right thing to do. Or a right thing to do. Or at least the only possible thing to do.

Gulien had always been there, her older brother, always ready to protect her, to stand between Oressa and anything that could harm her or frighten her, even between her and their father. And now their father was gone, and so was Gulien, and Oressa shied away from the awareness of that emptiness, but the emptiness was everywhere.

She tried to take comfort from the multitude of urgent tasks that faced them all, especially from the urgent need to get back to Caras and deal with Bherijda's remaining people.

They couldn't just fling themselves straightaway on the road and gallop through the night, unfortunately. There seemed to be a great many things to do, and a good many of them couldn't be done by anybody but Oressa. As soon as the Kieba took Gulien away with her, all those things seemed to crash down upon Oressa at once. At least it stopped her from worrying too much about Gulien. At least he seemed better. She *thought* he was better, though all that about having the wrong memories was really disturbing if she thought about it too hard.

But the Kieba had promised that Gulien would recover. Oressa clung to that reassurance, partly because she had so many other things to think about. Even though in those brief moments when she paused, it still astonished her that there were decisions to be made at all.

Even now she sometimes half expected time itself to stutter and stop, waiting, as she was waiting, for her father to reappear from the dust and smoke haze. And yet the world did not stop. She still saw that last look of his in her mind's eye: of irony or humor or scorn or whatever it had been. She felt that if she knew what expression it had been, she might have been better able to accept the fact of his death. But she could not decide. She wished she could talk to Gulien about him. But her brother was out of reach as well, and she had to try to accept that, too.

But she seldom had time to pause. She had to decide about Prince Bherijda's men, for one thing. They were happy to be offered any terms at all as long as they could surrender to Oressa rather than the Kieba. Had their positions been reversed, she would *never* have surrendered to Bherijda, but then, Bherijda had not been the kind of man to whom anyone would want to surrender. His men fell over themselves to surrender to her.

Bherijda's surviving senior officer now was a mere *karanat*, a lieutenant. He took down the last scorpion banner with his own hands and laid it and his sword on the ground at Oressa's feet. He was visibly surprised and relieved to be offered a chance to take back his sword, if not his banner, if he would take oath to Oressa as well.

"After all, where else can they go now?" Oressa said to Laasat. "He can take oath for himself and all the men. They can make individual oaths later, but I don't think we want to take time for that now, do we?"

"I think we need not. You're very generous to take them at all, and well do they know it," Laasat said grimly, as much for the young officer's benefit as for Oressa's. "They have no other prince to take them in now, nowhere else to go, and no hope but your generosity. But though you may return their swords and crossbows and arquebuses now, I would advise you wait to restore their supply of bolts and powder."

That seemed very wise to Oressa, who gave the *karanat* a stern look. The young man bowed his head and begged to be allowed to earn her good regard. Oressa said he and his people had certainly better try, and they might begin by spending the rest of the evening helping put out the smoldering fires they'd started, disposing of the livestock they'd slaughtered, and apologizing to the people they'd attacked and terrified and tried to murder. She said she was tempted to hang them all, except that, too, would take too much time. Making that threat made her feel strong and ruthless and like she might all of a sudden have somehow turned into her father. For a moment, taken by surprise by a storm of confusion and anger and possibly even grief, she couldn't think of anything else.

But the threat alone, or maybe just the fact of their defeat and their prince's defeat and death, seemed enough to make the scorpion soldiers behave. She spoke to them in Tamaj to be sure they understood. Few of Bherijda's men spoke Esse, not even the officers, and so at last she admitted she could manage in their language. Laasat didn't even blink; he only shook his head as though to say, *Of course.*

Oressa also took command of her father's Carastindin soldiers, since no one else could. There were a good number left, for they had stayed fairly well out of the battle, not knowing whom they should fight. She was almost but not quite surprised to find that they, too, were glad to take their direction from her.

"We have no other lord to whom we might answer now," their senior officer told Oressa, sounding rather lost about it. Oressa didn't take offense. She knew he meant, *Now that your father is dead.* He was an older man, devastated at the loss of his king and plainly relieved to have a Madalin left, even a girl, giving the orders. Oressa wished *she* had somebody she trusted to hand everything off to, but unfortunately there wasn't anybody.

She was so relieved that her father was dead. It was dreadful to be relieved at something like that. But whatever she found in Caras, she believed she could handle it, as long as she didn't have to face her father.

She could hardly believe . . . Gulien had always . . . He had never . . . Their father had been different with her brother than he had been with her. Or Gulien had been different with their father than she had been. She didn't know. It was too hard to think about. It was better to get on the road at last so that she could lose herself in motion and stop thinking.

They traveled as quickly as men could march. Oressa insisted on it, and no one argued. But when they were still more than a day's march from Caras, all three pairs of scouts they'd sent ahead returned, each within an hour of the others. They all said the same thing: There was an army outside Caras, and it was neither Carastind nor Tamaristan.

"Estenda!" Oressa said disbelievingly. *"Estenda!"* After the first moments, she wasn't surprised. She was *furious.* If any of the gods had still lived, she would have cursed Kelian in all their names, one after another. If she'd known the proper forms of the ancient curses, she might have done it anyway. Except it probably wasn't wise to take the time for cursing when they had to *do* something about that Estendan army. She had no idea what to do.

"Your militia commander at Addas was perhaps a little rigid," Laasat said. "I can't wish we'd remained in the north, but I fear his narrow-mindedness put him at a disadvantage."

Oressa laughed grimly. "No. No. I think some ambitious merchant-prince in Estenda was waiting his chance. He's probably dreaming of making himself into a real prince, or even a king. This is so *ridiculous.* All we've done, all we've faced, and now there's *this?* All I want is to get *home."* She was not quite sure whether she meant Caras or the palace or her own apartment or just that she wanted to find Gajdosik and make sure he was all right. But she knew she was outraged.

"Well, it's a nuisance, of course, but no more than that, I hope. After, as you say, what we've already faced," said Laasat.

"Well." Oressa had to agree that she would rather face any Estendan army than Bherijda's horrible artifact. "Do we have the numbers? Can we keep surprise? Can we get the Estendan soldiers out of Caras, do you suppose, or will we have to fight for the city house by house? I suppose we can go back and ask the Kieba for help—"

One of the scouts held up a hand, tentatively interrupting. "I don't think we need help, Your Highness. Them Estendan bastards aren't in Caras at all. The numbers aren't so far off, except we'll get reinforced from the city, and them Estendans, they're drawn up outside the walls where we can get to 'em from both sides—"

"Really? What have our people held them off with?" Oressa wondered aloud, but she was very pleased as well as astonished. She said to Laasat, "That *is* good, isn't it? Surely it means we can just, you know—"

"Catch them from the rear and by surprise and drive them back north so hard they'll outrun their own horses?" said Laasat. "Yes, I hope that's exactly what it means—if we're quick."

So they were quick. They left the wounded to follow more slowly, so their men were mostly in decent shape. The young *karanat* came to Oressa and begged her to put his men in the front of the combined force, and in the center, where the fighting would be hardest. Laasat and Gajdosik's other officers were doubtful: What if Bherijda's men did not hold? What if they even deliberately betrayed Oressa?

"We will not!" protested the *karanat*. "Please, Your Highness. We will fight for you."

"I suppose it will make a change from terrifying farmers," Oressa said, not very kindly. But she could see Bherijda's men must eventually be given a chance to earn back their pride. She straightened her shoulders and added, "Laasat will give orders that you and all your men should be supplied with shot and powder and bolts for your crossbows. Don't disappoint me."

"No," the *karanat* said earnestly. He bowed to the ground at her feet, which was what Tamaristans did to show their sincerity, and went away to bring his men up to their new position.

Estenda's army was indeed outside the city, its long moon-and-mountain banner snapping in the hot wind. But it seemed to be actually retreating, for some reason—a kind of wavering retreat, like its commanders hadn't made up their minds what they wanted to do. This made a lot more sense when they were close enough to see the red-tinged fog that drifted here and there in the city.

"Plague!" Laasat said, horrified.

"No . . . ," said Oressa. "No, I don't think it is."

"What?"

"I think . . . it's just smoke."

Laasat gave her a doubtful look. "It's red, Your Highness."

Oressa nodded. "Tinted smoke. Someone's been clever." She found herself smiling. Who but Gajdosik would have thought of so clever a plan, or put it into action so swiftly, before his enemies could even break through walls that were already breached?

Laasat gave the rolling smoke a hard look. "Well . . . ," he said. "Well, maybe you're right, at that. Maybe—" He cut that off. Then he said, "Well, as someone has been so good as to provide us with a clear target, I think it would be unappreciative not to take it."

"Yes, I think so too." Oressa waved her hand as a kind of blanket permission for Laasat to take over tactical command and listened with interest to the orders he gave. She thought she could learn tactics if she wanted to. She thought she might be good at it.

The Estendan army proved rather easy to rout. They hadn't expected an army to come suddenly out of the east, far less a combined force nearly equal to their own, riding under both sea-eagle and falcon banners. Besides, the Estendans were in a bad position if they were afraid to go into the city, and a worse one after another force emerged from Caras to harass them, probably fewer than a thousand men, but they drove aggressively forward, firing arquebuses in volley, each rank firing and then falling back to the rear to reload, and the Estendans broke in the face of the confident roaring of the arquebuses, so much more terrifying than crossbows. Oressa didn't think the Estendans actually outran their own horses when they retreated; in fact, they retreated in fairly good order. But they did retreat, and with very little fighting. She wished her people could follow and cut them to pieces. Maybe they *should* follow and cut them to pieces—it would probably be a good idea to teach Estenda's ambitious merchant-princes better manners.

"All the mounted soldiers we have," said Laasat, when she suggested this. "We want to punish them, and we want to press them and keep them moving, but we don't want them to really turn and fight. I'll send men—Carastindin men—to cut around them and alert the Addas militia, if there's anything left of it. With luck we can make them think twice before they try this again."

"It's not a matter of luck," Oressa said firmly. "We'll make sure they think *three* times before they take us so lightly."

As Oressa and her companions approached the gate, she was pleased but not at all surprised to find Gajdosik coming through the open gates to meet her, though all the banners showed the Madalin falcon. She *was* surprised to see Lord Paulin beside Gajdosik, apparently willing to take his orders. That was, she guessed, the whole point of Paulin's presence—to show that he was willing to take Gajdosik's orders. Those men riding under the falcon banner must be Paulin's own men, most of them—yes, nearly all of the Carastindin men in sight were wearing the Tegeres fox badge. She was frankly astonished. Putting his own house guard at Gajdosik's orders, that was more than casual or theoretical support. That was a *statement*.

Gajdosik carried no weapons—well, two of the fingers on his right hand were splinted, of course, so he probably couldn't handle a sword or even an arquebus. But he also wore an iron manacle around his left wrist. For all this, though, he looked grimly satisfied. Oressa understood that perfectly: After being beaten by one opponent after another, his stratagem had finally, decisively, defeated Estenda's army, and so he had begun to recover his pride. And he must also be vastly relieved to find that Oressa had brought him his own people and that they were safe. He couldn't stop himself smiling at her in relief and delight. She made no attempt to keep from smiling back.

"That was clever of you," she said, indicating the manacle.

"Prince Gulien and I mutually agreed upon the symbolism," Gajdosik replied smoothly. "And Lord Paulin and I agreed it would be as well to keep it for the . . . duration. Though I hope we will be able to dispense with it shortly."

He glanced past her, plainly looking for Gulien and probably for her father and maybe for Bherijda, too, though Oressa guessed he must be relieved to see no sign of his brother, at least. When he saw none of them, he went on with a little less assurance. "If I may ask, what . . . ? That is, I had wondered whether the Kieba might have been compelled to act. By Bherijda or by your father. I see they are both notably absent. But Prince Gulien? Surely—" He hesitated.

Oressa opened her mouth, but closed it again without speaking. She hardly knew how to say, *Yes, I killed your brother,* far less, *My father died saving me from your brother.* She'd thought she'd gotten used to the idea over the past days, but now, with the walls of Caras in front of them, it seemed impossible that her father should not be in his accustomed place within the palace, cool and high-handed and utterly in command of himself, as well as everything and everyone else. Except, sometimes, her.

Lord Paulin glanced from one of them to the other and, with a tact Oressa had not really expected, held his tongue.

She said finally, uncomfortably, "Gulien is . . . Gulien is all right. I . . . He . . ." She bit her lip, her eyes prickling, not knowing how to explain what had happened.

"Gulien!" exclaimed Lord Paulin, leaning forward in alarm. "Oressa, has something happened to your brother?"

"I don't . . . I don't really . . . He's not *dead,*" she added urgently, realizing how this must sound.

"I see you have somehow managed to acquire some of my brother's men," Gajdosik said, obviously changing the subject to give her time to recover. "You seem to have put them to good use in routing the Estendan troops. That was well done."

"Yes," said Oressa, intensely grateful to follow his lead. "But only because you set them up for us. Estenda! As though we needed another enemy this summer! I can't *believe* I ever liked Kelian!"

"Kelian?" said Gajdosik. He hesitated for a bare second, then said, "Well. I should have realized."

"We both should have!" agreed Oressa. "He brought—" She gestured north, after the retreating Estendan army. "All those, I'm sure. I hope he was with them today and got to enjoy the rout you arranged. Let him run with the Estendan soldiers if he will, and I hope he leaves his bones in the dust before he makes it to the highlands! At least they all had to run! The colored smoke was brilliant."

She glanced at Lord Paulin, including him in this, but he said at once, "It was indeed brilliant. I wish I could take credit for the idea, but it was Prince Gajdosik's plan from start to finish. The only difficult part was spreading the word widely enough among our own folk that we could be sure of avoiding panic in the city."

"Even with that complication, it seemed simpler than trying to stand off several thousand men with a mere few hundred. We also gave fifty men or so an emetic before sending them to engage the Estenda force— all volunteers!" Gajdosik added hastily at Oressa's horrified reaction. "It added a wonderful verisimilitude to our plague, to have men vomiting as they staggered toward the enemy. If the Estenda commander hadn't ordered a retreat, he'd have lost all his men to immediate mutiny."

Oressa laughed. Then she caught the somber, wary look in Gajdosik's eyes, and stopped laughing.

"Your brother?" he asked her again, gently.

Oressa shook her head, even though she again answered, "He's all right." But once more she found no way to go on from that simple, hopeful statement. At last she only nudged her horse toward the city gates, letting the men turn to follow her. She remembered only after she'd started forward that she had forgotten to tell Laasat what he should do with the soldiers, where they should go, that he should have Bherijda's men watched but not actually guarded; she should have made sure the Carastindin soldiers with Gajdosik understood the Tamaristans were to be regarded as allies and treated with respect—she started to turn, but then heard Gajdosik give all those orders, everything she would have said. She realized, from Lord Paulin's tight-lipped glance at Gajdosik's back, that this might be interpreted as a usurpation of her authority, or of Carastindin authority in her person. She said nothing, but only checked her horse and waited for Gajdosik to catch up with her.

He had clearly realized, too, belatedly, how his assumption of authority might seem. As soon as his horse came up even with hers, he began, "Your Highness, I apologize—"

Oressa lifted a hand to stop him. "No. That was well done. Listen, I'll tell you. I *can* tell you. Let me—" She looked away from him. Then she looked back and met his eyes. "Bherijda and some of his magisters and—and my father got into the Kieba's mountain, and Gulien, too, somehow. Something happened there. I don't understand precisely what, only none of the magisters came out again, and I think—I know— that Gulien did something to help the Kieba. I think he—well, I think he gave the Kieba his mind, or his soul, or something. She said she 'put him back.' I think she meant put him back into himself, somehow."

Gajdosik nodded grimly, clearly finding the idea as disturbing as she had. Lord Paulin rubbed his mouth and gave Oressa a little nod to encourage her to go on. Neither of them said anything.

"She tried to restore Gulien, but she couldn't restore him all the way. He's not—he's not—for a while he didn't recognize me." She was speaking faster now. "It was horrible. Even after he came back . . . He's not the same."

"I am sorry for that, then," Gajdosik said gently.

"And before that, before . . . Bherijda was horrible to me. I think he was trying to use something, something of the gods' power, something terrible, and I slapped him, and he tried to kill me, and my—my father got in the way, and Bherijda killed him, and I killed Bherijda—"

"*You* killed Prince Bherijda!" Lord Paulin exclaimed.

"I had this knife. A woman gave it to me." Oressa tried not to remember the way the knife had felt as it had gone into Bherijda's back. She swallowed, swallowed again, and fixed her eyes firmly on the ears of her horse before she said again, in a small voice, "So I killed your brother."

"Of course you did," said Gajdosik. "Good for you."

Oressa gave him a quick, sideways glance, but he obviously meant it. She finished, "And Bherijda's men all surrendered to me, so we came back here, and that's all, I think."

"I believe we would appreciate the long version, eventually," murmured Gajdosik. "Now, here we had some difficulty settling matters with Bherijda's garrison. However, Lord Paulin found it possible to work with me—"

"Because Gulien gave Prince Gajdosik tactical command and ordered the rest of us to respect that," Lord Paulin said bluntly. "I thought it was a terrible idea." He gave Gajdosik a sideways look. "I was wrong."

"Fortunately," Gajdosik said smoothly, "the Estendan troops appeared at about the moment that we'd finally sorted out the men Bherijda left to hold Caras, and though I doubt they meant to do anything so helpful, they did furnish us all with a common opponent. . . ."

They came around a last corner, and Oressa checked her horse sharply, staring at the palace. "Gajdosik!" she exclaimed. "The palace! What did you *do* to it?"

Gajdosik actually laughed; so, really, Oressa thought, it might have been almost worth blowing up nearly the entire remaining palace. But she was still appalled.

"You can rebuild it. With, no doubt, beautiful sturdy roofs, nearly flat, and a good deal of fancy work to lend good handholds."

Oressa rolled her eyes.

Lord Paulin dismounted, rather stiffly, from his horse, and took Oressa's reins with a slight but courtly bow. "In the meantime, Your Highness, may I offer you the use of my town house?" He nodded to it. It was quite near, its iron gates standing wide, a gracious and welcoming building, several stories, with its own stables and cistern and pigeon loft.

"It offers ample room for your household," Lord Paulin said earnestly. "Do me the honor to agree. I assure Your Highness that I and my staff will make the utmost effort to see to your comfort and security."

Oressa gazed at Lord Paulin in surprise. Then she wondered why she was surprised at all, because really, he was just the man to make such an offer—both ambitious and kind, and intelligent enough to support Gulien and now even Gajdosik. She gave him a little nod, finding that she liked him a good deal better now, after everything that had happened, than she had ever expected to. Just as long as she didn't have to *marry* him. She gave him her hand and let him help her down from her horse. Gajdosik swung down beside them without a word, beckoning men to come take the horses.

Sometime in the past days, Lord Paulin had turned an enormous upper-story room with a huge window and a wide balcony into a kind of war room. It was a beautiful room, but papers and maps littered every table and half the chairs. Lord Paulin told the servants to bring wine and rolls, fruit and cakes. He himself swept papers and maps off one table, two chairs, and a couch before he came to lead Oressa to a seat. He didn't hover over Gajdosik, but then Gajdosik did not appear to need anyone to hover over him. He leaned his hip against the largest table, seeming content for the moment to allow Lord Paulin to take the lead.

Paulin took the wine away from the servant who brought it and poured Oressa a cup with his own hands. This he offered to her with an old-fashioned courtesy that was well suited to his age and stature, both kind and punctilious. He said, "I'm sorry to hear of His Majesty's passing, Your Highness, but you say . . . you did say he died defending you from Bherijda?"

"Yes," whispered Oressa. A week ago she would have declared with absolute confidence, *I will never forgive my father anything, not if he goes down on his knees and begs me.* Now she said instead, "I don't understand why he . . . why he would do that."

Lord Paulin said gently, "I'm sure he knew his own mind and did exactly as he meant."

"He always did," Oressa agreed in a small voice.

Gajdosik said quietly, "Fathers are often difficult for their children to understand. Or forgive. But if he sacrificed himself in the end to protect Your Highness and his kingdom from my brother, then at least I will honor him for that."

Oressa nodded. She wasn't sure she could do the same, but she thought . . . she thought she might at least *try*.

"But now . . . ," said Lord Paulin. "Forgive me for speaking bluntly, but if His Majesty is gone and Prince Gulien is not . . . not well . . . I believe I understand accurately that His Highness is not well? Then, Your Highness, have you considered . . . ?" He hesitated again, his painstaking effort to explain the obvious failing at this point.

Oressa had never stepped into public view, not even after she attained her majority. She had stayed out of her father's way and therefore out of everyone's sight. Now Lord Paulin was trying to find a way to explain that if her brother wasn't here to take the throne, then she would have to step forward herself and take the throne. And that she would have to marry, because while Gulien could have ruled on his own account, a woman, especially a woman as young as Oressa, would be expected to present Carastind with an appropriate husband. It was ridiculous, no doubt, but Oressa knew perfectly well that this moment, after this terrible summer, after her people had lost first their king and then their prince, was not the time to challenge custom.

Lord Paulin obviously thought she would be too shy to do what she had to do, and he might be thinking that he had better make suggestions about whom she should marry. She could see he was embarrassed. That was part of his uncharacteristic hesitation.

He didn't know yet, because she hadn't had time to show him—she had barely had time to realize it herself—that whatever she chose to do, she had already stepped into the light. That she would never again be able or willing to step back into the shadows.

Lord Paulin said earnestly, "I . . . Your brother once suggested . . . but I don't believe you consider that we should suit. Yet you must marry, Your Highness, if you will be queen regnant."

"Oh," said Oressa, smiling at him, "I do know that, Lord Paulin. I think I can stand it." She looked at Gajdosik.

He was standing beside a chair, his arm resting along its back, his face turned down toward the floor, frowning. He might have looked indifferent, except for his stillness, which was not the quiet of indifference. He might have looked relaxed, except for the hard grip of his hand on the back of the chair. As though Oressa's gaze pulled at his, he lifted his head to meet her eyes.

"I certainly won't let you conquer Carastind," Oressa told him. "You'll have to marry me, you know. It's the only way you can be king. Though if you say a single word about gilded cages with every luxury, well, you can just find another princess to hand you a different kingdom."

"I have no wish to bring that particular custom to Carastind," Gajdosik assured her. "Not only would your people kill me for attempting anything of the kind, but you would surely escape any cage that might be built." He was not smiling. The expression in his eyes was too intense to be a smile. He said, "You will be an extraordinary queen. As my mother might have been, had she been permitted." But he gave Lord Paulin a wary look. "Even so, however, I am certain your people would, of course, prefer that you accept a worthy Carastindin lord."

Lord Paulin straightened ponderously. He no longer looked embarrassed, only exasperated and faintly amused. "I think that decision can safely be left to Her Highness. Besides, all our worthy Carastindin lords would resent any among them whom Her Highness might choose. In some ways, it's simpler to elevate a foreign prince. I'm confident Her Highness has sound judgment."

"Well, I hope so," Oressa said tartly. "Though I hope that in the years to come, my loyal and steadfast Carastindin lords will give us both the benefit of their good counsel."

"I think you may not only hope for that but demand it," Lord Paulin told her.

Oressa *did* like Paulin, she decided. Now that he had realized she was actually not stupid, she even thought she might learn to trust him. She said to Gajdosik, "So you see, I think Carastind will be willing to see a foreign prince marry their queen."

Gajdosik was starting to smile. It hadn't reached his mouth yet, but his eyes were alight. Even so, he said, "We did not begin well, you and I. You are confident in this decision?"

"Once my people are yours, you'll do anything to be sure they prosper," Oressa told him. "What, did you think I hadn't noticed your . . . your steadfastness? That's what I want for Carastind. Besides, you're too ambitious and ruthless to let you stay on this side of the Narrow Sea unless you're committed to Carastind." She hesitated and then added, unable to prevent a slight hesitation from coming into her tone, "As long as . . . that is, if . . . you think you can stand to be married to me."

Gajdosik's smile crooked just the corner of his mouth now. He looked at once very sober and highly entertained. He said, "I think I will be able to accommodate myself to the idea. Do you know . . . ? Do you *know* how my heart stopped when you leaped out that tower window?" He added thoughtfully, "But that was hardly the moment you caught my attention. When you promised me that you would take care of my people." He paused and then added, "No. Before that. I already knew I could trust you to take care of them for me. Because of your courage, and your wit, and your kindness. I think I had already noticed how brightly you shone in that stinking warehouse where you threw my words about bread back in my face."

"*I* noticed your confidence. Not to say arrogance." A blazing confidence filled Oressa right now, in fact. Not to say arrogance. She said smoothly, "Princesses always make purely political marriages, of course. Think of all the potential advantages of this one. They're quite breathtaking. Naturally that's my sole concern." It was taking considerable effort to tamp out her own smile, which wanted to turn into a ridiculous grin. She ought to be worried for Gulien. She ought to be concerned about what her less loyal and steadfast Carastind lords would think. She *really* ought to be worried about what new and deadly threat might come out of Tamarist. She ought to be absolutely *terrified* something might happen to the Kieba before Gulien was ready to take her place in that mountain.

Somehow at the moment she couldn't be afraid of anything. She stepped toward Gajdosik, laid a hand on his arm, stood on her toes, and whispered in his ear, "Of course, I did promise to tell you when I lied to you." She paused, and then added, in an even lower whisper, "That was a lie."

Gajdosik laughed out loud at this ambiguous assurance. He put his hand on her arm in turn, tentatively, as though not yet quite certain he had the right to touch her. When she didn't move away, he slid his hand down to her waist. He said huskily, "I would never hold a lady to such a promise."

"I never promised to actually tell you the truth," Oressa pointed out.

"That's all right, then." His eyes met hers. "Promise me you'll show me all the secret passages you have built into the new palace. . . ."

"As long as *you* promise not to stop me from climbing on roofs. . . ."

"As if I could stop you from doing anything. But I'll give you no reason to run from me."

Oressa laughed. She knew he was telling her the truth.

TURN THE PAGE FOR A SNEAK PEEK AT
WINTER OF ICE AND IRON

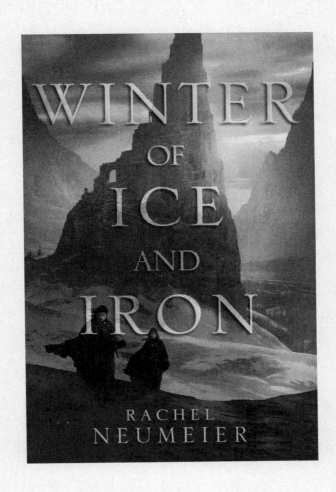

Jeneil inè Suon was a beautiful girl. Her beauty did not serve her well:
not as a child in her father's house and not in her youth and certainly not
when, as a woman grown, she caught the eye of Iheraïn terè Iönei Eänetaì.
The Iron Duke, the Wolf Duke, the Black Duke: Iheraïn Eänetaì, possibly the cruelest of all the lords of Pohorir. The very first lord of Eäneté
had possessed a difficult temperament that had unhappily found an
echo in the emerging Eänetén Power. The Immanent Power that formed
from those mountains, from their thin soils and their broken stones,
from their forests and creatures and the folk dwelling within their
small, scattered villages, had even from those earliest days exhibited a
savage disposition. That savagery had echoed back and forth between
the lords of Eäneté and their strengthening Immanent, until cruelty no
less than molten fire burned beneath the stone of its mountains.

Jeneil loved music and painting and small pretty songbirds: nothing
that flourished in the house of Iheraïn Eänetaì. Her lord permitted her
paints and canvas because these could be used silently and alone, and
because sometimes it amused him to take them away. Jeneil's mother
had taught her to love music, but her lord forbade instruments in his
house. When she sang, she had a voice pure as the voice of a lark—or

so said the servants of the house, pitying her. But she seldom sang after she entered the Black Duke's keeping, and never when her lord was anywhere in his house, because in that house she became as fragile and timid as a little bird.

Jeneil had always known fear. Her own father had taught her that lesson well. But in the Black Duke's house, she found that lesson refined. She grew more delicate every day she lived there. Even so, at first she stole moments of happiness; moments when, just for a little while, she forgot to be afraid. Small things might give Jeneil a moment of happiness: a spring crocus blooming through the snow, a bird coming to her hand for bread, a line flowing from her brush to the canvas in just the way she had imagined it.

She found love in that house too. She loved one of the duke's stewards, a young man named Gereth Murrel, for Jeneil had a generous and loving heart and she needed to love someone. He loved her in return. But for Jeneil this was a wistful and distant love, and for the young man a cruel one, for neither dared break her marriage vows. Iheraïn Eänetaì would have known, as he knew all things that occurred in his house and his city and his province.

Even so, Jeneil turned to the young steward for companionship in her misery, though she feared for him lest her lord destroy him as he sometimes destroyed her paintings. She turned to Gereth for comfort anyway, just as she turned to painting to create the illusion of freedom; just as she sang, when she dared, to distract herself from her unhappiness. But in the face of her fear, neither the love of the steward nor her own wistful thoughts of what her life might have been gave Jeneil reason enough to hold to life. A year after her marriage to the duke, she turned to her child-bed with relief, knowing she might die of the birth. She wished to die, because she no longer hoped for any other escape from her life.

There was nothing especially difficult about the birth. Jeneil Suon delivered the child, a son. When the midwife cut the cord and laid the child in her arms, Jeneil gazed for some time upon his small, wrinkled form. If she had borne a daughter, perhaps it would have been different. But even so young, this boy-infant had his father's black hair and, rather than the cloudy blue eyes of any common newborn, his father's yellow wolf eyes. So after gazing upon him for a little while, Jeneil set the child aside in his crib and turned her face to the wall. She died on her next breath.

When he was fourteen, Innisth terè Maèr Eänetaì tried for the first time to kill his father. He did not succeed. He found out instead something that he should have realized beforehand: that the Immanent Power of Eäneté protected the Duke of Eäneté from any ordinary attack.

No Immanent Power was concerned with action or achievement or triumph, not when it was young and new and first stretched itself out in the earth and stone and forests and creatures of its land. Such matters were human concerns. But Immanents took something of the character of those to whom they were tied. Ambition and domination and triumph had been the driving concern even for the first of the Maèr line. So Innisth should have realized that the Immanent Power would move to shield his father from any attack. Even an unexpected attack. Even an attack by the heir.

He also learned that it is a great deal easier and less painful to discover such things through logic than it is to learn them through trial and error. Both lessons proved useful, in time.

Innisth survived his father's punishment and the subsequent years of his youth. When he was twenty, he tried again to murder his father. This time he succeeded. This time he thought out his plan with cold deliberation, and when the opportunity presented itself, on the twenty-eighth day of the Month of Wolves, he seized his chance.

Wolf Month was the starving month, the bitter month, the month when winter stores grew lean and the new growth had not yet come, the month when the long haunting cries of the wolves drifted almost nightly from the high mountains. It was a hard month. The cold lingered. But one could look forward from the Month of Wolves to the approaching spring. It was a good month for sharp change, for renewal, for the rekindling of life out of grim silence. Perhaps that, too, drove Innisth to make and seize his chance.

This time, he knew that the Eänetén Immanent would block any attempt to stab or bludgeon or poison its master. But there was nothing it could do to preserve a man flung down a sheer thousand-foot cliff.

The Immanent Power of Eäneté came down upon Innisth after his father's death. By that time it was immensely strong, for the dukes of Eäneté had always, despite their cruelty, been intelligent enough to steward their province with an eye toward the prosperity of both land and people. It was not a Great Power such as ruled and bound lesser Immanences into a unified nation. It was not quite that. But it had learned ambition and pride—not in any mortal or human way, but in the way the soul of the land could learn such things from those most closely bound to it. Now only stark will could rule it.

Generally, a duke's heir mastered his Power while surrounded by supporters and allies, men and women bound to allied lesser Immanences, who knew best how to help a new heir survive the often brutal transference of the deep tie. Innisth Eänetaì mastered the Immanent of Eäneté alone, in the cold heights, lying in the trampled snow at the top of the ice-edged granite cliff. It was a cruel and ferocious Immanent, long shaped by the sharp-edged mountains and the high cutting winds of Eäneté and by the savagery of a long, long line of Eänetén dukes, none of whom had taught it much of gentleness.

But Innisth was his father's true son. He encompassed the Eänetén Power, and mastered it, and bound it, and he did not freeze to death there in the heights because Eänetaìsarè would not allow its master to die such a death.

By the time he got to his feet and brushed the snow off his face and out of his hair, it was nearly dusk. Innisth did not look toward the cliff edge where his father had fallen. He found his horse and his father's horse not far away, in the shelter of the firs in the lee of the mountain's high ridge. Though he was stiff with cold, he mounted and rode down the long steep way to the gate at the mouth of the pass.

The men stationed there knew immediately what had happened. At least, they knew the important part of what had happened. They knew because Innisth Eänetaì came out of the pass alone, leading his father's horse by its reins. And they knew because of the look on Innisth's face, or by some subtle difference in his manner, or perhaps because they could feel the dense, invisible presence of the Eänetén Power spreading out above and around him. They knelt there in the snow and made their vows.

Innisth did not accept an escort back to the house that was now his: the massive house that loomed, gray and thick-walled and forbidding, dominating the town below. He told the men where to look for his father's body. They took his orders with white-faced impassivity. He left his father's horse with them and rode his own black mare down from the gate of the pass toward that great grim house. He did not look back.

There were more men-at-arms at the courtyard gate, of course. They were not so quick to understand, until Innisth said, "I am now Eäneté." Then he said, "Send for my seneschal, and for your captain, and bid all the household staff assemble here in the courtyard."

It was cold, with the frigid stillness that sometimes lay across the mountains during the winter dusk. But the courtyard was the only place large enough for all the staff to assemble. And there were other advantages to the courtyard besides its sheer size. Even at night. "Light all the lanterns, and light torches," Innisth commanded the men-at-arms. They ran to obey.

If one included all the men-at-arms, the household staff comprised well over a hundred men and women. There were the stablemen and grooms, the huntsmen and kennel girls, the kitchen staff and scullery maids, the old women who stayed in the attics of the servants' quarters and spun wool and wove cloth, and the seamstresses who made the cloth into finished clothing. In the back of the assembly hovered the girls who endlessly polished the wooden floors and the brass doorknobs and the boys who clambered dangerously about on the outside walls to wash the house's many fine glass windows. To one side stood the house physickers and the grim old librarian with his assistant scribe. To the other side stood the men-at-arms, drawn up in their neat ranks, with their captain at their head. Before them all, with the torchlight casting his heavy features into unreadable shadow, stood Innisth's father's seneschal and his father's personal servants—including the special servants, with their rusty-black clothing that did not show blood.

They all knew the old duke was dead. Innisth did not have to tell them so. Word must have run through the house, even in the few moments they had required to assemble, but he believed they would have known anyway. He thought the empty space where his father should have stood echoed with the old duke's absence. To him it seemed that absence echoed through the entire house, louder than a shout. The assembled staff were utterly silent. They did not know yet how the shift of power from the old duke to the younger would affect them.

Innisth looked along the silent lines of the gathered staff. He said flatly, "Captain Tregeris," and beckoned with the crook of one finger.

The captain of the men-at-arms stepped out, approached Innisth, and saluted. He was not a young man, but not old; his shoulders were broad and his mouth narrow and he thought much of himself and little of others—except for Innisth's father, whom he had always feared and admired and sought to emulate. His eyes ran up and down Innisth's frame, curious and scornful, for he had, following the old duke's lead in this as in all else, never much regarded his son.

Innisth took one step forward, flicking his smallest knife out of his sleeve and into his hand. He stabbed the captain in the stomach and then stepped back while the man's mouth fell open and he sank down, quivering, his hands clutching at the hilt of the knife. The knife was small, but it was a vicious quilled blade, and when the captain steeled himself and jerked it out, a great dark gush of blood followed, and his breath followed it in a voiceless moan, and he died.

It had all been very quick, though at the same time the moment seemed to Innisth to stretch out and out, until he was half surprised that, when he looked up again, the whole assembly was still frozen in shocked quiet.

Innisth said, "Sergeant Etar."

There was a pause. Then the man he had named stepped out of the ranks and came forward to face him. Etar was nearly of an age with the dead man, perhaps twenty years Innisth's senior. In other ways he was not much like his former captain, for he was a plain man who did not seek to come near power. That was why he was still merely a sergeant, despite his age and competence. He met Innisth's eyes now, expressionless save for the tightness of his mouth.

Innisth said, "Captain Etar. The men-at-arms are yours. Over the coming days, you may set them in what order you think best. Dismiss men you do not think suited to your command; recruit other men as you see fit. I will expect you to inform me of what you do, but I do not expect I shall countermand your decisions. Is that clear?"

Small muscles around Etar's mouth twitched; that was the only sign of surprise. He gave a measured nod. "Your Grace."

Innisth sent him back to his men with a small gesture and said, not raising his voice, "Now, where is Gimil Sohoras? Where is my father's seneschal?" His voice, though not loud, fell into the echoing silence of the courtyard as clearly as a shout.

His father's seneschal was, of course, right there at the front of the assembly. He was a big man with heavy bones and heavy hands and a heavy voice. He glowered at Innisth and started to speak. Innisth lifted an eyebrow, and the man closed his mouth without a word.

"Gimil Sohoras," said Innisth, in that same quiet, carrying tone. "Though I appreciate your years of service to my father, I find I have no need of your service myself. You may have until dawn to gather all your possessions and leave Eäneté. You are not to count the girl Ranè among your possessions, however. She will remain here. Nor are you to damage her before you depart." There was a murmur from the gathering. Innisth pretended not to notice the young woman he had named, who turned and embraced an older woman. The woman eased Ranè away out of sight through the crowd. Innisth pretended not to notice that, either.

The big man stared at Innisth, plainly stunned. "But—"

"Or, of course, you may refuse to go," said Innisth. "That is certainly an option, if you prefer." He glanced thoughtfully down at the dead man who had been his father's captain and then once more regarded his father's seneschal.

The man closed his mouth.

"Dawn," Innisth reminded him. "Captain Etar will provide you with the assistance of two of his men. You would not wish to risk mistaking the hour as the sunrise approaches."

"No," said the man, his voice husky with suppressed rage. "No." He backed away awkwardly, nearly bumping into one of the men-at-arms Etar had sent to oversee his departure. He wheeled on the man, but then shot a wary glance at Innisth and smothered his anger.

"Gereth Murrel," said Innisth, naming a man who had been a factor and steward in the great house all Innisth's life. When the man made his way forward, Innisth met his eyes and smiled for the first time in all this long day.

Returning his smile, Gereth came forward to take the new duke's hand and kneel at his feet. "Innisth," he said, but very quietly. Then he said more loudly, "Your Grace. Command me."

Gereth was not young, being already in his fifties, but he was the man to whom everyone turned when they were in need. Quiet and methodical, Gereth was seldom noticed: a manner he had learned bitterly in this house and taught, as well as he could, to Innisth, when he had still been young enough to sometimes escape his father's notice. Innisth was confident that Gereth Murrel knew everything about running the house. And he knew the older man was kind.

Resting a hand briefly on the older man's shoulder, Innisth told him, "You are my seneschal," and another murmur, louder than the rest, whispered through the assembly.

Gereth said clearly, "Yes, Your Grace." His eyes searched his new duke's face. "Mastering Eänetaìsarè cannot have been easy. No one will challenge your right or your tie. There's no need for you to reorder the entire province tonight."

Innisth gave him another thin smile. "I have one or two more tasks before I rest. But you may certainly assign factors and stewards as you please. You will need an adequate staff, and I do not suppose you will find many of my father's factors suitable." He turned his hand palm-up: permission to rise.

Then he turned to his father's . . . special servants. He looked them over, one and then the next and then the third, and then raised his hand to signal to Captain Etar and said briefly, "Hang them all."

"But—!" protested one of the men, taking an involuntary step backward before stopping himself. Men-at-arms were already moving swiftly to seize them; Etar had plainly anticipated this order or one like it, and there would be no escape. The man flung himself to his knees instead, pleading. "But, Your Grace! We served your father well—we would gladly serve you—we only obeyed your father's commands, Your Grace—we had no personal animosity—I'm sure none of us ever wished—"

Innisth cut the man off with a lift of his hand. He said softly, "Yet I seem to remember a quite personal relationship between us. I advise you, do not protest overmuch. There are far more unpleasant fates than mere hanging. As you of all men are certainly aware."

The man closed his mouth.

"Be quick," Innisth said to his new captain, careful that his tone was merely impatient and held no trace of unease—though to himself he acknowledged that he would not truly be able to believe himself secure until these three servants, among all others, were dead. On that thought, he added to Etar, "And assemble a punishment detail. I do not care what failings the men have shown, but there should be at least half a dozen of them. I will see them, and you, downstairs. In half an hour."

There was the slightest stiffening of Etar's expression. But the captain only asked, "Tonight, Your Grace?" But he added immediately, "Of course it will be as Your Grace commands. Six men in half an hour."

Innisth had actually forgotten the time. If he had thought, he might have ordered Etar to bring his men downstairs in the morning, but he did not wish to seem indecisive, so he only gave a curt nod and turned to watch as the third of his father's torturers joined the other two in strangling death. It was not the death the man deserved, but it would do. It would do. He glanced across the courtyard toward the assembled staff. They were very quiet now. If anything, the silence had deepened. He met Gereth Murrel's wide gaze and said to him in a low voice, "I will speak to you further on matters of law and custom. Both will change now. You may advise me. Tomorrow. Late tomorrow."

Gereth bowed acknowledgment. "Your Grace."

"You are dismissed. You are all dismissed," added Innisth to the gathering, raising his voice. "Save for male servants of my household between the ages of twenty and thirty. The rest of you may all go." He paused, and then added flatly, "Go."

There was a general movement, not precisely a retreat, but nearly everyone was clearly glad to be permitted to escape without being singled out in any way. A few of the staff lingered, however, braver or more curious than the rest, or perhaps having friends among the young men whom Innisth had commanded to stay. Innisth pretended not to notice this minor disobedience. He said to the young men—there were fourteen of them, from a young groom to a senior huntsman—"I require a personal body servant. If any of you are not content with your current position, you may inform my seneschal of your interest. Your duties as my personal servant would be light, but various."

Only the stupidest of men could fail to understand, and even those would assuredly be enlightened by their fellows. Even now, a few of the sharper or more daring of them were exchanging significant glances. Innisth said, "This position will remain open until it is filled," and gestured dismissal.

The young men all edged away toward the staff entrance or toward the stable—none of them daring to speak, not yet, not while Innisth might overhear. But when Innisth turned to go into the house, he found the librarian's scribe in his way. He stopped, startled and prepared to be offended.

The youth clasped his hands in front of his belt, glanced down nervously, but then raised his gaze to meet Innisth's eyes. "Your Grace. I'm—I—if it pleases you, Your Grace, I would be glad to—to ask for the transfer of which you spoke."

Innisth looked the scribe up and down. He had the bony look of a boy who has not yet grown into himself. His clothing was plain but of good quality, as befit a young man who earned his bread with a quill rather than with the labor of his hands or a hunting bow. But he did not look delicate. His wrists were too big for his hands; his shoulders promised eventual strength. He was plain, with a rather ordinary face and untidy brown hair, but his gaze was sharp enough—though nervous, at the moment.

"Caèr Reiöft," Innisth said, pulling the name from his memory after a moment. "How old are you? Am I to understand that you have been dissatisfied with your place as a scribe?"

"Nineteen, Your Grace," the young man answered immediately. "But near enough twenty, if it pleases you. I don't mind the scribing, Your Grace, and if you wished me to—to write letters for you, or anything you wish, I would be glad to do that. But I would be glad— that is, I believe I understand the duties you will expect of a personal servant, and I would be very glad to serve Your Grace in any capacity that pleases you."

Innisth's eyes narrowed. "You mean: instead of the librarian. Is that what you mean?"

Reiöft took a quick breath. "I've no complaint of him, Your Grace. But I would—I've lived all my life in this house, Your Grace, and I would be glad to serve you, if you will have me. I know I'm not—I don't want to be presumptuous, Your Grace—"

Innisth lifted one hand a fraction, and Reiöft stopped. "We may at least try the arrangement," he said. "Inform Gereth of the matter. I am going downstairs for a little while. Then I will come up to my rooms. I will wish to bathe and rest. I will expect you to have everything ready for me."

Reiöft nodded swiftly. "Your Grace." He looked slightly stunned now that it was settled. His eyes were wide and vulnerable. Innisth liked that. He had never much noticed the young man before, but now he thought he might like him well enough. He gave him a brief nod of dismissal and walked away, for the black door and the narrow steps that led downstairs.

A long table, scarred by iron and knife, dominated the large antechamber of the old duke's dungeons. Beyond it stood an ornate chair with a high, carved back and carved arms and a cushion of black leather. The chair was a handsome piece, out of place in this room. Save for the space directly around the chair, the floor was matted with straw and sweet rushes, originally laid down to absorb blood and other matter, but left far too long. The stench of moldy straw and rotted blood and filth hung in the room; even the torches seemed to burn low and flicker unevenly in the close air. A vast fireplace took up most of the wall to the left, though at the moment no wood was arranged there. Tools of all sorts occupied racks and shelves along the wall to the right. In the far wall, an iron door stood open, leading to the small cells where the old duke's less fortunate prisoners might linger for . . . some time. There

Britain, 1936.

A mild-mannered civilian reporter with a dangerous secret may be the only one who can discover the truth behind a terrifying German plot to invade Britain—before it's too late.

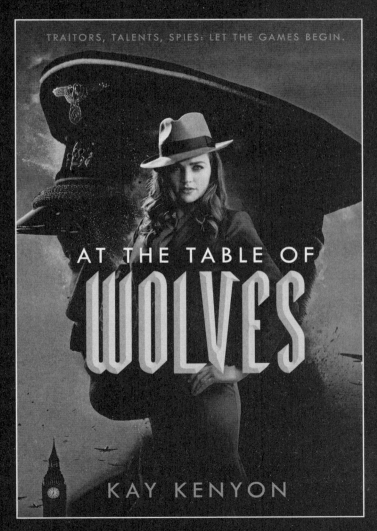

TRAITORS, TALENTS, SPIES: LET THE GAMES BEGIN.

AT THE TABLE OF
WOLVES

KAY KENYON

Tinker Tailor Soldier Spy meets *X-Men* in a classic espionage adventure.

tentative and hopeful, and though Innisth did not smile in return, he offered no rebuke to this familiarity. And he bought a lark from the first woman he encountered offering them for sale.

Innisth took the little bird out of its cage and held it in his hands for a moment, feeling its heartbeat rapid and delicate against his fingers. And then, in the middle of the market square, in full view of all his people, he opened his hands and let it fly.

The old duke's body was returned to the house, where it lay in state for a day and a night. The Immanent Power of Eäneté did not take it up, and thus the body was finally interred in the duke's garden of remembrance. Innisth did not attend the ceremony.

There were quiet celebrations all through Eäneté as the season eased from the Month of Wolves into the new spring. Nothing obtrusive. No one wanted to risk offending their new young duke. But on the twenty-eighth day of the Month of Bright Rains and then again on the twenty-eighth day of Apple Blossom Month, townspeople made cakes with brandy and berry preserves, then broke the cakes to share with strangers on the street. The wealthy bought lambs and young calves, took them up to the pine forests, slaughtered them there, and left them for the wolves. This might have been the old custom of propitiation, to turn wolf and misfortune aside, save that the month was wrong and the day was wrong. Innisth knew, though no one would say so, that it was a gesture of homage to the new Wolf Duke. Those who could not afford lambs bought larks and other songbirds in the market and set them free in a new custom that had, Innisth gathered, already become quite widespread.

"I believe some of the larks have been caught and released a dozen times by now," Gereth told Innisth, who lifted one shoulder in a deliberately disinterested shrug. But he was pleased. So he also rode down to the town on the twenty-eighth day of the next month, which was the Golden Hinge Month.

As the month ended, the world would enter the uncounted four days of the Golden Hinge, the days of good fortune and celebration during which spring turned to summer. Already the town was fragrant with baking and decorated with streamers of flowers. Delicate strands of blown robins' eggs had been draped over the lintels of doorways where marriages would take place during those golden days. Innisth strolled through the Open Market. No one had the temerity to offer him a bit of cake. But folk caught his eye and smiled as they bowed,

That was brave. Of course, Innisth had known Etar was brave. It took a moment of effort to appreciate that courage, to set down offense. There was a tiny stir among the men as they waited for his response, a general catch of breath. Their fear was . . . seductive, in a way Innisth had only half expected.

Nevertheless, at last he managed a thin smile. "So long as they respect my law and my commands, my own people will have nothing to fear from me, my captain. Neither your men nor my staff nor any of my folk." He made this a promise, flat and uncompromising, and swore to himself that he would keep that vow.

Captain Etar bowed his head briefly, accepting this assurance. If he let out a covert breath, Innisth couldn't tell it.

Setting aside the pressure of the Immanent as well as he could, Innisth made himself look around with careful consideration. "The cells," he told the captain. "Clean them all. If there are prisoners, inform me. If any could benefit from the attentions of a physicker, summon one. If any would best be granted a swift knife, then supply that need and, again, inform me." The men were once more looking faintly dismayed. He ignored them. He had, after all, told Etar to assemble a punishment detail.

"Your Grace," Etar acknowledged. "I think this will take more than one night's work, if I may say so."

"In this, I prefer thoroughness to speed."

Etar gave a nod. "I shall inform you when the task is completed, Your Grace."

Innisth returned the nod and left the men to their labor, turning back toward the narrow stairway. The stench of this place clung to him even after so brief a time, following at his heels as he mounted the steps and returned to the clean air above. He did want a bath now. Though . . . that was not all he wanted. But the bath, certainly, first. And then he would discover whether Caèr Reiöft did indeed understand the duties Innisth expected of his personal body servant. And then . . . and then, Innisth thought, he might at last be able to rest.

was no sound from beyond the iron door. Innisth could not remember whether his father currently held any prisoners in those cells, but if any were there, they were too cowed to make a sound when they heard men come into this antechamber.

Drawn up in an uneasy row waited the men-at-arms Innisth had ordered be brought to this place, and their new captain. The men were afraid, Innisth saw, but not terrified. That was Etar's influence. He met the new duke's gaze with level fortitude before inclining his head. "Your Grace."

Innisth gave him a small nod. He glanced around, his gaze catching on the chair. He nodded toward it. "Burn that."

"Your Grace?"

"Burn it." Innisth scuffed the toe of one boot through the filthy straw. "Clean away this mess. Clear the air. Burn cedar—burn incense, if necessary." He didn't actually care for incense, but better that than this current stench. "Scrub the floor. Clean and polish the table. Replace those torches with clean-burning lanterns and clean the soot off the walls."

The men were exchanging glances in which dismay and relief mingled. Even Captain Etar let his breath out. He gave Innisth a crisp nod. "Those?" He nodded toward the racks of whips and knives, irons and needles and clamps. "Shall we dispose of all of that as well?"

Innisth hesitated, wanting to say, *Yes, burn it all*. But Eänetaìsarè pressed him, drawn by this place with a force he had not entirely expected. The Immanent wanted blood and screaming; already he could tell he would eventually need to give it something of that kind. Already he could tell he would eventually want to.

"No," he said at last. "Clean away the old blood and rust. Sharpen the blades; replace anything worn or damaged and leave everything in good order."

Some of the relief faded. But Etar met his eyes and said quietly, "Of course it will be as Your Grace commands. But as your captain, I must ask that Your Grace leave the discipline of your men-at-arms in my hands."